EX LIBRIS

·ty Library

VINTAGE **CLASSICS**

VINTAGE CLASSICS

THE WAPSHOT CHRONICLE

John Cheever was born in Quincy, Massachusetts, in 1912, and went to school at Thayer Academy in South Braintree. He is the author of seven collections of stories and five novels. His first novel, *The Wapshot Chronicle*, won the 1958 National Book Award. In 1965 he received the Howells Medal for Fiction from the National Academy of Arts and Letters and in 1978 he won the National Book Critics Circle Award and the Pulitzer Prize. Shortly before his death in 1982 he was awarded the National Medal for Literature.

JOHN CHEEVER

The Wapshot Chronicle

VINTAGE BOOKS
London

Published by Vintage 1998

14

Copyright © John Cheever 1954, 1956, 1957

John Cheever has asserted his right under the Copyright, Designs and
Patents Act 1988 to be identified as the author of this work

First published in Great Britain by Harper in 1957
First published by Vintage in 1998

Vintage
Random House, 20 Vauxhall Bridge Road,
London SW1V 2SA

www.vintage-classics.info

Addresses for companies within The Random House Group Limited
can be found at: www.randomhouse.co.uk/offices.htm

The Random House Group Limited Reg. No. 954009

A CIP catalogue record for this book
is available from the British Library

ISBN 9780099275275

Penguin Random House is committed to a sustainable future for
our business, our readers and our planet. This book is made from
Forest Stewardship Council® certified paper.

Printed and bound in Great Britain by Clays Ltd, Elcograf S.p.A.

To M *with love:*

and with best wishes to practically everybody else I know

Four chapters of this book appeared in a slightly different form in *The New Yorker* magazine and the author is indebted to the editors of *The New Yorker*.

PART
ONE

CHAPTER I

St Botolphs was an old place, an old river town. It had been an inland port in the great days of the Massachusetts sailing fleets and now it was left with a factory that manufactured table silver and a few other small industries. The natives did not consider that it had diminished much in size or importance, but the long roster of the Civil War dead, bolted to the cannon on the green, was a reminder of how populous the village had been in the 1860's. St Botolphs would never muster as many soldiers again. The green was shaded by a few great elms and loosely enclosed by a square of store fronts. The Cartwright Block, which made the western wall of the square, had along the front of its second story a row of lancet windows, as delicate and reproachful as the windows of a church. Behind these windows were the offices of the Eastern Star, Dr Bulstrode the dentist, the telephone company and the insurance agent. The smells of these offices – the smell of dental preparations, floor oil, spittoons and coal gas – mingled in the downstairs hallway like an aroma of the past. In a drilling autumn rain, in a world of much change, the green at St Botolphs conveyed an impression of unusual permanence. On Independence Day in the morning, when the parade had begun to form, the place looked prosperous and festive.

The two Wapshot boys – Moses and Coverly – sat on a lawn on Water Street watching the floats arrive. The parade mixed spiritual and commercial themes freely and near the

Spirit of '76 was an old delivery wagon with a sign saying: GET YOUR FRESH FISH RROM MR HIRAM. The wheels of the wagon, the wheels of every vehicle in the parade were decorated with red, white and blue crepe paper and there was bunting everywhere. The front of the Cartwright Block was festooned with bunting. It hung in folds over the front of the bank and floated from all the trucks and wagons.

The Wapshot boys had been up since four; they were sleepy and sitting in the hot sun they seemed to have outlived the holiday. Moses had burned his hand on a salute. Coverly had lost his eyebrows in another explosion. They lived on a farm two miles below the village and had canoed upriver before dawn when the night air made the water of the river feel tepid as it rose around the canoe paddle and over their hands. They had forced a window of Christ Church as they always did and had rung the bell, waking a thousand songbirds, many villagers and every dog within the town limits including the Pluzinskis' bloodhound miles away on Hill Street. 'It's only the Wapshot boys.' Moses had heard a voice from the dark window of the parsonage. 'Git back to sleep.' Coverly was sixteen or seventeen then – fair like his brother but long necked and with a ministerial dip to his head and a bad habit of cracking his knuckles. He had an alert and a sentimental mind and worried about the health of Mr Hiram's cart horse and looked sadly at the inmates of the Sailor's Home – fifteen or twenty very old men who sat on benches in a truck and looked unconscionably tired. Moses was in college and in the last year he had reached the summit of his physical maturity and had emerged with the gift of judicious and tranquil self-admiration. Now, at ten o'clock, the boys sat on the grass waiting for their mother to take her place on the Woman's Club float.

Mrs Wapshot had founded the Woman's Club in St Botolphs and this moment was commemorated in the parade each year. Coverly could not remember a Fourth of July when his mother had not appeared in her role as founder. The float was simple. An Oriental rug was spread over the floor of a truck or wagon. The six or seven charter members sat in folding chairs, facing the rear of the truck. Mrs Wapshot stood at a lectern, wearing a hat, sipping now and then from a glass of water, smiling sadly at the charter members or at some old friend she recognized along the route. Thus above the heads of the crowd, jarred a little by the motion of the truck or wagon, exactly like those religious images that are carried through the streets of Boston's north end in the autumn to quiet great storms at sea, Mrs Wapshot appeared each year to her friends and neighbors, and it was fitting that she should be drawn through the streets for there was no one in the village who had had more of a hand in its enlightenment. It was she who had organized a committee to raise money for a new parish house for Christ Church. It was she who had raised a fund for the granite horse trough at the corner and who, when the horse trough became obsolete, had had it planted with geraniums and petunias. The new high school on the hill, the new firehouse, the new traffic lights, the war memorial – yes, yes – even the clean public toilets in the railroad station by the river were the fruit of Mrs Wapshot's genius. She must have been gratified as she traveled through the square.

Mr Wapshot – Captain Leander – was not around. He was at the helm of the SS *Topaze,* taking her down the river to the bay. He took the old launch out on every fine morning in the summer, stopping at Travertine to meet the train from Boston and then going across the bay to Nangasakit, where there were a white beach and an amusement park. He had been many things in his life; he had been a partner in the table-silver company and had legacies from relations, but nothing much had stuck to his fingers and three years ago Cousin Honora had arranged for him to have the captaincy of the *Topaze* to keep him out of mischief. The work suited him. The *Topaze* seemed to be his creation; she seemed to mirror his taste for romance and nonsense, his love of the seaside girls and the long, foolish, brine-smelling summer days. She had a sixty-foot water line, an old Harley engine with a single screw and enough room in her cabin and on her decks for forty passengers. She was an unseaworthy hulk that moved – Leander said so himself – like real estate, her decks packed with school children, whores, Sisters of Mercy and other tourists, her wake sewn with hard-boiled-egg shells and sandwich papers and her bones shaking so wildly at each change of speed that the paint flaked off her hull. But the voyage seemed to Leander, from his place at the helm, glorious and sad. The timbers of the old launch seemed held together by the brilliance and transitoriness of summer and she smelled of summery refuse – sneakers, towels, bathing suits and the cheap fragrant matchboard of old bathhouses. Down the bay she went over water that was sometimes the violet color of an eye to where the land wind brought aboard the music of the merry-go-round and where you could see the distant shore of Nangasakit – the scrim of nonsensical rides, paper lanterns, fried food and music that breasted the Atlantic in such a fragile jumble that it seemed like the rim of flotsam, the starfish and orange skins that came up on the waves. 'Tie me to the mast, Perimedes,' Leander used to shout when he heard the merry-go-round. He did not mind missing his wife's appearance in the parade.

There were some delays about the commencement of the parade that morning. These seemed to center around the Woman's Club Boat. One of the charter members came up the street to ask Moses and Coverly if they knew where their mother was. They said they hadn't been home since dawn. They were beginning to worry when Mrs Wapshot appeared suddenly in the doorway of Moody's drugstore and took her place. The Grand Marshal blew his whistle, the drummer with his head in a bloody bandage played a measure and the fifes and drums began to squeal, discharging a dozen pigeons from the roof of the Cartwright Block. A little wind came off the river, bringing into the square the dark, raw smell of mud. The parade picked up its scattered bones and moved.

The fire-department volunteers had been up until midnight, washing and polishing the gear of the Niagara Hose Company. They seemed proud of their work, but under some enjoinder to appear serious. The fire truck was followed by old Mr Starbuck, who sat in an open car wearing the uniform of the GAR, although it was well known that he had never had anything to do with the Civil War. Next came the Historical Society float where a direct – an authenticated – descendant of Priscilla Alden sweated under a heavy wig. She was followed by a truckful of lighthearted girls from the table-silver company who scattered coupons into the crowd. Then came Mrs Wapshot, standing at her lectern, a woman of forty whose fine skin and clear features could be counted among her organizational gifts. She was beautiful but when she tasted the water from the glass on her lectern she smiled sadly as if it were bitter for, in spite of her civil zeal, she had a taste for melancholy – for the smell of orange rinds and wood smoke – that was extraordinary. She was more admired among the ladies than the men and the essence of her beauty may have been disenchantment (Leander had deceived her) but she had brought all the resources of her sex to his infidelity and had been rewarded with such an air of wronged nobility and luminous vision that some of her advocates sighed as she passed through the square as if they saw in her face a life passing by.

Then some hoodlum – it must have been one of the foreigners who lived across the river – set off a firecracker under the rump of Mr Pincher's old mare and she bolted. In recalling this disaster much later the people of St Botolphs would recall its fortunate aspects. They would say how providential it had been that none of the women and children who lined the route of the parade had been trampled. The float had been only a few feet from the junction of Water and Hill streets and the horse took off hell for leather in this direction with old Mr Pincher shouting whoaa, whoaa. The first marchers had their backs to the accident and while they could hear the cries of excitement and the noise of hoofs they did not guess the magnitude of the disaster and the fifes went on squealing. Mr Starbuck went on bowing to the left and the right, the girls from the table-silver company went on scattering coupons into the crowd. As the wagon heaved up Hill Street Sarah Wapshot's lectern could be seen to go over and with it her water pitcher and glass; but none of the ladies of the Woman's Club was cowardly or foolish and they took a firm hold on some nonportable part of the wagon and trusted in the Lord. Hill Street was then a dirt road and that being a dry summer the horse's hoofs beat up such a pillar of dust that in a few minutes the float was gone.

CHAPTER 2

The Harcourts and the Wheelwrights, the Coffins and the Slaters, the Lowells and the Cabots and the Sedgewicks and the Kimballs – yes, even the Kimballs – have all had their family histories investigated and published and now we come to the Wapshots, who would not want to be considered without some reference to their past. A cousin by marriage had had the name traced back to its Norman beginnings – Vaincre-Chaud. The declension from Vaincre-Chaud through Fanshaw, Wapeshaw, Wapshafftes, Wapshottes and Wapshot had been found in Northumberland and Dorsetshire parish records. In St Botolphs it was given the catarrhal pronunciation 'Warpshart.' The branch of the family that concerns us was founded by Ezekiel Wapshot, who emigrated from England aboard the *Arbella* in 1630. Ezekiel settled in Boston, where he taught Latin, Greek, and Hebrew and gave lessons on the flute. He was offered a post in the Royal Government but he judiciously refused, establishing a family tradition of thoughtful regret that would – three hundred years later – chaff Leander and his sons. Someone wrote of Ezekiel that he 'abominated periwigs and had the welfare of the Commonwealth always upon his conscience.' Ezekiel begat David, Micabah and Aaron. Cotton Mather spoke the eulogy at Ezekiel's grave.

David begat Lorenzo, John, Abadiah and Stephen. Stephen begat Alpheus and Nestor. Nestor – a leftenant in the war with England – was tendered a decoration by General Washington

which he declined. This was in the tradition established by
Ezekiel and while these regrets sprang in part from a candid
assessment of the man's self-knowledge there was also some
Yankee shrewdness here, for to be conspicuous – to be a
hero – might entail some untoward financial responsibilities.
No man of the family had ever accepted an honor and in
upholding this tradition of unworthiness the ladies of the
family had so enlarged it that when they dined out they merely
picked at their food, feeling that to refuse the sandwiches at
tea or the chicken on Sunday – to refuse anything – was a
mark of character. The ladies were always hungry when they
left the dinner table but their sense of purpose was always
refreshed. In their own bailiwick, of course, they ate like
wolves.

Nestor begat Lafayette, Theophilus, Darcy and James. James
was captain of the first *Topaze* and later a 'merchant' in the
trade with the West Indies. He begat three sons and four
daughters but Benjamin is the only one that concerns us here.
Benjamin married Elizabeth Merserve and begat Thaddeus
and Lorenzo. Elizabeth died when Benjamin was seventy. He
then married Mary Hale and begat Aaron and Ebenezer. In St
Botolphs the two sets of children were known as 'first crop'
and 'second crop.'

Benjamin prospered and was responsible for most of the
additions to the house on River Street. Among his relics were
a phrenological chart and a portrait. In the phrenological chart
the circumference of his head was given as twenty-three and
one-half inches 'from the occipital spinalis to individuality.' He
measured six and one-half inches from the 'orifice of his ear
to benevolence.' His brain was calculated to be unusually large.
Among his largest propensities were amativeness, excitability
and self-esteem. He was moderately secretive and showed no
signs of marvelousness, piety and veneration. In the portrait
he appeared with yellow sideburns and very small blue
eyes, but his descendants, studying the picture and trying to
divine what, buried beneath the hair ornaments, the man
had been, always came away with an impression of harshness

and dishonesty – an uneasy feeling that was increased by the conviction that Benjamin would have detested his descendants in their gabardine suits. The force of mutual disapproval in the portrait was so great that it was kept in the attic. Benjamin had not been painted in the uniform of a captain. Far from it. He appeared in a yellow velvet cap, trimmed with fur, and a loose green velvet gown or bathrobe as if he, bred on that shinbone coast and weaned on beans and codfish, had translated himself into some mandarin or hawk-nosed Renaissance prince, tossing bones to the mastiffs, jewels to the whores and swilling wine out of golden goblets with his codpiece busting its velvet bows.

Along with the phrenological paper and the portrait were the family journals, for all the Wapshots were copious journalists. There was hardly a man of the family who had doctored a sick horse or bought a sailboat or heard, late at night, the noise of rain on the roof without making a record of these facts. They chronicled the changes in the wind, the arrival and departure of ships, the price of tea and jute and the death of kings. They urged themselves to improve their minds and they reproached themselves for idleness, sloth, lewdness, stupidity and drunkenness, for St Botolphs had been a lively port where they danced until dawn and where there was always plenty of rum to drink. The attic was a fitting place for these papers, for this barny summit of the house – as big as a hayloft – with its trunks and oars and tillers and torn sails and broken furniture and crooked chimneys and hornets and wasps and obsolete lamps spread out at one's feet like the ruins of a vanished civilization and with an extraordinary spiciness in the air as if some eighteenth-century Wapshot, drinking Madeira and eating nuts on a sunny beach and thinking about the passing of the season, had tried to capture the heat and light in a flask or hamper and had released his treasure in the attic, for here was the smell of summer without its vitality; here seemed to be the lights and sounds of a summer preserved.

Benjamin was remembered in the village – unjustly, to be sure – for an incident that took place on his return from

Ceylon in the second *Topaze*. His son Lorenzo gave a good account of this in his journal. There were four volumes of these, bound in boards with this introduction. – I, Lorenzo Wapshot, being 21 years of age and thinking that it will be for my amusement to keep a sort of journal of my time and situation and the various events that may take place as I proceed along through life have concluded to make a minutes on this book daily of all circumstances that may transpire respecting not only my own concerns but of those throughout the town of St Botolphs as far as I can conveniently ascertain. – It was in the second volume of the journal that he reported the events leading up to his father's famous return.

This day (Lorenzo wrote) we received news of the ship Topaze, my father Captn. She has been overdue three mos. Brackett esq. from the brig Luna tells us now that her rigging was much damaged by a tempist and that she was at Samoa 2 mos. for repairs, and can now be expected any day. Mother and Aunts Ruth and Patience hearing there was a heavy surf at Hales Point I harnessed the chaise and drove thence.

This day we were waited upon by David Marshman, 1st mate of the brig Luna who asked to speak privately with Mother and was shown into the back parlor for this purpose. He was served no tea and upon leaving Mother was rejoined by her sisters and much whispering ensued. None of the ladies took supper and I ate alone in the kitchen with the Chinaman. In the evening I walked to Cody's store and weighed myself. I weigh 165 lbs.

This day pleasant and warm; winds southerly. During the day the following vessels arrived viz: The Resiliance from Gibralter, Captn Tobias Moffet. The Golden Doge from New Orleans. Captn Robert Folger. The Venus from Quito. Captn Edg. Small. The Unicorn from Antwerp. Captn Josh Kelley. Bathed in river. This afternoon the thirsty earth was refreshed with a most charming shower.

This day at about noon there was a cry of fire and lo the top of Mr Dexter's house was discovered to be ignited. Water however was immediately applied in such copious quantities that its progress was directly stopped. A trifling damage was done to the roof. Walked this evening to Cody's store and weighed myself. I weigh 165 lbs. While I was at Cody's Newell Henry drew me aside with further news of the Topaze. He had the damnable effrontery to tell me my father's delay was occaisioned by no damage to his rigging but by his addiction to immoral practices viz drinking intemperately and indulging in lewdness with the natives whereupon I kicked him in the arse and walked home.

Was waited upon this morning at the counting house by Prince esq. president of the Birch Rod Club an organization of young men from hereabouts for the promotion of manly conduct and high moral character. Was brought before the club in the evening on the complaint of Henry esq. for kicking him in the arse. 1st mate Marshman of the brig Luna testified as to the veracity of Henry's allegation and H. Prince, serving as prosecutor for the defense made a most elegant and moving condemnation of gossip of all kinds whether or not they be a kernel of truth in it and the jury found for me and fined the plaintiff 3 doz fine apples. Upon returning home found Mother and sisters drinking rum punch.

This day clear at dawn. Captn Webb's little boy was trod upon by a horse and died before candlelight. Went to Cody's store and got weighed. I weigh 165 lbs. Walked with ladies in the pasture. Mother and sisters drinking rum punch.

This day was engaged in the gardain wheeling maneur. Mother and sisters drinking rum punch. It is Marshman's tale of Samoa that has undone them but they should not judge the absent unkindly nor forget that the flesh lusteth contrary to the spirit. I have spent considerable of my leisure time in this past year in the improvement of my mind but I find that much of it has been spent extremely foolish and that walking in the pasture at dusk with virtuous, amiable and genteel young ladies I experience none but swineish passions. I commenced to read Russell's Modern Europe sometime last summer. I have read the first two vols which I find very interesting and I shall improve the first opportunity to complete the work. By a retrospective view of the past may I find wisdom to govern and improve the future more profitably. To accomplish this and improve my character may the Almighty Ruler of the Universe grant His assistance and guide and direct me in all good things.

This day a wild animal caravan arrived at the River House and I went there in the evening to see the curiosities. At half-past six the gates to the tent were open, previous to which many had gathered and stood crouded together with their gallants like a vast flock of sheep when gathered before the shearer. It was absolutely disgusting to see delicate females and those too of the first respectability as well as many comely, strait and tall lads crouded and jammed and pushing and shoving in keeping their stations near the entrance of the tent and endeavoring to obtain as near a position as possible. The gate was at length opened and then it was a rush. The utmost exertions of several gate-keepers were hardly competent to regulate and prune the flood of ingression and the tent soon became filled to stuffing. Luckily I obtained a situation where by looking between several heads I could see the curiosities which included 1 lion, 3 monkies, 1 leopard and a learned bear this dumb beast having been taught to dance to music and add a sum of figures.

This day at 8 am Sam Trowbridge rode over from Saul's Hill with the news that the Topaze was sighted. There was much livliness and stirring both at home and in the town amongst her other owners. Rode down-river with Judge Thomas in his chaise and was carried out to the Topaze by John Pendleton. Found father in fine spirits and has brought me as a present one rich sword called a kriss. Drank maderia in the cabin with father and judge Thomas. The cargo is jute. The ship was walked up and made fast and the gangplank put down to where mother and sisters were waiting to greet father. They carried umbrellas. As father approached the ladies Aunt Ruth raised her umbrella high in the air and brought it down most savagely upon the back of his head. Aunt Hope beat him angrily on the port side and Mother charged him from the bow. When the ladies had done Father was taken directly by chaise to Dr Howland's surgery where three stitches was taken in his ear and where he spent the night with me for company and where we drank wine and ate nuts and passed the time cheerfully in spite of his pain.

The early volumes of Lorenzo's journals were the best – accounts of the liveliness in the river and summer evenings when the St Botolphs horse guards could be heard drilling on the green – and this was in a way surprising since he succeeded in improving his mind, served two terms in the state legislature and founded the St Botolphs Philosophical Society, but learning did nothing for his prose and he would never write as well again as he had written about the wild-animal caravan. He lived to be eighty, never married and left his savings to his niece Honora, the only daughter of his younger brother Thaddeus.

Thaddeus went out to the Pacific on what may have been a voyage of expiation. He and his wife Alice remained there for eighteen years as missionaries, distributing copies of the New Testament, supervising the construction of coral block churches, healing the sick and burying the dead. Physically neither Thaddeus nor Alice was what is usually called to mind by the dedicated missionary. They beamed out of the family photographs – a handsome goodhumored couple. They were dedicated, and in his letters Thaddeus reported approaching an island in an outrigger one evening where naked and beautiful women waited on him with ropes of flowers. 'What a challenge to my piety,' he wrote.

Honora was born on Oahu and sent to St Botolphs, where she was raised by her Uncle Lorenzo. She had no children. Ebenezer had no children but Aaron begat Hamlet and Leander. Hamlet had no legal issue and Leander married Sarah Coverly and begat Moses and Coverly, whom we have seen watching the parade.

CHAPTER 3

Mr Pincher's horse galloped along Hill Street for about a hundred yards – maybe two – and then, her wind gone, she fell into a heavyfooted trot. Fatty Titus followed the float in his car, planning to rescue the charter members of the Woman's Club, but when he reached them the picture was so tranquil – it looked like a hayride – that he backed his car around and returned to the village to see the rest of the parade. The danger had passed for everyone but Mr Pincher's mare. God knows what strains she had put on her heart and her lungs – even on her will to live. Her name was Lady, she chewed tobacco and she was worth more to Mr Pincher than Mrs Wapshot and all her friends. He loved her sweet nature and admired her perseverance, and the indignity of having a firecracker exploded under her rump made him sore with anger. What was the world coming to? His heart seemed to go out to the old mare and his tender sentiments to spread over her broad back like a blanket.

'Lady's going home,' he called over his shoulder to Mrs Wapshot. 'She wants to get home and I'm going to let her.'

'Couldn't you let us off?' Mrs Wapshot asked.

'I ain't going to stop her now,' Mr Pincher said. 'She's had a lot more to put up with than the rest of you. She wants to get home now and I ain't going to stop her.'

Mrs Wapshot and her friends resigned themselves to the news of their captivity. After all, none of them had been hurt.

The water pitcher was broken and the lectern had been upset, but the lectern was whole. Lady's stable was on Hewitt Street, they knew, which meant going over the hill and through the back country to River Street; but it was a fine day and a good opportunity to enjoy the salt air and the summer scenery, and anyhow they didn't have any choice.

The old mare had begun the pull up Wapshot Hill and from here, above the trees, they had an excellent view of the village in the valley. To the northeast lay the brick walls of the table-silver factory, the railroad bridge and the morose, Victorian spire of the depot. Toward the center of town was a less sentimental spire – the Unitarian Church, founded in 1780. Its clock struck the half hour as they traveled. The bell had been cast in Antwerp and had a sweet, clear note. A second later the bell at Christ Church (1870) struck the half hour with a gloomy note that sounded like a frying pan. This bell came from Altoona. A little below the crown of the hill the wagon rolled past old Mrs Drinkwine's charming white house with her picket fence buried in red roses. The whiteness of the house, the feathery elms, the punctual church bells – even the faint smell of the sea – encouraged in these travelers a tendency to overlook the versatility of life as if it was only common sense to forget that Mrs Drinkwine had once been a wardrobe mistress for Lee and J. J. Shubert and knew more about the seamy side of life than Louis-Ferdinand Céline.

But it was difficult, from the summit of Wapshot Hill, not to spread over the village the rich, dark varnish of decorum and quaintness – to do this or to lament the decadence of a once boisterous port; to point out that the Great Pissmire was now Alder Vale and that the Mariner's Jug was now the Grace Louise Tearoom. There was beauty below them, inarguable and unique – many fine things built for the contentment of hardy men – and there was decadence – more ships in bottles than on the water – but why grieve over this? Looking back at the village we might put ourselves into the shoes of a native son (with a wife and family in Cleveland) coming home for some purpose – a legacy or a set of Hawthorne or a football sweater – and swinging through the streets in good weather what would it matter that the blacksmith shop was now an art school? Our friend from Cleveland might observe, passing through the square at dusk, that this decline or change in spirit had not altered his own humanity and that whatever he was – a man come for a legacy or a drunken sailor looking for a whore – it did not matter whether or not his way was lighted by the twinkling candles in tearooms; it did not change what he was.

But our friend from Cleveland was only a visitor – he would go away, and Mr Pincher and his passengers would not. Now, past Mrs Drinkwine's and over the crown of the hill, the west of the village spread out below them – farmland and woods and in the distance Parson's Pond, where Parthenia Brown had drowned herself and where the icehouse, useless now, stood with its ramp sloping down into the blue water. They could see, from this high land, that there were no walls or barriers around the village and yet, as the wagon started slowly down the west side of Wapshot Hill and they approached Reba Heaslip's house, they might wonder how Reba could have carried on her life in a place that was not walled. Whenever Reba was introduced to a stranger she exclaimed: 'I was BORN in the inner sanctum of the Masonic Temple.' What she meant, of course, was that what was now the Masonic Temple had been her father's house, but would her jolting and exclamatory style have gotten her very far in a place like Chicago? She was a passionate antivivisectionist and was dedicated to the alteration or suppression of the celebration of Christmas – a holiday that seemed to her to inculcate and perpetuate ruinous improvidence, false standards and economic depravity. On Christmas Eve she joined her enthusiasms and went among the carol singers, passing out antivivisectionist tracts. She had been arrested twice by what she called the 'fascist police.' She had a white house like Mrs Drinkwine's and a sign was nailed to her door. THIS IS THE HOUSE OF A VERY OLD LADY WHO HAS GIVEN THE LAST TEN

YEARS OF HER LIFE TO THE ANTIVIVISECTIONIST CAUSE. MANY
OF THE MEN OF HER FAMILY DIED FOR THEIR COUNTRY. THERE
IS NOTHING OF VALUE OR INTEREST HERE. SALUTE YOUR FLAG!
ROBBERS AND VANDALS PASS BY! The sign was weathered and
had hung there for ten years and the ladies hardly noticed it.

On Reba's front lawn there was a skiff planted with
petunias.

Going down the west side of Wapshot Hill with the full
Weight of the wagon forward on the shafts the mare picked
her way slowly. Beyond Reba's there was a patch of woodland,
charmingly dappled with sunlight, and this grove had on
them all, even on Mr Pincher, a happy effect as if it were
some reminder of paradise – some happy authentication of
the beauty of the summer countryside – for it was the kind
of scene that most of them had hanging on their parlor walls
and yet this was no photograph or painting through which
they traveled with the spotty lights flowing over them. It was
all real and they were flesh and blood.

Beyond the woods they came to Peter Covell's place.

Peter was a farmer. He had a small cash crop – sweet
corn, gladioli, butter and potatoes – and in the past he had
made some money building stone walls. A powerful man of
perhaps seventy with rusty tools, a collapsed barn, chickens
in his kitchen, cats in his parlor, lusty and sometimes drunk
and always clean-spoken, he had pulled stones out of the
earth with a mare that was older than Lady and had set them
together into walls that would outlive the village, whatever its
destiny. Dam the river and flood it for a reservoir (this could
happen) and in the summer droughts people would drive or
fly – this being in the future – to see the pattern of Covell's
walls as they appeared above the receding water; or let the
scrub take hold, maple saplings and horse brier, and fishermen
and hunters, climbing the walls, would say that this must have
been pasture once upon a time. His daughter Alice had never
married, she loved the old man so, and even now on Sunday
afternoons they climbed the hill hand in hand, carrying a
spyglass to watch the ships in the bay. Alice raised collies. A

sign hung on the house: COLLIES FOR SALE. Who wanted collies? She would have done better raising children or selling eggs.

All the unsold collies barked at the wagon as it went by.

Beyond Covells' there was Brown's River – a little stream or brook with a wooden bridge that set up peals of false thunder as they crossed it. On the other side of the river was the Pluzinskis' farm – a small brown house with glass ornaments on the lightning rods and two rose trees in the front yard. The Pluzinskis were hardworking foreigners who kept to themselves although their oldest son had won a scholarship at the Academy. Their farm, rectilinear and self-contained, was the opposite of Peter Covell's place as if, although they could not speak English, they had come much more naturally to the valley land than the old Yankee.

Beyond Pluzinskis' the road turned to the right and they could see the handsome Greek portico of Theophilus Gates' house. Theophilus was president of the Pocamasset Bank and Trust Company and as an advocate of probity and thrift he could be seen splitting wood in front of his house each morning before he went to work. His house was not shabby, but it needed paint, and this, like his wood splitting, was meant to put honest shabbiness above improvident show. There was a FOR SALE sign on his lawn. Theophilus had inherited from his father the public utilities of Travertine and St Botolphs and had sold them at a great profit. On the day these negotiations were completed he came home and put the FOR SALE sign on his grass. The house, of course, was not for sale. The sign was only meant to set in motion a rumor that he had sold the utilities at a loss and to help preserve his reputation as a poor, gloomy, God-fearing and overworked man. One more thing. When Theophilus invited guests for the evening they would be expected, after supper, to go into the garden and play hide-and-go-seek.

As they passed Gates' the ladies could see in the distance the slate roof of Honora Wapshot's house on Boat Street. Honora would not appear to them. Honora had once been introduced to the President of the United States and wringing his hand she had said: 'I come from St Botolphs. I guess you must know where *that* is. They say that St Botolphs is like a pumpkin pie. No upper crust. . . .'

They saw Mrs Mortimer Jones chasing up her garden path with a butterfly net. She wore a bulky house dress and a big straw hat.

Beyond the Joneses' was the Brewsters' and another sign: HOME-MADE PIE AND CAKES. Mr Brewster was an invalid and Mrs Brewster supported her husband and had sent her two sons through college with the money she made as a baker. Her sons had done well but now one of them lived in San Francisco and the other in Detroit and they never came home. They wrote her saying that they planned to come home for Christmas or Easter – that the first trip they made would be the trip to St Botolphs – but they went to Yosemite National Park, they went to Mexico City, they even went to Paris, but they never, never came home.

At the junction of Hill and River streets the wagon turned right, passing George Humbolt's, who lived with his mother and who was known as Uncle Peepee Marshmallow. Uncle Peepee came from a line of hardy sailors but he was not as virile as his grandfathers. Could he, through yearning and imagination, weather himself as he would have been weathered by a passage through the Straits of Magellan? Now and then, on summer evenings, poor Uncle Peepee wandered in his bare skin among the river gardens. His neighbors spoke to him with nothing more than impatience. 'Go home, Uncle Peepee, and get some clothes on,' they said. He was seldom arrested and would never be sent away for to send him away would reflect on the uniqueness of the place. What could the rest of the world do for him that could not be done in St Botolphs?

Beyond Uncle Peepee's the Wapshot house could be seen in the distance and River Street itself, always a romantic picture, seemed more so on this late holiday morning. The air smelled of brine – the east wind was rising – and would presently give to the place a purpose and a luster and a sadness too, for

while the ladies admired the houses and the elms they knew
that their sons would go away. Why did the young want to
go away? Why did the young want to go away?

Mr Pincher stopped long enough for Mrs Wapshot to climb
down from the wagon. 'I shan't thank you for the ride,' she
said, 'but I will thank Lady. It was her idea.' This was Mrs
Wapshot's style, and smiling good-by she stepped gracefully
up the walk to her door.

CHAPTER 4

Rosalie Young took the road to the shore that morning, unknown to the Wapshots as you are unknown to me, early, early, long before the parade had begun to form in St Botolphs, way to the south. Her date stopped for her in his old convertible at the rooming house in the city where she lived. Mrs Shannon, the landlady, watched them drive away through the glass panels of her front door. Youth was a bitter mystery to Mrs Shannon but today the mystery was deepened by Rosalie's white coat and the care she had taken in painting her face. If they were going swimming, the landlady thought, she wouldn't have worn her new white coat, and if they weren't going swimming why did she carry a towel – one of Mrs Shannon's towels? They might have been going to a wedding or an office picnic, a ball game or a visit to relations. It made Mrs Shannon sad to know that she couldn't be sure.

But it was always difficult for a stranger to guess Rosalie's destination, she approached each journey with such great expectations. Sometimes in the autumn her date would tell his parents that he was going hunting and would then take Rosalie – who was under no kind of surveillance once she left the rooming house – out for a night in a tourist cabin on the turnpike, and when he picked her up on those Saturday afternoons she usually wore a chrysanthemum and an oak leaf pinned to her lapel and carried a small suitcase with an Amherst or Harvard label stuck to it as if all the pleasures of a football week end – the game, the tea dance, the faculty reception and the prom – were what she was expecting. She was never disappointed nor was she ever disabused. There was never a point, when she hung up her coat in the tourist cabin while he tried to burn off the damp with a fire, where the difference between this furtive evening and the goal-post snake dance would depress her, nor did she ever seem to reach a point where these differences challenged or altered her expectations. Most of her expectations were collegiate and now, as they found their way out of the city, she began to sing. Popular music passed directly from the radio and the bandstand into some retentive space in her memory, leaving a spoor of cheerful if repetitious and sentimental lyrics.

Going out of the city they passed those congested beaches that lie within its limits and that spread, with a few industrial interruptions, for miles to the south. Now, in the middle of the morning, the life of the beaches was in full swing and the peculiar smell of cooking grease and popcorn butter was stronger than any emanations of the Atlantic Ocean that seems there, held in the islands of a sinking coast, to be a virile and a sad presence. Thousands of half-naked bathers obscured the beach or hesitated knee deep in the ocean as if this water, like the Ganges, were purifying and holy so that these displaced and naked crowds, strung for miles along the coast, gave to this holiday and carnival surface the undercurrents of a pilgrimage in which, as much as any of the thousands they passed, Rosalie and her date were involved.

'You hungry?' he said. 'You want something to eat now? Ma gave us enough for three meals. I've got some whisky in the glove case.'

The thought of the picnic hamper reminded her of his plain, white-haired mother, who would have sent along something of herself in the basket – watchful, never disapproving, but saddened by the pleasures of her only son. He had his way. His neat, bleak and ugly bedroom was the axis of their house and the rapport between this man and his parents was so intense and tacit that it seemed secretive to Rosalie. Every

room was dominated by souvenirs of his growth; guns, golf
clubs, trophies from schools and camps and on the piano some
music he had practiced ten years ago. The cool house and his
contrite parents were strange to Rosalie and she thought that
his white shirt that morning smelled of the yellow varnished
floors where he took up his secretive life with Ma and Pa. Her
date had always had a dog. He had, in his lifetime, run through
four dogs, and Rosalie knew their names, their habits, their
markings and their tragic ends. On the one time that she had
met his parents the conversation had turned to his dogs and
she had come to feel that they thought of his relationship to
her – not maliciously or harmfully, but because these were the
only terms they could find – as something like the exchange
between him and a dog. I feel absolully like a dog, she said.

They drove through a few holiday village squares where
newspapers were stacked outside the one open drugstore and
where parades were forming. Now they were in the country,
a few miles inland, but there was not much change in feeling,
for the road was fenced with stores, restaurants, gift shops,
greenhouses and tourist cabins. The beach to which he was
taking her was unpopular because the road was rough and
the beach was stony, but he was disappointed that day when
he found two other cars in the clearing where they parked,
and they unloaded the hamper and followed a crooked path
to the sea – the open sea here. Pink scrub roses grew along
the path and she felt the salt air form on her lips and tasted
it with her tongue. There was a narrow, gravelly beach at a
break in the cliffs and then below them they saw a couple
like themselves and a family with children and then beyond
them the green sea. Turning away self-consciously from the
privacy he so sorely wanted then and that the cliffs all around
them made available he carried the picnic hamper, the whisky
bottle and the tennis ball down onto the beach and settled
himself in full view of the other bathers as if this momentary
gesture toward simple, public pleasure was made for the sake
of whatever his mother had been able to wrap up of herself
in the sandwiches. Rosalie went behind a stone and changed

from her clothes into a bathing suit. He was waiting for her at the edge of the water and when she had made sure that all her hair was under her bathing cap she took his hand and they walked in.

The water was cruelly cold there, it always was, and when it got up to her knees she dropped his hand and dived. She had been taught to swim a crawl but she had never unlearned a choppy, hurried stroke and with her face half buried in the green she headed out to sea for ten feet, turned, surface-dived, shouted with pain at the cold and then raced toward the beach. The beach was sunny and the cold water and the heat of the sun set her up. She dried herself roughly with a towel, snatched off her cap and then stood in the sun, waiting for its heat to reach her bones. She dried her hands and lighted a cigarette and he came out of the sea then, dried only his hands and dropped down beside her.

Her hair was yellow and she was fair – long limbed and full breasted with a skittish look that even in the robes of a choir girl, which she had worn, made her look high-tailed and undressed. He took her hand and raised it and brushed her arm, covered with the light hair of an early down, with his lips. 'I'd adore to pick blueberries,' she said loudly and for the benefit of the others on the beach. 'I'd adore to pick blueberries but let's take your hat and we'll put the blueberries in that.'

They climbed the stones above the beach, hand in hand, but the search for a privacy that would satisfy her was lengthy and they went from place to place until finally he stopped her and she agreed, timidly, that there was probably nothing better. He took her bathing suit off her shoulders and when she was naked she lay down cheerfully, gladly in the sunny dirt to take the only marriage of her body to its memories that she knew. Tenderness and good nature lingered between them after they were done and she leaned on his shoulder while she stepped back into her bathing suit and they returned hand in hand to the beach. They went swimming again and unwrapped the sandwiches that his worried mother had made them the night before.

There were deviled eggs and chicken joints, sandwiches, cakes, cookies, and when they had eaten what they could they put the rest away in the hamper and he jogged down the beach and pitched the tennis ball to her from there. The light ball wavered in the wind but she caught it and threw it back to him with a wing that, like her swimming stroke, was short of what was needed, and he caught the ball with a flourish and threw it back to her. Now the catching and the throwing, the catching and the throwing took on a pleasant monotony and through it she felt the afternoon passing. The tide was going out, leaving on the beach seriations of coarser gravel and strands of kelp whose flower shapes burst with a shot when she crushed them between her fingers. The family group had begun to gather their possessions and call to their children. The other couple lay side by side, talking and laughing. She lay down again and he sat beside her and lighted a cigarette, asking, now, now, but she said no and he walked off toward the water. She looked up and saw him swimming in the waves. Then he was drying himself beside her and offering her a cup of whisky but she said no, no, not yet, and he drank it himself and looked out to sea.

Now the pleasure steamers, fat, white, crowded and unseaworthy, that had set out that morning were returning. (Among these was the *Topaze*.) The swell of the sea had quieted a little. Her date drank off his whisky and wrung the paper cup in his hand. The couple on their left were getting up to go and when they had gone he asked again now, now, and she said no, led on by some vague vision of continence that had appeared to her. She was weary of trying to separate the power of loneliness from the power of love and she was lonely. She was lonely and the sun drawing off the beach and the coming night made her feel tender and afraid. She looked at him now, holding in at least one chamber of her mind this vision of continence. He was staring out to sea. Lechery sat like worry on his thin face. He saw the leonine reefs in the sea like clavicles and women's knees. Even the clouds in heaven wouldn't dissuade him. The pleasure boats looked to him like

voyaging whorehouses and he thought that the ocean had a
riggish smell. He would marry some woman with big breasts,
she thought – the daughter of a paper hanger – and go on
the road selling disinfectants. Yes, yes, she said, yes now.

Then they drank some more whisky and ate again and now
the homing pleasure boats had disappeared and the beach and
all but the highest cliffs lay in the dark. He went up to the car
and got a blanket, but now the search for privacy was brief;
now it was dark. The stars came out and when they were
done she washed in the sea and put her white coat on and
together, barefoot, they went up and down the beach, carefully
gathering the sandwich papers, bottles and egg shells that they
and the others had left, for these were neat, good children of
the middle class.

He hung the wet bathing suits on the door of the car to dry,
patted her gently on the knee – the tenderest gesture of them
all – and started the car. Once they had got onto the main
road the traffic was heavy and many of the cars they passed
had, like his, bathing suits hung from the door handles. He
drove fast, and she thought cleverly, although the car was old.
Its lights were weak and with the lights of an approaching car
filling the pupils of his eyes he held to the road precariously,
like a blind man running. But he was proud of the car – he
had put in a new cylinder head and supercharger – proud
of his prowess in negotiating the dilapidated and purblind
vehicle over the curving roads of Travertine and St Botolphs,
and when they had gotten free of the traffic and were on a
back road that was not, to his knowledge, patrolled, he took
it as fast as it would go. The speed made Rosalie feel relaxed
until she heard him swear and felt the car careen and bump
into a field.

CHAPTER 5

The heart of the Wapshot house had been built before the War of Independence, but many additions had been made since then, giving the house the height and breadth of that recurrent dream in which you open a closet door and find that in your absence a corridor and a staircase have bloomed there. The staircase rises and turns into a hall in which there are many doors among the book shelves, anyone of which will lead you from one commodious room to another so that you can wander uninterruptedly and searching for nothing through a place that, even while you dream, seems not to be a house at all but a random construction put forward to answer some need of the sleeping mind. The house had been neglected in Leander's youth, but he had restored it during his prosperous years at the table-silver company. It was old enough and large enough and had seen enough dark acts to support a ghost but the only room that was haunted was the old water closet at the back of the upstairs hall. Here a primitive engine, made of vitreous china and mahogany, stood by itself. Now and then – sometimes as often as once a day – this contraption would perform its functions independently. There would be the clatter of machinery and the piercing whinny of old valves. Then the roar of waters arriving and the suck of waters departing could be heard in every room of the house. So much for ghosts.

The house is easy enough to describe but how to write a summer's day in an old garden? Smell the grass, we say. Smell the trees! A flag is draped from the attic windows over the front of the house, leaving the hall in darkness. It is dusk and the family has gathered. Sarah has told them about her journey with Mr Pincher. Leander has brought the *Topaze* in to port. Moses has raced his sailboat at the Pocamasset club and is spreading his mainsail on the grass to dry. Coverly has watched the table-silver-company ball game from the barn cupola. Leander is drinking bourbon and the parrot hangs in a cage by the kitchen door. A cloud passes over the low sun, darkening the valley, and they feel a deep and momentary uneasiness as if they apprehended how darkness can fall over the continents of the mind. The wind freshens and then they are all cheered as if this reminded them of their recuperative powers. Malcolm Peavey is bringing his catboat up the river and it is so still that they can hear the sound she makes as she comes about. A carp is cooking in the kitchen, and, as everyone knows, a carp has to be boiled in claret with pickled oysters, anchovies, thyme, marjoram, basil and white onions. All of this can be smelled. But as we see the Wapshots, spread out in their rose garden above the river, listening to the parrot and feeling the balm of those evening winds that, in New England, smell so of maidenly things – of orris root and toilet soap and rented rooms, wet by an open window in a thunder shower; of chamber pots and sorrel soup and roses and gingham and lawn; of choir robes and copies of the New Testament bound in limp morocco and pastures that are for sale, blooming now with rue and fern – as we see the flowers, staked by Leander with broken hockey sticks and mop and broom handles, as we see that the scarecrow in the cornfield wears the red coat of the defunct St Botolphs Horse Guards and that the blue water of the river below them seems mingled with our history, it would be wrong to say as an architectural photographer once did, after photographing the side door, 'It's just like a scene from J. P. Marquand.' They are not like this – these are country people, and in the center of the gathering sits Aunt

Adelaide Forbes, the widow of a schoolteacher. Hear what Aunt Adelaide has to say.

'Yesterday afternoon,' says Aunt Adelaide, 'about three o'clock, three or three thirty – when there was enough shade in the garden so's I wouldn't get sunstroke, I went out to pull some carrots for my supper. Well, I was pulling carrots and suddenly I pulled this very unusual carrot.' She spread the fingers of her right hand over her breast – her powers of description seemed overtaken, but then they rallied. 'Well, I've been pulling carrots all my life, but I never seen a carrot like this. It was just growing in an awdinary row of carrots. There wasn't no rocks or anything to account for it. Well, this carrot looked like – I don't know how to say it – this carrot was the spit and image of Mr Forbes' parts.' Blood rushed to her face but modesty would not halt nor even delay her progress. Sarah Wapshot smiled seraphically at the twilight. 'Well, I took the other carrots into the kitchen for my supper,' Aunt Adelaide said, 'and I wrapped this unusual carrot up in a piece of paper and took it right over to Reba Heaslip. She's such an old maid I thought she'd be interested. She was in the kitchen so I give her this carrot. That's what it looks like, Reba, I said. That's just what it looks like.'

Then Lulu called them in to supper where the smell of claret, fish and spices in the dining room would make your head swim. Leander said grace and served them and when they had all tasted the carp they said that it hadn't a pondy taste. Leander had caught the carp with a rig of his own invention, baited with stale doughnuts. They talked about other carp that had been taken from the fresh-water inlet to the river. There were six in all – six or seven. Adelaide would remember one that the others couldn't recall. Leander had caught three and Mr Dexter had caught two and a mill hand who lived on the other side of the river – a Pole – had caught one. The fish had come from China to St Botolphs to be used in ornamental garden pools. In the '90's they had been dumped into the stream to take their chances and their chances had been good enough. Leander was saying that he knew there were more carp when they all heard the crash that, considering the dilapidation of the car, sounded extraordinarily rich as if some miscreant had put an ax through the lid of a jewel box. Leander and his sons got up from the table and went out the side door.

It was a vast summer night. There was an unusual softness to the dark air and the bland starlight and an unusual density to the darkness so that even on his own land Leander had to move cautiously to keep from stumbling over a stone or stepping into a brier patch. The car had gone off the road at the bend and run into an elm in the old field. Its red tail lamp and one of its headlights were still burning and in this light the grass and the leaves on the elm shone a bright green. Steam, as they approached the car, was escaping from the radiator and hissing, but as they crossed the field this hissing lessened and when they reached the car it had stopped, although the smell of the vapors was still in the air.

'He's dead,' Leander said. 'He's dead. What a Christly mess. Stay here, Moses. I'll go up to the house and call the police. You come with me, Coverly. I want you to drive Adelaide home. They'll be enough trouble without her. He's dead,' he muttered, and Coverly followed him up the field and across the road to the house where all the windows were being lighted, one by one.

Moses seemed stunned. There was nothing for him to do and then a sound of crackling – he thought Leander or someone had returned and stepped on some brush, crossing a field – made him spin around but the field and the road were empty and he turned back to the car and saw a fire under the vents of the hood. At the same time the clammy smell of dirty steam and rubber was joined by the smell of heated metal and burning paint and while the hood contained the fire its paint began to blister. Then he seized the dead man's shoulders and tried to pull him out of the car while the fire crackled with the merriment of a hearth fire in a damp house at the end of the day and began to throw a golden light on the trees. The fear of an explosion that might send Moses to join the dead man made his movements hasty and constrained and while he wanted to get away from the fire he could not leave the man there on his pyre and he pulled and pulled until the body, released, sent them both backward into the field. There was sand there at the edge of the path and now he scooped this up with his hands and threw it onto the fire. The sand checked the fire and now he loaded it onto the hood and then knocked the hood open with a stick and threw sand onto the cylinder head until the fire was out and his fear of an explosion was ended and he was left alone in the field, he thought, with the wrecked car and the dead man. He sat down, exhausted, and saw that all of the windows of the farm across the road were lighted and then heard, north of the four corners, a siren and knew that Leander had got the police. He would sit there and catch his breath and his strength, he thought, until they came, when he heard the girl saying from somewhere in the darkness: I'm hurt, Charlie, I've hurt myself. Where are you? I'm hurt, Charlie. For a moment Moses thought: I'll leave her too; but when she spoke again he pushed himself to his feet and went around the car, looking for her. Charlie, she said, I've hurt myself, and then he found her and thinking that Moses was the dead man she said: Charlie, oh Charlie, where are we? and began to cry and he knelt beside her where she lay on the ground. By then the sound of the siren had passed the four corners and was bearing down the road and then he heard, from the darkness, Leander's voice and the voices of the police and saw their flashlights playing over the field — idly, inquisitively — heard their sighs as their idle, inquisitive lights touched the dead man and heard one of them tell another to go to the house and get a blanket. Then they began, idly, to discuss the fire, and Moses called to them and they brought their inquisitive lights over to where he knelt beside the girl. Now they played their lights on the girl, who kept up a bitter light sobbing and who, with her fair hair, seemed very young. 'Don't move her, don't touch her,' a policeman said importantly. 'She may have sustained some internal injuries.' Then one of them told another to get a stretcher and they put her on the stretcher – she was still sobbing – and carried her past the wrecked car and the dead man who was now covered with a blanket toward the many lights of the house.

Remember that crash on 7B – one of them said, but the question was put nervously and the others didn't answer. The strangeness of the night, the probing lights, the distant sound of fireworks and the dead man they had left in the field had unsettled them all and had unmanned at least one of them and now they followed closely the one course open to them: to bring the girl into the lighted house. Mrs Wapshot stood in her door, her face composed in a sorrowful smile – an involuntary choice of expression with which she always confronted the unknown. She assumed that the girl was dead; more than that she assumed that she was the only child of a devoted couple, that she was engaged to marry a splendid man and that she had been standing at the threshold of a rich and useful life. But most of all she thought that the girl had been a child, for whenever Mrs Wapshot saw a drunkard lying on the street or a whore tapping her windowpane the deep sadness she always felt in her breast lay in the recollection that these unfortunates had once been fragrant children. She was unsettled, but she restored herself with a kind of imperiousness as she spoke to the policemen when they carried the stretcher through the open door. 'Take her to the spare room,' she said, and when they hesitated, since they had never been in the house before and had no idea of where the spare room might be, she spoke as if they were stupid and had compounded the tragedy. 'Take her up to the spare room,' she commanded, for to Mrs Wapshot all the world knew, or ought to know, the floor plan of West Farm. The 'up' helped them and with this they started for the stairs.

The doctor was telephoned and he came over and the girl was put in the spare-room bed. Small stones and sand had cut the skin of her arms and shoulders and when the doctor came there was some indecision about whether he should first pronounce the man in the field dead or look at the girl but he decided on the girl and they all waited in the downstairs hall.

'Get her something hot, get her something hot,' they heard him tell Mrs Wapshot, and she came down and made some tea in the kitchen. 'Does that hurt?' they heard him ask the girl. 'Does that hurt, does that hurt you at all?' and to all of this she answered no. 'Now, what is your name,' he asked her, and she said, 'Rosalie Young,' and she gave an address in the city. 'It's a rooming house,' she said. 'My folks live in Philadelphia.' 'Do you want me to notify your parents?' the doctor said, and she said warmly, 'No, please don't, there isn't any reason why they should know.' Then she began to cry again and Sarah Wapshot gave her the tea and the front door opened quietly and in came Emmet Cavis, the village undertaker.

Emmet Cavis had come to St Botolphs as a traveling salesman for the gold-bead factory. He had impressed the village with his urbanity and his sharp clothes for those were the days when it was the responsibility of a drummer to represent for the people of isolated places the turbulence and color of urban life. He had made a few trips and had then returned with a mortician's diploma and had opened up an undertaking parlor and furniture store. Whether or not it had entered into his calculations, this transformation from a jewelry salesman to an undertaker had worked in his favor, for everything that he was associated with as a salesman – jewelry, promiscuity, travel and easy money – set him apart from the rest of the population and seemed, to the farm women at least, to be suitable attributes for the Angel of Death.

In his dealings with bewildered families he had, in the exchange of furniture and property for his services, been guilty now and then of sharp and dishonest practice; but it is a custom of that country to regard craft and dishonesty with respect. His cunning made him seem formidable and intelligent and like any good Yankee he had never trimmed the bereaved without remarking on The Uncertainty of All Earthly Things. He had retained and improved upon all his gifts as a commercial traveler and was the life of the village square. He could gossip brilliantly, tell a story in dialect and comfort a poor woman whose only child had been drowned in the surf. He put up, unwillingly, with the habits of mind his occupation had formed and when he spoke with Leander he judged him to be good for another fifteen years, but he suspected that his insurance policies might have elapsed and that the funeral would be modest if the two boys didn't interfere, as was sometimes the case, and insist on a cremation. What would the Day of Judgment be with nothing but ashes to show? He shook hands all around – neither hearty enough to be offensive nor diffident enough to seem sly – and then left the house with two policemen.

He told them what to do. Beyond opening the doors of the hearse he didn't raise a finger himself. 'He goes right in there, boys, right on that platform. Just give him a push. Just give him a push there.' He slammed the doors and tried the handle. He had the biggest car in St Botolphs, as if first among the powers of death was richness, and he climbed into the driver's seat and drove slowly away.

CHAPTER 6

By morning the news of the accident was known to almost everyone in St Botolphs. The young man's death filled them with sadness; and they asked what Honora Wapshot would think of the stranger at the farm. Now it was only natural that they should think of Honora, for this childless matriarch had done much more for the family than give Leander the *Topaze*. She had, as they said, the wherewithal, and Moses and Coverly were, on a contingent basis, her heirs. It is not my fault that New England is full of eccentric old women and we will merely give Honora her due.

She was born, as we know, in Polynesia, and raised by her Uncle Lorenzo in St Botolphs. She attended Miss Wilbur's Academy. 'Oh, I was an awful tomboy,' she often said of her youth, covering a smile with her hand and thinking, probably, of upset privies, tin cans tied to dog tails and other small-town pranks. She may have missed the tender love of her parents, who died in Polynesia, or been oppressed by her elderly uncle or been forced by something such as loneliness into the ways of a maverick but these were her ways. You could say of Honora that she had never subjected herself to the discipline of continuousness; but we are not dealing here with great cities and civilizations but with the society of an old port whose population diminished year by year.

After her graduation from Miss Wilbur's, Honora moved with Lorenzo into the city, where he served in the state

37

legislature and where she occupied herself in social-service work that seemed to be mostly of a medical nature. She claimed that these were her proudest years and as an old lady she often said that she wished she had never given up social work, although it was hard to imagine why she should long, with such snarling and bitterness, for the slums. She liked, at times, to reminisce about her experiences as a samaritan. These tales could take your appetite away and make your body hair bristle, but this may have been no more than that attraction to morbidity that overtakes many good women late in life. We hear them on buses and trains, in kitchens and restaurants, talking in such sad and musical voices about gangrene that they only seem to express their dismay at discovering that the body, in spite of all its ringing claims to the contrary, is mortal. Cousin Honora did not feel that she should use a medical vocabulary and so she had worked out a compromise. What she did was to pronounce the first syllables of the word in question and mumble the rest. Thus hysterectomy became hystermumblemumble, suppuration became suppurmumblemumble and testicles became testimumblemumbles.

When Lorenzo died he left Honora with a much larger trust than she might have expected. The Wapshot family had never — never in the darkest night with the owls chanting — discussed this sum. A month or two after Lorenzo's death Honora married a Mr de Sastago who claimed to be a marquis and to have a castle in Spain. She sailed for Europe as a bride but she returned in less than eight months. Of this part of her life she only said: 'I was once married to a foreigner and was greatly disappointed in my expectations. . . .' She took her maiden name again and settled down in Lorenzo's old house on Boat Street. The best way to understand her is to watch her during the course of a day.

Honora's bedroom is pleasant. Its walls are painted a light blue. The high, slender posts of her bed support a bare wooden frame that is meant to hold a canopy. The family has urged her to have this removed because it has fallen several times and might crash down in the middle of the night and brain the old lady while she dreams. She has not heeded these warnings and sleeps peacefully in this Damoclean antique. This is not to say that her furniture is as unreliable as the furniture at West Farm but there are three or four chairs around her house which, if you should be a stranger and sit in them, will collapse and dump you onto the floor. Most of her furniture belonged to Lorenzo and much of it was bought during his travels in Italy for he felt that this New World where he lived had sprung from the minds of Renaissance men. The dust that lies on everything is the world's dust, but the smell of salt marshes, straw floor matting and wood smoke is the breath of St Botolphs.

Honora is waked this morning by the whistling of the 7:18 as it comes into the station and, half asleep she mistakes this sound for the trumpeting of an angel. She is very religious and has joined with enthusiasm and parted with bitterness from nearly every religious organization in Travertine and St Botolphs. Hearing the train she sees in her mind an angel in snowy robes with a slender trumpet. She has been called, she thinks cheerfully. She has been summoned to some unusual task. She always expected as much. She rises up on her pillows to hear the message and the train hoots again. The image of a locomotive replaces the angel, but she is not very disappointed. She gets out of bed, dresses and sniffs the air, which seems to smell of lamb chops. She goes down to breakfast with a good appetite. She walks with a stick.

A fire is burning in her dining room this July morning and she warms her hands at this to get the chill of age out of her bones. Maggie, her cook, brings a covered dish to the table and Honora, expecting lamb chops, is disappointed to discover a perch. This makes her very irritable, for she is subject to severe attacks of irritability, night sweats and other forms of nervousness. She does not have to admit these infirmities for if she feels out of sorts she can throw a dish at her cook. She bangs the metal cover against the platter now, like a cymbal, and when Maggie comes into the room she exclaims, 'Perch.

Whatever made you think I wanted perch for breakfast? Perch.
Take it away. Take it away and cook me some bacon and eggs
if it's not too much trouble.' Maggie removes the fish and sighs,
but not with any real despair. She is used to this treatment.
People often ask why Maggie remains with Honora. Maggie
is not dependent on Honora – she could get a better job
tomorrow – and she does not love her. What she seems to
recognize in the old lady is some naked human force, quite
apart from dependence and love.

Maggie cooks some bacon and eggs and brings them to
the table. She announces then that there has been an accident
near West Farm. A man was killed and a young woman was
taken into the house. 'Poor soul,' Honora says of the dead, but
she says nothing else. Maggie hears the mailman's step on the
walk and the letters fall through the brass slot and spill onto
the floor. She picks up the mail – there are a dozen letters
– and puts them on the table beside Honora's plate. Honora
hardly glances at her mail. There may be letters here from old
friends, checks from the Appleton Trust Company, bills, pleas
and invitations. No one will ever know. Honora glances at
the pile of envelopes, picks them up and throws them into
the fire. Now we wonder why she burns her mail without
reading it, but as she goes away from the fireplace back to
her chair the light of a very clear emotion seems to cross her
face and perhaps this is explanation enough. Admiring that
which is most easily understood we may long for the image
of some gentle old woman, kind to her servant and opening
her letters with a silver knife, but how much more poetry
there is to Honora, casting off the claims of life the instant
they are made. When she has stowed away her breakfast she
gets up and calls over her shoulder to Maggie, 'I'll be in the
garden if anyone wants me.'

Mark, her gardener, is already at work. He comes to work
at seven. 'Good morning, Mark,' Honora says gaily, but Mark
is deaf and dumb. Before she employed Mark, Honora ran
through every gardener in the village. The last one before
Mark was an Italian who behaved badly. He threw down his

rake and shouted, 'She'sa no good, working for you, Missa Honora. She'sa no good. She'sa planta this, she'sa pullupa that, she'sa changes her mind every five minutes, she'sa no good.' When he finished he went out of the garden leaving Honora in tears. Maggie ran out of the kitchen and took the old lady in her arms, saying, 'You mustn't pay any attention to him, you mustn't pay any attention to him, Miss Wapshot. Everybody knows how wonderful you are. Everybody knows what a wonderful woman you are.' Mark, being deaf, is protected from her interference and when she tells him to move all the rose bushes she might as well be talking to a stone.

It is hard for Honora to get down on her knees, but she does this and works in her garden until the middle of the morning. Then she goes into the house, quietly washes her hands, gets a hat, gloves and a bag and goes out through her garden to the four corners, where she catches a bus to Travertine. Whether this fairly stealthy departure is calculated or not no one will ever know. If Honora asks people for tea and is not home when they, wearing their best clothes, arrive, she has not consciously done something that will make them feel ill at ease, but she has acted characteristically. At any rate a few minutes after she leaves her garden a trust officer of the Appleton Bank rings her front doorbell. During the years in which she has lived on the income from Lorenzo's trust, Honora has never signed a form approving the bank's management. Now the trust officer has been told not to leave St Botolphs until he has her signature. He rings the doorbell for some time before Maggie throws open a window and tells him that Miss Wapshot is in the garden. Talking with Mark is hopeless, of course, and when he rings the doorbell again Maggie shouts at him, 'If she ain't in the garden I don't know where she's at but she might be at the farm where the other Wapshots live. That's over on Route 40. A big house beside the river.' The trust officer starts for Route 40 just as Honora boards the bus for Travertine.

Honora doesn't put a dime into the fare box like the rest of the passengers. As she says, she can't be bothered. She sends the transportation company a check for twenty dollars each Christmas. They've written her, telephoned her and sent representatives to her house, but they've gotten nowhere. The bus is decrepit and the seats and several of the windows are held together with friction tape. Jarring and rattling, it gives, for a vehicle, an unusual impression of frailty. It is one of those lines that seem to carry the scrim of the world – sweet-natured but browbeaten women shoppers, hunchbacks and drunks. Honora looks out the window and at the river and the houses – those poignant landscapes against which she has played out most of her life and where she is known as the Wonderful Honora, the Splendid Honora, the Grand Honora Wapshot. When the bus stops at the comer in Travertine she goes up the street to Mr Hiram's fish market. Mr Hiram is in back, opening a crate of salt fish. Honora goes around and behind the counter to where there is a small tank of sea water for lobsters. She puts down her bag and stick, rolls up one sleeve and plunges her hand into the tank, coming up with a good four-pound lobster just as Mr Hiram comes in from the back. 'Put that down, Miss Honora,' he shouts. 'They ain't pegged, they ain't pegged yet.'

'Well, they don't seem to be doing me any harm,' says Honora. 'Just get me a paper bag.'

'George Wolf just brought them in,' says Mr Hiram, scurrying around for a paper bag, 'and if one of those four pounders tooka hold of you you could lose a finger.'

He holds the paper bag open and Honora drops the lobster into this, turns and plunges her hand into the tank again. Mr Hiram sighs, but Honora comes up quickly with another lobster and gets it into the bag. When she has paid Mr Hiram she carries her lobsters out to the street and walks to the comer where the bus is waiting to pick up passengers for St Botolphs. She hands the bag of lobsters to the bus driver. 'Here,' she says. 'I'll be back in a few minutes.'

She starts for the dry-goods store but, as she walks by the five-and-ten-cent store, the smell of frankfurters draws her in. She sits at the counter. 'Your frankfurters smell so deliciously,' she tells the clerk, 'that I can't resist having one. Our Cousin Justina used to play the piano in here, y'know. Oh, if she knew I remembered, she'd die. . . .' She eats two frankfurters and a dish of ice cream. 'That was delicious,' she tells the counter girl, and gathering up her things she starts down the street again toward the bus stop when she notices the sign above the Neptune movie theater: ROSE OF THE WEST. What harm can there be, she thinks, in an old lady going to a movie, but when she buys her ticket and steps into the dark, bad-smelling theater she suffers all the abrasive sensations of someone forced into moral uncleanliness. She does not have the courage of her vices. It is wrong, she knows, to go into a dark place when the world outside shines with light. It is wrong and she is a miserable sinner. She buys a box of popcorn and takes an aisle seat in the last row – a noncommittal position that seems to lighten her burden of guilt. She munches her popcorn and watches the movie suspiciously.

In the meantime Maggie is keeping her lunch warm on the back of the stove and her lobsters, battling for life in the paper bag, have made the trip to St Botolphs and are now on their way back to Travertine. Mr Burstyn, the trust officer, has driven to West Farm. Sarah has been courteous and helpful. 'I haven't seen Honora myself,' she says, 'but she's expected. She's interested in some furniture in the barn. She may be there.' He walks down the driveway to the barn. Mr Burstyn is a city boy and the size of the barn and its powerful smells make him homesick. A large yellow spider on the barn floor comes straight toward him and he makes a wide circle around the insect. There is a staircase up to the loft. Two of the lifts are broken and a third is about to break and when he gets up into the loft there is no one there although it would be hard to make sure, for the loft is lighted by a single window hung thickly with spiderwebs and drifted with hayseed.

Honora sits through the movie twice. When she leaves the theater she feels weary and sad like any sinner. The lobby of the theater slopes like a kind of tunnel down toward the sidewalk. There is a small stretch here of some slippery composition stone and on it a spot of water or moisture from the iceman's load or a child's pop bottle. Someone may even have spat. Honora slips on this and crashes down onto the stone. Her purse flies in one direction and her stick in another and her three-cornered hat comes down over her nose. The girl, the woman, the hag, in fact, in the ticket window sees all of this and her heart seems to stop beating for she sees here, in the fallen old woman, the ruthlessness of time. She fumbles around for the key to the cash register and locks up the money. Then she opens the door to her little tower, sanctuary or keep and hurries to where Honora lies. She kneels beside her. 'Oh, Miss Wapshot,' she says. 'Dear Miss Wapshot.'

Honora raises herself by the arms and gets to her knees. Then slowly she swings her head around to this samaritan. 'Leave me alone,' she says. 'Please leave me alone.' The voice is not harsh or imperious. It sounds small, plaintive, the voice of a child with some inner trouble; a plea for dignity. Now more and more people come to her side. Honora is still on her hands and knees. 'Please leave me alone,' she tells the gathering. 'Please mind your own business. Please go away and leave me alone.' They recognize that what she is expressing is the privateness of pain and they move back. 'Please leave me alone,' she says, 'please mind your own business.' She straightens her hat and, using her stick for a support, gets to her feet. Someone hands her the purse. Her dress is torn and dirty but she walks straight through the gathering to the corner where the bus to St Botolphs is waiting. The driver who took her to Travertine earlier in the day has gone home to supper and has been replaced by a young man. 'What,' Honora asks him, 'have you done with my lobsters?'

The bus driver tells her that the lobsters have been delivered and he has the good sense not to ask for her fare. So they travel up the River Road to St Botolphs and Honora gets off at the four corners and enters her garden by the back gate.

Mark has done a good job. The paths and the flower beds look neat in the twilight – for it is nearly dark. The day has pleased her and she liked the movie. By half-closing her eyes she can still see the colored plains and the Indians riding down from the butte. Her kitchen windows are lighted and open on this summer night and as she approaches them she sees Maggie sitting at the kitchen table with Maggie's younger sister. She hears Maggie's voice. 'Perch,' says Maggie. 'Perch, she says, rattling the dish cover and breathing smoke and fire. Whatever in the world made you think I wanted perch for breakfast? For weeks she's been telling me how she'd like a bit of perch and I bought a couple from the little Townsend boy yesterday with my own money and I cooked it for her nicely and all the thanks I get is this. Perch, she says. Whatever made you think I wanted perch for breakfast!'

Maggie is not bitter. Far from it; she and her sister are laughing uproariously at the memory of Honora who stands now outside the lighted windows of her own house in the dusk. 'Well then,' says Maggie, 'I hear Mr Macgrath coming up the walk and putting the mail into the slot and so I go down the hall to get her letters and I give them to her and you know what she does?' Maggie rocks back and forth in her chair with laughter. 'She takes these letters – there must be twelve of them altogether – and throws them into the fire. Oh Lord, she's better than a three-ring circus.'

Honora walks past the window on the soft grass but they have not heard her; they are laughing too loudly. Halfway down the house she stops and leans heavily, with both hands, on her cane, engrossed in an emotion so violent and so nameless that she wonders if this feeling of loneliness and bewilderment is not the mysteriousness of life. Poignance seems to drench her until her knees are weak and she yearns so earnestly for understanding that she raises her head and says half a prayer. Then she gathers her forces, enters the front door and calls cheerfully down the hall, 'It's me, Maggie.' Upstairs in her bedroom she drinks a water glass full of port and while she is changing her shoes the telephone rings. It is poor Mr Burstyn, who has taken a room at the Viaduct House, which is no place for a respectable man to stay. 'Well if you want to see me, come and see me,' Honora says. 'I'm not very hard

to find. Excepting to visit Travertine I haven't been out of
St Botolphs in nearly seven years. You can go and tell those
men at the bank that if they want someone to talk with me
they'd better get someone with more gumption than it takes
to find an old lady.' Then she hangs up the receiver and goes
down to supper with a good appetite.

CHAPTER 7

The morning light and the bruit of the family going around the upstairs hallway woke the girl. She felt at first the strangeness of the place, although there were not many places with which she was familiar any more. The air smelled of sausage and even the morning light – golden with all its blue shadows – seemed foreign in a way that pained her and she remembered waking up on her first night at camp to find that she had wet the bed. Then she remembered the accident – all that – but not in detail; it loomed up in her mind like a boulder, too big to be moved and too adamant to be broken and have its contents revealed. All that stood in her mind like a dark stone. The sheets – linen and damp – brought her back to the pain of strangeness and she wondered why a person should feel, in the world where she was meant to live, so miserable and abraded. She got up out of bed to discover that her whole body was lame and sore. In the closet she found her coat and some cigarettes in the pocket. The taste of smoke diminished the painful sense of strangeness by a little and she carried a clamshell for an ash tray to the side of her bed and lay down again. She shivered, she trembled, she tried unsuccessfully to cry.

Now the house, or the part of it where she lay, was quiet. She heard a man calling good-by. On the wall she noticed that stuck behind the picture of a little Dutch girl were some palm fronds from Palm Sunday and she hoped that this was not the house of a priest. Then, in the downstairs hall, she heard the telephone ring and someone shouted, 'Hello, Mabel. I may not be coming over today. No, she ain't paid me yet. She don't have any money. They get all their money from Honora. She don't have any money. No, I can't borrow no more money on my insurance. I told you, I told you, I did ass them, I assed them. Well, I need shoes myself the way she expects me to go upstairs and downstairs fifty times a day. They got somebody here now. Did you hear about the accident? There was an accident here last night. A car went off the road and a man was killed. Terrible. Well, he had a girl with him and they brought her in here and she's here now. I'll tell you later. I SAID I'LL TELL YOU LATER. They got her here now and that makes more work for me. How's Charlie? What are you going to have for supper? Don't have the meat loaf. You don't have enough of it. I said, don't have the meat loaf. Open a can of salmon and make Charlie a nice salad. There isn't enough meat loaf. I just told you. Open a can of salmon and get some of those nice rolls from the bakery. Make him a pie for dessert. They got nice pie apples now. Is he still constipated? They got pie apples, they have so got pie apples, I saw them day before yesterday, they got pie apples at Tituses'. You go down to Tituses' and get some pie apples and make him an apple pie. Do what I tell you. I'll tell you about the accident when I see you. I don't know how long she's going to stay. I don't know. I got to make the beds now. Good-by . . .'

After this the house was quiet again and then she heard someone climbing the stairs and the pleasant noise of dishes on a tray. She put out her cigarette. 'Good morning,' Mrs Wapshot said. 'Good morning, Rosalie. I'm going to call you Rosalie. We don't stand on ceremony here.'

'Good morning.'

'The first thing I want you to do is to let me telephone your parents. They'll be worried. But what am I talking about? That's not the first thing I want you to do. The first thing I want you to do is to eat a nice breakfast. Let me fix your pillows.'

'Oh, I'm awfully afraid that I can't eat anything,' the girl said. 'It's awfully nice of you but I just couldn't.'

'Well, you don't have to eat everything on the tray,' Mrs Wapshot said kindly, 'but you've got to eat something. Why don't you try and eat the eggs? That's all you have to eat; but you must eat the eggs.'

Then the girl began to cry. She laid her head sidewise on the pillow and stared into the corner of the room where she seemed to see a range of high mountains her look was so faraway and heart-breaking. The tears rolled down her cheeks. 'Oh, I'm sorry,' Mrs Wapshot said. 'I'm very sorry. I suppose you were engaged to him. I suppose . . .'

'It isn't that,' the girl sobbed. 'It's just about the eggs. I can't *bear* eggs. When I lived at home they made me eat eggs for breakfast and if I didn't eat my eggs for breakfast well then I had to eat them for dinner. I mean everything I was supposed to eat and couldn't eat was always juss piled up on my dinner plate and the eggs were disgusting.'

'Well, is there anything you would like for breakfast?' Mrs Wapshot asked.

'I'd love some peanut butter. If I could have a peanut-butter sandwich and a glass of milk . . .'

'Well, I think that can be arranged,' Mrs Wapshot said, and carrying the tray and smiling she went out of the room and down the stairs.

She felt no resentment at this miscarriage of her preparations and was happy to have the girl in her house, as if she was, at bottom, a lonely woman, grateful for any company. She had wanted a daughter, longed for one; a little girl sitting at her knees, learning to sew or making sugar cookies in the kitchen on a snowy night. While she made Rosalie's sandwich it seemed to her that she possessed a vision of life that she would enjoy introducing to the stranger. They could pick blueberries together, take long walks beside the river and sit together in the pew on Sunday. When she took the sandwich upstairs again Rosalie said that she wanted to get up. Mrs Wapshot protested but Rosalie's pleading made sense. 'I'd just feel so much better if I could get up and walk around and sit in the sun; just feel the sun.'

Rosalie dressed after breakfast and joined Mrs Wapshot in the garden where the old deck chairs were. 'The sun feels so good,' she said, pushing up the sleeves of her dress and shaking back her hair.

'Now you must let me call your parents,' Sarah said.

'I just don't want to call them today,' the girl said. 'Maybe tomorrow. You see, it always bothers them when I'm in trouble. I just don't like to bother them when I'm in trouble. And they'll want me to come home and everything. You see Daddy's a priest — rector really, I mean communion seven days a week and all that.'

'We're low church here,' Mrs Wapshot said, 'but some people I could name would like to see a change.'

'And he's absolutely the most nervous man I ever knew,' Rosalie said. 'Daddy is. He's always scratching his stomach. It's a nervous ailment. Most men's shirts wear out at the collar, I guess, but Daddy's shirts wear out where he scratches himself.'

'Oh, I think you ought to telephone them,' Mrs Wapshot said.

'It's just because I'm in trouble. They always think of me as making trouble. I went to this camp — Annamatapoiset — and I had this sweater with an A on it for being such a marvelous camper and when Daddy saw it he said I guess that A stands for Always in Trouble. I just don't want to bother them.'

'It doesn't seem right.'

'Please, *please*.' She bit her lip; she would cry and Mrs Wapshot swiftly changed the subject. 'Smell the peonies,' she said. 'I love the smell of peonies and now they're almost gone.'

'That sun feels so good.'

'Do you have a position in the city?' Mrs Wapshot asked.

'Well, I was going to this secretarial school,' Rosalie said.

'You planned to be a secretary?'

'Well, I didn't want to be a secretary. I wanted to be a painter or a psychologist but first I went to Allendale School and I couldn't bear the academic adviser so I never really made up my mind. I mean he was always touching me and fiddling with my collar and I couldn't bear to talk with him.'

'So then you went to secretarial school?'

'Well, first I went to Europe, I went to Europe last summer with some other girls.'

'Did you like it?'

'You mean Europe?'

'Yes.'

'Oh I thought it was divine. I mean there were some things I was disappointed in, like Stratford. I mean it was just another small town. And I couldn't bear London but I adored the Netherlands with all those divine little people. It was terribly quaint.'

'Shouldn't you telephone this secretarial school you go to and tell them where you are?'

'Oh no,' Rosalie said. 'I flunked out last month. I blew up on exams. I knew all the material and everything but I just didn't know the words. The only words I know are words like divine and of course they don't use those words on exams and so I never understood the questions. I wish I knew more words.'

'I see,' Mrs Wapshot said.

Rosalie might have gone on to tell her the rest of it and it would have gone something like this: I mean it just seems that all I ever heard about was sex when I was growing up. I mean everyone told me it was just marvelous and the end of all my problems and loneliness and everything and so naturally I looked forward to it and then when I was at Allendale I went to this dance with this nice-looking boy and we did it and it didn't stop me from feeling lonely because I've always been a very lonely person so we kept on doing it and doing it because I kept thinking it was going to keep me from being lonely and then I got pregnant, which was dreadful, of course, with Daddy being the priest and so virtuous and prominent, and they nearly died when they found out and they sent me to this place where I had this adorable little baby although they told everyone I was having an operation on my nose and afterwards they sent me to Europe with this old lady. . . .

Then Coverly came down the lawn from the house. 'Cousin Honora called,' he said, 'and she's coming for tea or after supper, maybe.'

'Won't you join us?' Mrs Wapshot asked. 'Coverly, this is Rosalie Young.'

'How do you do,' he said.

'Hello.' He had that spooky bass voice meant to announce that he had entered into the kingdom of manhood, but Rosalie knew that he was still outside the gates and sure enough, while he stood there smiling at her he raised his right hand to his mouth and began thoughtfully to chew on a callus that had formed at the base of his thumb.

'Moses?'

'He's at Travertine.'

'Moses has been sailing every day of his vacation,' Mrs Wapshot said to Rosalie. 'It's just as though I didn't have an older son.'

'He wants to win a cup,' Coverly said. They stayed in the garden until Lulu called them into lunch.

After lunch Rosalie went upstairs and lying down in the still house she fell asleep. When she woke the shadows on the grass were long and downstairs she could hear men's voices. She went down and found them all in the garden, once more, all of them. 'It's our out-of-door sitting room,' Mrs Wapshot said. 'This is Mr Wapshot and Moses. Rosalie Young.'

'Good evening, young lady,' Leander said, charmed by her fairness, but not at all foxy. He spoke to her with a triumphant and bright disinterestedness as if she had been the daughter of an old friend and drinking companion. It was Moses who was surly — who hardly looked at her, although he was polite enough. It made Mrs Wapshot unhappy to see any impediment in the relationships of the young. They ate cold carp in the homely dining room, half lighted by the summer twilight, half by what seemed to be an inverted bowl of stained glass, pieced together mostly out of gloomy colors. 'These napkins are more holy than righteous,' Mrs Wapshot said, and most of her conversation at the table was made up of just such chestnuts, saws and hoary puns. She was one of those women who seemed to have learned to speak by rote. 'May I please be excused,' Moses mumbled as soon as he had cleared his plate, and he was out of the dining room and had one foot in the night before his mother spoke.

'Don't you want any dessert, Moses?'

'No, thank you.'

'Where are you going?'

'Over to Pendletons'.'

'I want you home early. Honora is coming.'

'Yes.'

'I wish Honora would come,' Mrs Wapshot said.

Honora will not come — she is hooking a rug — but they do not know and so rather than dwell with the Chekhovian delays of this family watching the night come in we might climb the stairs and pry into things of more pertinence. There is Leander's bureau drawer, where we find a withered rose — once yellow — and a wreath of yellow hair, the butt end of a Roman candle that was fired at the turn of the century, a boiled shirt on which an explicit picture of a naked woman is drawn in red ink, a necklace made of champagne corks and a loaded revolver. Or we might look at Coverly's book shelf — *War and Peace, The Complete Poetry of Robert Frost, Madame Bovary, La Tulipe Noire.* Or still better we might go to the Pocamasset Trust Company in the village where Honora's will lies in a safe deposit box.

CHAPTER 8

Honora's will was no secret. 'Lorenzo left me a little something,' she had told the family, 'and I have to consider his wishes as well as my own. Lorenzo was very devoted to the family and the older I grow the more important family seems to me. It seems to me that most of the people I trust and admire come from good New England stock.' There was more of the same; and then she said that since Moses and Coverly were the last of the Wapshots she would divide her fortune between them, contingent upon their having male heirs. 'Oh, the money will do so much good,' Mrs Wapshot had exclaimed, while institutes for the blind and the lame, homes for unwed mothers and orphan asylums danced in her head. The news of their inheritance did not elate the boys – it did not seem at first to penetrate or alter their feelings toward life, and Honora's decision only seemed to Leander to be a matter of course. What else would she have done with the money? But, considering the naturalness of her choice, it came as a surprise to everyone that it should lead them into something as unnatural as anxiety.

On the winter after Honora had made her will Moses came down with a severe case of mumps. 'Is he all right?' Honora kept asking. 'Will he be all right?' Moses recovered but that summer a little gasoline stove in the galley of their sailboat exploded, burning Coverly in the groin. They were on tenterhooks again. However, these forthright assaults on

the virility of his sons did not trouble Leander as much
as those threats to the continuation of the family that lay
beyond his understanding. Such a thing happened when
Coverly was eleven or twelve and went with his mother
to see a performance of *A Midsummer Night's Dream*. He
was transported. When he got back to the farm he would
be Oberon. Girdling himself with a loose arrangement of
neckties, he tried flying from the back stairs into the parlor,
where his father was adding up the monthly accounts. He
couldn't fly, of course, and landed in a pile on the floor – his
neckties undone – and while Leander did not speak to him
angrily he felt, standing above his naked son in the presence
of something mysterious and unrestful – Icarus! Icarus! – as if
the boy had fallen some great distance from his father's heart.

Leander would never take his sons aside and speak to
them about the facts of life, even although the continuation
of Honora's numerous charities depended upon their virility.
If they looked out of the window for a minute they could
see the drift of things. It was his feeling that love, death and
fornication extracted from the rich green soup of life were
no better than half-truths, and his course of instruction was
general. He would like them to grasp that the unobserved
ceremoniousness of his life was a gesture or sacrament toward
the excellence and the continuousness of things. He went
skating on Christmas Day – drunk or sober, ill or well –
feeling that it was his responsibility to the village to appear
on Parson's Pond. 'There goes old Leander Wapshot,' people
said – he could hear them – a splendid figure of continuous
and innocent sport that he hoped his sons would carry on. The
cold bath that he took each morning was ceremonious – it
was sometimes nothing else since he almost never used soap
and got out of the tub smelling powerfully of the sea salts in
the old sponges that he used. The coat he wore at dinner, the
grace he said at table, the fishing trip he took each spring, the
bourbon he drank at dark and the flower in his buttonhole
were all forms that he hoped his sons might understand and
perhaps copy. He had taught them to fell a tree, pluck and

dress a chicken, sow, cultivate and harvest, catch a fish, save money, countersink a nail, make cider with a hand press, clean a gun, sail a boat, etc.

He was not surprised to find his ways crossed and contested by his wife, who had her own arcane rites such as arranging flowers and cleaning closets. He did not always see eye to eye with Sarah but this seemed to him most natural, and life itself appeared to regulate their differences. He was impulsive and difficult to follow – there was no telling when he would decide that it was time for the boys to swim the river or carve the roast. He went trout fishing each spring at a camp in the wilderness near the Canadian border and decided one spring that the time had come for Moses to accompany him. For once Sarah was angry and stubborn. She didn't want Moses to go north with his father and on the evening before they were to leave she said that Moses was sick. Her manner was seraphic.

'That poor boy is too ill to go anywhere.'

'We're going fishing tomorrow morning,' Leander said.

'Leander, if you take this poor boy out of a sickbed and up to the north woods I'll never forgive you.'

'There won't be anything to forgive.'

'Leander, come here.'

They continued their discussion or quarrel behind the closed doors of Sarah's bedroom but the boys – and Lulu – could hear their angry and bitter voices. Leander got Moses out of bed before dawn on the next day. He had already packed the bait and fishing tackle and they started for the Langely ponds in the starlight while Sarah was still asleep.

It was May when they left – the valley of the West River was all in bloom – and they had had a brace or more of those days when the earth smells like a farmer's britches – all timothy, manure and sweet grass. They were north of Concord when the sun came up and they stopped in some town in New Hampshire for lunch. They were far north of the lush river valley by then. The trees were bare and the inn where they stopped still seemed to be in the throes of a cold winter.

The place smelled of kerosene and the waitress had a runny nose.

They were in the mountains then, the stony rivers full of black water – melted snow – and the sheen of reflected blue from the sky didn't much soften the impression of cold. Coming up into a pass Moses raised his head cheerfully to the voluptuous line of the mountains, the illusory blue, thunderous and deep, but the loud noise of wind in the bare trees reminded him of the gentle valley they had left that morning – shadbush and lilac and already some arbutus underfoot. They had then got to the approaches of French Canada – those farms and towns that seem, from the winter's cold and tedium, utterly unprotected: St Evariste, St Methode, the bleak country of the Holy Ghost, exposed to the lash of winter. Now the north wind was bitter, the clouds were a cheerless white and here and there on the ground he saw patches of old snow. They reached the village of Langely late in the day where the old launch – the *Cygnet* – that would take them uplake and into the wilderness was tied to a wharf and which Moses now loaded with their duffel bags and fishing tackle.

There was nothing at Langely but a post office and a store. It was late; it would be dark soon. The post-office windows were lighted but the shores of the lake were uninhabited and dark. Moses looked at the old launch, tied up at the wharf, her long bow and her helm shaped like a steering wheel. He recognized in the length of her mahogany bow, with its brass funnel and brass-bound bulkhead, that she was one of those boats built years ago, for the leisurely comings and goings of another generation of summer people. Four wicker chairs stood side by side on her deep stern deck. Weathered and raveled and threadbare, they had carried – how long ago? – women in summer dresses and men in flannels out to see the sun go down. Now her paint was dirty and her varnish was dim and she bemoaned her dereliction by rubbing the wharf in the northerly wind.

His father came down the path with the groceries and an old man followed him. It was the old man who took off the lines and pushed the boat into deep water with a hook. He must have been eighty. His teeth were gone and his mouth had sunk, accentuating the little thrust of his chin. He blinked his eyes behind a pair of dirty glasses and poked his tongue out between his lips and when he got her into forward and full speed ahead he settled himself very stiffly. It was a seven-mile voyage to the camp. They carried their things up to a ramshackle place with a chimney made of soup cans and they lighted a fire and a lamp. Squirrels had gotten into the mattress. Mice and rats and porcupines had come and gone. Below them Moses heard the old man start the motor of his *Cygnet* and head back for the post office. The icy light of the after-glow, the noise of the launch as it faded and the smells of the stove all were so unlike their beginnings that morning in St Botolphs that the world seemed to fall into two pieces or halves.

Here on this half were the deep lake, the old man with his superannuated *Cygnet* and the dirty camp. Here were salt and catsup and patched blankets and canned spaghetti and dirty socks. Here was a pile of rusted tin cans around the steps; here were *Saturday Evening Post* covers fixed with roofing nails to the bare walls beside the Fisherman's Prayer, the Fisherman's Lexicon, the Lament of the Fisherman's Widow, the Fisherman's Crying Towel and all the other inane and semicomic trash that has been published about fishing. Here was the smell of earthworms and gut, kerosene and burned pancakes, the smell of unaired blankets, trapped smoke, wet shoes, lye and strangeness. On the table near where he stood someone had stuck a candle into a root and beside this was a detective story, its first chapters eaten by mice.

On the other half was the farm at St Botolphs, the gentle valley and the impuissant river and the rooms that smelled now of lilac and hyacinth and the colored engraving of San Marco and all the furniture with claw feet. There were the Canton bowls full of forget-me-nots, the damp linen sheets, the silver on the sideboard and the loud ticking of the clock in the hall. The difference seemed more strenuous than if he had crossed the border from one mountain country into another, more strenuous he guessed because he had not realized how deep his commitment to the gentle parochialism of the valley was – the east wind and the shawls from India – and had never seen how securely conquered that country was by his good mother and her kind – the iron women in their summer dresses. He stood, for the first time in his life, in a place where their absence was conspicuous and he smiled, thinking of how they would have attacked the camp; how they would have burned the furniture, buried the tin cans, holystoned the floors, cleaned the lamp chimneys and arranged in a glass slipper (or some other charming antique) nosegays of violets and Solomon's-seal. Under their administration lawns would reach from the camp to the lake, herbs and salad greens would flourish at the back door and there would be curtains and rugs, chemical toilets and clocks that chimed.

His father poured himself some whisky and when the stove was hot he took some hamburgers and cooked them on the lid, turning them with a rusty spoon as if he was following some ritual in which he disregarded his wife's excellent concepts of hygiene and order. When supper was finished the loons on the lake had begun to cry and these cries seemed to bring into the cabin, overheated now from the stove, a fine sense of their remoteness. Moses walked down toward the lake, pissed in the woods and washed his hands and face in water that was so cold his skin was still stinging when he undressed and climbed in between two dirty blankets. His father blew out the lamp and got into bed himself and they fell asleep.

The fishing was not at Langely, it was in the ponds deeper in the woods, and they left for Folger's Pond at six the next morning. The wind was still northerly and the sky was overcast. They crossed the lake in a dinghy with a two-cylinder motor, heading for Kenton's swamp. Halfway across the lake the old dinghy sprang a leak. Moses sat in the stern, bailing with a bait can. At Lovell's Point his father throttled down the motor and turned the leaky boat into a great swamp. It was an ugly and a treacherous place but the landscape seemed to Moses enthralling. Rank on rank of dead trees lined the shore – tall, catatonic and ashen, they looked like the statuary of some human disaster. When the water got shallow Leander tipped the motor into the boat and Moses took the oars. The noise of setting them into the locks startled a flight of geese. 'A little to port,' his father said, 'a little more to port . . .' Looking over his shoulder, Moses saw where the swamp narrowed to a stream and heard the roar of some falls. Then he saw the shapes of stones through the water, his oars struck and the bow grazed the shore.

He pulled the boat up and made it fast to a tree while his father examined a scraping of boat's paint on a stone near where they landed. It seemed to be last year's paint. Then Moses saw how anxious his father was to be the first man into the woods and while he unloaded the gear Leander looked around the trail for footprints. He found some but when he scraped them with a knife he saw that they were lined with mold and had been made by hunters. Then he started briskly up the trail. Everything was dead; dead leaves, dead branches, dead ferns, dead grass, all the obscenity of the woods death, stinking and moldy, was laid thickly on the trail. A little white light escaped from the clouds and passed fleetly over the woods, long enough for Moses to see his shadow, and then this was gone.

The trail went uphill. He got hot. He sweated. He watched his father's head and shoulders with feelings of admiration and love. It was the middle of the morning when they saw the clearing ahead of them through the trees. They pushed up the last slope and there was the pond and they were the first to have seen it since the hunters in the fall. The place was ugly but it had the exalting ugliness of the swamp. Leander looked into the bushes and found what he wanted – an old duck-shooting battery. He told Moses to get some wood for a fire and when the fire was lighted he took a can of tar out of his pack, rigged a crane of green wood over the fire and heated the tar. Then he swabbed the boat's seams with hot tar which hardened quickly in the cold. They floated the battery and rowed out onto the water against the north wind. In spite of the tar the battery leaked but they baited their hooks and began to troll.

Five minutes later Leander's rod bent, and with a grunt he set his hook and with Moses keeping the boat in motion he played a big trout that rose, a hundred feet to their stern, and then sounded and fought, taking his last sanctuary in the dim shade of the battery. Then Moses caught a fish and within an hour or so they had a dozen trout between them. Then it began to snow. For three hours they trolled in the snow squall without a strike, eating their dry sandwiches at noon. This was an ordeal and Moses had the sense to see that it was part of their trip. In the middle of the afternoon the squall blew off and then Leander had a strike. Then the fish began to bite again and before the sky began to darken they each had their limit. They pulled the battery up onto the banks – stupefied and brute tired – and stumbled down the trail to the lake, reaching this not much before dark. The wind had backed around to the northeast and from beyond the mouth of the swamp they could hear the roar of water but they crossed safely, with Moses bailing, and made the boat fast by her bow and stern. Moses lighted a fire while his father gutted four trout and fried them on the stove lid and when they had finished supper they mumbled their good nights, put out the lamp and went to bed.

That was a good trip and they returned to St Botolphs with enough fish for all their friends and relations. On the next year it was time for Coverly to go. Coverly did have a runny nose, as it happened, but Sarah didn't mention this. However, late on the evening before they left, she came into his room carrying a cookbook and put it into his pack. 'Your father doesn't know how to cook,' she said, 'and I don't know what you'll eat for four days so I'll give you this.' He thanked her, kissed her good night and left with his father before dawn. The trip was the same – the stop for lunch and whisky, and the long voyage up the lake in the *Cygnet*. At the camp Leander threw some hamburgers onto the stove lid and when they had

finished supper they went to bed. Coverly asked if he could
read.

'What's your book, son?'

'It's a cookbook,' Coverly said, looking at the cover. 'Three
hundred ways of preparing fish.'

'Oh Goddamn it to hell, Coverly,' Leander roared. 'Goddamn
it to hell.' He took the book out of his son's hands, opened
the door and threw it out into the night. Then he blew out
the lamp, feeling once more — Icarus, Icarus — as if the boy
had fallen away from his heart.

Coverly knew that he had offended his father but guilt
would have been too exact a word for the pain and uneasiness
he felt and this pain may have been aggravated by his
knowledge of the conditions of Honora's will. The sense was
not only that he had failed himself and his father by bringing
a cookbook to a fishing camp; he had profaned the mysterious
rites of virility and had failed whole generations of future
Wapshots as well as the beneficiaries of Honora's largess — the
Home for Aged Sailors and the Hutchens Institute for the
Blind. He was miserable, and he would be made miserable
again by the feeling that his human responsibilities had been
abnormally enlarged by Honora's will. This was some time
later, a year, perhaps, and anyhow later in the year and the
matter was a simple one, simpler than fishing — the village
fair which he attended late in August with his father as he
always did. (Moses had planned to go, but he grounded the
Tern on a sandbar and didn't get home until ten.) Coverly had
an early supper in the kitchen. He wore his best white ducks
and a clean shirt and had his allowance in his pocket. Leander
gave him a toot on the whistle when the *Topaze* rounded the
bend and swung the boat over to the dock, putting her into
half-speed and then neutral but just touching the dock long
enough for Coverly to jump aboard.

There was only a handful of passengers. Coverly went up
to the cabin and Leander let him take the wheel. The tide
was going out and they moved against it slowly. It had been a
hot day and now there were cumulus clouds or thunderheads

standing out to sea in a light of such clearness and brilliance that they seemed unrelated to the river and the little village. Coverly brought the boat up to the wharf neatly and helped Bentley, the deck hand, make her fast, and knocked together the old deck chairs, upholstered with carpet scraps, and lashed a tarpaulin over the pile. They stopped in Grimes' bakery, where Leander ate a plate of baked beans. 'Baked beans, the musical fruit,' the old waitress said. 'The more you eat, the more you toot.' The mild crudeness of the joke had kept it fresh for her. Walking up Water Street toward the fairgrounds Leander let several loud farts. It was a summer evening so splendid that the power it had over their senses was like the power of memory and they could have kicked up their heels with joy when they saw ahead of them the matchboard fence and within it and above it the lights of the fair, burning gallantly against some storm clouds in which lightning could be seen to play.

Coverly was excited to see so many lights burning after dark and by the apparatus for the tightrope artist – a high pole secured by guy wires with a summit of fringed platforms and pedestals, all of it standing in the glare of two up-angled searchlights in whose powdery beams moth millers could be seen to swim like scraps of gum paper. There a girl with powdery skin and straw hair and a navel (Leander thought) deep enough to put your thumb into, and with rhinestones burning blue and red at her ears and breasts, walked and rode a bicycle over the tightwire, pushing her hair back now and then and hurrying a little it seemed, for the thunder was quickening and the gusty wind smelled clearly of rain and now and then people who were anxious or old or wearing their best clothes were leaving the bleachers and looking for shelter although not a drop of rain had fallen. When the high-wire act was over Leander took Coverly down to the head of the midway, where the argument for the cootch show had begun.

Burlymaque, burlymaque, see them strip the way you like, see them do the dance of the ages. If you're old you'll go

home to your wife feeling younger and stronger and if you're
young you'll feel happy and full of high spirits as youth should
feel, said a man whose sharp face and sharp voice seemed
wholeheartedly dedicated to chicanery and lewdness and who
spoke to the crowd from a little red pulpit although they stayed
at a safe distance from him as if he were the devil himself or
at least the devil's advocate, a serpent. Lashed to poles at his
back and billowing in the rain wind like idle sails were four
large paintings of women in harem dress, so darkened by time
and weather that the lights played on them to no purpose and
they might have been advertising cough syrup and cure-alls.
In the center was a gate in which some lights spelled GAY
PAREE – the gate scuffed and battered from its long summer
travels up and down New England. Burlymaque, burlymaque,
hootchie cootch, hootchie cootch, said the devil, striking the
top of his little red pulpit with a roll of unsold tickets. I'm
going to ask the little ladies out here just once more, just one
more time, to give you some idea, a little idea of what you'll
see when you get inside.

Reluctantly, talking among themselves, shyly, shyly, as children
called on to recite 'Hiawatha' or the 'Village Blacksmith,' a pair
of girls, dressed in skirts of some coarse, transparent cloth like
the cloth hung at cottage windows, side by side for company,
one adventuresome and one not so, their breasts hung lightly
in cloth so that you could see the beginning of the curve,
climbed up onto a ramshackle platform, the boards of which
gave under their weight, and looked boldly and cheerfully
into the crowd, one of them touching the back of her hair to
keep it from blowing in the rain wind and holding with her
other hand the opening in her skirt. They stood there until the
pimp released them with the words that the show was about
to begin, about to begin, last chance, your last chance to see
these beauties dance, and Coverly followed his father up to
the stand and then into a little tent where perhaps thirty men
were standing apathetically around a little stage not so unlike
the stage where he had seen his beloved Judy hit Punch over
the head when he was younger. The roof of the tent was so

shot with holes that the lights of the carnival shone through it like the stars of a galaxy – an illusion that charmed Coverly until he remembered what they were there for. Whatever it was, the crowd seemed sullen. Leander greeted a friend and left Coverly alone and listening to the pimp outside. 'Burlymaque, hootchie cootch – I'm going to ask these little ladies out here just one more time before the show begins. . . .'

They waited and waited while the girls climbed up onto the platform and down again – up and down and the evening and the fair passed outside. A little rain began to fall and the walls of the tent to luff but the water did not cool the tent and sent up only in Coverly's mind memories of some mushroom-smelling forest where he wished he was. Then the girls retired, one of them to crank a phonograph and the other to dance. She was young – a child to Leander – not pretty but so fully in possession of the bloom of youth that it couldn't have mattered. Her hair was brown and as straight as a cow hand's except at the side where she had made two curls. She swore when she pricked her finger with a pin that held her skirt together and went on dancing with a drop of blood on her thumb. When she dropped her skirt she was naked.

Then, in this moth-eaten tent, filled with the fragrance of trampled grass, the rites of Dionysus were proceeding. A splintered tent post served for the symbol on the plate – that holy of holies – but this salute to the deep well of erotic power was step by step as old as man. The lowing of cattle and the voices of children came through the thin canvas walls that hid them. Coverly was rapt. Then the girl picked the cap off a farm hand in the front row and did something very dirty. Coverly walked out of the tent.

The fair was persevering in spite of the rain, which had left a pleasant, bitter smell in the air. The merry-go-round and the Ferris wheel were still turning. At his back Coverly could hear the scratchy music of the cootch show where his father was. To get out of the rain he wandered into the agricultural exhibit. There was no one there but an old man and nothing that he wanted to see. Squashes, tomatoes, corn and lima beans were arranged on paper plates with prizes and labels. The irony of admiring squashes, under the circumstances, was not wasted on him. 'Second prize. Olga Pluzinski,' he read, staring miserably at a jar of tomato pickles. 'Golden Bantam Corn. Raised by Peter Covell. Second prize, Jerusalem Artichokes . . .' He could still pick out, past the noise of the merry-go-round and the rain, the music where the girl was dancing. When the music stopped he went back and waited for his father. If Leander had seen Coverly leave the tent he didn't say so, but they walked to the village where the car was parked in silence. Coverly remembered his feelings at Langely. He had not only jeopardized his own rights – generations of unborn Wapshots were in jeopardy as well as the aged and the blind. He had even endangered that fitting and proper old age to which his parents were entitled and might have imperiled their way of life at West Farm. Everyone was asleep when they got home and they drank some milk, mumbled their good nights and went to bed.

But Coverly's troubles were not over. He dreamed about the girl. It was a humid day when he woke with a salt fog drifting upriver and catching, like bits of carded wool, in the firs. There was nothing about the morning into which he could escape. The rags of fog seemed to turn his mind and his body back onto themselves and their troubles. He groped among the piles of clothing on the floor to find his worsted bathing trunks. They were wet and smelled of a dead sea – the damp wool felt like a corruption on his skin and, thinking piously of saints and others who practiced mortification, Coverly drew them up over his groin and went down the back stairs. But even the kitchen that morning – the one room in the house that could be counted on to generate light and sense in the overcast – seemed like an abandoned hulk, dirty and cold, and Coverly went out the back door and down through the garden to the river. The tide was low and the mudbanks were exposed and reeking, but not so stinking, it seemed to Coverly, as the damp worsted wrapped around his loins so that, with every movement he made, and warmed now by his own miserable flesh, new odors of decayed sea water were discharged. He went out to the tip of the diving board and stood there on a scrap of potato sacking, warming the skin of his chest with the skin of his arms and looking up and down the cold, fog-hung valley where a little mortifying drizzle had begun to form and drop like the condensation of moisture in some subterranean prison. He dived and swam, shivering, out to the middle of the river and then ran back up through the wet garden, wondering if the joy of life was in him.

The boys took their mother to church at eleven and Coverly got vehemently to his knees but he was not halfway through his first prayer when the perfume of the woman in the pew ahead of him undid all his work of mortification and showed him that the literal body of Christ Church was no mighty fortress, for although the verger had shut the oak doors and the only windows open were not big enough for a child to enter by, the devil, so far as Coverly was concerned, came and went, sat on his shoulder, urged him to peer down the front of Mrs Harper's dress, to admire the ankles of the lady in front and to wonder if there was any truth in the rumors about the rector and the boy soprano. His mother nudged him with her elbow when it was time for communion but he looked at her palely and shook his head. The sermon was grueling and through it all Coverly's mind turned over tirelessly the words of an obscene double limerick about a bishop.

Late in the day, when the family were drinking tea, Coverly went out to the back of the house. He smelled a clearing wind and heard it stir in the trees and saw the overcast rise, the miserableness of that day carried off and a band of yellow light spill out of the west. Then he knew what he had to do and he made his preparations; he washed his armpits and emptied his bank. He had enough money to pay for her favors. He would join the blessed company of men, so lightly screened by canvas from the lowing of cattle and the voices of children. He walked, he ran, he walked again, he took a short cut over the Waylands' pasture to the dirt road to the fairgrounds, wondering why the simplicity of life had not appeared to him sooner.

It was dark by the time he reached the dirt road and in spite of the clearing wind it seemed to be a starless night. He did not stop or hesitate until he saw at the gates to the fairgrounds that all the lights were out. The fair was over, of course, and the carnival had gone. The gates hung open and why not, for after the cakes and squashes, the kewpie dolls and the exhibitions of needlework had been removed what was there to guard? With so many dark lanes and tree-shaded places not even the most harassed lovers would seek the shelter of the fairgrounds which, tenanted in these times no more than three or four days each year and nearly as old as Leander, breathed out into the night air the smell of rotted wood. But Coverly went on, into the space where the smell of trampled grass lingered in the air, down the ruts of the midway to where, or where as best he could see in the dark, she had gone through her rites. Oh, what can you do with a boy like that?

As for Moses, it was only a matter of chance that he was not already a father.

CHAPTER 9

Henry Parker brought Rosalie's clothes out from the city in his produce truck and she stayed on at the farm, although she talked about going on to Chicago to visit a girl she had known in Allendale. But her plans to go, whenever she made them, seemed to render the old square house and the valley in such a fine, golden light and to arouse such tenderness in her for everything she saw that she stayed on. Sometimes, walking on a beach and when there is no house near, we smell late in the day, on the east wind, lemons, wood smoke, roses and dust; the fragrance of some large house that we must have visited as children, our memories are so dim and pleasant – some place where we wanted to remain and couldn't – and the farm had come to seem like this for Rosalie.

She liked the old house best when it rained. When she woke in the morning and beard the noise of rain on the many roofs and skylights it was always with a great sense of comfort. She planned to read on the rainy days – to catch up on my reading, she said. All the books she chose were ambitious, but she never got through the first chapter. Sarah tried gently to direct her. *Middlemarch* is a very nice book or have you tried *Death Comes for the Archbishop*? After breakfast Rosalie would settle herself in the back parlor with some book and in the end she would take the old comic sections out of the woodbox and read these. She sometimes went into the village, where she was pleased to find that there was no question about her

identity. You must be the young lady who's staying with the
Wapshots, everyone said. She tried to be helpful around the
house, sweeping the living room and wandering around with a
dust cloth, but she was at that time of life when the ornaments
and moveables of middle age seemed like thorns and stones in
her path and she was always knocking things over. She secretly
did not understand why Mrs Wapshot should bring so many
flowers into the house and put them into vases and pitchers
that kept tipping over. Her laughter was loud and sweet and
almost everyone was glad to hear her voice; even her most
distant footstep. She was good-natured about everything
including the water pump, which broke down several times.
When this happened Coverly drew water from a well near
the woodshed for Rosalie and Mrs Wapshot to wash with but
the men took their baths in the brook.

Honora had never come to judge her. This was a family joke.
'You can't go to Chicago until you've seen Cousin Honora,'
Leander said. The drill and stir of rain on the roofs assured
her that her idle life at the farm was natural – that she was
charged with nothing more than letting time slip through her
hands. When she thought of her friend she tried to rationalize
his death as we will, stumbling onto such conclusions as that
it was time for him to go; he was meant to die young; and
other persuasive and consoling sentimentalities. She dreamed
of him once. She woke from a sound sleep, feeling that he
was in trouble. It was late and the house was dark. She could
hear the brook and in the woods an owl – a small and gentle
chant. He is in trouble, she thought then, lighting a cigarette,
and she seemed to see him, his back to her, naked in that he
was defenseless, and lost, she could see, by the way he held his
head and shoulders – lost or blinded, and wandering in some
maze or labyrinth in great pain. She could not help him – she
saw that – although she could feel the pain of his helplessness
in the way he moved his hands like a swimmer. She supposed
that he was being punished although she didn't know what
sins he had committed. Then she went back to bed and to

sleep but the dream was over as if he had wandered out of her ken or as if his wandering had ended.

Leander took her off for a day on the *Topaze*. It was lovely seaside weather and she stood on the forward deck while Leander watched her from the wheelhouse. A stranger approached her as they started across the bay and Leander was happy to see that she paid him very little attention and when he persisted she gave him a chilly smile and climbed up to the wheelhouse. 'This is absolutly the funniest old boat I've ever seen,' she said.

Now Leander did not like to have people speak critically of the *Topaze*. Her light words made him angry. His respect for the old boat might be a weakness but he thought that people who did not appreciate the *Topaze* were lightheaded. 'I'm starving,' Rosalie said. 'All this *salt* air. I could eat an ox and it isn't ten o'clock.' Leander's feelings were still smarting from her first words. 'At the lake at this camp where I went to,' she said, 'there was a kind of boat that took people around, but it wasn't as much fun as this. I mean I didn't know the captain.' She sensed the mistake she had made in speaking lightly of the *Topaze* and now she tried to make amends. 'And the other boat wasn't as seaworthy,' she said. 'I suppose she's awfully seaworthy. I mean I suppose she was built in the days when people knew how to build seaworthy boats.'

'She's thirty-two years old this spring,' Leander said proudly. 'Honora doesn't spend more than two or three hundred dollars on her a season and she's brought her passengers through thick and thin without harming a hair on their heads.'

They went ashore together at Nangasakit and Leander watched her eat four hot dogs and wash them down with tonic. She didn't want to ride on the roller-coaster and he guessed that her ideas of pleasure were more sophisticated. He wondered if she drank cocktails in lounges. In speaking of her home she had spoken both of wealth and meanness and Leander guessed that her life had been made up of both. 'Mother gives an enormous garden party, every summer,' she had said, 'with an orchestra sort of hidden in the bushes and millions of delicious cakes,' and an hour later she had said, speaking of her own ineptitude as a housekeeper, 'Daddy cleans the bathrooms at home. He gets into these old clothes and gets down on his hands and knees and scrubs the floors and tubs and everything. . . .' The hired orchestra and the housecleaning priest were equally strange to Leander and interested him, mostly in that her background seemed to stand between Rosalie and her enjoyment of Nangasakit. He would have liked to ride on the roller-coaster himself and he was disappointed when she refused. But they walked on the wrecked sea wall above the white sand and the green water and he was happy in her company. He thought – like Sarah – how much he would have liked a daughter, and the images of her career formed swiftly in his mind. She would marry, of course. He even saw himself throwing rice at her as she ran down the steps of Christ Church. But somehow her marriage went wrong. Her husband was killed in the war perhaps or turned out to be a drunk or a crook. In any case she came back to take care of Leander in his old age – to bring him his bourbon and cook his meals and listen to his stories on stormy nights. At three o'clock they went back to the boat.

Everyone liked Rosalie but Moses, who stayed out of her way and was surly with her when they met. Mrs Wapshot kept urging him to take her sailing and he always refused. It may have been that he associated her with that first night in the pasture and the fire or that – and this was more likely – that she seemed to him to be his mother's creation, to have stepped out of Sarah's brow. He spent most of his time at the Pocamasset boat club, where he raced the *Tern,* and he sometimes went fishing in the brook that flowed from Parson's Pond down behind the barn into the West River.

He planned to do this one morning and was up before dawn, although his chances of catching any fish that late in the summer were slim. It was dark when he made himself some coffee and pulled on his waders in the kitchen, his head full of pleasant recollections of other, similar, early mornings; the camp at Langely and skiing – the suffocating heat in ski lodges and the bad food and the running. Drinking coffee in the dark kitchen (the windows had begun to show some light) reminded him of all these things. He got some gear out of the hall closet, hitched his boots to his belt and trudged up the fields, planning to walk to Parson's Pond and then fish the stream down with wet flies, which were the only flies he had been able to find.

He cut into the woods a little below Parson's Pond. Other fishermen had made a path. It was humid in the woods and the smell of vegetation was heady and his heart seemed to rise when he heard the noise of water – like the garbled voices of prophets – and saw the first pool. His bladder was full, but he would save that for good luck if he needed it. He was so anxious to get a fly into the water that he had to reproach himself for haste. He had to put on leader and tie some respectable knots. While he did this he saw a trout traveling upstream – no more than the flicker of an eyelid – and somehow determined like a dog at evening with a newspaper in its mouth.

There were rags of mist over the water that early in the morning and what was that smell, he wondered, as strong as tanbark and much finer? He let himself into the brook, making sure of his footing, and made a fair cast. At least he was pleased himself and if he had been a trout he would have struck, his gastric juices flowing freely until he felt the hook in his jaw. He gathered in his line and made another cast, wading so deep in the pool that his crotch got wet, a blessing, he thought, hoping that the cold water would discourage his mind from ever leaving such simple pleasures, for with his maturity Moses had found in himself a taste for the grain and hair of life. He snagged a fly and then tying another waded on through some swift, shallow water into another pool, the prettiest of them all, but one where he had never caught a fish. The granite around the pool was square, like quarry stone, the water was black and slow – moving, overhung here and there with fir and wild apple, and although Moses knew that it was a pool where he wasted his time he could not convince himself that it was not inhabited by trout – whole families of shrewd two-pounders with undershot jaws. From this dark pool he waded through white water again to a place with meadowy banks where Turk's-cap lilies and wild roses grew and where it was easy to cast. While he was fishing this pool the sun came up and out – a flood of golden light that spread all through the woods and sank into the water so that every blue stone and white pebble showed – flooded the water with light until it was as golden as bourbon whisky – and the instant this happened he got a strike. His footing was bad. He nearly fell down, swearing loudly, but his rod was bent and then the trout surfaced with a crash and made for the logs at the mouth of the pool, but Moses kept him away from these, the fish zooming this way and that and the thrill of its life shooting up into Moses' arms and shoulders. Then, as the fish tired and he got out his landing net, he thought: What a life; what a grand life! He admired the rosy spots on the fish, broke its back and wrapped it in fern, ready now for a big day, a day in which he would catch his limit or over. But he fished that pool for an hour without getting another strike and then waded on to the next and the next, about as reflective as a race-track tout, but not insensitive to the stillness of the woods around him, the loud, prophetic noise of water and then, by looking down to the pool below him to the fact that he was not alone. Rosalie was there.

She had come to bathe; she was really washing herself, rubbing soap between her toes and sitting naked in the warm sun on a stone. He snapped his reel so that she would not hear him take in the line and waded carefully, not to make any noise, to the banks of the pool where she could not see him but where he could see her through the leaves. He watched his gleaming Susanna, shamefaced, his dream of simple pleasure replaced by some sadness, some heaviness that seemed to make his mouth taste of blood and his teeth ache. She did not go in for washing much more than her feet. The water was too cold or the sun was too warm. She stood, picked a leaf off her buttocks and went into the green woods; vanished. Her clothes would be there. His head was confused and the smell of the dead trout in his pocket seemed like something from his past. He unwrapped the fish and washed it in the running water, but it looked like a toy. After a decent interval he went back to the farm, where his mother was waiting to ask him to bring water from the well, and after lunch he asked Rosalie to go sailing. 'I'd adore to,' she said.

They went down to Travertine in the old car and she knew more about sailing than he had expected. While he pumped the boat dry she put the battens into his sail and kept out of the way. There was a fresh southwest wind blowing and he took the racecourse, running for the first buoy with the wind at his stern, his centerboard up. And then the wind backed around to the east and the day darkened as swiftly as breath obscures a piece of glass. He took a wide tack for the second buoy but the water was rough and suddenly everything was sullen, angry and dangerous, and he could feel the pull of the old sea – the ebb tide – on his hull. Waves began to break over the bow and every one of them soaked Rosalie.

She hoped that he would head back for the boat club and she knew that he wouldn't. She had begun to shake with the cold and she wished she had never come. She had wanted his attention, his friendship, but as the hull rose clumsily and made an ominous thump and another sea broke over her shoulders she had some discouraging thoughts about her past and her hopes. Without a loving family, without many friends, dependent mostly upon men for her knowledge and guidance, she had found them all set on some mysterious pilgrimage that often put her life into danger. She had known a man who liked to climb mountains and as the *Tern* heeled over and shipped another sea she remembered her mountain-climbing lover; the crusts of fatigue in her mouth, the soreness of her feet, the dry sandwiches and the misty blue view from the summits that only raised in her mind the question of what she was doing there. She had tramped after bird watchers and waited home for fishermen and hunters and here she was on the *Tern*, half frozen and half drowned.

They rounded the second buoy and started back for the boat club and as they approached the mooring Rosalie went up to the bow. What happened was not her fault although Moses might have blamed her if he hadn't seen it. As she pulled the skiff toward her the light painter broke. The skiff rested thoughtfully, it seemed, in the chop for a second or two and then eased its bow around to the open sea and headed in that direction, nodding and dancing in the rough. Moses kicked off his sneakers and dived in, striking out for the skiff, and swam after it for some distance until he realized that the skiff was traveling more rapidly on the ebb tide and the wind than he could swim. Then he turned his head and saw the full scope of his mistake. When the painter broke the mooring had been lost and now, with her sails down and Rosalie calling to him, the *Tern* was heading out to the open sea.

It was foggy then. He could barely see the beach and the lights of the Pocamasset club and he struck out for these, but not hurriedly, for the ebb tide was strong and there were limits to his strength. He saw someone come out onto the porch of the boat club and he waved and shouted but he couldn't be heard or seen and after floating for a minute to rest he began the long haul to shore. When he felt sand under his feet it was a sweet sensation. The old committee boat was tied up to the wharf and he threw off the lines and headed her out into the fog, trying to guess the course the *Tern* would take. Then he let the motor idle and began to shout: 'Rosalie, Rosalie, Rosalie, Rosalie . . .'

She answered him in a little while and he saw the outlines of the *Tern* and told her what line to throw him, and lifted her, in his arms, off the bow. She was laughing and he had been so anxious that her cheerfulness seemed to him like a kind of goodness that he had not suspected her to have. Then they picked up the skiff and headed for shore and when the *Tern* was moored they went into the old clubhouse that looked as if it had been put together by old ladies and mice and had, in fact, been floated down the river from St Botolphs. Moses built a fire and they dried themselves here and would have

remained if old Mr Sturgis hadn't come into the billiard room
to practice shots.

Honora finished her hooked rug that afternoon – a field
of red roses – and this and the gloomy sea-turn decided her
to go to West Farm at last and be introduced to the stranger.
She cut across the fields in the rain from Boat Street to River
Street and let herself in the side door calling, 'Hello. Hello. Is
anyone home?' There was no answer. The house was empty.
She was not nosy, but she climbed the stairs to the spare room
to see if the girl might be there. The hastily made bed, the
clothes scattered on chairs, and the full ash tray made her feel
unfriendly and suspicious and she opened the closet door.
She was in the closet when she heard Moses and Rosalie
coming up the stairs, Moses saying, 'What harm can there be
in something that would make us both feel so good?' Honora
closed the closet door as they came into the room.

What else Honora heard – and she heard plenty – does
not concern us here. This is not a clinical account. We will
only consider the dilemma of an old lady – born in Polynesia,
educated at Miss Wilbur's, a philanthropist and samaritan – led
by no more than her search for the truth into a narrow closet
on a rainy afternoon.

CHAPTER 10

No one saw Honora leave the house that day and if they had they wouldn't have been able to tell whether or not she was crying with the rain streaming over her face as she stamped across Waylands' pasture to Boat Street. The violence of her emotion may have stemmed from her memories of Mr de Sastago, whose titles and castles turned out to be air. Her life had been virtuous, her dedication to innocence had been unswerving and she had been rewarded with a vision of life that seemed as unsubstantial as a paper match in a fairly windy place. She did not understand. She did not, as you might expect, take out her bewilderment on Maggie. She changed into dry clothes, drank her port and after supper she read the Bible.

At ten o'clock Honora said her prayers, turned out the light and got into bed. As soon as she turned out the light she felt wakeful and alert. It was the dark that made her wakeful. She was afraid of it. She looked boldly into the dark to assure herself that there was nothing to be afraid of but there seemed, in the dark, to be a stir, an increase of movement as if figures or spirits were arriving and gathering. She cleared her throat. She tried shutting her eyes, but this only heightened the illusion that the dark was populated. She opened her eyes again, determined to look squarely at the fantasy since she could not escape it.

The figures, although she couldn't see them clearly, were not numerous. There seemed to be twelve or fourteen – enough to circle her bed. They seemed to dance. Their movements were ugly and obscene and by looking narrowly into the dark she was able to recognize their forms. There were pumpkin heads cut with a dog-tooth smile; there were the buckram masks of cats and pirates that are sold to children at Halloween; there were skeletons, masked executioners, the top-heavy headdresses of witch doctors that she had seen photographed in the *National Geographic* magazine; there was everything that had ever seemed to her strange and unnatural. I am Honora Wapshot! she said aloud. I am a Wapshot. We have always been a hardy family.

She got out of bed, turned on a light and lighted the fire in her hearth, holding out her arms to the warmth. The light and the fire seemed to scatter the grotesques. I am a Wapshot, she said again. I am Honora Wapshot. She sat by the fire until midnight and then she went to bed and fell asleep.

Early in the morning she dressed and after breakfast hurried through her garden to catch the bus to Travertine. The rain was over but the day was sullen; the tail of the storm. There were only a few other passengers. One of these, a woman, left her seat in the rear when they had been traveling for a few minutes and sat down beside Honora. 'I'm Mrs Kissel,' she said. 'You don't remember me, but I recognized you. You're Honora Wapshot. I have a very embarrassing thing to tell you but I noticed when you got on the bus –' Mrs Kissel lowered her voice to a whisper – 'that your dress is undone all down the front. It's very embarrassing but I always think it's best to tell people.'

'Thank you,' Honora said. She clutched her coat over her dress.

'I always think it's best to tell people,' Mrs Kissel went on. 'Whenever people tell me I'm always grateful. I don't care who they are. It reminds me of something that happened to me. Some years ago Mr Kissel and I went up to Maine for his vacation. Mr Kissel comes from Maine. He graduated from Bowdoin College. We went up in the sleeping cars. The train arrived at the station early in the morning and I had the most awful time getting my clothes on in that berth. I'd never been in a sleeping car before. Well, when we got off the train there were quite a few people there on the platform. The stationmaster was there, waiting for the mail, I guess, or something like that. Well, he came right over to me. I'd never seen him before in my life and I couldn't imagine what he wanted. Well, he came right over to me and he said "Madam," he said in a low voice, "Madam, your corset is undone."' Mrs Kissel lifted her head and laughed for an instant like a young, young woman. 'Oh, I'd never seen him before,' she said, 'and I never saw him again, but he came right over to me and told me that and I didn't resent it. Oh, I didn't resent it at all. I thanked him and went into the ladies' room and fixed it and then we took a carriage to the hotel. Those were the days when they had carriages.'

Honora turned and stared at Mrs Kissel, seized with jealousy, her neighbor seemed so simple and good and to have so few problems on her mind. They were at Travertine then and when the bus stopped Honora got off and marched up the street to the sign painter's.

CHAPTER 11

Early the next morning Leander walked down the fish-smelling path to the wharf where the *Topaze* lay. A dozen passengers were waiting to buy their tickets and go aboard. Then he noticed that a sign had been hung on his wheelhouse. Then he thought at once of Honora and wondered what she had up her sleeve. The sign was painted on wood and must have cost five dollars. NO TRESPASSING, it said. THIS YACHT FOR SALE. FOR FURTHER INFORMATION SEE HONORA WAPSHOT 27 BOAT STREET. For a second his heart sank; his spirit seemed to wither. Then he was angry. The sign was hung, not nailed, to the wheelhouse, and he seized it and was about to throw it into the river when he realized that it was a good piece of wood and could be used for something else. 'There won't be any voyage today,' he told his passengers. Then he put the sign under his arm and strode through the group to the square. Of course most of the tradespeople in the village knew about the sign and most of them watched Leander. He saw no one and it was a struggle for him to keep from talking loudly to himself. He was, as we know, in his sixties; a little stooped, a little inclined to duck-foot, but a very handsome old man with thick hair and a boyish mien. The sign was heavy and made his arm lame and he had to change it from side to side before he got to Boat Street. His spirits by this time were fulminating. There wasn't much common sense left in him. He pounded on Honora's door with the edge of the sign.

Honora was sewing. She took her time getting to the door. First she reached for her stick and went around the parlor gathering up all the photographs of Moses and Coverly. She dumped these onto the floor behind the sofa. The reason she did this was that, although she liked having photographs of the boys around, she never wanted any of the family to catch her in such an open demonstration of affection. Then she straightened her clothes and started for the door. Leander was pounding on it. 'If you mar the paint on my door,' she called to him, 'you'll pay for it.' As soon as she opened the door he stormed into the hall and roared, 'What in Christ's name is the meaning of this?'

'You don't have to be profane,' she said. She put her hands over her ears. 'I won't listen to profanity.'

'What do you want from me, Honora?'

'I can't hear a word you say,' she said. 'I won't listen to swearing.'

'I'm not swearing,' he shouted. 'I've stopped swearing.'

'She's mine,' Honora said, taking her hands down from her ears. 'I can do anything I want with her.'

'You can't sell her.'

'I can too,' Honora said. 'The D'Agostino boys want to buy her for a fishing boat.'

'I mean she's my usefulness, Honora.' There was nothing pleading in his voice. He was still shouting. 'You gave her to me. I'm used to her. She's my boat.'

'I only loaned her to you.'

'Goddamn it, Honora, the members of a family can't backbite one another like this.'

'I won't listen to swearing,' Honora said. Up went her hands again.

'What do you want?'

'I want you to stop swearing.'

'Why did you do this? Why did you do this behind my back? Why didn't you tell me what was on your mind?'

'She belongs to me, I can do anything I want with her.'

'We've always shared things, Honora. That rug belongs to me. That rug's mine.' He meant the long rug in the hall.

'Your dear mother gave that rug to me,' Honora said.

'She loaned it to you.'

'She meant me to have it.'

'That's my rug.'

'It's nothing of the kind.'

'Two can play at this game as well as one.' Leander put down the sign and picked up an end of the rug.

'You put down that rug, Leander Wapshot,' Honora shouted.

'It's my rug.'

'You put down that rug this instant. Do you hear me?'

'It's mine. It's my rug.' He pulled the folds of the rug, which was long and so dirty that the dust from its warp made him sneeze, toward the door. Then Honora went to the other end of the rug, seized it and called for Maggie. When Maggie came out of the kitchen she grabbed Honora's end – they were all sneezing – and they all began to pull. It was a very unpleasant scene, but if we accept the quaintness of St Botolphs we must also accept the fact that it was the country of spite fences and internecine quarrels and that the Pinchot twins lived until their death in a house divided by a chalk line. Leander lost, of course. How could a man win such a contest? Leaving Honora and Maggie in possession of the rug he stormed out of the house, his feelings in such a turmoil that he did not know where to go, and walking south on Boat Street until he came to a field he sat down in the sweet grass and chewed the succulent ends of a few stalks to take the bitterness out of his mouth.

During his lifetime Leander had seen, in the village, the number of sanctuaries for men reduced to one. The Horse Guards had disbanded; the Atlantic Club was shut; even the boat club had been floated down to Travertine. The only place left was the Niagara Hose Company, and he walked back to the village and climbed the stairs beside the fire engine to the meeting room. The smell of many jolly beefsteak suppers was in the air, but there was no one in the room but old Perley Sturgis and Perley was asleep. On the walls were many photographs of Wapshots: Leander as a young man; Leander and Hamlet; Benjamin, Ebenezer, Lorenzo and Thaddeus. The photographs of himself as a young man made him unhappy and he went and sat in one of the Morris chairs near the window.

His anger at Honora had changed to a pervasive sense of uneasiness. She had something up her sleeve and he wished he knew what it was. He wondered what she could do and then he realized that she could do anything she pleased. The Topaze and the farm were hers. She paid the school bills and the interest on the mortgage. She had even filled the cellar with coal. She had offered to do all this in the kindest imaginable way. I have the wherewithal, Leander, she had said. Why shouldn't I help my only family? It was his fault – he couldn't blame her – that he had never expected consequence for this largess. He knew that she was meddlesome but he had overlooked this fact, borne along on his conviction of the abundance of life – carp in the inlet, trout in the streams, grouse in the orchard and money in Honora's purse – the feeling that the world was contrived to cheer and delight him. A ragged image of his wife and his sons appeared to him then – thinly dressed and standing in a snowstorm – which was, after all, not so outrageous since couldn't Honora, if she wanted, let them all experience hunger? This image of his family roused in him passionate feelings. He would defend and shelter them. He would defend them with sticks and stones; with his naked fists. But this did not change the facts of possession. Everything belonged to Honora. Even the rocking horse in the attic. He should have led his life differently.

But out of the window he could see the blue sky above the trees of the square and he was easily charmed with the appearance of the world. How could anything go wrong in such a paradise? 'Wake up, Perley, wake up and we'll play some backgammon,' he shouted. Perley woke up and they played backgammon for matchsticks until noon. They had some lunch in the bakery and played backgammon some more. In the middle of the afternoon it suddenly occurred to Leander that all he needed was money. Poor Leander! We cannot endow him with wisdom and powers of invention that he does not have and give him a prime-ministerial breadth of mind. This is what he did.

He crossed the square to the Cartwright Block and climbed the stairs. He said good afternoon to Mrs Marston in the telephone-company office – a pleasant white-haired widow surrounded by many potted plants that seemed to bloom and flourish in the fertile climate of her disposition. Leander spoke to her about the rain and then went down the hall to the doctor's office, where a WALK IN sign hung from the doorknob like a bib. In the waiting room there was a little girl with a bandaged hand, leaning her head against her mother's breast, and old Billy Tompkins with an empty pill bottle. The furniture seemed to have been brought in from some porch, and the wicker chair in which Leander sat squeaked as loudly as if he had sat down on a nest of mice. The pack, hedges and jumpers of a fox hunt appeared on the wallpaper and in these repeated images Leander saw a reflection on the vitality of the village – a proneness to dwell on strange and different ways of life The door to the inner office opened and a dark-skinned young woman who was pregnant came out. Then the child with the bandaged hand was led in by her mother. She was not in the office long. Then Billy Tompkins went in with his empty pill bottle. He came out with a prescription and Leander went in.

'What can I do for you, Captain Wapshot?' the doctor asked.

'I was playing backgammon with Perley Sturgis at the fire-bouse,' Leander said, 'and I had an idea. I wondered if you could give me a job.'

'Oh, I'm afraid not,' the doctor said pleasantly enough. 'I don't even have a nurse.'

'That wasn't the kind of work I had in mind,' Leander said. 'Can anyone hear us?'

'I don't believe so,' the doctor said.

'Take me for an experiment,' Leander said. 'Please take me. I've decided that's what I want to do. I'll sign anything. I won't tell anyone. Operate on me. Do anything you want. Just give me a little money.'

'You don't know what you're talking about, Captain Wapshot.'

'Take me,' Leander said. 'I'm a very interesting specimen. Pure Yankee stock. Think of the blood in my veins. State senators. Scholars. Sea captains. Heroes. Schoolmasters. You can make medical history. You can make a name for yourself. You'll be famous. I'll give you the family history. I'll give you a regular pedigree. I don't care what you do with me. Just give me a little money.'

'Please get out of here, Captain Wapshot.'

'It would help humanity some, wouldn't it?' Leander asked. 'It would help humanity. Nobody has to know. I won't tell anybody. I promise I won't tell anybody. I'll promise on the Bible. You can have a laboratory nobody knows about. I won't tell anyone. I'll go there whenever you say. I'll go there nights if you want me. I'll tell Mrs Wapshot I'm traveling.'

'Please get out of here, Captain Wapshot.'

Leander picked up his hat and left. In the square a woman, from the other side of the river, was calling in Italian to her son. 'Speak English,' Leander told her. 'Speak English. This is the United States.' He drove back to the farm in the old Buick.

He was tired, and happy to see the lights of the farm. He was hungry and thirsty and his appetite seemed to embrace the landscape and the house. Lulu had burned something. There was a smell of burned food in the hall. Sarah was in the back parlor.

'Did you see the sign?' she asked.

'Yes,' Leander said. 'Was she here today?'

'Yes. She was here this afternoon.'

'She hung it on the wheelhouse,' Leander said. 'I guess she hung it there herself.'

'What are you talking about?'

'The sign.'

'But it's on the gatepost.'

'What do you mean?'

'The sign's on the gatepost. She put it there this afternoon.'

'She wants to sell the farm?'

'Oh, no.'

'What is it, what is it then? What in hell is it?'

'Leander. Please.'

'I can't talk with anyone.'

'You don't have to talk like that.'

'Well, what is it? Tell me, Sarah, what is it?'

'She thinks that we ought to take in tourists. She's spoken to the Pattersons and they make enough money taking in tourists to go to Daytona every year.'

'I don't want to go to Daytona.'

'We have three extra bedrooms,' Sarah said. 'She thinks we ought to let them.'

'That old woman has not got a scrap of the sense of the fitness of things left in her head,' Leander shouted. 'She'll sell my boat to foreigners and fill my house with strangers. She has no sense of fitness.'

'She only wants. . .'

'She only wants to drive me out of my head. I can't make head nor tail of what she's doing. I don't want to go to Daytona. What makes her think I want to go to Daytona?'

'Leander. Please. Shhh . . .' In the dusk she saw the headlights of a car come up the drive. She went down the hall to the side door and onto the stoop.

'Can you put us up?' a man called cheerfully.

'Well, I believe so,' Sarah said. Leander followed her down the hall but when he heard the stranger, veiled by the dark, close the door of his car, he stepped back from the door.

'What do you charge?' the man asked.

'Whatever's customary,' Sarah said. 'Perhaps you'd like to look at the rooms?' A man and a woman came up the stairs.

'All we want are comfortable beds and a bathroom,' the man said.

'Well, the bed has a nice hair mattress,' Sarah said thoughtfully, 'but there's some rust in the hot-water tank and we've had an awful time with the water pump this month, but I'd like you to see the rooms.'

She opened the screen door and stepped into the hall to be followed by the strangers and Leander, standing there and trapped, opened the hall closet and crashed into the dark with its collection of old coats and athletic equipment. He heard the strangers enter his house and follow Sarah up the stairs. Just then the old water closet sounded the opening notes of a performance of unusual vehemence. As this noise abated Leander heard the stranger ask, 'Then you don't have a room with a private bath?'

'Oh no,' Sarah said, 'I'm sorry,' and there was sorrow in her voice. 'You see this is one of the oldest houses in St Botolphs and our bathroom is the oldest in the county.'

'Well, what we were looking for was a place with a private bathroom,' the stranger said, 'and . . .'

'We always like to have a private bathroom,' his wife said gently. 'Even when we travel on trains we like to have one of those compartments.'

'*De gustibus non est disputandum*,' Sarah said sweetly, but her sweetness was forced.

'Thank you for showing us the rooms.'

'You're quite welcome.'

The screen door slammed and when the car had gone down the drive Leander came out of the closet. He strode down the drive to where a sign, TOURIST HOME, was hung on his gatepost. It was about the size and quality of the sign on the *Topaze* and raising it in the air with all his might he brought it down on the stones, splitting the sign in two and jarring his own bones. Later that night he walked over to Boat Street.

Honora's house was dark but Leander stood squarely in front of it and called her name. He gave her a chance to put on a wrapper and then shouted her name again.

'What is it, Leander?' she asked. He couldn't see her, but her voice was clear enough and he knew she had come to the window. 'What do you want?'

'Oh you're so high and mighty these last days, Honora. Don't forget that I know who you are. I can remember you feeding swill to the pigs and coming back from Waylands' with the milk pails. I have something to tell you, Honora. I have something important to tell you. It was a long time ago. It was right after you came back from Spain. I was standing in front of Moodys' with Mitch Emerson. When you walked through the square Mitch said something about you. I couldn't repeat what he said. Well, I took him out behind the lumberyard, Honora, and I walloped him until he cried. He weighed fifty pounds more than me and all the Emersons were hardy, but I made him cry. I never told you that.'

'Thank you, Leander.'

'And other things, too. I've always been dutiful towards you. I would have gone to Spain and killed Sastago if you'd asked me. There's not a hair on my body that has not turned white in your service. So why do you devil me?'

'Moses has to go,' Honora said.

'What?'

'Moses has to go out in the world and prove himself. Oh, it's hard for me to say this, Leander, but I think it's right. He hasn't raised a finger all summer except to indulge himself, and all the men of our family went out into the world when they were young; all the Wapshots. I've thought it over and I think he'll want to go but I'm afraid he'll be homesick. Oh, I was so homesick in Spain, Leander. I'll never forget it.'

'Moses is a good boy,' Leander said. 'He'll do well anywhere.' He straightened up, thinking proudly of his son. 'What did you have in mind?'

'I thought he might go to someplace like New York or Washington, someplace strange and distant.'

'That's a bully idea, Honora. Is that what all the trouble's been about?'

'What trouble?'

'Are you going to sell the *Topaze?*'

'The D'Agostino boys have changed their minds.'

'I'll talk it over with Sarah.'

'It won't be easy for any of us,' Honora said, and then she sighed. Leander heard the tremulous sound, shaken and breaking like smoke and seeming to arise from such a deep base of the old lady's spirit that age had not changed its tenderness or its purity, and it affected him like the sigh of a child.

'Good night, Honora dear,' he said.

'Feel that lovely breeze.'

'Yes. Good night.'

'Good night, Leander.'

CHAPTER 12

Moses' career at college had been unexceptional and – but for a few friendships – there was nothing about it that he would miss; not the skimmed milk on his porridge or Dunster House upended like a sow above the threadbare waters of the Charles. He wanted to see the world. For Leander the world meant a place where Moses could display his strong, gentle and intelligent nature; his brightness. When he thought of his son's departure it was always with feelings of pride and anticipation. How well Moses would do! Honora had tradition at her back, for all the men of the family had taken a growing-up cruise – Leander's father included – rounding the Horn before they shaved, some of them, and on the homeward voyage lewdly straddling the beauties of Samoa, who must have begun to show some signs of wear and tear. Sarah's habitual reliance on sad conclusions – life is only a casting off and we only live from day to day – helped her to bear the pain of having her first born plucked from his home. But where did all of this leave poor Coverly?

The relationship between the two brothers had been stormy until a year or so ago. They had fought bare fisted and with sticks, stones and iceballs. They had reviled one another and had thought of the world as a place where the other would be exposed as an evil-tempered fraud. Then all this bad feeling had turned to tenderness and a brotherhood had bloomed that had all the symptoms of love – the pleasure of nearness and the pain of separation. They even took long walks together on the beach at Travertine, airing their most intimate and improbable plans. The knowledge that his brother was leaving gave Coverly his first taste of love's dark side; it was gall. He didn't see how he could live without Moses. Honora made the arrangements. Moses would go to Washington and work for a Mr Boynton who was in some way indebted to her. If Moses had any regrets or hints of regrets they were lost in the confusion of his feelings and overridden by his passionate wish to get out of St Botolphs and try his strength in the world.

Sarah gathered those things that she thought Moses might need when he took up his life in a strange place – his confirmation certificate, a souvenir spoon he had bought at Plymouth Rock, a drawing of a battleship he had made when he was six, his football sweater, prayer book, muffler and two report cards – but, hearing him shout loudly up the stairs to Coverly, she sensed, in the notes of his voice, that he would leave these things behind him and she put them away again. The closeness of Moses' departure drew Sarah and Leander together and refreshed those charming self-deceptions that are the backbone of many long-lived marriages. Leander felt that Sarah was frail and on the evenings before Moses left he brought her a shawl to shield her from the night air. Sarah felt that Leander had a beautiful baritone voice and now with Moses going away she wished he would take up his music again. Sarah was not frail – she had the strength of ten – and Leander could not carry the simplest tune. 'You have to remember about the night air,' Leander told her when he brought her the shawl, and, looking up at him admiringly, Sarah would say, 'It's a shame the boys have never heard you sing.'

There was a farewell party. The men drank bourbon and the ladies had ginger ale and ice cream. 'I came over by Waylands' pasture,' Aunt Adelaide Forbes said, 'and that pasture's just covered with cowflops. I have never seen so many cowflops in my whole life. There's just cowflops everywhere. You can't hardly take a step without ending up in a cowflop.' Everyone was there and Reba Heaslip came up to Rosalie and said, 'I was BORN in the inner sanctum of the Masonic Temple.' They all talked about their travels. Mr and Mrs Gates had been to New York and had paid eighteen dollars a day for a room where you couldn't swing a cat around in. Aunt Adelaide had been taken to Buffalo when she was a child. Honora had been to Washington. Mildred Harper, the church organist, played the piano, and they sang from the old hymnal and song books – 'Silver Threads Among the Gold,' 'Beulah Land' and 'In the Gloaming.' While they were singing Sarah saw Uncle Peepee Marshmallow's face in the window but when she went out onto the stoop to ask him in he had fled. Moses, going into the kitchen for a drink, found Lulu crying. 'I ain't crying because you're going away, Moses,' she said. 'I'm crying because I had this bad dream last night. I dreamed I give you this gold watch and you broke it on some stones. Ain't that silly of me? Of course I don't have the money to buy you a gold watch and even if I did you aren't the kind of boy that'd break it, but just the same I dreamed this dream where I give you this gold watch and you broke it on some stones.'

Moses left the next night on the 9:18, but there was no one to see him off but his parents. Rosalie was in her room, crying. 'I won't go to the station,' Honora had said in the same tone of voice she used at family funerals when she said that she would not go to the grave. No one knew where Coverly was but Sarah suspected that he was taking a walk on the beach at Travertine. Standing on the platform they could hear in the distance the noise of the train coming up the east banks of the river, a sound that made Sarah shiver, for she was at an age when trains seemed to her plainly to be the engines of separation and death. Leander put a hand on Moses' shoulder and gave him a silver dollar.

Moses' feelings were strenuous but not sad and he did not remember the skimming fleet at the ten-minute signal before a race or the ruined orchards where he hunted grouse or Parson's Pond and the cannon on the green and the water of the river shining between the hardware store and the five-

and-ten-cent store where Cousin Justina had once played the piano. We are all inured, by now, to those poetic catalogues where the orchid and the overshoe appear cheek by jowl; where the filthy smell of old plumage mingles with the smell of the sea. We have all parted from simple places by train or boat at season's end with generations of yellow leaves spilling on the north wind as we spill our seed and the dogs and the children in the back of the car, but it is not a fact that at the moment of separation a tumult of brilliant and precise images – as though we drowned – streams through our heads. We have indeed come back to lighted houses, smelling on the north wind burning applewood, and seen a Polish countess greasing her face in a ski lodge and heard the cry of the horned owl in rut and smelled a dead whale on the south wind that carries also the sweet note of the bell from Antwerp and the dishpan summons of the bell from Altoona but we do not remember all this and more as we board the train.

Sarah began to cry when Moses kissed her. Leander put an arm around her shoulder but she would have none of it and so they stood apart when Moses said good-by. As soon as the train started, Coverly, who had boarded it in Travertine, came out of the toilet where he was hidden and joined his brother and past the table-silver factory they went, past old Mr Larkin's barn with this legend painted on it: BE KIND TO ANIMALS, past the Remsens' fields and the watermans' dump, past the ice pond and the hair-tonic works, past Mrs Trimble's the laundress, past Mr Brown's who ate a slice of mince pie and drank a glass of milk when the 9:18 rattled his windows, past the Howards' and the Townsends' and the grade crossing and the cemetery and the house of the old man who filed saws and whose windows were the last of the village.

CHAPTER 13

It never rains but it pours. After saying good-by to Moses, Leander and Sarah came home to find this letter from Coverly on the hall table.

'Dear Mother and Father, I have gone away with Moses. I know that I should have told you and that not telling you was like lying but this is only the second lie I have ever told and I will never tell another. The other lie I told was about the screwdriver with the black handle. I stole it from Tinicum's hardware store. I love Moses so much that I couldn't be in St Botolphs if he wasn't there. But we are not going to be together because we thought that if we separated we would have a better chance of proving our self-reliance to Cousin Honora. I am going to New York and work for Cousin Mildred's husband in his carpet factory and as soon as I have a place to live in I will write and tell you my address. I have twenty-five dollars.

'I love you both and would not want to hurt your feelings and I know there is no place finer in the world than St Botolphs and our house and when I have made my mark I am coming back. I wouldn't be happy anywhere else. But now I am old enough to go out in the world and make my fortune. I can tell this because I have so many ideas about life where I never had any ideas before. I have taken the framed copy of Kiplings IF with me and I will think about this and about all the great men I have read about and I will go to Church.

'Your loving son, Coverly.'

And two days later Rosalie's parents telephoned to say that they would pick up Rosalie in an hour. They were driving to Oysterville. Soon after this a long black car that would have opened Emmet Cavis' eyes came up the driveway at West Farm and Rosalie ran down the path to greet her parents. 'Where did you get that green dress?' Sarah heard Mrs Young ask her daughter. It was the first or at least the second thing she said. Then they got out of the car and Rosalie, blushing and as confused and embarrassed as a child, introduced them to Sarah. As soon as Mrs Young had shaken Sarah's hand she turned to Rosalie and asked, 'Guess what I found yesterday? I found your scarab bracelet. I found it in my top bureau drawer. Yesterday morning before we had planned to go to Oysterville I decided to clean out my top bureau drawer. I just took the whole thing and dumped it out onto my bed – just dumped it out onto my bed and lo and behold there was your scarab bracelet.'

'I'll go up and finish packing,' said Rosalie, blushing and blushing, and she went in, leaving Sarah with her parents. The rector was a pursy man in clericals and sure enough, while they stood there, he began to scratch his stomach. Sarah disliked quick and unkind judgments and yet there seemed to be some striking stiffness and dryness in the man and something so pompous, monotonous and crusty in the notes of his voice that she felt irritable. Mrs Young was a short woman, a little plump, and decked out with furs, gloves and a hat sewn with pearls – one of those middle-aged women of means, it seems, whose emptyheadedness smacks of tragedy. 'The funny thing about the scarab bracelet,' she said, 'was that I thought Rosalie lost it in Europe. She went abroad last year, you know. Eight countries. Well, I thought she lost her bracelet in Europe and I was so surprised to find it in my bureau drawer.'

'Won't you come in?' Sarah asked.

'No thank you, no thank you. It's a quaint old house, I can see that. I love quaint old things. And some day when I'm old and James has retired I'm going to buy a quaint, run-down old house like this and do it all over myself. I love quaint old run-down places.'

The priest cleared his throat and felt for his wallet. 'We have a little pecuniary matter to settle,' he said, 'before Rosalie comes down. I've talked it over with Mrs Young. We thought that twenty dollars might help repay you for . . .' Then Sarah began to cry, to cry for them all – Coverly, Rosalie and Moses and the stupid priest – and she felt such a sharp pain in her breast that it seemed as if she was weaning her children. 'Oh, you must excuse me for crying,' she sobbed. 'I'm terribly sorry. You must excuse me.'

'Well, here's thirty dollars then,' the priest said, handing her the bills.

'Oh, I don't know what's come over me,' Sarah sobbed. 'Oh dear. Oh dear.' She threw the money into the garden. 'I've never been so insulted in my life,' she sobbed, and went into the house.

Upstairs in the spare room Rosalie, like Mrs Wapshot, was crying. Her bags were packed but Sarah found her lying face down on the bed and she sat beside her and put a hand tenderly on her back. 'You poor child,' she said. 'I'm afraid they're not very nice.'

Then Rosalie raised her head and spoke, to Sarah's astonishment, in anger. 'Oh, I don't think you should talk like that about people's parents,' she said. 'I mean they are my parents, after all, and I don't think it's very nice of you to say that you don't like them. I mean I don't think that's very fair. After all they've done everything for me like sending me to Allendale and Europe and everybody says he's going to be a bishop and . . .' She turned then and looked at Sarah tearfully and kissed her good-by on the cheek. Her mother was calling her name up the stairs. 'Good-by, Mrs Wapshot,' she said, 'and please say good-by to Lulu and Mr Wapshot for me. I've had a perfectly divine time . . .' Then to her mother she called, 'I'm coming, I'm coming, I'm coming, I'm coming,' and she banged with her suitcases down the stairs.

PART
TWO

PART
TWO

Chapter 14

Writer's epistolary style (Leander wrote) formed in tradition of Lord Timothy Dexter, who put all punctuation marks, prepositions, adverbs, articles, etc., at end of communication and urged reader to distribute same as he saw fit. West Farm. Autumn day. 3 P.M. Nice sailing breeze from NW quarter. Golden light. Glittering riffle on water. Hornets on ceiling. An old house. Roofs of St Botolphs in distance. Old river-bottom burg today. Family prominent there once. Name memorialized in many things in vicinity; lakes, roads, hills even. Wapshot Avenue now back street in honkytonk beach resort further south. Smell of hot dogs, popcorn, also salt air and grinding music from old merry-go-round calliope. Matchwood cottages for rent by day, week or season. Such a street named after forebear who rode spar in Java sea for three days, kicking at sharks with bare feet.

There's nothing but the blood of shipmasters and schoolteachers in writers' veins. All grand men! A true pork and beaner and something of a curiosity these days. Memories important or unimportant as the case may be but try in retrospect to make sense of what is done. Many skeletons in family closet. Dark secrets, mostly carnal. Cruelty, illicit love, candor, but no dirty linen. Decisions of taste involved. Voided bladder so many times; brushed teeth so many times; visited Chardon Street fancy house so many times. Who cares? Much modern fiction distasteful to writer because of above.

There may have been literature of New England port –
factory town also – period of 70's and upwards, but if so I
have never found same. Shipyards prospering in writer's early
youth. Oak chips three feet deep in yards at foot of River
Street. Lumber moved by oxen. Noise of adzes, hammers,
heard all summer. Heartening sounds. Noise of seams being
calked heard in late August. Soon will come the winter cold.
Launching in September. Ships once crewed with flower of
native youth, crewed then with lascars, Kanakas and worse.
Bad times in offing. Grandfather on deathbed cried: 'Shipping
is dead!' Prosperous master. Writer raised among souvenirs
of salt-water riches. Velvet cushions on deep window seats;
now bare. Long garden in rear of house once upon a time.
Geometric flower pots. Paths at right angles. Low box hedge.
Four inches high. Father's fancy poultry. Fantails. Homers.
Tumblers. No dung-heap stuff. Man to care for garden and
birds in times gone by. Local character. Good man. Been to
sea. Wonderful stories. Flying fish. Porpoises. Pearls. Sharks.
Samoan girls. Beached six months in Samoa. Paradise. Never
put his pants on once in six months. Let the pigeons out each
afternoon. Each type separately. Tumblers interested writer
most.

Sad times sometimes; sometimes gay. Thunderstorms.
Christmas. Sounds of fish horn with which writer was
called home to supper. Sailed with father on small schooner.
Zoe. Moored at river in foot of garden on summer months.
High sided; small, counter stern. Short overhang bow. Good
cabin with transom and small galley. Thirty-foot water line.
Moderate sail plan. Mainsail, foresail, two jibs set on jib-stay.
One good-sized. She was dry in rough weather. She moved
very well off the wind, quartering it or before it wing and
wing, but 'on the wind' or 'up the wind' as they say today,
she moved like real estate. Did not hold at all close going to
windward and sagged off badly. Schooner crewed by Daniel
Knight. Retired sailor. Old then. About five feet eight. 170
lbs. Broad-beamed and lively. Remembered square-riggers,
Calcutta, Bombay, China, Java. Went out to Zoe in tender. First

ceremony on getting aboard was meeting in cabin of father and crew. Libation of Barkham's rum and molasses. I was not in at slicing of mainbrace; but I can smell it now. More savory world then, than today. Smell of ship's-bread bakery. Green coffee beans roasted once a week. Perfumery of roasted coffee floated miles downriver. Lamp smoke. Smell of cistern water. Lye from privy. Wood fires.

Family consisted of self and brother, ten years my senior. Difference in ages seemed abysmal in early life. Later diminished. Brother named Hamlet after Prince of Denmark. Offshoot of father's devotion to Shakespeare. Unlike gloomy Prince, however. Very frisky. Played baseball for hose company; also lacrosse. Won many foot races. Much loved by mother. Later the darling of Chardon Street hookers. Familiar figure at the Narragansett House bar. Good fighter both with gloves in gymnasium and bare fisted in street when necessary.

In warm months writer slept in attic, surrounded by boyish museum of minerals and curiosities. Also facsimile of Chinese junk carved in ivory. Two feet long. Three balls of ivory within one another. Large as an apple. Brain corals. Sea shells as big as melons. Others like peas. Held to the human ear there was a sound like surf breaking on shore. Some shells with spikes. Two tame crows among cherished possessions. Taken from nest on Hale's island in April. Swordfish spur and eye socket. Powerful odor from same. Attic illuminated by skylight, approached by several steps. Fine view of river to the sea.

Sturgeon in river then. About three feet long. All covered with knobs. Leap straight up in air and fall back in water. Viewed from horse car running then between St Botolphs and Travertine. One bobtailed car. You got in at the back end. Dingey Graves was driver. Been to sea. One voyage to Calcutta. Gave me free rides always and sometimes let me drive the horse. Hold the reins and see the sturgeon leap. Boyish happiness. Dingey was lovelorn. Harriet Atkinson was the object of his passion. She was of the first families but Dingey's financial and scholastic rating was a blank. They loved but never wedded. In such a place many dark lanes for

lovers' meeting. Wooded river banks and groves. Love child
raised by old-maid sister. Harriet exiled to Dedham. Dingey
led life of quiet desperation, driving horse car.

Dingey was nephew of Jim Graves, prop of old River House
on waterfront. Honest gambler. Big chested. 5′11″. 200 lbs.
Dark hair. River House bar very popular. Good liquor or so
I was told. Ten cents per drink. Hard stuff. You got the bottle.
Customers poured their own. Some lager. Cool lager. Some
stock ale. Also native product. Barkham's rum. Made here for
many years. No cocktails; mixed drinks served. Uncle Jim
Graves never walked. Rode in hacks or barouches. Pair of
horses. Never singles. Always one or more companions with
him. Quiet. Much dignity. Wore good-sized diamond stud in
necktie on boiled stiff shirt front. Also large ruby ring with
stone inside hand. Always had big roll but never vulgar display.
Clothes of excellent quality in style of those days. Prince
Albert coat and some double-breasted vests with cutaway.
Hair a bit long according to today's fashions. Mustache. Not
walrus. Silk hat. Cards. Faro. Stud poker. Wheel. Sweatboard.
No dice used as craps. Went with Uncle Jim and Dingey
when of age to fancy house on Chardon Street, next door to
sulphur, brimstone, deep-water Baptist Church. Whore with
up-country accent. Lowell girl. Big thighs. Breath smelled
of violets. Could hear the singing in the church. Uncle Jim
ordered champagne by the basket. Well liked everywhere. Big
shot. Big wagers. Big drinks. Never lost his head or legs. Never
noisy. Died broke. Third-floor room of River House. Spare
room. Cold. Went to see him. Forsaken by all. Like Timon. All
fair-weather friends scattered. Not bitter. Gentleman to the
end. Skin of ice in water pitcher. Shy flakes of snow falling.

On last summer of youth spent in valley J. G. Blaine,
Presidential candidate, came to dinner. Sunday. Cousin Juliana
visiting. Poor relation. Carried ivory ruler in apron pocket and
gave writer cut on wrist when whistled on Sunday, went up
stairs two at a time, said 'awful' for 'good.' 'Awful nice pudding.'
Crack! Porgies schooling in river then. Mackerel sharks –
fourteen, fifteen feet long – chased porgies up to town dock

in middle of afternoon. Big excitement. Ran up river bank
to village. Water foaming white. Mysteries of the deep. Grand
thunderstorm came down from the hills. Fierce rain. Stood
under apple tree. Grand sunset after. Sharks went downriver
with tide. Beautiful hour. Skies all fiery. Stagecoach horns and
train whistles. (Trains running then regularly.) Church bells
ringing. Everybody and his grandmother out to see departure
of sharks. Walked home in twilight. Wished for gold watch
and chain on evening star. Venus? House ablaze with light.
Carriages. Remembered Mr Blaine for dinner. Late. Afraid of
Juliana's ruler.

Front hall lamp lighted first time in two years. Moth millers
all around lamp. Hall carpet seldom walked on. Felt coarse
under bare feet. Barefooted most of summer. Five or six lamps
burning in parlor. Grand illumination for those times. Splendid
company. Mr Blaine. Heavy man. Mother in garnet dress, later
made into curtains. Something wrong. Juliana in best black
dress, gold beads, lace cap, etc., squatted on floor. Big cigar
in left hand. Speaking gibberish. Writer got upstairs without
being seen. Troubled in spirit. Attic bedroom smelled of trunks,
also swordfish spur. Would send you into the street on rainy
weather. Made water in pot. No bathrooms at all. Washed
in rain water collected in large tubs at back of house. Much
troubled by spectacle of Juliana. Later voices on driveway.
Men talking; lighting carriage lamps. Dogs barking for miles
upriver.

In morning asked Bedelia. Hired girl. Never ask parents.
Children seen, not heard. Very solemn, Bedelia. 'Miss Juliana's
a famous seer. She talks with the dead through the spirit of
an Indian. Last night she talked with Mr Blaine's mother and
the little Hardwich boy who was drowned in the river.' Never
understood pious old lady talking with the dead. Can't think
clearly about it now. Watched all day for Juliana. Didn't appear
for noon meal. Tired out from talking with the dead. Showed
up for supper. Same uniform. Black dress. Gray hair in little
curls. Lace cap. Said grace in loud voice. 'Dear Lord we thank
Thee for these Thy blessings.' Ate with good appetite. Always

smelled like pantry, Juliana did. Cinnamony smell. Savory, sage
and other spices. Not unpleasant. Watched for signs of seer,
but saw only strict old lady. Dewlaps. Poor relation.

One more Indian. Joe Thrum. Lived on hoopskirts of town.
Painted face orange. Smelly hut. Wore silk shirt. Big brass rings
in ears. Dirty. Ate rats or so writer believed. Last of savages.
Hate Indians, even in Wild West show. Great-great-grandfather
killed by same at Fort Duquesne. Poor Yankee! How far from
home. Strange water. Strange trees. Led into clearing at edge
of water stark naked at 4 P.M. Commenced fire-torture. 8 P.M.,
still living. Cried most piteously. Hate Indians, Chinamen, most
foreigners. Keep coal in bathtub. Eat garlic. Trail smell of Polish
earth, Italian earth, Russian earth, strange earth everywhere.
Change everything. Ruin everything.

This was the first chapter of Leander's autobiography or
confession, a project that kept him occupied after the *Topaze*
was put up the year his sons went away.

CHAPTER 15

You come, as Moses did, at nine in the evening to Washington, a strange city. You wait your turn to leave the coach, carrying a suitcase, and walk up the platform to the waiting room. Here you put down your suitcase and crane your neck, wondering what the architect had up his sleeve. There are gods above you in a dim light and, unless there are some private arrangements, the floor where you stand has been trod by presidents and kings. You follow the crowds and the sounds of a fountain out of this twilight into the night. You put down your suitcase again and gape. On your left is the Capitol building, flooded with light. You have seen this so often on medallions and post cards that it seemed incised on your memory only now there is a difference. This is the real thing.

You have eighteen dollars and thirty-seven cents in your pocket. You have not pinned the money to your underwear as your father suggested but you keep feeling for your wallet to make sure that it hasn't been lifted by a pickpocket. You want a place to stay and, feeling that there will not be one around the Capitol, you start off in the opposite direction. You feel springy and young – your shoes are comfortable and the good, woolen socks you wear were knitted by your dear mother. Your underwear is clean in case you should be hit by a taxicab and have to be undressed by strangers.

You walk and walk and walk, changing your suitcase from hand to hand. You pass lighted store fronts, monuments,

theaters and saloons. You hear dance music and the thunder of
tenpins from an upstairs bowling alley and wonder how long it
will be before you begin to play a role against this new scene.
You will have a job, perhaps in that marble building on your
left. You will have a desk, a secretary, a telephone extension,
duties, worries, triumphs and promotions. In the meantime
you will be a lover. You will meet a girl by that monument
on the corner, buy her some dinner in that restaurant across
the street and be taken home by her to that apartment in the
distance. You will have friends and enjoy them as these two
men, swinging down the street in shirt sleeves, are enjoying
one another. You may belong to a bowling club that bowls
in the alley whose thunder you hear. You will have money to
spend and you may buy that raincoat in the store window on
your right. You may – who knows? – buy a red convertible
like that red convertible that is rounding the corner. You may
be a passenger in that airplane, traveling southeast above the
trees, and you may even be a father like that thin-haired man,
waiting for the traffic light to change, holding a little girl by
one hand and a quart of strawberry ice cream in the other. It
is only a question of days before the part begins, you think,
although it must in fact have begun as soon as you entered
the scene with your suitcase.

You walk and walk and come at last to a neighborhood
where the atmosphere is countrified and domesticated and
where signs hang here and there, advertising board and rooms.
You climb some stairs and a gray-haired widow answers the
door and asks your business, your name and your former
address. She has a vacancy, but she can't climb the stairs
because of a weak heart or some other infirmity and so you
climb them alone to the third floor back where there is a
pleasant-enough room with a window looking into some
back yards. Then you sign a register and hang your best suit
in the closet; the suit that you will wear for your interview
in the morning.

Or you wake – like Coverly – a country boy in the biggest
city in the world. It's the hour when Leander usually begins

his ablutions and the place is a three-dollar furnished room, as small or smaller than the closets of your home. You notice that the walls are painted a baneful green which can't have been chosen because of its effect on a man's spirit – this is always discouraging – and so must be chosen because it is cheap. The walls seem to be sweating but when you touch the moisture it is as hard as glue. You get out of bed and look out of your window onto a broad street where trucks are passing, bringing produce up from the markets and railroad yards – a cheerful sight but one that you, coming from a small town in New England, regard with some skepticism, even with compassion, for although you have come here to make your fortune you think of the city as a last resort of those people who lack the fortitude and character necessary to endure the monotony of places like St Botolphs. It is a city, you have been told, where the value of permanence has never been grasped and this, even early in the morning, seems to be a pitiful state of affairs.

In the hallway you find a wash basin where you shave your beard and while you are shaving a stout man joins you and watches critically. 'You gotta stretch your skin, sonny,' the stranger says. 'Look. Let me show you.' He takes a fold of his skin and pulls it tight. 'Like that,' he says. 'You gotta stretch it, you gotta stretch your skin.' You thank him for his advice and stretch your lower lip, which is all you have left to shave. 'That's the way to do it,' the stranger says. 'That's the way. If you stretch your skin you'll have a nice, clean shave. Last you all day.' He takes over the wash basin when you are finished and you go back to your room and dress. Then you climb down the stairs to a street full of shocks and wonders, for in spite of its Philosophical Society your home town was a very small place and you have never seen a high building or a dachshund; you have never seen a man in suede shoes or a woman blow her nose into a piece of Kleenex; you have never seen a parking meter or felt the ground under your feet shaken by a subway, but what you first notice is the fineness of the sky. You have come to feel – you may have been told – that the beauties of heaven centered above your home, and now you are surprised to find, stretched from edge to edge of the dissolute metropolis, a banner or field of the finest blue.

It is early. The air smells of cheap pastry, and the noise of trucking – the clatter of tail gates – is loud and cheerful. You go into a bakery for some breakfast. The waitress smiles at you openly and you think: Perhaps. Maybe. Later. Then you go out onto the street once more and gawk. The noise of traffic has gotten louder and you wonder how people can live in this maelstrom: how can they stand it? A man duckfoots past you wearing a coat that seems to be made out of machine waste and you think how unacceptable such a coat would be in St Botolphs. People would laugh. In the window of a tenement you see an old man in an undershirt eating something from a paper bag. He seems to be by-passed so pitilessly by life that you feel sad. Then, in crossing the street, you are nearly killed by a truck. Safe on the curb again you wonder about the pace of life in this big city. How do they keep it up? Everywhere you look you see signs of demolition and creation. The mind of the city seems divided about its purpose and its tastes. They are not only destroying good buildings; they are tearing up good streets; and the noise is so loud that if you should shout for help no one would hear you.

You walk. You smell cooking from a Spanish restaurant, new bread, beer slops, roasting coffee beans and the exhaust fumes of a bus. Gaping at a high building you walk straight into a fire hydrant and nearly knock yourself out. You look around, hoping that no one saw your mistake. No one seems to have cared. At the next crossing a young woman, waiting for the light to change, is singing a song about love. Her song can hardly be heard above the noise of traffic, but she doesn't care. You have never seen a woman singing in the street before and she carries herself so well and seems so happy that you beam at her. The light changes and you miss your chance to cross the street because you are stopped in your tracks by a host of young women who are coming in the opposite direction. They must be going to work but they don't look anything like the table-silver girls in St Botolphs. Not a single one of them is under the charge of modesty that burdens the beauties in your New England home. Roses bloom in their cheeks, their hair falls in soft curls, pearls and diamonds sparkle at their wrists and throats and one of them – your head swims – has put a cloth rose into the rich darkness that divides her breasts. You cross the street and nearly get killed again.

You remember then that you must telephone Cousin Mildred who is going to get you a job in the carpet works but when you go into a drugstore you find that all the telephones have dials and you have never used one of these. You think of asking a stranger for help but this request would seem to expose – in a horrible way – your inexperience, your unfitness to live in the city, as if your beginnings in a small place were shameful. You overcome these fears and the stranger you approach is kind and helpful. On the strength of this small kindness the sun seems to shine and you are thrilled by a vision of the brotherhood of man. You call Cousin Mildred but a maid says that she is sleeping. The maid's voice makes you wonder about the circumstances of your cousin's life. You notice your rumpled flannel pants and step into a tailor shop to have them pressed. You wait in a humid little fitting room walled with mirrors, and, pantless, the figure you see is inescapably intimate and discouraging. Suppose the city should be bombed at this moment? The tailor hands in your trousers, warm and cozy with steam, and you go out again.

Now you are on a main avenue and you head, instinctively, for the north. You have never seen such crowds and such haste before. They are all late. They are all bent with purpose and the interior discourse that goes on behind their brows seems much more vehement than anything in St Botolphs. It is so vehement that here and there it erupts into speech. Then ahead of you you see a girl carrying a hat box – a girl so fair, so lovely, so full of grace and yet frowning so deeply as if she doubted her beauty and her usefulness that you want to run after her and give her some money or at least some reassurance. The girl is lost in the crowd. Now you are passing, in the store windows, those generations of plaster ladies who

have evolved a seasonal cycle of their own and who have posed
at their elegant linen closets and art galleries, their weddings
and walks, their cruises and cocktail parties long before you
came to town and will be at them long after you are dust.

You follow the crowd north and the thousands of faces
seems like a text and a cheerful one. You have never seen
such expensiveness and elegance and you think that even
Mrs Theophilus Gates would look seedy in a place like this.
At the park you leave the avenue and wander into the zoo.
It is like a paradise; greenery and water and innocence in
jeopardy, the voices of children and the roaring of lions and
in the underpasses obscenities written on the walls. Leaving
the park you are surprised at the display of apartment houses
and you wonder who can live in them all and you may even
mistake the air-conditioning machinery for makeshift iceboxes
where people keep a little milk and a quarter of a pound of
butter fresh. You wonder if you will ever enter such a building
– have tea or supper or some other human intercourse there.
A concrete nymph with large breasts and holding a concrete
lintel on her head causes you some consternation. You blush.
You pass a woman who is sitting on a rock, holding a volume
of the Beethoven sonatas in her lap. Your right foot hurts.
There is probably a hole in your sock.

North of the park you come into a neighborhood that
seems blighted – not persecuted, but only unpopular, as if it
suffered acne or bad breath, and it has a bad complexion –
colorless and seamed and missing a feature here and there. You
eat a sandwich in one of those dark taverns that smells like
a *pissoir* and where the sleepy waitress wears championship
tennis sneakers. You climb the stairs of that great eyesore,
the Cathedral of St John The Divine, and say your prayers,
although the raw walls of the unfinished basilica remind you
of a lonely railroad station. You step from the cathedral into a
stick-ball game and in the distance someone practices a sliding
trombone. You see a woman with a rubber stocking waiting
for a bus and in the window of a tenement a girl with yellow
bangs.

Now the people are mostly colored and the air rings with jazz. Even the pills and elixirs in the cut-rate drugstore jump to boogie-woogie and on the street someone has written in chalk: JESUS THE CHRIST. HE IS RISEN. An old woman on a camp stool sings from a braille hymnal and when you put a dime into her hands she says, God bless you, God bless you. A door flies open and a woman rushes into the street with a letter in her hand. She stuffs it into a mailbox and her manner is so hurried and passionate that you wonder what son or lover, what money-winning contest or friend she has informed. Across the street you see a handsome Negress in a coat made out of cloth of gold. 'Baloney John and Pig-fat's both dead,' a man says, 'and me married five years and still don't have a stick of furniture. Five years.' 'Why you always comparing me to other girls?' a girl asks softly. 'Why you always telling me this one and that one is better than me? Sometimes it seems you just take me out to make me miserable, comparing me to this one and that one. Why you always comparing me to other girls?'

Now it is getting dark and you are tired. There is a hole for sure in your sock and a blister on your heel. You decide to go home by subway. You go down some stairs and board a train, trusting that you will end up somewhere near where you began, but you won't ask directions. The fear of being made ridiculous – a greenhorn – is overpowering. And so, a prisoner of your pride you watch the place names sweep by: Nevins Street, Franklin Avenue, New Lots Avenue.

CHAPTER 16

Writer enterprising although perhaps immodest to say so (Leander wrote). Bought sick calf in spring for two dollars. Nursed. Fatted. Sold in autumn for ten. Sent money to Boston for two-volume encyclopedia. Walked to post office to get same. Barefoot through autumn night. Heart beating. Remember every step of way on bare feet. Sand, thistles. Coarse and silky grass. Oyster shells and soft dirt. Unwrapped books outside of town on river path. Read in fading light. Dusk. Aalborg. Seat of a bishopric. Aardwolf. Aaron. Never forget. Never will forget. Joy of learning. Resolved to read whole encyclopedia. Memorize same. Memorable hour. Fires going out in west. Fires lighted on moon. Loved valley, trees and water. River smelled of damp church. Turn your hair gray. Grand night. Sad homecoming.

Father's star descending. Handsome man. Straight. Black haired. People said was spoiled and idle but never believed same. Loved same. Made four voyages to East Indies. Proud. Cousins found work for him in gold-bead factory but he refused. Why not? He was a proud man, not meant to make gold beads. Many family conferences. Dark country of visiting relations. Whispering in the parlor. No money, no supper, no wood for fires. Father sad.

And a grand and glorious autumn that was too. Leaves coming down like old cloth; old sails; old flags. Solid curtain of green in summer. Then north wind takes it away, piece by piece. See roofs and steeples, buried since June in leaves. Everywhere gold. Midas-like. Poor father! Mind coarsened with sorrow. Trees covered with gold bank notes. Gold everywhere. Gold knee deep on the ground. Dust in his pockets. Bits of thread. Nothing more. Uncle Moses came to the rescue. Mother's brother. Big, fat man. Uncouth. Ran wholesale business in Boston. Sold novelties to four-corner stores. Threads and needles. Buttons. Ginghams. A booming voice like a preacher. Shiny trousers. Threadbare. Walked the four miles from Travertine to St Botolphs to save eight-cent horsecar fare. Famous walker. Once walked from Boston to Salem to foreclose on a creditor. Slept in livery stable. Walked home. Offered father house in Boston. Work. 'The cities is where the money is, Aaron!' Father hated Moses. Had no choice. Moses always spoke of losses. Sad. Lost four thousand dollars one year. Lost six thousand dollars next year. Lived in big square house in Dorchester with For Sale sign on same. Wife made underwear of flour sacks. Two sons; both dead.

Good-by to St Botolphs then. Let the tame crows go. Loaded few possessions onto wagon including Hallet & Davis rosewood piano. No room for swordfish spur, shells or corals. House for sale but no customers. Too big. Old-fashioned. No bathrooms. Furniture packed in Tingleys' wagon night before departure. Horses stabled in barn. Slept last time in attic. Waked by sound of rain 4 A.M. Sweet music. Left homestead by dawn's early light. Forever? Who knows? Brother and writer to ride on tail gate of wagon. Mother and father to travel by cars. Little wind before dawn. Boxed compass. Not enough to fill your sails. Stirring leaves. Good-by. Reached house on Pinckney Street after dark. Run-down place. Stair lifts rotted. Windows broken. Moses there. Shiny pants. Preacher's voice. 'The house is not in good repair, Aaron, but surely you're not afraid of a little hard work.' Slept first night on floor.

Went to visit Moses in Dorchester following Sunday. Walked all the way. Horsecars running but mother thought if he could walk to Salem and back we could walk to Dorchester. Burden of poor relations to set good example. Late winter morning.

Overcast. Wind from north, northeast. Cold. Out in farming country barking dogs followed us. Strange figures we cut. Dressed for church, marching up dirt roads. Reached Uncle Moses' at two. Big house but Uncle Moses and Aunt Rebecca lived in kitchen. Sons, both dead. Moses carrying wood from shed to cellar. 'Help me, boys, and I'll pay you,' he says. Hamlet, father and me carried wood all afternoon. Got bark all over our best clothes. Mother was in the kitchen sewing. Night falls. Cold winds. Moses leads us over to the well. 'Now we'll have a drink of Adam's ale, boys. There's nothing more refreshing.' This was our payment. A drink of cold water. Started home at dark. Miles to go. Nothing to eat since breakfast. Sat down on the way to rest. 'He's a Christly skin, Sarah,' father says. 'Aaron,' mother says. 'He buys and sells on the exchange like a prince,' father says, 'and he pays me and my sons with a cup of water for carrying his Christly firewood all afternoon.' 'Aaron,' mother says. 'He's known everywhere in the trade as a skin,' father says. 'He counts to make ten thousand and when he only makes five he claims to have lost five. All the goods he sells are shoddy and damaged in the loom. When his sons were sick he was too stingy to buy the medicine and when they died he buried them in pine-wood coffins and marked their graves with a slate.' Mother and Hamlet walked on. Father put an arm around shoulders; held me tight. Mixed feelings, all deep, all good. Love and consolation.

Father. How to describe? Stern faced, sad hearted. Much loved, never befriended. Aroused pity, tenderness, solicitude, admiration among associates. Never stalwart friendship. Child of bold seafaring men. First tasted love in Samoa. Honest as the day was long. Perhaps unhappily married. Standards different in those times. Fatalistic. Never quarreled. Only Irish. Perhaps fastidious principles. Hatred for Moses deepened. Worked hard but complained of sharp practice. Mother's sisters often at house. Whispering. Father complained of numerous visitors. 'My latchstring's always out for my relations,' Mother said. Father often played checkers with writer. Shrewd checker player. Faraway looks.

Writer entered Latin school. Stood at head of class of forty. (Report card attached.) Country boy in high-water britches. Delivered newspapers in winter before dawn. Moon still in sky. Played on Common. Lacrosse. Snowball fights. Skating. Some baseball. Vague rules. No river embankment then. Copley Square was a dump. Full of hoopskirt wires. River at low tide smelled of sea gas. Trust writer was cheerful. Happy. Excepting father no unhappy memories. Hard now to reconstruct. Epizootic epidemic. (1873.) All horses in city killed. Few oxen imported but little sound of wheels, hoofs. Only street callers. Coalie-oilee man. Knife sharpener. Played checkers late with father. Heard bells ring. Church bells but no church. Loud. From all corners of the compass. Praise, Laud and Honor. Among bells sounds of people running. Went with father to roof. Excitement fast growing. Bells louder on roof. Glory be to God on the highest. Clamor. Saw great fire at waterfront; Great Boston Fire.

Ran downstairs, down Pinckney Street with father. Boston's burning! Joined hose company on Charles Street. Ran at father's side all the way to waterfront. First more smoke than flame. Hellish smell of burning chattels. Shoes, wallpaper, clothes, plumage. Joined bucket brigade. Eyes sore from smoke. Coughing. Father made writer rest back of safety cordon, but rejoined brigade later. Worked most of night. Walked home at dawn. Dead tired. Smoky city. You could see from Washington and Winter streets through to the harbor. Old South Church was scorched. Way through to Fort Hill were smoking ruins. Dawn-light reddish in smoke. Bad smell. Tents on Common for refugees. Strange sight. Babies crying. Fires for cooking. Clink of water buckets like ghostly cowbells. Scenes of upheaval, suffering and humor. Down Charles Street the scavengers. Worse than Indians. Armies of thieves. Sewing machines, dishes, celluloid collars, two dozen left shoes, ladies' hats. Barbarians all. Hit the feathers at sunrise.

Moses burned out. Heavily insured. Cleared ten thousand. Expected to clear twenty. Claimed to have lost ten. Crocodile tears. Well-known skin. Opened up new business six weeks later in new building. Continued sharp practice. Father complaining. Aunts and cousins in and out of house like dog's hind leg. Whispering. Father not home for supper. Not home after. Never ask questions. No sign of father for three days. Church on Sunday. Took walk. Grand and glorious spring day after New England rains. Cheerful. Passed brick house near junction of Pinckney and Cedar. Heard woman's voice calling, 'Boy, boy, oh you!' Looked up to window. Saw naked woman. Big brindle bush of hair like beard. Plain face. Man enters picture. Strikes woman. Draws curtains. Went on walking to river. Resolved never to walk by house looking for woman again. Resolved to keep mind clean, body healthy. Ran a mile on riverbank. Had clean thoughts. Admired sky. Water. God's creation. Walked straight back to junction of Pinckney and Cedar streets. All resolves broken. Shame faced. Looked in window and saw woman again. Dressed now in voluminous house dress. Picking leaves off geranium plants in window. Later found name was Mrs Trexler. Member of church in good standing. Poor soul.

Walked home at dusk. No father. Uncle Jared playing flute. Mother at rosewood piano. Sterling silver flute. *Faite en France*. Acis and Galatea. Writer heard music from room. Later Jared's farewells. Was called then to kitchen where mother and brother were having confab. Smelled trouble. Mother, saintly old woman. God bless her! Never one to admit unhappiness or pain. Cried at music, sunsets. Never human things. Remember her at West River, wiping away tears while she watched sunsets, colored clouds. Dry eyed at all funerals. Asked me to sit down. 'Your father has abandoned us,' she said. 'He left me a note. I burned it in the fire. Moses knows. He says we can stay on here if we persevere. Your school days are over. You will go to work. Hamlet is going to California. We will never talk about your father again.'

Writer first tasted sorrow then. Bewilderment. The first of many hard knocks. Noticed kitchen. Dartmouth pump. Stain on ceiling like South America. Mother's sewing bag made from scrap of old silk dress worn at St Botolphs in happy summertime. Printing on stove; Pride of the Union. Saw everything. Gray in mother's hair. Cracks in floor. Smoke on lamp chimney. A poor Yankee trait. Writer remembers turning point in life as cracked dishes, soot on glass, coal stove and pump.

Writer looked for work next morning. Plans afoot for Hamlet's trip. Joined a company. Cousin Minerva put up the cash, sailed in June. Hamlet, mother's favorite. Planned to begin sending money home in seven months. Save us all. Big farewell party for Hamlet. Moses, head cheese. All the rest too. Jared, Minerva, Eben, Rebecca, Juliana, many more. Jared did sleight of hand. Pulled brooch out of Minerva's topknot. Made watch disappear. Took same out of vase made of lava from Mount Vesuvius. Mead to drink. Homemade. Delicious. Mother played piano. Hamlet sang. Sympathetic tenor voice:

> Youth and pleasure go together,
> Soon will come the winter cold

Not a dry eye in the house. A dark night. Many lamps. Parting is such sweet sorrow. Not sweet for me.

Father gone. Hamlet sailing away. Writer left alone with dear old mother. God bless her! Stern company though. Writer led clean life. Cold bath every morning. Stone Hills boat club. Single-oared shells. Gymnasium twice a week. Missed father, brother. Father most. Lonely places. Bedroom hallway. Staircase turning. Looked for father in crowds. Straight back. Black coat. Walking home from work. Always looked for father in crowds. Looked in stations both north and south. Looked on waterfront. Watched disembarkations of all kinds. Passenger ships. Fishing boats. Ghosts rattle chains. Live in castles. Gauzy things with kindly voices mostly. Partial to blue light. Vanish at cock's crow. God give me such a ghost I cried.

Asked mother once for news of father but received no reply. Spoke later of old times. Asked me if I remembered St Botolphs. Reminisced. Plums on Hales Island. Picked a bushel basket every year. Recalled famous church picnic with twenty-one varieties of pie. Sails. All good things. House still

empty. Falling down. Old mother's eyes brightened. First time
she ever seemed gay. Laughing, talking about old river-bottom
place, Godforsaken. Took advantage of high spirits and asked
once more for father. 'Is he living or dead?'

'Remember one night last autumn when we had steak and
tomatoes for supper?' she said. 'The Boston police notified me
while you were at work the day before that your father had
been found dead in a Charles Street lodging. I made all the
arrangements with no help from anyone. Early in the morning
I took the body in the cars to St Botolphs. Mr Frisbee said
the words. No one else was there at the grave. Then I came
home on the cars and cooked a good supper for you so you
wouldn't think that anything was wrong.'

Blow to feelings not improved by receipt of enclosed letter
from Hamlet: 'Hello old scout. We reached this happy land after
traveling 7 months and 9 days. I stood the trip well although
the hardships of the voyage exceeded my anticipations. Out
of a company of thirty, seven of our brother argonauts were
taken by the grim reaper. My own skin is hale and hearty and
we're a whip-cracking, bushy-bearded, sun-burned brotherhood, bound to make our million or go to H——.

'We made the passage from the Isthmus to San Francisco
in the company of many women and children, going to be
reunited with their loved ones. There is nothing in the world
like the arrival of a ship in San Francisco to pluck at your
heart-strings. I wish you could get out here and see the
sights. I pity you in that musty old burg, compared to which
San Francisco is an honest to G——d beehive. However the
necessities of life were costly – board was four dollars a day
and we lingered in San Francisco only a week and then came
north where provisions still set me back two dollars a day.
When you see Cousin Minerva don't spare the hard facts.

'Among us is an Irishman whose name is Clancy and is
from Dedham. He is come out here to find a dowery for his
daughter so that she can marry into the 'edicated' classes. There
are also 3 carpenters, 2. shoemakers, a blacksmith and many
other trades represented including the genteel art of music

for one of the company has brought his violin with him and entertains us at night with symphonius strains. We had no sooner settled here than Howie Cockaigne and me got to work with our pick-axes in the bed of the river and when we had been digging for less than an hour two Mexicans came along and offered to buy the digging for an ounce of flour-gold and so we took the offer and had our first gold in less time than it takes to tell and you see that with gold selling at $5.60 an ounce and if our luck holds out we will be making forty or fifty dollars per day. Now under Captain Marsons leadership we are making a race in the river and turning its course so that we will be able to take the gold out of the dry bed.

'Don't expect many letters from me Old Scout because this happy land is still wild and as I am writing you now the ground is my chair and the night is my roof. But oh its a grand feeling to be out here and even with the professor playing symphonius strains on his violin and bringing back to me the sweet remembrance of all by-gone days there isn't a king or a merchant prince in the whole world that I envy for I always knew I was born to be a child of destiny and that I was never meant to be subservient to the wealth, fame, power, etc. of others or to wring my living from detestable, low, degrading, mean and ordinary kinds of business.'

Chapter 17

To create or build some kind of bridge between Leander's world and that world where he sought his fortune seemed to Coverly a piece of work that would take strength and perseverance. The difference between the sweet-smelling farmhouse and the room where he lived was abysmal. They seemed to have come from the hands of different creators and to deny one another. Coverly thought about this one rainy night on his way to Cousin Mildred's, wearing a rented tuxedo. 'Come for dinner,' she had asked him, 'and then we'll go to the opera. That ought to be fun for you. It's Monday night so you'll have to dress. Everyone dresses on Mondays.' Cousin Mildred's apartment was in one of those large buildings that Coverly, on his first day, had wondered if he would ever penetrate. Looking up at the building Coverly realized that by all the standards of St Botolphs it would be condemned as expensive, pretentious, noisy and unsafe. It could not be compared to a nice farm. He took an elevator to the eighteenth floor. He had never approached such an altitude and he entertained himself with some imaginary return to St Botolphs where he regaled Pete Meacham with a description of this city of towers. He felt worldly and saturnine like a character in a movie. A pretty maid let him in and took him into a parlor for which he was completely unprepared. The walls were half-paneled like the dining-room walls at West Farm. Most of the furniture he recognized since most of it had been stored in the hayloft when he was a boy. There, over the mantelpiece, hung old Benjamin himself, in his peignoir or Renaissance costume, staring out into the room with that harsh and naked look of dishonesty that had made him so unpopular with the family. Most of the lamps had come from the barn or the attic and Grandmother Wapshot's old moth-eaten sampler ('Unto Us a Son Is Given') was hanging on the wall. Coverly was studying old Benjamin's stare when Cousin Mildred blew in – a tall, gaunt woman in a red evening dress that seemed cut to display her bony shoulders. 'Coverly!' she exclaimed. 'My dear. How nice of you to come. You look just like a Wapshot. Harry will be thrilled. He adores Wapshots. Sit down. We'll have something to drink. Where are you staying? Who was the woman who answered the telephone? Tell me all about Honora. Oh, you do look like a Wapshot. I would have been able to pick you out in a crowd. Isn't it nice to be able to recognize people? There's another Wapshot in New York. Justina. They say she used to play the piano in the five-and-ten-cent store but she's very rich now. We've had Benjamin cleaned. Don't you think he looks better. Did you notice? Of course, he still looks like a crook. Have a cocktail.'

The butler passed Coverly a cocktail on a tray. He had never drunk a martini cocktail before and to conceal his inexperience he raised the glass to his lips and drained it. He didn't cough and sputter but his eyes swam with tears, the gin felt like fire and some oscillation or defense mechanism in his larynx began to palpitate in such a way that he found himself unable to speak. He settled down to a paroxysm of swallowing. 'Of course, this isn't my idea of a decent room at all,' Cousin Mildred went on. 'It's all Harry's idea. I'd much rather have called in a decorator and gotten something comfortable but Harry's mad for New England. He's an adorable man and a wizard in the carpet business, but he doesn't come from anyplace really. I mean he doesn't have anything nice to remember and so he borrows other people's memories. He's really more of a Wapshot than you or I.'

'Does he know about Benjamin's ear?' Coverly asked hoarsely. It was still hard for him to speak.

'My dear, he knows the family history backwards and forwards,' Cousin Mildred said. 'He went to England and had the name traced back to Vaincre-Chaud and he got the crest. I'm sure he knows more about Lorenzo than Honora ever did. He bought all these things from your mother and I must say he paid for them generously and I'm not absolutely sure that your mother – I don't mean to say that your mother was untruthful – but you know that old traveling desk that always used to be full of mice? Well, your mother wrote and said that it belonged to Benjamin Franklin and I don't ever remember having heard that before.'

This hint or slur at his mother's veracity made Coverly feel sad and homesick and annoyed with his cousin's rattling conversational style and the pretensions of simplicity and homeliness in her parlor and he might have said something about this, but the butler refilled his glass again and when he took another gulp of gin the oscillations in his larynx began all over again and he couldn't speak. Then Mr Brewer came in – he was much shorter than his wife – a jolly pink-faced man with a quietness that might have been developed to complement the noise she made. 'So you're a Wapshot,' he said to Coverly when they shook hands. 'Well, as Mildred may have told you, I'm very much interested in the family. Most of these things come from the homestead in St Botolphs. That cradle rocked four generations of the Wapshot family. It was made by the village undertaker. That tulip-wood table was made from a tree that stood on the lawn at West Farm. Lafayette rode under this tree in 1815. The portrait over the mantelpiece is of Benjamin Wapshot. This chair belonged to Lorenzo Wapshot. He used it during his two terms in the state legislature.' With this Mr Brewer sat down in Lorenzo's chair and at the feel of this relic beneath him a smile of such sensual gratification spread over his face that he might have been squeezed between two pretty women on a sofa. 'Coverly has the nose.' Cousin Mildred said. 'I've told him that I could have picked him out in a crowd. I mean I would have known that he was a Wapshot. It will be so nice having him work for you. I mean it will be so nice having a Wapshot in the firm.'

It was quite some time before Mr Brewer replied to this but he smiled broadly at Coverly all during the pause and so it was not an anxious silence and during it Coverly decided that he liked Mr Brewer tremendously. 'Of course, you'll have to start at the bottom,' Mr Brewer said.

'Oh, yes sir,' Coverly exclaimed; his father's son. 'I'll do anything sir. I'm willing to do anything.'

'Well, I wouldn't expect you to do anything,' Mr Brewer said, tempering Coverly's earnestness, 'but I think we might work out some kind of apprenticeship, so to speak – some arrangement whereby you could decide if you liked the carpet business and the carpet business could decide if it liked you. I think we can work out something. You'll have to go through personnel research. We do this with everyone. Grafley and Harmer do this for us and I'll make you an appointment for tomorrow. If they're done with you on Monday you can report to my office then and go to work.'

Coverly was not familiar with a correct dinner service, but by watching Cousin Mildred he saw how to serve himself from the dishes that the waitress passed and he only got into trouble when he was about to drop his dessert into his finger bowl, but the waitress, by smiling and signaling, got him to move his finger bowl and everything went off all right. When dinner was finished they went down on the elevator and were driven through the rain to the opera.

It is perhaps in the size of things that we are most often disappointed and it may be because the mind itself is such a huge and labyrinthine chamber that the Pantheon and the Acropolis turn out to be smaller than we had expected. At any rate, Coverly, who expected to be overwhelmed by the opera house, found it splendid but cozy. Their seats were in the orchestra, well forward. Coverly had no libretto and he could not understand what was going on. Now and then the plot would seem to be revealed to him but he was always mistaken and in the end more confused than ever. He fell asleep twice. When the opera ended he said good night and thank you to Cousin Mildred and her husband in the lobby, feeling that it would be to his disadvantage to have them drive him back to the slum where he lived.

Early the next morning Coverly reported to Grafley and Harmer, where he was given a common intelligence-quotient test. There were simple arithmetical problems, blocks to count and vocabulary tests, and he completed this without any difficulty although it took him the better part of the morning. He was told to come back at two. He ate a sandwich and wandered around the streets. The window of a shoe-repair place on the East Side was filled with plants and reminded him of Mrs Pluzinski's kitchen window. When he returned to Grafley and Harmer he was shown a dozen or so cards with drawings or blots on them — a few of them colored — and asked by a stranger what the pictures reminded him of. This seemed easy, for since he had lived all his life between the river and the sea the drawings reminded him of fish bones, kelp, conch shells and other simples of the flood. The doctor's face was inexpressive and he couldn't tell if he had been successful. The doctor's reserve seemed so impenetrable that it irritated Coverly that two strangers should be closeted in an office to cultivate such an atmosphere of inhumanity. When he left he was told to report in the morning for two more examinations and an interview.

In the morning he found himself in stranger waters. Another gentleman — Coverly guessed they were all doctors — showed him a series of pictures or drawings. If they were like anything they were like the illustrations in a magazine although they were drawn crudely and with no verve or imagination. They presented a problem to Coverly, for when he glanced at the first few they seemed to remind him only of very morbid and unsavory things. He wondered at first if this was a furtive strain of morbidity in himself and if he would damage his chances at a job in the carpet works by speaking frankly. He wondered for only a second. Honesty was the best policy. All the pictures dealt with noisome frustrations and when he was finished he felt irritable and unhappy. In the afternoon he was asked to complete a series of sentences. They all presented a problem or sought an attitude and since Coverly was worried about money – he had nearly run through his twenty-five dollars – he completed most of the sentences with references to money. He would be interviewed by a psychologist on the next afternoon.

The thought of this interview made him a little nervous. A psychologist seemed as strange and formidable to him as a witch doctor. He felt that some baneful secret in his life might be exposed, but the worst he had ever done was masturbate and looking back over his life and knowing no one of his age who had not joined in on the sport he decided that this did not have the status of a secret. He decided to be as honest with the psychologist as possible. This decision comforted him a little and seemed to abate his nervousness. His appointment was for three o'clock and he was kept waiting in an outer room where many orchids bloomed in pots. He wondered if he was being observed through a peephole. Then the doctor opened a double or soundproof door and invited Coverly in. The doctor was a young man with nothing like the inexpressive manners of the others. He meant to be friendly, although this was a difficult feeling to achieve since Coverly had never seen him before and would never see him again and was only closeted with him because he wanted to work in the carpet factory. It was no climate for friendship. Coverly was given a very comfortable chair to sit in, but he cracked his knuckles nervously. 'Now, suppose you tell me a little about yourself,' the doctor said. He was very gentle and had a pad and a pencil for taking notes.

'Well, my name is Coverly Wapshot,' Coverly said, 'and I come from St Botolphs. I guess you must know where that is. All the Wapshots live there. My great-grandfather was Benjamin Wapshot. My grandfather was Aaron. My mother's family are Coverlys and . . .'

'Well I'm not as interested in your genealogy,' the doctor said, 'as I am in your emotional make-up.' It was an interruption, but it was a very courteous and friendly one. 'Do you know what is meant by anxiety? Do you have any feelings of anxiety? Is there anything in your family, in your background that would incline you to anxiety?'

'Yes sir,' Coverly said. 'My father's very anxious about fire. He's awfully afraid of burning to death.'

'How do you know this?'

'Well, he's got this rig up in his room,' Coverly said. 'He's got this suit of clothes – underwear and everything – hanging up beside his bed so in case of fire he can get dressed and out of the house in a minute. And he's got buckets full of sand and water in all the hallways and the number of the fire department is painted on the wall by the telephone and on rainy days when he isn't working – sometimes he doesn't work on rainy days – he spends most of the day going around the house sniffing. He thinks he smells smoke and sometimes it seems to me that he spends nearly a whole day going from room to room sniffing.'

'Does your mother share this anxiety?' the doctor asked.

'No sir,' Coverly said. 'My mother loves fires. But she's anxious about something else. She's afraid of crowds. I mean she's afraid of being trapped. Sometimes on the Christmas holidays I'd go into the city with her and when she got into a crowd in one of those big stores she'd nearly have a fit. She'd get pale and gasp for breath. She'd pant. It was terrible. Well then she'd grab hold of my hand and drag me out of there and go up some side street where there wasn't anybody and sometimes it would be five or ten minutes before she got her breath back. In any place where my mother felt she was confined she'd get very uneasy. In the movies, for instance – if anybody in the movies was sent to jail or locked up in some small place why my mother would grab her hat and her purse and run out of that theater before you could say Jack Robinson. I used to have to sprint to keep up with her.'

'Would you say that your parents were happy together?'

'Well, I really never thought of it that way,' Coverly said. 'They're married and they're my parents and I guess they take the lean with the fat like everybody else but there's one thing she used to tell me that left an impression on me.'

'What was that?'

'Well, whenever I had a good time with Father – whenever he took me out on the boat or something – she always seemed to be waiting for me when we got home with this story. Well, it was about, it was about how I came to be, I suppose you'd say. My father was working for the table-silver company at the time and they went into the city for some kind of banquet. Well, my mother had some cocktails and it was snowing and they had to spend the night in a hotel and one thing led to another but it seems that after this my father didn't want me to be born.'

'Did your mother tell you this?'

'Oh, yes. She told me lots of times. She told me I shouldn't trust him because he wanted to kill me. She said he had this abortionist come out to the house and that if it hadn't been for her courage I'd be dead. She told me that story lots of times.'

'Do you think this had any effect on your fundamental attitude toward your father?'

'Well, sir, I never thought about it but I guess maybe it did. I sometimes had a feeling that he might hurt me. I never used to like to wake up and hear him walking around the house late at night. But this was foolish because I knew he wouldn't hurt me. He never punished me.'

'Did she punish you?'

'Well, not very often, but once she just laid my back open. I guess perhaps it was my fault. We went down to Travertine swimming – I was with Pete Meacham – and I decided to climb up on the roof of the bathhouse where we could see the women getting undressed. It was a dirty thing to do but we hadn't even hardly got started when the caretaker caught us. Well my mother took me home and she told me to get undressed and she took my great-grandfather's buggy whip – that was Benjamin – and she just laid my back open. There was blood all over the wall. My back was such a mess she got scared, but of course she didn't dare call a doctor because it would be embarrassing, but the worst thing was I couldn't go swimming for the rest of that summer. If I went swimming people would see these big sores on my back. I wasn't able to go swimming all that summer.'

'Do you think this had any effect on your fundamental attitude toward women?'

'Well, sir, where I come from, I think it's hard to take much pride in being a man. I mean the women are very powerful. They are kind and they mean very well, but sometimes they get very oppressive. Sometimes you feel as if it wasn't right to be a man. Now there's this story they tell about Howie Pritchard. On his wedding night he's supposed to have put his foot into the chamber pot and pissed down his leg so his wife wouldn't hear the noise. I don't think he should have done that. If you're a man I think you ought to be proud and happy about it.'

'Have you ever had any sexual experiences?'

'Twice,' Coverly said. 'The first time was with Mrs Maddern. I don't suppose I should name her but everybody in the village knew about her and she was a widow.'

'Your other experience?'

'That was with Mrs Maddern too.'

'Have you ever had any homosexual experiences?'

'Well, I guess I know what you mean,' Coverly said. 'I did plenty of that when I was young but I swore off it a long time ago. But it seems to me that there's an awful lot of it around. There's more around anyhow than I expected. There's one in this place where I'm living now. He's always asking me to come in and look at his pictures. I wish he'd leave me alone. You see, sir, if there's one thing in the whole world that I wouldn't want to be it's a fruit.'

'Now would you like to tell me about your dreams?'

'I dream about all kinds of things.' Coverly said. 'I dream about sailing and traveling and fishing but I guess mostly what you're interested in is bad dreams, isn't it?'

'What do you mean by bad dreams?'

'Well, I dream I do it with this woman,' Coverly said. 'I never saw this woman in real life. She's one of those beautiful women you see on calendars in barbershops. And sometimes,' Coverly said, blushing and hanging his head, 'I dream that I do it with men. Once I dreamed I did it with a horse.'

'Do you dream in color?' the doctor asked.

'I've never noticed,' Coverly said.

'Well, I think our time is about up,' the doctor said.

'Well, you see, sir,' Coverly said, 'I don't want you to think that I've had an unhappy childhood. I guess what I've told you doesn't give you a true picture but I've heard a little about psychology and I guessed what you wanted to know about were things like that. I've really had an awfully good time. We live on a farm and have a boat and plenty of hunting and fishing and just about the best food in the world. I've had a happy time.'

'Well, thank you, Mr Wapshot,' the doctor said, 'and good-by.'

On Monday morning Coverly got up early and had his pants pressed as soon as the tailor shop opened. Then he walked to his cousin's office in midtown. A receptionist asked if he had an appointment and when he said that he hadn't she said that she couldn't arrange one until Thursday. 'But I'm Mr Brewer's cousin,' Coverly said. 'I'm Coverly Wapshot.' The secretary only smiled and told him to come back on Thursday morning. Coverly was not worried. He knew that his cousin was occupied with many details and surrounded by executives and secretaries and that the problems of this distant Wapshot might have slipped his mind. His only problem was one of money. He didn't have much left. He had a hamburger and a glass of milk for supper and gave the landlady the rent that night when he came in. On Tuesday he ate a box of raisins for breakfast, having heard somewhere that raisins were healthful and filling. For supper he had a bun and a glass of milk. On Wednesday morning he bought a paper, which left him with sixty cents. In the help-wanted advertisements there were some openings for stock clerks and he went to an employment agency and then crossed town to a department store and was told to return at the end of the week. He bought a quart of milk and marking the container off in three sections drank one section for breakfast, one for lunch and one for dinner.

The hunger pains of a young man are excruciating and when Coverly went to bed on Wednesday night he was doubled up with pain. On Thursday morning he had nothing to eat at all and spent the last of his money having his pants pressed. He walked to his cousin's office and told the girl he had an appointment. She was cheerful and polite and asked him to sit down and wait. He waited for an hour. He was so hungry by this time that it was nearly impossible for him to sit up straight. Then the receptionist told him that no one in Mr Brewer's office knew about his appointment but that if he would return late in the afternoon she might be able to help him. He dozed on a park bench until four and returned to the office and while the receptionist's manner remained cheerful her refusal this time was final. Mr Brewer was out of town. From there Coverly went to Cousin Mildred's apartment house but the doorman stopped him and telephoned upstairs and was told that Mrs Brewer couldn't see anyone; she was just leaving to keep an engagement. Coverly went outside the building and waited and in a few minutes Cousin Mildred came out and Coverly went up to her. 'Oh yes, yes,' she said, when he told her what had happened. 'Yes, of course. I thought Harry's office must have told you. It's something about your emotional picture. They think you're unemployable. I'm so sorry but there's nothing I can do about it, is there? Of course your grandfather was second crop.' She unfastened her purse and took out a bill and handed it to Coverly and got into a taxi and drove away. Coverly wandered over to the park.

It was dark then and he was tired, lost and despairing – no one in the city knew his name – and where was his home – the shawls from India and the crows winging their way up the river valley like businessmen with brief cases, off to catch a bus? This was on the Mall, the lights of the city burning through the trees and dimly lighting the air with the colors of reflected fire, and he saw the statues ranged along the broad walk like the tombs of kings – Columbus, Sir Walter Scott, Burns, Halleck and Morse – and he took from these dark shapes a faint comfort and hope. It was not their minds or their works he adored but the kindliness and warmth they must have possessed when they lived and so lonely and so bitter was he then that he would take those brasses and stones for company. Sir Walter Scott would be his friend, his Moses and Leander.

Then he got some supper – this friend of Sir Walter Scott – and in the morning went to work as a stock clerk for Warburton's Department Store.

CHAPTER 18

Moses' work in Washington was highly secret – so secret that it can't be discussed here. He was put to work the day after he arrived – a reflection perhaps of Mr Boynton's indebtedness to Honora or a recognition of Moses' suitability, for with his plain and handsome face and his descendance from a man who had been offered a decoration by General Washington, he fitted into the scene well enough. He was not smooth – the Wapshots never were – and compared to Mr Boynton he sometimes felt like a man who eats his peas off a knife. His boss was a man who seemed to have been conceived in the atmosphere of career diplomacy. His clothes, his manners, his speech and habits of thought all seemed so prescribed, so intricately connected to one another that they suggested a system of conduct. It was not, Moses guessed, a system evolved at any of the eastern colleges and may have been formed in some foreign-service school. Its rules were never shown to Moses, so he could not abide by them, but he knew that rules must underlie this sartorial and intellectual diffidence.

Moses was happy at the boardinghouse that he had picked by chance, and found it tenanted mostly by people of his own age: the sons and daughters of mayors and other politicians; the progeny of respectable ward heelers who were in Washington, like himself, as the result of some indebtedness. He did not spend much time at the boardinghouse for he found that much of his social, athletic and spiritual life was ordained by the agency where he worked. This included playing volleyball, taking communion and going to parties at the X Embassy and the Z Legation. He was up to all of this although he was not allowed to drink more than three cocktails at any party and was careful not to make eyes at any woman who was in government service or on the diplomatic list, for security regulations had clapped a lid on the natural concupiscence of a city with a large floating population. On the autumn week ends he sometimes drove with Mr Boynton to Clark County, where they went riding and sometimes stayed for dinner with Mr Boynton's friends. Moses could stay on a horse, but this was not his favorite sport. It was a chance to see the countryside and the disappointing southern autumn with its fireflies and brumes, all of which stirred in him a longing for the brilliance of autumn at West Farm. Mr Boynton's friends were hospitable people who lived in splendid houses and who, without exception, had made or inherited their money from some distant source such as mouthwash, airplane engines or beer; but it was not in Moses to sit on some broad terrace and observe that the bills for this charming picture had been footed by some dead brewer; and as for brewing he had never drunk such good bourbon in his life. It was true that, having come from a small place where a man's knowledge of his neighbors was intimate and thorough, Moses sometimes experienced the blues of uprootedness. His knowledge of his companions was no better than the knowledge travelers have of one another and he knew, by then, enough of the city to know that, waiting for a bus in the morning, the swarthy man with a beard and a turban might be an Indian prince in good standing or he might be a rooming-house eccentric. This theatrical atmosphere of impermanence – this latitude for imposture – impressed him one evening at an embassy concert. He was alone and had gone, at the intermission, out onto the steps of the building to get some air. As he pushed open the doors he noticed three old women on the steps. One was so fat, one so thin and haggard and one had such a foolish countenance that they looked like a representation of human folly. Their evening clothes reminded him of the raggle-taggle elegance of children on Halloween. They had shawls and fans and mantillas and brilliants and their shoes seemed to be killing them. When Moses opened the door they slipped into the embassy – the fat one, the thin one and the fool – so wary, so frightened and in such attitudes of wrongdoing that Moses watched. As soon as they got inside the building they fanned out and each of them seized a concert program that had been left on a chair or fallen to the floor. By this time a guard saw them and as soon as they were discovered they headed for the door and fled, but they were not disappointed, Moses noticed. The purpose of their expedition had been to get a program and they limped happily down the driveway in their finery. You wouldn't see anything like that in St Botolphs.

The man who had the room next to Moses in the boardinghouse was the son of a politician from somewhere in the West. He was competent and personable and an ideal of thrift and continence. He did not smoke or drink and saved every penny of his salary toward the purchase of half a saddle horse that was stabled in Virginia. He had been in Washington for two years and he invited Moses into his room one night and showed him a chart or graph on which he had recorded his social progress. He had been to dinner in Georgetown eighteen times. His hosts were all listed and graded according to their importance in the government. He had been to the Pan-American Union four times: to the X Embassy three times: to the B Embassay one time (a garden party) and to the White House one time (a press reception). You wouldn't find anything like that in St Botolphs.

The intense and general concern with loyalty at the time when Moses arrived in Washington had made it possible for men and women to be discharged and disgraced on the evidence of a breath of scandal. Old-timers like to talk about the past when even the girls in the Library of Congress – even the archivists – could be booked for a clandestine week end at Virginia Beach, but these days were gone or at least in suspense for government servants. Public drunkenness was unforgivable and promiscuity was death. Private industry went its own way and a friend of Moses' who was in the meat-packing industry once made him this proposition: 'I've got four dirty girls coming up from the shirt factory in Baltimore Saturday and I'm going to take them out to my cabin in Maryland. How about it? Just you and me and the four of them. They're pigs but they're not bad looking.' Moses said no thanks – he would have said so anyhow – but he envied the meat packer his liberty. This new morality was often on his mind and by thinking about it long enough he was able to make some dim but legitimate connection between lechery and espionage, but this understanding did nothing to lessen this particular loneliness. He even wrote to Rosalie, asking her to visit him for a week end, but she never answered. The government was full of comely women but they all avoided the dark.

Feeling lonely one night and having nothing better to do he went out for a walk. He headed for the center of town and went into the lobby of the Mayflower to buy a package of cigarettes and to look around at a place that, for an its intended elegance, only reminded him of the vastness of his native land. Moses loved the lobby of the Mayflower. A convention was meeting and red-necked and self-respecting men from country towns were gathering in the lobby. Listening to them talk made him feel closer to St Botolphs. Then he left the Mayflower and walked deeper into the city, and hearing music and being on a fool's errand he stepped into a place called the Marine Room and looked around. There were a band and dance floor and a girl singing. Sitting alone at a table was a blonde woman who seemed pretty at that distance and who looked as if she didn't work for the government. Moses took the table beside her and ordered a whisky. She did not see him at first because she was looking at herself in a mirror on the wall. She was turning her head, first one way and then another, raising her chin and taking the tips of her fingers and pushing her face into the firm lines that it must have had five or six years ago. When she had finished examining herself Moses asked if he could join her and buy her a drink. She was friendly – a little flurried – but pleased. 'Well, it would be very nice to have your company,' she said, 'but the only reason I'm here is because Chucky Ewing, the band leader, is my husband and when I don't have anything better to do I just come down here and kill time.' Moses joined her and bought her a drink and after a few farewell looks at herself in the mirror she began to talk about her past. 'I used to vocalize with the band myself,' she said, 'but most of my training is operatic. I've sung in night clubs all over the world. Paris. London. New York . . .' She spoke, not with a lisp, but with an articulation that seemed childish. Her hair was pretty and her skin was white but this was mostly powder. Moses guessed that it would have been five or six years since she could be called beautiful but since she seemed determined to cling to what she had been he was ready to string along. 'Of course, I'm really not a professional entertainer,' she went on. 'I went to finishing school and my family nearly died when I started entertaining. They're very stuffy. Old family and all that sort of thing. Cliff dwellers.' Then the band broke and her husband joined them and was introduced to Moses and sat down.

'What's the score, honey?' he asked his wife.

'There's a table in the corner drinking champagne,' she said, 'and the six gentlemen by the bandstand are drinking rye and water. They've each had four. There're two tables of Scotch and five tables of bourbon and some beer drinkers over on the other side of the bandstand.' She counted the tables off on her fingers, still speaking in a very dainty voice. 'Don't worry,' she told her husband. 'You'll gross three hundred.'

'Where's the convention?' he said. 'There's a convention.'

'I know,' she said. 'Sheets and pillowcases. Don't worry.'

'You got any hot garbage?' he asked a waiter who had come over to their table.

'Yes sir, yes sir,' the waiter said. 'I've got some delicious hot garbage. I can give you coffee grounds with a little sausage grease or how about some nice lemon rinds and sawdust?'

'That sounds good,' the band leader said. 'Make it lemon rinds and sawdust.' He had seemed anxious and unhappy when he came to the table but this leg-pulling with the waiter cheered him up. 'You got any dishwater?' he asked.

'We got all kinds of dishwater,' the waiter said. 'We got greasy dishwater and we got dishwater with stuff floating around in it and we got moth balls and wet newspaper.'

'Well, give me a little wet newspaper with my sawdust,' the band leader said, 'and a glass of greasy dishwater.' Then he turned to his wife. 'You going home?'

'I believe that I will,' she said daintily.

'Okay, okay,' he said. 'If the convention shows I'll be late. Nice to have met you.' He nodded to Moses and went back to the bandstand, where the other players had begun to stray in from the alley.

'Can I take you home?' Moses asked.

'Well, I don't know,' she said. 'We just have a little apartment in the neighborhood and I usually walk but I don't think there'd be any harm in you walking me home.'

'Go?'

She got a coat from the hat-check girl and talked with the hat-check girl about a four-year-old child who was lost in the woods of Wisconsin. The child's name was Pamela and she had been gone four days. Extensive search parties had been organized and the two women speculated with deep anxiety on whether or not little Pamela had died of exposure and starvation. When this conversation ended, Beatrice – which was her name – started down the hall, but the hat-check girl called her back and gave her a paper bag. 'It's two lipsticks and some bobby pins,' she said. Beatrice explained that the hat-check girl kept an eye on the ladies' room and gave Beatrice whatever was left there. She seemed ashamed of the arrangement, but she recuperated in a second and took Moses' arm.

Their place was near the Marine Room – a second-story bedroom dominated by a large cardboard wardrobe that seemed on the verge or in the process of collapse. She

struggled to open one of its warped doors and exposed a
magpie wardrobe – maybe a hundred dresses of all kinds.
She went into the bathroom and returned, wearing a kind
of mandarin coat with a dragon embroidered up the back
out of threads that felt thorny to Moses' hands. She yielded
easily but when it was over she sobbed a little in the dark
and asked, 'Oh dear, what have we done?' Her voice was as
dainty as ever. 'Nobody ever likes me except in this way,' she
said, 'but I think it's because I was brought up so strictly. I was
brought up by this governess. Her name was Clancy. Oh, she
was so strict. I was never allowed to play with other children
. . .' Moses dressed, kissed her good night and got out of the
building without being seen.

CHAPTER 19

Back at the farm Leander had banked the foundations of the old house with seaweed and had hired Mr Pluzinski to clear the garden. His sons wrote him once or twice a month and he wrote them both weekly. He longed to see them and often thought, when he was drinking bourbon, of traveling to New York and Washington, but in the light of morning he couldn't find it in himself to ever leave St Botolphs again. After all, he had seen the world. He was alone a lot of the time, for Lulu was spending three days a week with her daughter in the village and Mrs Wapshot was working three days a week as a clerk in the Anna Marie Louise Gift Shoppe in Travertine. It was made clear to everyone, by Sarah's mien, that she was not doing this because the Wapshots needed money. She was doing it because she loved to, and this was the truth. All the energies that she possessed – and that she had used so well in improving the village – seemed to have centered at last in an interest in gift shops. She wanted to open a gift shop in the front parlor of the farmhouse. She even dreamed of this project, but it was something Leander wouldn't discuss.

It was hard to say why the subject of gift shops should excite, on one hand, Sarah's will to live, and on the other, Leander's bitterest scorn. As Mrs Wapshot stood by a table loaded with colored-glass vases and gave a churchly smile to her friends and neighbors when they came in to spend a little money and pass the time, her equilibrium seemed wonderfully secure. This love of gift shops – this taste for ornamentation – may have been developed by the colorless surface of that shinbone coast or it may have been a most natural longing for sensual trivia. When she exclaimed – about a hand-carved salad fork or a hand-painted glass – 'Isn't it lovely?' she was perfectly sincere. The gossip and the company of the customers let her be as gregarious as she had ever been in the Woman's Club; and people had always sought her out. The pleasure of selling things and putting silver and bills into the old tin box that was used for this purpose pleased her immensely, for she had sold nothing before in her life but the furniture in the barn to Cousin Mildred. She liked talking with the salesmen and Anna Marie Louise asked her advice about buying glass swans, ash trays and cigarette boxes. With some money of her own she bought two dozen bud vases that Anna Marie Louise had not wanted to buy. When the bud vases came she unpacked the barrel herself, tearing her dress on a nail and getting excelsior all over the place. Then she washed the vases and, arranging a paper rose in one, put it into the window. (She had had a lifelong aversion to paper flowers, but what could you do after the frosts?) Ten minutes after the vase had been put in the window it was sold and in three days they were all gone. She was very excited, but she could not talk it over with Leander and could only tell Lulu in the kitchen.

To have his wife work at all raised for Leander the fine point of sexual prerogatives and having made one great mistake in going into debt to Honora he didn't want to make another. When Sarah announced that she wanted to work for Anna Marie Louise he thought the matter over carefully and decided against it. 'I don't want you to work, Sarah,' he said. 'You don't have anything to say about it,' Sarah said. That was that. The question went beyond sexual prerogatives into tradition, for much of what Sarah sold was ornamented with ships at sea and was meant to stir romantic memories of the great days of St Botolphs as a port. Now in his lifetime Leander had seen, raised on the ruins of that coast and port, a second coast and port of gift and antique shops, restaurants, tearooms and

bars where people drank their gin by candlelight, surrounded
sometimes by plows, fish nets, binnacle lights and other relics
of an arduous and orderly way of life of which they knew
nothing. Leander thought that an old dory planted with
petunias was a pretty sight but when he stepped into a newly
opened saloon in Travertine and found that the bar itself was
made of a bifurcated dory he felt as if he had seen a ghost.

He spent much time in his pleasant room on the southwest
corner of the house, with its view of the river and the roofs
of the village, writing his journal. He meant to be honest and
it seemed, in recording his past, that he was able to strike a
level of candor that he had only known in his most lucky
friendships. Young and old, he had always been quick to get
out of his clothes, and now he was reminded of the mixed
pleasures of nakedness.

Writer went to work day after confab about poor father
(he wrote). Rose before dawn as usual. Got morning papers
for delivery and looked at help-wanted ads. Vacancy at J. B.
Whittier. Big shoe manufacturer. Finished newspaper route.
Washed face. Put water on hair. Inked hole in sock. Ran all
the way to Whittier's office. They were on the second story of
frame building. Center of town. First person there. Only little
light in sky. Spring dawn. Two other boys joined me, looking
for same job. Birds singing in trees of Common. Glorious
hour. Clerk – Grimes – opened door at eight o'clock. Let
in applicants. Took me to Whittier's office. Half-past eight.
Beard the lion. Heavy man, seated at desk with his back to
door. He did not turn. Spoke over shoulder. 'Can you write
a letter? Go home and write a letter. Bring it in tomorrow
morning. Same time.' End of interview. Waited in outer office
and watched two applicants go in and out with same results.
Watched other applicants go home. Asked clerk – slender-
faced – for sheet of paper and use of pen. Obliged. Headed
paper J. B. Whittier. Wrote imaginary creditor. Asked to see
boss again. Clerk helpful. Bearded lion for second time. 'I've
written my letter, sir.' Reached for letter but did not turn.
Read letter. Passed brown envelope over shoulder. Addressed

to broker. Brewster, Bassett & Co. 'Deliver this and wait for
the receipted bill.' Ran all the way to broker's. Caught breath
while waiting for receipted bill. Ran all the way back. Gave
bill to Whittier. 'Sit down there in the corner,' he says. Sat
there for two hours without being noticed. More despotism
in business in those days. Merchants often erratic. Tyrannical.
No unions. Finally spoke at end of two hours. 'I want you
in there.' Points to outer office. 'Clean out the spittoons and
then ask Grimes what to do. He'll keep you busy.'

Pleasant memories all, even spittoons. Beginning business
life. Full of self-confidence. Resolved to succeed. Kept
journal of maxims. Always run. Never walk. Never walked
in Whittier's presence. Always smile. Never frown. Avoid
unclean thoughts. Buy mother gray silk dress. Turn of century
approaching. Progress everywhere. New World. Dirigible in
Music Hall. Phonograph in Horticultural Hall. First arc light
on Summer Street. Had to change carbon stick every day.
Early demonstration of telephone at Concord and Lexington
Festival. Cold. Big crowds. No food. Rode to Boston on
rooftop of train coach. Whittier bona-fide merchant prince.
Factory in Lynn. Office in Boston. Shoe prices from 67 cents
a pair to $1.20. All sold to jobbers from West. South. Business
in excess of a million a year. Worked from 7 to 6. Smiling.
Running. Learning.

Grimes head clerk. Best friend in office. Slender man. Silky
hair. Monkey fingered, horny minded, sad. At times tiresome.
Spoke often of wife. Conjugal bliss. Color in eyes deepened.
Licked lips. Knew about Turkish customs. French customs.
Armenian customs, etc. Sometimes tiresome as already said
above. Writer captivated by thought of wife. Golden headed.
Slut perhaps? Went home with Grimes for supper to meet
same. Excited. Grimes unlocked door. Woman spoke from
parlor. Heavy voice. Excitement gone. Big broad-shouldered
woman. Red cheeks. Heavy boots caked with mud. 'There's
pork chops and greens for supper,' she says. 'I want to be at
the hall at eight.' Grimes puts on apron. Cooks supper. Runs
between table and stove. Runs between stove and table. Wife

stows away big meal; big eater. Not much to say. Puts on heavy coat and tramps off to meeting in muddy boots. A feminist. Grimes washes dishes. Monkey-fingered man. Sad.

Found self, although not yet of legal age, powerfully attracted to opposite sex. Picked up hooker on riverbank. Big hat. Dirty linen. Girlish airs, but not young. What matter. Writer on fool's errand. Red hair. Green eyes. Talked. 'What a pretty sky,' says she. 'My how nice the river smells,' says she. Very ladylike. River smells of mudbanks. Bad breath of the sea. Low tide. French kissed. Groin to groin. Put hand in front of dress. Little boys in bushes giggled. Tomfools. Walked in dusk, hip to hip. 'I have a little room on Belmont Street,' she says. No thanks. Took her to railroad embankment. Cinders. Cornflowers. Stars. Big weeds like tropical vegetation. Samoa. S——d her there. Grand and glorious feeling. Forget for an hour all small things. Venalities. Money worries. Ambitions. Felt refreshed, generous toward sainted old mother. Hooker named Beatrice. Met often afterwards. Later went to New York. Rattled her glass rings on Twenty-third Street windows. Winter nights. Tried to find her later. Disappeared. Above may be in bad taste. If so, writer apologizes. Man born to trouble as the sparks fly upward.

Smells. Heat. Cold. All things like that most clearly remembered. Air in office fetid in wintertime. Coal stoves. Walking home to supper through cold. Joyous. Air in streets straight from snow-capped mountains. Washington. Jefferson. Lafayette. Franconia. Etc. Like mountain city in winter. Inhale smell of dead leaves on Common. Inhale north wind. Sweeter than any rose. Never get enough of sun and moon. Always sad to shut door. Got week's vacation in July. Grimes informed writer purpose was to give another boy – relation of Whittier's – chance at job. No good. Went to St Botolphs with mother. Stayed with cousins. House still empty. Porch falling down. Garden overgrown. Few roses. Swam in river. Sailed. Caught three-pound trout in Parson's Pond. Much pleasure walking on lonely beaches. Happy hours. Waves roar, rattle like New York, New Haven & Hartford. Underfoot dead skates. Sea grass shaped like bull whips, flowers, petticoats. Shells, stones, sea tack. All simple things. In the golden light memories of paradise perhaps; youth, surely, innocence. On beaches the joy and gall of perpetual youth. Even today. Smell east wind. Hear Neptune's horn. Always raring to go. Pack sandwiches. Bathing suit. Catch ramshackle bus to beach. Irresistible. In blood perhaps. Father read Shakespeare to waves. Mouthful of pebbles. Demosthenes?

Planned life carefully. Gym. Sailing in summer. Read Plutarch. Never missed a day at the office. Not once. Raise in salary. Increase of responsibility. Other signs of success. A winter night. Clerks going home. Cleaning pens. Banking fires. Whittier called me in to sanctum sanctorum. Coarse-faced man. Strong. Suffered from flatulence. Kept whisky keg in corner of office. Drank from bunghole with straw. Kept me waiting half hour. Footsteps of last clerk – Grimes – heard going downstairs. 'You like the business, Leander?' he says. 'Yes sir.' 'Don't be so damned eager,' he says. 'You look like a house nigger.' Clears throat. Uses spittoon. Slumps suddenly in chair. Sad? Sickness? Bad news? Bankruptcy? Failure? Worse? 'I have no son,' he says. 'I'm sorry, Mr Whittier.' 'I have no son,' he says again. Raises big face. Tears all over cheeks. Tears running from eyes. 'Work hard,' he says. 'Trust me. I'll treat you like a son. Now good night my boy.' Pats me. Sends me home.

Mingled feelings of ambition and tenderness. My heart in the business. Whittier and Wapshot. Wapshot & Co. In love with the shoe business. Do anything for the boss. Visions of saving him from burning building, wrecked ship. Angry heirs at reading of will. Success ordained. Hurried through supper. Read Plutarch in cold room. Kept on gloves. Hat. Breath smoked. Got to office half hour early, next day. Ran. Smiled. Wrote letters. Shared lunch pail with Grimes. 'How are you getting along with J. B.?' he asks. 'All right,' I said. 'Has he asked you in yet and told you that he doesn't have a son?' Grimes said. 'No,' I said. 'Well, he will,' Grimes said. 'He'll ask you in to his office late some day and tell you to work hard and trust him and he'll treat you like a son. He does it to everybody. Even Old Man Thomas. He's seventy-three years old. That's old for a son.'

Writer tried to conceal hurt feelings. Grimes knew. Tried to turn experience to use. Continued to play role of eager son. Insincere but rules of business. Conceal natural independence. Seem dutiful. Obedient. As a result received many father-to-son talks. Advice typical of merchants at time. 'Never extend credit to man with long hair. Never trust cigarette smokers; men with low-cut shoes.' Business a religion. Full of shrewdness. Superstition too. In daydreams began to think of marrying Whittier's daughter. Only child. Harriet. Tried to discourage above ideas but received encouragement from old man himself. Asked to Whittiers' for dinner.

Bought black suit. When dressed on historic night went into kitchen to say good-by to mother. Hamlet not heard from. Anxious over favorite son. 'Be sure and wipe your mouth with a napkin,' she said. 'I guess you know enough to get to your two feet when any ladies or older people come into the room. We come from a mannerly family. We weren't always poor. Be sure and use your napkin.'

Walked to Whittiers' house in south end. Manservant opened door and took coat. House still standing. Now a slum. Good-sized house but not palatial as appeared then. Hothouse flowers. Wallpaper. Clock struck. Counted chimes. Fourteen. Mrs Whittier met me at door of parlor, drawing room. Slender, gracious woman. Two necklaces. Four bracelets. Three rings. Greeted boss, then daughter. One necklace. Two bracelets. Two rings. Big girl. Horse-faced. Hopes dashed. No room for love, marriage. Human needs not so simple. Also had forgotten to empty bladder. Miserable. Spoil everything. Counted pictures on walls. Fourteen. All beautiful. Still lifes. Storms at sea. Italian or Egyptian woman at well. French priests playing dominoes. Foreign landscapes. Wallpaper even on ceiling.

Ate big dinner. Elegant surroundings but manners not so good as West Farm. Whittier broke wind twice. Both times loud. After repast Mrs Whittier sang. Put on spectacles. Stood bright lamps on table. Sang of love. Shrill voice. Spectacles. Bright lamps made hostess seem old, pinched. After concert, writer said good night. Walked home. Found mother still in kitchen. Sewing by lamplight. Old now. Longing for Hamlet. 'Did you have a nice time? Did you remember to use your napkin? Does your own home look ugly and dark? When I was a girl, I was younger than you, I went to visit my Brewster cousins in Newburyport. They had carriage horses, servants, a big house. When I came back to St Botolphs my home looked ugly and dark. It made me thoughtful.'

Father-to-son talk four weeks later, at dark as customary. Clerks leaving. Fires dying. 'Sit down, Leander, sit down,' he said. 'I told you that if you trusted me and worked hard I'd treat you like a son, didn't I? I never told that to anybody else. You know that, don't you? You believe me, don't you? Now I'm going to show you what I mean. Business practice is changing. I'm going to send a salesman on the road. I want you to be that salesman. I want you to go to New York for me, representing me. I want you to call on my customers, just as if you were my son. Take orders. Behave like a gentleman. When you go to New York I want you to realize what you're doing. I want you to realize that J. B. Whittier is more than a business. I want you to think of the firm as if it was your mother; our mother. I want you to think of it as if this dear old lady needed money and you were going to New York to make some money for her. I want you to comport yourself and dress yourself and talk as if you were representing this dear old lady. When you order your meals and stay in a hotel I want you to spend your money as if you realized it all belonged to this little old lady.' Liberal display of the waterworks. We understood one another.

Sing of the night boats. All that writer knows. Fall River, Bangor, Portland, Cape May, Baltimore, Lake Erie, Lake Huron, Saint Louis, Memphis, New Orleans. Floating palaces. Corn-husk mattresses. Music over water. One-night card games, one-night friendships, one-night girls. All gone with dawn's early light. First passage calm. Ocean like glass. Many lights glittering on water. Sparse lights on shore line. People watching palace drift by from porches, lawns, bridges, cupolas. Set their clocks by her. Shared cabin with stranger. Put watch, cash and checks in sock, put sock on foot. Slept on corn-husk mattress yearning for night-boat nymphs. Going to big city to make fortune for little old lady. J. B. Whittier & Co.

Checked in at Hoffman House as ordered. First customer gave order for eight hundred dollars. Second customer slightly higher. Sold five thousand dollars in three days. Wired for confirmation on last orders. Slept every night with watch, cash, etc., in sock. Returned on train, tired but happy. Went straight to office. J. B. waiting. Fell on writer's neck. Return of prodigal. Conquering hero. Took favorite son to Parker House for dinner. Whisky, wine, fish, flesh and fowl. Later to Chardon Street fancy house. Second visit. First time with Jim Graves. Died in St Botolphs as stated above. Baptists still singing. 'Lead, Kindly Light.' Appeared to be favorite hymn.

White-haired boy. Advice sought on manufacturing, merchandising, etc. Subject of marriage finally broached. Same place, same time of day as other confidential talks. 'You planning to marry, my boy,' he says, 'or are you going to remain a bachelor all your life?' 'I plan to marry and raise a family, sir,' I said. 'Shut the door and sit down,' he said. 'Have you got a young lady?' he asks. 'No sir,' I said. 'Well, I've got the young lady for you,' he said. 'She lives with her parents in Cambridge. She's a Sunday-school teacher. She's no more than eighteen years old. Have a drink of whisky.' He walked to the keg in the corner. Took turns at the straw. Sat down again. 'Man born of woman,' he said, 'hath but a short span and he is full of misery.' Waterworks beginning. Liberal display of tears. 'I wronged this young lady, Leander. I forced her. But she'll make you a good wife.' Loud sobbing. 'She's not flighty or loose. I was the first one. You marry her and I'll give you a thousand dollars. You don't marry her and I'll see that you get no work in Boston or anyplace else where my name is known. Tell me on Monday. Go home and think it over.' Got to his feet. Heavy man. Spring on swivel chair boomed. 'Good

night, my boy,' he said. Down the curved stairs slowly. Night
air smelled of mountains, but not for me. Colorless, hateful,
northern city. All black but for gaslights; mustard-colored
blankets on livery-stable hacks. Dirty snow underfoot. Gruel
of snow; horse manure. Five years wasted in business. Father
dead. Hamlet never coming home. Sole support of sainted
old mother. What to do? Ate supper with mother. Went
upstairs to cold room. Put on Mackinaw. Looked through
book of resolutions. Avoid unclean thoughts. Run, never
walk. Smile. Never frown. Go to gymnasium twice a week.
Buy your mother a gray silk dress. No help here. Thought of
Albany. Find work there. Lodgings. Begin life again. Decided
on Albany. Pack on Sunday. Leave on Monday. Never see
Whittier again. Went downstairs. Mother by stove in kitchen.
Sewing. Mentioned Albany. 'I hope you don't have any plans
for going there,' she said. 'You've been a good boy, Leander,
but you take after your father. It was always his feeling that
if he could go someplace where he wasn't known he would
become rich and happy. It was a great weakness. He was a
weak man. If you want to go away at least wait until I die.
Wait until Hamlet comes home. Remember that I'm old. I
mind the cold. Boston is my only home.'

Went to church on Sunday. God would be conscious of
my trial. Got to my knees. Prayed for once with a full heart.
Feast of Saint Mark. Lesson from Saint John. Looked around
church wondering what symbol would reveal choice. Gordian
knots, sheep and lions' heads, doves, swastikas, crosses, thorns
and wheels. Watchful all through service. Nothing. Ask a stone.
'I prayed for you,' mother said. Took arm. 'Albany is full of
Irishmen and other foreigners. You won't go there.' Jared came
later. Played Acis and Galatea. Hated music. Was Acis hungry?
Was Galatea sole support of aged mother? Mortals bad worse
trouble.

Woke before dawn on Monday. Two, three A.M. Irresolute
and sleepless. Sat at window to try and reach decision. City
sleeping. Few lights. Innocent-looking prospect. Remembered
West Farm. Good old summertime! Remembered father.

Life made unbearable by lack of coin. Moral of whole career
appeared to be: Make Money. Hell hath no fire that burns like
need. Poverty is the root of all evil. Who is the thief? A poor
man. Who is the drunkard? A poor man too. Who makes his
daughter spread her legs to strangers on Chardon Street? The
poor man. Who leaves his son fatherless? The poor man.

Such reasoning quieted moral qualms somewhat although
decision went against deepest instincts. Romantic perhaps.
Dreamed often of fair wife, waiting in rose bower at end of
day. White cottage. Lovebirds in flowering trees. Nellie Melba's
embonpoint. All this lost. Saw no other course, however. Gentle
light appearing in sky. Dusk. Sound of early-bird horsecar
coming up Joy Street. Went first thing in morning to Whittier.
'I'm game, sir,' says I. Told me his plans. Go to visit girl that
evening. Marry her in week or two. When time comes for
accouchement take her to address in Nahant. Leave baby there.
Infanticide? After birth of baby one thousand dollars would
be deposited in National Trust Co., New York City, to writer's
account.

Put on best black suit after supper and walked to address
given in Cambridge. Spring night. Temperature in the sixties.
South wind sounding in still-bare trees like kettle drums. Many
stars. Gentle light. Unlike winter constellations. House on
hoopskirts of Cambridge. Half-starved dogs barked at writer's
footsteps. No sidewalks. Bare planks on mud. Small house
among trees. Knocked woefully on door. Tall man opened.
White hair. Sideburns. Drawn face. Sick perhaps? Sallow wife
at back, holding lamp. Wick lying in yellow coal oil. How-
do-you-dos ended, followed old couple into parlor, saw future
wife.

Pretty child. Hair like raven's wing. Snow-white complexion.
Slender wrists. Felt pity, sympathy too. Rolled by old wind-
breaking goat in bushes after Sunday-school picnic. Boss was
unpopular, even among Chardon Street beauties. Babes in the
wood; she and me. 'Father was reading from the Bible' says
her mother. 'Luke,' says the old man. 'Chapter seven; verse
thirty-one.' Reads the Bible for an hour. Closed with prayers.

Everybody on their knees. Said good-by then. 'Good-by, Mr Wapshot' were the only words spoken by future spouse. Walked home, wondering: Was she stupid? Could she cook?

Took Clarissa to church following Sunday. In company with her parents. On way there made proposal of marriage. 'I would like to marry you, Mr Wapshot,' she said. Some happiness then. Picture was not hopeless. Thought ahead to time after baby's birth. Stormy weather coming but why not peace and quiet after? Church was deep-water Baptist. Sunny day. Fell asleep during sermon. Late that evening told mother of plans. Sainted old lady did not bat an eyelash. Never told her facts in case. Laconism, like blindness, seems to develop other faculties. Powers of divination. Married following Sunday in Church of Ascension. Father Masterson tied bond. Fine old character. Mother only witness. God bless dear old lady. Went from church to North Station. Took cars to Franconia.

Tedious journey in local. Stopped at every back yard. So it seemed. Backside of every barn on way painted with advertisements. Elixirs. Liver pills. Old circus posters. Dried codfish. Tea. Coffee. Back of barn in St Botolphs painted: Boston Store. Rock bottom prices.

Young black-haired wife, dressed in best. Made all own clothes. Great sweetness; grace. Remember slenderness of wrists, ankles. Fleeting joy, sadness on face. Much openness. Real meaning of beauty all flow from lovely woman. Poetry. Music. Makes everything touched upon seem like revelation. Writer's hand. Ugly train coach. 'I once rode to Swamscott in the cars,' she said. Musical voice made journey seem like poem. Swans. Music of harps. Fountains. Swamscott not much and trains to same like trains everywhere. Fragrant, supple child, carrying seed of troll. Deep feeling of pity. Also lead in pencil.

Arrival in Franconia. Took hack to boardinghouse. Eight dollars per week. American plan. North country. Cold nights even in midsummer. Pick-up supper in gloomy dining room. No matter. Love blind to cold pudding, sallow-faced landlady, stains on ceiling. Bridal chamber big farmhouse bedroom.

Cumbrous bedstead painted with purple grapes. Iron wood stove blazing. Undressed in light, heat of fire.

No fishing in vicinity. Walked with bride in hills. Beautiful scenery. Milky-blue hills in distance. Old lakes. Old mountains. Poignant country, north of mill towns. Then booming. Later ruined. (Unable to meet competition from south and west.) So-called marginal farming. Sam Scat. Stony fields. Most hill towns abandoned even then. Foundation holes, mined buildings in deep woods. Homesteads, schoolhouses, churches even. Woods in vicinity still wild. Deer, bears, some lynx. Young wife picked nosegay of posies from gardens planted by farmers' wives. Departed then. English roses. Sweet William. Lemon lilies. Phlox and primrose. Brought some back to bridal chamber. Put in water pitcher. Real love of flowers. Haying weather perfect. Writer worked in fields with farmer, sons. Thunderstorm at end of day. Dark clouds mounting. Cock's crow. Deep sound of stone hills falling. Get hay into barn before rain. Forked lightning. Heavy wagon reaches safety just as first drops fall. Encircling sound. Long after nightfall, departure of rain, embrace of wife returns to writer all good things. Magic of haying weather. Heat of sun. Chill of storm.

Vacation ends all too soon. Bid good-by to hills, fields, cow pastures, Elysian fields with real sorrow. Pinckney Street, Whittier, Grimes, etc. Sainted old mother was tender with wife, never so tender with anyone but Hamlet. Never spoke of trouble but seemed to sense babe-in-wood situation. Nothing of convenience in marriage, however. Made in heaven; so it seemed. Sweet child woke with writer in early mornings. Darned socks, made marriage bed sweet, cleaned lamp chimneys, waxed rosewood piano. Thought often of future. Dispose of troll-child and raise own family. Live in rose-covered cottage after demise of sainted old mother. In church writer often thanked God for sweetness of spouse. Prayed with full heart. Never had occasion to thank same for anything else. Wife sang sometimes in evening, accompanied by sainted old mother on Hallet & Davis rosewood piano.

Voice modest in range but true pitch and oh so clear. Sweet, good, loving, kindly, spirit.

Little troll very lively. Abdomen swollen, but no disfigurement. Easily fatigued during dog days. Accouchement expected in October. Sent message to office one afternoon. Left office at three. Found bags packed, both wife's and writer's. Took late train to Nahant. Hired livery to Rutherford farm. Reached there nine o'clock or later. Dark house. Smelled salt in wind. Heard harsh, regular noise of waves. Used both bell pull and knocker. Door opened by sallow-faced woman in nightdress, wrapper. Hair in rags. 'I don't know, your names,' says she. 'I don't want to know them. The sooner you get out of here the better.' Lighted lamp. Unpacked bags. Went to bed. Wife slept poorly. Often spoke in sleep. Unclear words. Listened all night to troubled speaking; also moiling of sea. Seemed from sound of waves to be flat, stony beach. Distinguished rattling, knocking sound of stones. Milk-pail, cattle sounds before dawn. Woke early. Washed in cold water. 'You'll take your meals in kitchen,' said sallow-faced landlady. 'So far as you're able you'll do your own work. I'm not going to be picking up after you.'

Husband of same introduced self at breakfast. 5'6" 125 pounds. Runty. Poor specimen. Appeared to be henpecked. Former livery-stable proprietor or so claimed. Tales of prosperity. Once possessed biggest wardrobe in Nahant. Sixty-four horses. Seven grooms on payroll. All lost in epidemic. Documents of splendor displayed. Receipted feed bill for one thousand dollars. Also tailor bill, butcher bill, grocery bill, etc. All gone. Walked with Clarissa on beach. Dear wife gathered colored stones, shells in skirt. Day slow to pass. Situation seemed like Gordian knot and to cut same dreamed of future. Painted rosy picture of country cottage, children gathered around knees, pleasant life. Net result of such wool-gathering was to make wife weep.

Labor pains began at seven. Wet bed. Broke waters or some such term. Writer unfamiliar, even today, with obstetrical lingo. 'Our Father who art in heaven,' said Clarissa. Prayed continuously. Pain arduous. First experience with such things. Held wife in arms when seizures commenced. Sallow-faced landlady waited in next room. Sound of rocking chair. 'Put blanket over her mouth,' she said. 'They'll hear her up at the Dexter place.' Most violent seizure at eleven. Suddenly saw blood, baby's head. Landlady rushed in. Drove me away. Called henpecked husband to bring water, rags, etc. Much coming and going. Sallow-faced landlady emerged at 2 A.M. 'You have a little daughter,' says she. Magical transformation! Butter wouldn't melt in mouth. Went in to see baby. Sleeping in soapbox. Clarissa also sleeping. Kissed brow. Sat in chair until morning. Went for walk on beach. Clouds shaped like curved ribbing of scallop shell. Light pouring off sea into same. Form of sky still vivid in memory. Returned to room on tiptoe. Opened door. Clarissa in bed, smiling. Masses of dark hair. Baby at breast, swollen with milk. Writer cried for first time since leaving West River. 'Don't cry,' Clarissa says. 'I'm happy.'

Heavy step of sallow-faced landlady. Transformation still in order. 'God bless you, you dear, sweet little girl,' she says to the baby. High, squeaky voice. 'Look at her dear little fingers,' says she. 'Look at her dear little toes. I'll take her now.' 'Let her suck for a little while,' says Clarissa. 'Let her finish her dinner,' says I. 'Well, you ain't going to take the baby with you,' says she, 'and since you ain't going to take the baby with you and since she ain't going to be your baby there's no point in your suckling her.' 'Let her suck for a little while longer,' says Clarissa. 'I'm not one to judge others,' says she, 'and I don't put my nose in their business but if you hadn't done wrong you wouldn't be coming out here to have your baby in this Godforsaken place and when a baby drinks milk from a mother who's done wrong all the wickedness and sinfulness and lustfulness goes right into the baby through its mother's milk,' says she. 'You've got a wicked tongue,' I said, 'and we'd appreciate it if you'd leave us alone now.' 'Let her suck for a little while longer,' Clarissa said. 'I'm only doing what I'm paid to do,' she said, 'and what's more she's God's little creature and it ain't fair to have her imbibing all the weaknesses of another the first thing in her life.' 'Leave us alone,' I said. 'She's right, Leander,' Clarissa said and she took the child off her pretty breast and gave it to the intruder. Then she turned her face away and cried.

She cried all the day long; she cried all night. She cried the bed full of tears. In the morning I helped her dress. She was too weak to dress herself, too weak even to lift her dark hair, and I lifted it for her and held it while she put it up with pins. There was a nine-o'clock train to Boston and I sent a message for a livery to pick us up in time to get it. Then I packed the valises and carried them out to the side of the road. Then I heard the landlady screaming: 'You, you, where is she?' Oh, she looked then like a harpy. 'She's run away. Go up to the Dexters', go up the Dexter path. I'll go down by the shell road. We've got to head her off.' Off she goes in her muddy boots. Off goes former livery-stable proprietor with his manure fork. Pursued quarry over horizon. Heard baby crying in garden. Whimper, really. She had flown; but she had not gone far.

Pear tree in garden pruned to look like fountain, sunshade perhaps. Graceful tent of leaves. Under this she sat. Bodice unbuttoned. Camisole unlaced. Child at breast. Fretful crying. Did not speak; she and me. Eyes only. No explanations, names even. Child sucking, but crying also. A little rain began to fall; but not on us. Pear tree served as adequate shelter. Baby fell asleep. How long we sat there I don't know. Half hour perhaps. Watched oyster-shell road darken in rain. Still no drops touched us. 'I have more tears than milk,' she said. 'I have more tears than milk. I've cried my breasts dry.' Carried sleeping baby, sheltered by head, shoulders from rain, back to soapbox in kitchen near stove. Took livery to station.

Have no wish to dwell on sordid matters, sorrows, etc. Bestiality of grief. Times in life when we can count only on brute will to live. Forget. Forget. (By this Leander meant to say that Clarissa was drowned in the Charles River that night.)

Took cars to St Botolphs next morning with old mother and poor Clarissa.

Overcast day. Not cold. Variable winds. South, southwest. Hearse at station. Few rubbernecks watching. Father Frisbee said the words. Old man then; old friend. Purple face. Skirts blowing in wind. Showed old-fashioned congress boots. Thick stockings. Family lot on hill above river. Water, hills, fields restore first taste of sense. Never marry again. Roof of old house visible in distance. Abode of rats, squirrels, porcupines. Haunted house for children. Wind slacked off in middle of prayer. Distant, electrical smell of rain. Sound amongst leaves; stubble. Hath but a short span, says Father Frisbee. Full of misery is he. Rain more eloquent, heartening and merciful. Oldest sound to reach porches of man's ear.

CHAPTER 20

The fat man who had given Coverly pointers on how to shave had begun to come into Coverly's room at night after supper and give him advice on how to get ahead in the world. He was a widower who had a house somewhere to the north where he went for week ends and who pinched pennies by living in the rooming house so that he would have a comfortable retirement. He had a job with Civil Service and it was his feeling that Coverly should get on the Civil Service lists. He brought him those newspapers that list Civil Service openings and kept pointing out opportunities for high-school graduates or opportunities for specialists who had been trained by the Civil Service schools in the city. There was a demand that year for Tapers and he pointed this out to Coverly as his best bet. The government would pay half of Coverly's tuition at the MacIlhenney Institute. It was a four-month course and if he passed his exams he would be taken into government service at seventy-five dollars a week. Advised and encouraged by his friend, Coverly enrolled in some night classes on Taping. This involved the translation of physics experiments into the symbols – or tape – that could be fed into a computation machine.

Coverly's schedule went like this. He punched Warburton's time clock at half-past eight and went down a back staircase into the basement. The air was spectacularly bad: the reek and the closeness of a department store backstage. The other

stock boys were of varying ages – one of them was in his
sixties – and they were all amused by Coverly's catarrhal accent
and his references to life in St Botolphs. They unpacked the
merchandise as it came in and kept it flowing up the freight
elevators to the departments overhead. When there were sales
they worked sometimes as late as midnight, unloading racks of
fur-trimmed coats or cartons of bed sheets. On three nights
a week, when Coverly had finished work at Warburton's, he
signed the monitor's book at the MacIlhenney Institute. This
was in the fourth floor of an office building that seemed to
contain a good many other schools – institutes of portrait
photography, journalism and music. The only elevator that
ran in the evening was a freight elevator, operated by an old
man in overalls who could, by pursing his lips, give a fairly
good imitation of a French horn. He performed the *William
Tell* Overture while he took his passengers up and down
and he liked to be complimented. There were twenty-four
students in Coverly's class and the instructor was a young
man who seemed to have put in a hard day himself by the
time he got to them. The first lecture was an orientation talk
on cybernetics or automation, and if Coverly, with his mildly
rueful disposition, had been inclined to find any irony in
his future relationship to a thinking machine, he was swiftly
disabused. Then they got to work memorizing the code.

This was like learning a language and a rudimentary
one. Everything was done by rote. They were expected
to memorize fifty symbols a week. They were quizzed for
fifteen minutes at the opening of each class and were given
speed tests at the end of the two-hour period. After a month
of this the symbols – like the study of any language – had
begun to dominate Coverly's thinking, and walking on the
street he had gotten into the habit of regrouping numbers
on license plates, prices in store windows and numerals on
clocks so that they could be fed into a machine. When the
class ended he sometimes drank a cup of coffee with a friend
who was going to school five nights a week. His name was
Mittler and his second enrollment was at Dale Carnegie's and

Coverly was very much impressed with how likeable Mittler had learned to make himself. Moses came over one Sunday to visit Coverly and they spent the day banging around the streets and drinking beer but when it came time for Moses to go back the separation was so painful for both of them that Moses never returned. Coverly planned to go to St. Botolphs for Christmas but he had a chance to work overtime on Christmas Eve and he took it, for he was in the city, after all, to make his fortune.

All things of the sea belong to Venus; pearls and shells and alchemists' gold and kelp and the riggish smell of neap tides, the inshore water green, and purple further out and the joy of distances and the roar of falling masonry, all these are hers, but she doesn't come out of the sea for all of us. She came for Coverly through the swinging door of a sandwich shop in the Forties where he had gone to get something to eat after classes at the MacIlhenney Institute. She was a thin, dark-haired girl named Betsey MacCaffery – raised in the badlands of northern Georgia – an orphan, her eyes red that night from crying. Coverly was the only customer in the shop. She brought him a glass of milk and a sandwich in an envelope and then went to the far end of the counter and began to wash glasses. Now and then she took a deep, tremulous breath – a sound that made her seem to Coverly, as she bent over the sink, tender and naked. When he had eaten half his sandwich he spoke to her:

'Why are you crying?'

'Oh Jesus,' she said. 'I know I shouldn't be here crying in front of strangers, but the boss just came in and found me smoking a cigarette and he gave me hell. There wasn't anybody in the store. It's always slow this late on rainy nights, but he can't blame me for that, can he? I don't have anything to do with the rain and I just can't stand out there in the rain asking people to come in. Well, it was slow and there hadn't been anybody in for nearly twenty – twenty-five or thirty minutes – and so I went out back and lighted a cigarette and then he came right in, sniffing like a pig, and gave me hell. He said these awful things about me.'

'You shouldn't pay any attention to what he says.'

'You English?'

'No,' Coverly said. 'I come from a place called St Botolphs. It's a small town, north of here.'

'The reason I asked was you don't talk like the others. I come from a small town myself. I'm just a small-town girl. I guess maybe that's the trouble with me. I don't have this thick skin you need to get along with in the city. I had so much trouble this week. I just took this apartment with my girl friend. I have or perhaps I should say I had this girl friend, Helen Bent. I thought she was my true-blue friend; true-blue. She certainly led me to believe she was my best friend. Well, since we were such good friends it seemed sensible for us to take an apartment together. We were inseparable. That's what people used to say about us. You can't ask Betsey unless you ask Helen, they used to say. Those two are inseparable. Well, we took this apartment together, my girl friend and I. That was about a month ago; a month or six weeks. Well, just as soon as we got moved in and settled and about to enjoy ourselves I discover that the whole thing is just a scheme. The only reason she wants to share this apartment with me is so she can meet men there. Formerly she was living with her family out in Queens. Well, I don't have any objections to having a boy friend now and then but it was only a one-room apartment and she was having them in every night and naturally it was very embarrassing for me. There were men going in and out of there so much that it didn't seem like home to me. Why, sometimes when it was time for me to go home to my own apartment where I was paying rent and had all my own furniture I'd just feel so heavyhearted about busting in on her with one of her friends that I'd go and sit in a late movie. Well, I finally spoke to her. Helen, I said, this place doesn't seem like home to me. There's no sense in my paying rent, I said, if I have to take up residence in a movie house. Well, she certainly showed her true colors. Oh, the spiteful things she said. When I come home the next day she's gone, television set and all. I was glad to see the last of her, of course, but I'm stuck with this apartment with nobody to share the rent and in a job like this I don't have any occasion to make girl friends.'

She asked Coverly if he wanted anything more. It was nearly time to close and Coverly asked if he could walk her home.

'You sure come from a small town, all right,' she said. 'Anybody could tell you come from a small town, asking if you can walk me home, but it so happens I just live five blocks from here and I do walk home and I don't guess it would do me any harm, providing you don't get fresh. I've had too much of freshness. You've got to promise that you won't be fresh.'

'I promise,' Coverly said.

She talked on and on while she made the preparations for closing the store and when these were finished she put on a hat and coat and stepped with Coverly out into the rain. He was delighted with her company. What a citizen of New York, he thought — walking a counter girl home in the rain. As they approached her house she reminded him of his promise not to be fresh and he didn't ask to come up, but he asked her to have dinner with him some night. 'Well, I'd adore to,' she said. 'Sunday's my only night off but if Sunday's all right with you I'd adore to have dinner with you on Sunday night. There's this nice Italian restaurant right around the corner we can go to — I've never been there, but this former girl friend of mine told me it was very good — excellent cooking, and if you could pick me up at around seven . . .' Coverly watched her walk through the lighted hall to the inner door, a thin girl and not a very graceful one, feeling, as surely as the swan recognizes its mate, that he was in love.

CHAPTER 21

Northeaster (Leander wrote). Wind backed from SW. 3rd equinoctial disturbance of season. All in love is not larky and fractious. — In the attic the broken harp-string music of water dropping into pails and pans had begun and, feeling chilled and exposed to the somber view of the river in the rain, he put away his papers and went down the stairs. Sarah was in Travertine. Lulu was away. He went into the back parlor, where he was completely absorbed in building and lighting a fire — in watching how it caught, in sniffing the perfume of clean wood and feeling the heat as it reached his hands and then went through his clothes. When he was warm he went to the window to see the dark day. He was surprised to see a car turn in the gates and come up the drive. It was one of the old sedans from the taxi stand at the station.

The car stopped at the side door and he saw a woman lean forward and talk to the driver. He did not recognize the passenger — she was plain and gray-haired — and he guessed that she was one of Sarah's friends. He watched her from the window. She opened the door of the car and walked up, through the thin curtain of rain that fell from the broken gutters, to the door. Leander was glad for any company and he went down the hall and opened the door before she rang.

He saw a very plain woman, her coat darkened at the shoulders with rain. Her face was long, her hat was trimmed gaily with hard white feathers, like the feathers that are used to balance badminton birds, and her coat was worn. Leander had seen, he thought, hundreds of her kind. They were the imprimatur of New England. Dutiful, pious and hardy, they seemed to have patterned their spirits after the weeds that grow in high pastures. They were the women, Leander thought, after whom the dirty boats of the mackerel fleet were named: Alice, Esther, Agnes, Maybelle and Ruth. That there should be feathers in her hat, that an ugly pin made of seashells should be pinned to her flat breast, that there should be anything feminine, any ornament on such a discouraging figure, seemed to Leander touching.

'Come in,' Leander said. 'I expect you're looking for Mrs Wapshot?'

'I think you're the gentleman I'm looking for,' she said with a look so troubled and shy that Leander glanced down at his clothes. 'I'm Miss Helen Rutherford. Are you Mr Wapshot?'

'Yes, I'm Leander Wapshot. Come in, come in out of the rain. Come into the parlor. I have a little fire.' She followed Leander along the hall and he opened the door to the back parlor. 'Sit down,' he said. 'Sit in the red chair. Sit by the fire. Give your clothes a chance to dry out.'

'You have quite a big house here, Mr Wapshot,' she said.

'It's too big,' Leander said. 'Do you know how many doors there are in this house? There are one hundred and twenty-two doors in this house. Now what was it that you wanted to see me about?'

She made a sniffling sound as if she had a cold or might even have been crying and began to unbuckle a heavy brief case that she carried.

'Your name was given to me by an acquaintance. I'm an accredited representative of the Institute for Self-Improvement. We still have a few subscriptions open for eligible men and women. Dr Bartholomew, the director of the institute, has divided human knowledge into seven branches. Science, the arts – both the cultural arts and the arts of physical well-being – religion . . .'

'Who gave you my name?' Leander asked.

'Dr Bartholomew thinks it's more a question of inclination than background,' the stranger said. 'Many people who've been fortunate enough to have a college education are still ineligible by Dr Bartholomew's standards.' She spoke without emphasis or feeling, almost with dread, as if she had come about something else, and she kept her eyes on the floor. 'Educators all over the world and some of the crowned heads of Europe have endorsed Dr Bartholomew's methods and Dr Bartholomew's essay on 'The Science of Religion' is in the Royal Library in Holland. I have a picture of Dr Bartholomew here and . . .'

'Who gave you my name?' Leander asked again.

'Daddy,' she said. 'Daddy gave me your name.' She began to wring her hands. 'He died last summer. Oh, he was good to me, he was like a real daddy, there wasn't anything in the world that he wouldn't do for me. He was my best beau. On Sundays we used to take walks together. He was awfully intelligent but they cheated him. They did him out of everything. He wasn't afraid, though, he wasn't afraid of anything. Once we went to a show in Boston. That was on my birthday. He bought these expensive seats. They were supposed to be in the orchestra but when we came to sit in them they put us in the balcony. We paid for orchestra seats – he told me – and we're going down and sit in that orchestra. So he took my hand and we went downstairs and he told the usher – he was one of those stuck-up fellows – we paid for orchestra seats and we're going to sit in that orchestra. I miss him so much it's all I can think about. He never let me go anywhere without him. And then he died last summer.'

'Where is your home?' Leander asked.

'Nahant.'

'Nahant?'

'Yes. Daddy told me everything.'

'What do you mean?' Leander said.

'Daddy told me everything. He told me how you came there after dark, like thieves, he said, and about how Mr Whittier paid for everything and how Mother kept me from drinking her wicked milk.'

'Who are you?' Leander said.

'I'm your daughter.'

'Oh no,' Leander said. 'You're lying. You're a crazy woman. Get out of here.'

'I'm your daughter.'

'Oh no,' Leander said. 'You've thought this all up, you and those people in Nahant. You've made it all up. Now get out of my house. Leave me alone.'

'You walked on the beach,' she said. 'Daddy remembered everything so's you'd believe me and give me money. He even remembered the suit you had. He said you had a plaid suit. He said you walked on the beach and picked up stones.'

'Get out of my house,' Leander said.

'I won't go away from here until you give me money. You never once asked was I living or dead. You never gave me a thought. Now I want some money. After Daddy died I sold the house and I had a little money and then I had to take this work. It's hard for me. It's too hard for me. I'm not strong. I'm out in all weathers. I want some money.'

'I don't have anything to give you.'

'That's what Daddy said. He said you'd try to get out of helping me. Daddy told me that's what you'd say, but he made me promise to come and see you.' Then she stood and picked up her brief case. 'God will be your judge,' she said at the door, 'but I know my rights and I can bring you into court and blacken your name.' Then she went down the hall and when she got to the door Leander called after her, 'Wait, wait, wait, please,' and went down the hall. 'I can give you something,' he said. 'I have a few things left. I have a jade watch fob and a golden chain and I can show you your mother's grave. It's in the village.'

'I would spit on it,' she said. 'I would spit on it.' Then she went out of the house to where the taxi was waiting and drove away.

CHAPTER 22

A week or ten days after his dinner with Betsey, Coverly moved into her apartment. This took a lot of persuasion on Coverly's part but her resistance pleased him and seemed to express the seriousness with which she took herself. His case was based – indirectly – on the fact that she needed someone to look out for her, on the fact that she did not have, as she had said herself, the thickness of skin the city demanded. Coverly's feelings about her helplessness were poetic and absorbing and when he thought of her in her absence it was with a mixture of pity and bellicoseness. She was alone and he would defend her. There was this and there was the fact that their relationship unfolded with great validity and this informal marriage or union, played out in a strange and great city, made Coverly very happy. She was the beloved; he was the lover – there was never any question about this and this suited Coverly's disposition and gave to his courtship and their life together the liveliness of a pursuit. Her search for friends had been arduous and disappointing and it was these disappointments and exasperations that Coverly was able to redress. There was no pretentiousness in her – no memories of either hunt balls or razorback hogs – and she was ready and willing to cook his supper and warm his bones at night. She had been raised by her grandmother, who had wanted her to be a schoolteacher, and she had disliked the South so much that she had taken any job to get out of it. He recognized her

defenselessness, but he recognized, at a much deeper level, het
human excellence, the touching qualities of a wanderer, for she
was that and said so and while she would play all the parts of
love she would not tell him that she was in love. On the week
ends they took walks, subway and ferryboat rides, and talked
over their plans and their tastes, and late in the winter Coverly
asked her to marry him. Betsey's reaction was scattered,
tearful and sweet, and Coverly wrote his plans in a letter to
St Botolphs. He wanted to marry as soon as he had passed his
civil-service examinations and had been assigned to one of
the rocket-launching stations where Tapers were employed. He
enclosed a photograph of Betsey, but he would not bring his
bride to St Botolphs until he was given a vacation. He took
these precautions because it had occurred to him that Betsey's
southern accent and sometimes fractious manner might not go
down with Honora and that the sensible thing to do would
be to marry and produce a son before Honora saw his wife.
Leander may have sensed this – his letters to Coverly were
all congratulatory and affectionate – and it may have been at
the back of his mind that with Coverly married they might
soon all be on Easy Street. It would be way at the back of
his mind. Sarah was heartbroken to know that Coverly would
not be married at Christ Church.

Coverly passed his exams with flying colors in April and was
surprised when the MacIlhenney Institute had a graduation
ceremony. This was held in the fifth floor of the building
in an academy of piano teaching where two classrooms
had been thrown together to make an auditorium. All of
Coverly's classmates appeared with their families or their wives,
and Betsey wore a new hat. A lady, a stranger to them all,
played 'Pomp and Circumstance' on the piano and as their
names were called they went up to the front of the room and
got their diplomas from Mr MacIlhenney. Then they went
down to the fourth floor where they found Mrs MacIlhenney
standing by a rented tea urn and a plate of Danish pastry.
Coverly and Betsey were married the next morning at the
Church of the Transfiguration. Mittler was the only witness

and they spent a three-day honeymoon on an island cottage that Mittler owned and loaned them. Sarah wrote Coverly a long letter about what she would send him from the farm when he was settled – the Canton china and the painted chairs – and Leander wrote a letter in which he said, among other things, that to make a son was as easy as blowing a feather off your knee. Honora sent them a check for two hundred dollars, but no message.

Coverly passed his Civil Service examinations and was qualified as a Taper. He knew, by then, the location of most of the rocket-launching bases in the country and as soon as he was settled he would send for Betsey and they would begin their marriage. Although Coverly's status was civilian his assignment was cut at an army base and he was given transportation by the air force. His orders were cut in code. A week after his marriage he boarded an old C-54 with bucket seats and found himself, next day, in an airfield outside San Francisco. His feeling then was that he would be sent to Oregon or flown back to one of the desert stations. He telephoned Betsey and she cried when she heard his voice but he assured her that in a week or ten days they would be together again in a house of their own. He was very uxorious and lay down each night in his army bunk with Betsey's specter, slept with her shade in his arms and woke each morning with powerful longings for his sandwich – shop Venus and wife. There was some delay about the second stage of his journey and he was kept at the air-force base in San Francisco for nearly a week.

We all, man and boy, know what a transient barracks looks like and there would be no point in enumerating this barrenness. The fact that Coverly was a civilian did not give him any freedom and whether he went to the officers' club or the movies he had to report his whereabouts to the orderly room. He could see the hills of San Francisco across the bay and, thinking that this city – or some firing grounds in the vicinity – would be his destination, he wrote hopefully to Betsey about her coming West. 'It was cold in the barracks last night and I sure wish you'd been in bed with me to warm it up.' And so forth and so on. He lived among a dozen or so men who seemed to have been withdrawn from permanent installations in the Pacific because they were unfit. The most articulate of these was a Mexican who had not been able to stomach army food because there were no peppers in it. He told his story to anyone who would listen. As soon as he started eating army food he lost weight. He knew what the trouble was. He needed peppers. He had eaten peppers all his life. Even his mother's milk had been peppery. He pleaded with army cooks and doctors to get him some peppers but they wouldn't take his pleas seriously. He wrote to his Momma and she sent him some pepper seeds in an envelope and he planted them around an anti-aircraft gun emplacement where the soil was rich and where there was plenty of sun. He watered them and tended them and they had just begun to sprout when the commanding officer ordered them to be plowed under. It was unmilitary to raise vegetables on a gun emplacement. This order broke the Mexican's spirit. He lost weight; he became so emaciated that he had to be sent to the infirmary; and now he was being discharged from the army as a mental incompetent. He would have been happy to serve his flag, he said, if he could have peppers in his food. His plaint seemed reasonable enough but it got tiresome night after night and Coverly usually stayed out of the barracks until the lights were off.

He ate his meals at the officers' club, lost or won a dollar at the gambling machines, drank a glass of ginger ale at the bar and went to the movies. He saw Westerns, gangster careers, tales of happy and unhappy love both in brilliant colors and in black and white. He was sitting in the movies one evening when the public-address system called: 'Attention, attention everybody. Will the following men report to Building Thirty-two with their gear. Private Joseph Di Gacinto. Private Henry Wollaston. Lieutenant Marvin Smythe. Mister Coverly Wapshot . . .' The audience hooted and whistled and called, 'You'll be sorreee,' as they went out into the dark. Coverly got his valise and went over to Building Thirty-two and was driven with the rest of the men to the airfield. They all had some theory about their destination. They were going to Oregon, Alaska or Japan. It had never occurred to Coverly that he might be leaving the country and he was worried. He pinned his hopes on Oregon but decided that if his destination was Alaska Betsey could follow him there. As soon as they boarded the plane the doors were shut and they taxied down the runway and took off. It was an old transport with a conservative speed, Coverly guessed, and if their destination was Oregon they would reach there before dawn. The plane was hot and stuffy and he fell asleep, and waking at dawn and looking from the port he saw that they were high over the Pacific. They flew westward all day, shooting crap and reading the Bible, which was all they had to read, and at dusk they picked up the lights of Diamond Head and landed on Oahu.

Coverly was assigned a bunk in another transient barracks and told to report to the airfield in the morning. No one would tell him if his travels were over, but he guessed, from the looks of the orderly-room clerks, that he had some way to go. He got rid of his valise and hitched a ride on a weapons carrier into Honolulu. It was a hot, stale-smelling night with thunder in the mountains. Memories of Thaddeus and Alice, of Honora and old Benjamin came to him and he walked in the footsteps of many Wapshots, but this was not much of a consolation. Half a world lay between him and Betsey, and all his plans of happiness, children, and the honor of the family name seemed cruelly suspended or destroyed. He saw a sign on a wall that said: AIRMAIL. AN ORCHID LEI TO YOUR SWEETHEART FOR AS LITTLE AS THREE DOLLARS. This would be a way of expressing his tender feelings for Betsey and he asked an MP near the old palace where he could get a lei. He followed the MP's directions and rang the bell of a house where a fat woman in evening clothes let him in. 'I want a lei,' Coverly said sadly.

'Well, you come to the right place, honey,' she said. 'You come right in. You come right in and have a drink and I'll fix you up in a few minutes.' She took his arm and led him into a little parlor where some other men were drinking beer.

'Oh, I'm sorry,' Coverly said suddenly. 'There's some mistake. You see, I'm married.'

'Well, that don't make no difference,' the fat lady said. 'More'n half the girls I got working for me's married and I been happily married for nineteen years myself.'

'There's been a mistake,' Coverly said.

'Well, make up your mind,' the fat woman said. 'You come in here telling me you want to get laid and I'm doing the best I can for you.'

'Oh, I'm sorry,' Coverly said, and he was gone.

In the morning he boarded another plane and flew all day. A little before dark they circled for a landing and out of the ports Coverly could see, in the stormy light, a long, scimitar-shaped atoll with surf breaking on one coast, a huddle of buildings and a rocket-launching platform. The airstrip was small and the pilot took three passes before he made a landing. Coverly swung down from the door and crossed the strip to an office where a clerk translated his orders. He was on Island 93 – an installation that was half military and half civilian. His tour of duty would be nine months with a two-week vacation at a rest camp in either Manila or Brisbane; take your pick.

CHAPTER 23

Moses was promoted and he bought a car and rented an apartment. He worked hard at his office and still had a lot of nightwork assigned to him by Mr Boynton. He saw Beatrice about once a week. This was a pleasant and irresponsible arrangement for he discovered very soon that Beatrice's marriage had gone on the rocks long before he had stepped into the Marine Room. Chucky was going around with the girl who sang in the band and Beatrice liked to talk about his perfidy and ingratitude. She had given him the money to organize the band. She had supported him. She had even bought his clothes. Beatrice meant to speak bitterly, but it wasn't in her. The dainty way in which she shaped her words seemed to exclude from them any of the deeper notes of human trouble. She had trouble – plenty of it – but she couldn't get it into her voice. She was thinking of traveling and spoke of beginning a new life in Mexico, Italy or France. She said she had plenty of money although if this was so Moses wondered why she put up with a broken-down cardboard wardrobe and wore such dilapidated furs. Going unexpectedly to her apartment one night, Moses was not let in until he had cooled his heels in the hallway for some time. From the noises inside he figured that she was entertaining another caller and when he was finally let in he wondered if his rival was hidden in the bathroom or stuffed into the wardrobe. But he was not in any way concerned with the life she led and he stayed long enough to smoke a cigarette and then went out to a movie.

It was the kind of relationship that was useful and peaceable enough until Moses began to lose interest and then Beatrice got ardent and demanding. She couldn't reach him at his office but she called his apartment, sometimes nightly, and when he went to see her she would cry and tell him about her artificial and socially ambitious mother and the sternness of Clancy. She moved from her apartment to a hotel and he helped carry her bags. She moved from this hotel to another and he helped her again. One early evening when he had just come in from supper she telephoned to say that she had gotten a singing engagement in Cleveland and would Moses put her on the train? He said that he would. She said she was home and gave him another address and he took a taxi.

The address was a delicatessen. He thought that perhaps her mother, in somewhat reduced circumstances, might have taken an apartment above the store, but there was no apartment entrance and he looked into the delicatessen. There in the back, dressed in a hat and coat and surrounded by suitcases, sat Beatrice. She was crying and her eyes were red. 'Oh, thank you for coming, Moses dear,' she said, as daintily as ever. 'I'll be ready to go in just a minute. I want to catch my breath.'

The room where she sat was the kitchen of the delicatessen. There were two other people there. Beatrice didn't explain or introduce them but Moses recognized one as Beatrice's mother. The resemblance was marked, although she was a very stout woman with a florid and handsome face. She wore an apron over her dress and her shoes were broken. The other woman was thin and old. This was Clancy. Here were the origins of Beatrice's splendid and unhappy memories. Her governess was a delicatessen cook.

The two women were making sandwiches. Now and then they spoke to Beatrice, but she didn't reply. They didn't seem troubled by her tear-stained face or her silence and the atmosphere in the kitchen was of a spent and ancient misunderstanding. The contrast between the stories Beatrice had told him of her unhappy childhood – her elegant and callous mother – and the clear lights of the delicatessen made her dilemma as keen and touching as the troubles of a child.

It was a fine delicatessen. The acid smell of pickles in brine came from some barrels near the door. Fresh sawdust had been scattered on the floor by Clancy – a little of it still clung to her apron – and from the door to the rear of the place, from the floor to the ceiling, were stacked cans of vegetables and fruit, shrimps, stone crabs, lobster meat, soups and chickens. There were baked turkeys and fowl in the glass cases, hams, turban-shaped rolls in the bread bins, sliced cucumbers in vinegar, creamed cheese, rollmops, smoked salmon, whitefish and sturgeon, and from this abundance of acid and appetizing smells poor Beatrice had invented an unhappy childhood with a hardhearted mother and a stern governess.

A little sob came from Beatrice. She took a paper napkin from a container on the table and blew her nose into it. 'If you could get a taxi and take my suitcases out, Moses dear,' she said. 'I'm too weak.' He knew what her suitcases contained – that magpie wardrobe – and when he lifted them they felt like stone. He carried the bags out to the curb and got a cab and Clancy followed with a large paper bag full of sandwiches. 'She'll eat them on the train,' Clancy said to Moses. Beatrice said nothing to either her mother or the cook and in the taxi she sobbed some more and kept blowing her nose into the paper napkin.

Moses carried her bags through the station and put them on the Cleveland train and then Beatrice kissed him good-by daintily and began to cry in earnest. 'Oh dear Moses, I've done something awful, and I have to tell you. You know how they always investigate people, I mean they ask everybody you know about you, and a man came to see me one afternoon and I told him this long story about how you took advantage of me and promised to marry me and took all my money but I had to tell them something because they would have thought I was immoral if I didn't and I'm sorry and I hope nothing bad happens to you.' Then the conductor shouted all aboard and the train pulled out for Cleveland.

CHAPTER 24

And now we come to the wreck of the *Topaze*.

This happened on May 3o – her first voyage of the year. For two weeks Leander and the hired hand – Bentley – had been getting her into shape. The lilac was in bloom and in St Botolphs there were hedges of lilac – there were whole groves and forests of it blooming the length of River Street and growing wild around the cellar holes on the other side of the hill. Going to the wharf in the early mornings Leander saw that the children walking to school all carried branches of lilac. He wondered if they gave it to their teachers, who must have lilac trees themselves, or used it to decorate the classrooms. All that week he saw children carrying lilac branches to school. Early on the morning of the thirtieth he cut some lilac himself and took it to the cemetery and then he went down to the *Topaze*.

Bentley had worked as a hired hand for Leander before. He was a young man who had been to sea and who had a bad name. He was known by everyone to be the illegitimate son of Theophilus Gates by a woman who called herself Mrs Bentley and who lived in a two-family house near the table-silver factory. He was one of those neat, taciturn and competent seamen who tear the world to pieces about once a month. Landladies in many cities had admired him for his cleanliness, sobriety and industry until he would come home some rainy night with three bottles of whisky in a paper bag and drink them, one after the other. Then he would break the windows, piss on the floor and erupt in such a volcano of bitterness and obscenity that the police were usually called and he would start all over again in some other city or furnished room.

Another passenger or crew member that day was Lester Spinet, a blind man who had learned to play the accordion at the Hutchens Institute. It was Honora's idea that he should work on the *Topaze*, and she planned to pay him a salary herself. Leander was naturally pleased to have music on his boat and displeased at himself that he disliked the sound of the blind man's cane and the way he looked. Spinet was a heavy man with a massive head and face canted upward, as if some traces of light still reached his eyes. Spinet and Bentley were waiting for Leander that morning when he got to the wharf and they took on some passengers including an old lady with some lilac branches wrapped in a newspaper. The sky and the river were blue and it was everything, or almost everything, that a holiday should be, although it was a little close or humid and mixed with the smell of lilacs that came down from the river banks was a sour smell like the smell of wet paper. It might storm.

At Travertine he took on more passengers. Dick Hammersmith and his brother were on the wharf in bathing trunks, diving for coins, but there wasn't much business. As he headed for the channel he saw that the beach in front of the Mansion House was crowded and heard the shrieks of a child who was being ducked by her father. 'Daddy isn't going to hurt you, Daddy only wants you to see how nice the water feels,' the man said while the child's cries grew higher and more desperate. He passed through the channel between Hale and Gull rocks into the lovely bay, green inshore, blue in the deeper water and as purple as wine at forty fathoms. The sun shone and the air was warm and fragrant. From the wheelhouse he could see the passengers settling themselves on the forward deck with the charm and innocence of all holiday crowds. They would be dispersed, he knew, once he headed up into the wind, and he took a wide tack after the channel so that he would have their company for as long as possible. There were families with children and families without but very few old people had bought tickets that day. Bucks were photographing their girls and fathers were photographing their wives and children and although Leander had never taken a picture in his life he felt kindly toward these cameramen or anyone else who made a record of such a lighthearted thing as the crossing to Nangasakit. There was among the passengers, he guessed, a man with a wig or toupee, and turning the boat up into the wind he watched the stranger grab for his hairpiece and secure it to his head with a cap. At the same time many women grabbed for their skirts and hats, but the damage was done. The fresh breeze scattered them all. They gathered up their papers and their comic books and carrying deck chairs went over to the leeward side or back to the stern and Leander was alone.

The fact of his aloneness reminded Leander of Helen Rutherford, whom he had seen the night before. He had worked late on the boat and had gone into Grimes' bakery to get his supper. While he was eating he looked up and saw her standing at the window, reading the menu that was posted there. He got up from the table and went out to speak with her – he didn't know what he would say – but as soon as she recognized him she backed away from him in fear, saying, 'Get away from me, get away from me.'

In the spring dusk the square was deserted. They were alone. 'I only want to . . .' Leander began.

'You want to hurt me, you want to hurt me.'

'No.'

'Yes, you do. You want to harm me. Daddy said you would. Daddy said for me to be careful.'

'Please listen to me.'

'Don't you move. Don't you come near me or I'll call the police officer.'

Then she turned and walked up the Cartwright Block as if the soft air of evening were full of flints and missiles – a queer, frightened limp – and when she had turned up a side street Leander went back to the bakery to pay for his supper.

'Who's the nut?' the waitress asked. 'She's been around here telling everybody she's got this secret that will set the river on fire. Oh, I hate nuts.'

When Bentley came up to the wheelhouse, Leander saw that he had been drinking. Considering his own habits he had a long nose for the smell of rotted fruit that clung to the lips of someone else. Bentley still preserved the preternatural neatness of a man who is often tempted and deeply familiar with sloth. His curly hair shone with grease, his pale face was clean shaven with razor nicks on his neck and he had washed and scrubbed his denims until they were threadbare and smelled nicely of soap, but mixed with the smell of soap was the smell of whisky and Leander wondered if he would have to make the return voyage alone.

He could see the white walls of Nangasakit then and hear the music of the merry-go-round. On the wharf there was an old man with a card in his hat advertising the four-, five- and six-course shore dinners at the Nangasakit House. Leander stepped out of the wheelhouse and shouted his own refrain. 'Return voyage at three thirty. Return voyage at three thirty. Please give yourself plenty of time to get back to the boat. Return voyage at three thirty. Please give yourself plenty of time to get back to the boat. . . .' The last to leave the boat was Spinet, who tapped his way down the wharf with a stick. Leander went to his cabin, ate a sandwich and fell sound asleep.

When he woke it was a little before three. The air was quite dark and he saw that it would storm. He poured some water into a basin and splashed his face. Going out onto the deck he saw a fog bank a mile or so out to sea. He wanted a hand on the return voyage and he put on his cap and walked up to Ray's Café, where Bentley usually did his drinking. Bentley was in no shape at all. He was not even in the bar but was sitting in a small back room with a bottle and a glass. 'I guess you muss think I'm drunk,' he began, but Leander only sat down wearily, wondering where he could get a deck hand in fifteen minutes. 'You think I'm no good, but I got this girl out in Fort Sill, Oklahoma,' Bentley said. 'She thinks I'm good. I call her parrot. She's got this big nose. I'm going back to Fort Sill, Oklahoma, and love my parrot. She's got this two thousand dollars in the bank she wants to give me. You don't believe me, do you? You think I'm no good. You think I'm drunk, but I got this girl out in Fort Sill, Oklahoma. She loves me. She wants to give me this two thousand dollars. I call her parrot. She's got this big nose. . . .' It was not his fault, Leander knew, that he was a bastard, and it might not even be his fault that he was a cheerless bastard, but Leander needed a deck hand and he went out to the bar and asked Marylyn if her kid brother would want to pick up a dollar for the return voyage. She said sure, sure the kid was crazy to make a nickel, and she telephoned her mother and her mother opened the kitchen door and shouted for the boy but he couldn't be found and Leander walked back to his ship.

He watched his passengers come aboard with interest and some tenderness. They carried trophies – things they had won – thin blankets that would not keep the autumn cold from your bones; glass dishes for peanuts and jelly; and animals made out of oilcloth and paper, some of them with diamond eyes. There was a pretty girl with a rose in her hair and a man and his wife and three children, all of them wearing shirts made of the same flowered cloth. Helen Rutherford was the last to come aboard, but he was in the wheelhouse and didn't see her. She wore the same pot-shaped hat, ornamented with shuttlecock feathers, had the same seashell pinned to her breast and carried the old brief case.

Helen Rutherford had been trying to sell Dr Bartholomew's wisdom in the cottages of Nangasakit for a week. On the morning of this, her last day, she had wandered into a neighborhood that seemed more substantial than anything else in the little resort. The houses were small – no bigger than bungalows – and yet all of them declaring by their mansards and spool railings and their porch latticework arched like the vents to a donjon that these were not summerhouses; these were places where men and women centered their lives and where children were conceived and reared. The sight might have cheered her if it hadn't been for the dogs. The place was full of dogs; and it had begun to seem to Helen that her life was a martyrdom to dogs. As soon as her footsteps were heard the dogs began to bark, filling her with timidity and self-pity. From morning until night dogs sniffed at her heels, snapped at her ankles, bit the skirts of her best gray coat and tried to run off with her brief case. As soon as she entered a strange neighborhood dogs that had been sunning themselves peacefully in clothesyards or sleeping by stoves, dogs who had been chewing bones or daydreaming or sporting with one another would give up their peaceful occupations and sound the alarm. She had dreamed many times that she was torn to pieces by dogs. It seemed to her that she was a pilgrim and the soles of her shoes were so thin that she was virtually barefoot. She was surrounded, day after day, by strange houses and people and hostile beasts, and like a pilgrim she was now and then given a cup of tea and a piece of stale cake. Her lot was worse than a pilgrim's for God alone knew in which direction her Rome, her Vatican would appear.

The first dog to come at her that day was a collie who snarled at her heels, a sound that frightened her more than a loud, straightforward bark. The collie was joined by a small dog who seemed friendly, but you could never tell. It was a friendly-seeming dog who had torn her coat. A black dog joined these two and then a police dog, woofing and belling like a hound from hell. She walked half a block, trailed by four dogs, and then all but the collie went back to their occupations. The collie was still a little behind, snarling at her heels. She hoped, she prayed, that someone would open a door and call him home. She turned to speak to him. 'Go home, doggie,' she said. 'Go home, good doggie, go home, nice doggie.' Then he sprang at her coat sleeve and she struck at him with her brief case. Her heart was beating so that she thought she would die. The collie sank his teeth into the old leather of the brief case and began a tug of war. 'Leave that poor lady alone, you nasty cur,' Helen heard someone say. A stranger appeared at her right with a kettle of water and let the dog have it. The dog went howling up the street. 'Now you come into the house for a few minutes,' the stranger said. 'You come in and tell me what you're selling and rest your feet.'

Helen thanked the stranger and followed her into one of the little houses. Her savior was a short woman with eyes of a fine, pale blue and a very red face. She introduced herself as Mrs Brown and in order to receive Helen she took off an apron and hung it over the back of a chair. She was a little woman with an extravagantly curved figure. Her breasts and buttocks stretched the cloth of her house dress. 'Now tell me what it is that you're selling,' she said, 'and I'll see if I want any.'

'I'm an accredited representative for Dr Bartholomew's Institute for Self-Improvement,' Helen said. 'There are still a few subscriptions open for eligible men and women. Dr Bartholomew feels that a college education is not a requirement. He feels . . .'

'Well, that's good,' Mrs Brown said, 'because I'm not what you would call an educated woman. I graduated from the Nangasakit High School, which is one of the best high schools in the world – known all over the world – but the amount of education I got through learning is nothing to the amount of education that runs in my blood. I'm directly descended from Madame de Staël and many other well-educated and distinguished men and women. I suppose you don't believe me, I suppose you think I'm crazy, but if you'll notice that picture on the wall – it's a picture post card of Madame de Staël – and then notice my own profile you'll see the resemblance, no doubt.'

'There are many four-colored portraits of famous historical men and women,' Helen said.

'I'll stand right up beside the portrait so's you'll be sure to see the resemblance,' Mrs Brown said, and she went across the room and stood beside the card. 'I guess you must have seen the resemblance by now. You see the resemblance, don't

you? You must see it. Everybody else does. A man came by
here yesterday selling hot-water heaters and told me I looked
enough like Madame de Staël to be her twin. Said we looked
like identical twins.' She smoothed her house dress and then
went back and sat on the edge of her chair. 'It's being directly
descended from Madame de Staël and other distinguished men
and women,' she said, 'that accounts for the education in my
blood. I have very expensive tastes. If I go into a store to buy
a pocketbook and there's a pocketbook for one dollar and a
pocketbook for three dollars my eye goes straight to the one
that costs three dollars. I've preferred expensive things all my
life. Oh, I had great expectations! My great-grandfather was
an ice merchant. He made a fortune selling ice to the niggers
in Honduras. He wasn't a man to put much stock in banks
and he took all his money to California and put it into gold
bullion and coming back his ship sank in a storm off Cape
Hatteras, gold and all. Of course it's still there – two and a
half million dollars of it – and it's all mine, but do you think
the banks around here would loan me the money to have it
raised? Not on your life. There's over two and one half million
dollars of my very own lying there in the sea and there's not
a man or woman in this part of the country with enough
gumption or sense of honor to loan me the money to raise
my own inheritance. Last week I went up to St Botolphs to
see this rich old Honora Wapshot and she . . .'

'Is she related to Leander Wapshot?'

'She's the very same blood. Do you know him?'

'He's my father,' Helen said.

'Well, for land's sakes, if Leander Wapshot's your father what
are you doing going from door to door, trying to sell books?'

'He's disowned me.' Helen began to cry.

'Oh, he has, has he? Well, that's easier said than done. It's
crossed my mind to disown my own children, but I don't
know how to go about it. You know what my daughter –
my very own daughter – did on Thanksgiving Day? We all
sat down to the table and then she picked up this turkey, this
twelve-pound turkey, and she threw it onto the floor and she

jumped up and down on it and she kicked it from here to there and then she took the dish with the cranberry sauce in it and she threw it all over the ceiling – cranberry sauce all over the ceiling – and then she began to cry. Well, I thought of disowning her then and there but it's easier said than done and if I can't disown my own daughter how's it Leander Wapshot can disown his? Well,' she said, getting to her feet and tying on her apron again, 'I've got to get back to my housework now and I can't spend any more time talking but my advice to you is to go to that old Leander Wapshot and tell him to buy you a decent pair of shoes. Why, when I saw you walking down the street with the dogs behind you and the holes in your shoes I didn't feel it would be Christian not to come to your help but now that I know you're a Wapshot it seems that your own flesh and blood could come to your aid. Good-by.'

Leander blew the warning whistle for his last voyage. From the wheelhouse he could see the rain falling onto the roller-coaster. He saw Charlie Matterson and his twin brother throw a tarpaulin over the last section of cars to come down. The merry-go-round was still turning. He saw the passengers in one of the boats of the Red Mill look up in surprise, as they were debouched from the mouth of a plaster-of-Paris ogre, to find it raining. He saw a young man gaily cover his girl's head with a newspaper. He saw people in the cottages up on the bluff lighting their kerosene lamps. He thought how sad it was that on this, their first trip away from home in so many years, it should rain. There were no stoves or fireplaces in the cottages. There was no escape from the damp and the doleful sounds of the rain for the matchboard walls of the cottages, salt soaked and tight, would resound when you touched them like the skin of a drum and you would hardly have settled down to a two-handed game of whist before the roof began to leak. There would be a leak in the kitchen and another over the card table and another over the bed. The vacationers could wait for the mailman, but who would write to them? – and they couldn't write letters themselves for all their envelopes would be stuck together. Only the lovers, their bedposts jingling loudly and merrily, would be spared this gloom. On the beach Leander saw the last parties surrender, calling to one another to remember the blanket, remember the bottle opener, remember the thermos and the picnic basket, until there was no one left but an old man who liked to swim in the rain and a young man who liked to walk in the rain and whose head was full of Swinburne and whose nickname was Bananas. Leander saw the Japanese, who sold fans and back scratchers, take in his silk and paper lanterns. He saw people standing in restaurant doorways and waitresses at windows. A waiter took in the naked tables of the Pergola Cantonese Restaurant and he saw a hand part some window curtains in the Nangasakit House, but he couldn't see the face that looked out. He saw how the waves, that had been riding in briskly, subsided in the rain so that they barely lapped the shore. The sea was still. Then the old man, who was standing waist deep in the water, suddenly turned and struggled up the beach, feeling the inward pull of the storm sea. He saw the gladness with which Bananas was watching these signs of danger. Then the sea, with a roar of stone, drew out beyond the line of sand to the stony beginnings of the harbor bottom, forming a wave that, when it broke (the first of a barrage that would sound all night), shook the beach and scooted up after the heels of the old man. He took off the lines and blew the whistle. Spinet started to play 'Jingle Bells' as the *Topaze* went out to sea.

There was a channel at Nangasakit – a granite breakwater bearded with sea grass and a bell buoy rocking in the southwest sea, white foam spilling over the float as it tipped. The bell, Leander knew, could on this wind be heard inland. It could be heard by the card players rearranging pots and pans under their leaky roof, by the old ladies in the Nangasakit House and even by the lovers above the merry jingling of their bedposts. It was the only bell Leander had ever heard in his dreams. He loved all bells: dinner bells, table bells, doorbells, the bell from Antwerp and the bell from Altoona had all heartened and consoled him but this was the only bell that chimed on the dark side of his mind. Now the charming music fell astern, fainter and fainter, lost in the creaking of the old hull and the noise of seas breaking against her bow. Out in the bay it was rough.

She took the waves head on, like an old rocking horse. Waves broke over the glass of the wheelhouse so that Leander had to keep one hand on the windshield wiper to see. The water pouring down the decks began to come in at the cabin. It was dirty weather. Leander thought of the passengers – the girl with the rose in her hair and the man with three children, all wearing shirts cut of the same cloth as his wife's summer dress. And what about the passengers themselves, sitting in the cabin? Were they frightened? They were, nine times out of ten, their fear clothed lightly in idle speculation. They fished for their key rings and their small change, gave their privates a hitch and, if they had some talisman, a silver dollar or a St Christopher medal, they rubbed it with their fingers. St Christopher, be with us now! They readjusted their garters if they wore them, tightened the knots in their shoelaces and their neckties and wondered why their sense of reality should seem suspended. They thought of pleasant things: wheat fields and winter twilights, when five minutes after the lemony yellow light in the west was gone the snow began to fall, or hiding jelly beans under the sofa cushions on Easter Eve. The young man looked at the girl with the rose in her hair, remembering how generously she had spread her legs for him and now how fair and gentle she seemed.

In the middle of the bay Leander turned the boat toward Travertine. It was the worst of the trip, and he was worried. The following sea punished her stern. Her screw shook the hull at the crest of every wave and in the hollow she slipped to port. He set his bow on Gull Rock, which he could see clearly then, the gull droppings on top and the sea grass fanning out as the waves mounted and swallowed the granite pile. Beyond the channel he would be all right with nothing ahead of him but the run up the calm river to home. He put his mind on this. He could hear the deck chairs smashing against the stern rail and she had taken in so much water that she heeled. Then the rudder chain broke with the noise of a shot and he felt the power of the helm vanish into thin air beneath his hands.

There was a jury rudder in the stern. He thought quickly enough. He put her into half speed and stepped into the cabin. Helen saw him, and she began to shriek. 'He's a devil, he's a devil from hell that one there. He'll drown us. He's afraid of me. For eighteen weeks, nineteen on Monday, I've been out in all weathers. He's afraid of me. I have information in my possession that could put him into the electric chair. He'll drown us.' It was not fear that stopped him, but a stunning memory of her mother's loveliness – the farm near Franconia and haying on a thundery day. He went back into the wheelhouse and a second later the *Topaze* rammed Gull Rock. Her bow caved in like an egg shell. Leander reached for the whistle cord and blew the distress signal.

They heard his whistle in what had been the parlor and was now the bar of the Mansion House and wondered what Leander was up to. He had always been prodigal with his whistle, tooting it for children's birthday parties and wedding anniversaries or at the sight of an old friend. It was one of the waiters in the kitchen – a stranger to the place – who recognized the distress signal and ran out onto the porch and gave the alarm. They heard him at the boat club and someone started up the old launch. As soon as Leander saw the boat leave the wharf he went back to the cabin, where most of the passengers were putting on life jackets, and told them the news. They sat quietly until the boat came alongside. He helped them aboard, including Spinet, including Helen, who was sobbing, and the boat chugged off.

He unscrewed the compass box from its stand and got his binoculars and a bottle of bourbon out of his locker. Then he went up to the bow to see the damage. The hole was a big one and the following sea was worrying her on the rocks. As he watched she began to ease off the rocks and he could feel the bow settle. He walked back toward the stern. He felt very tired – almost sleepy. His animal spirits seemed collapsed and his breathing, the beating of his heart felt retarded. His eyes felt heavy. In the distance he saw a dory coming out to get him rowed by a young man – a stranger – and through this feeling of torpor or weariness he felt as if he watched the approach of someone of uncommon beauty – an angel, or a ghost of himself when he had been young and full of mettle. Tough luck, old-timer, the stranger said, and the illusion of ghosts and angels vanished.

Leander got into the dory. He watched the *Topaze* ease off the rocks and start up the channel herself with the sea pounding at her stern; and derelict and forsaken she seemed, like those inextinguishable legends of underwater civilizations and buried gold, to pierce the darkest side of his mind with an image of man's inestimable loneliness. She was heading through the channel, but she wouldn't make it. As each wave pushed her forward, she lost some buoyancy. Water was breaking over her bow. And then, with more grace than she had usually sailed, her stern upended – there was a loud clatter of deck chairs knocked helter-skelter along the sides of her cabin and down went the *Topaze* to the bottom of the sea.

CHAPTER 25

Leander wrote to both his sons. He did not know that Coverly was in the Pacific and it took three weeks for his letter to be forwarded to Island 93. Moses didn't get his father's letter at all. He was fired as a security risk ten days after Beatrice left for Cleveland. It was at a time when these dismissals were summary and unexplained and if there was some court of appeal Moses did not, at that time, have the patience or the common sense to seek it out. An hour after he had received his discharge he was driving north with all his possessions in the back of his car. The anonymity of his discharge gave it oracular proportions, as if some tree or stone or voice from a cave had put the finger on him, and the pain of being condemned or expelled by a veiled force may have accounted for his rage. He was far from the green pastures of common sense. He was angry at what had been done to him and angry at himself for having failed to come to reasonable terms with the world and he was deeply anxious about his parents, for if the news should get back to Honora that he had been discharged for reasons of security he knew they would suffer.

What he did was to go fishing. It may have been that he wanted to recapture the pleasures of his trips to Langely with Leander. Fishing was the only occupation he could think of that might refresh his common sense. He drove straight from Washington to a trout pond in the Poconos that he had visited before and where he was able to rent a cabin or shack that was as dilapidated as the camp at Langely. He ate some supper, drank a pint of whisky and went for a swim in the cold lake. All this made him feel better and he went to bed early, planning to get up before dawn and fish in the Lakanana River.

He was up at five and drove north to the river, as anxious to be the first fisherman out as Leander had been anxious to be the first man in the woods. The sky was just beginning to fill with light. He was disappointed and perplexed then when a car ahead of him turned off and parked on the road shoulder that led to the stream. Then the driver of the car ahead hurried out of his car and looked over his shoulder at Moses in such agony and panic that Moses wondered – so soon after dawn – if he had crossed the path of a murderer. Then the stranger unbuckled his belt, dropped his trousers and relieved himself in full view of the morning. Moses gathered up his tackle and smiled at the stranger, happy to see that he was not another trout fisherman. The stranger smiled at Moses for his own reasons; and he took the path to the water and didn't see another fisherman that day.

Lakanana Pond emptied into the river and the water, regulated by a dam, was deep and turbulent and in many places over a man's head. The sharp fall of the land and the granite bed of the stream made it a place where there was nowhere a respite from the loud noise of water. Moses caught one trout in the morning and two more late in the day. Here and there a bridle path from the Lakanana Inn ran parallel to the stream and a few riders hacked by but it was not until late in the day that any of them stopped to ask Moses what he had caught.

The sun by then was below the trees and the early dark seemed to deepen the resonance of the stream. It was time for Moses to go and he was taking in his line and putting away his flies when he heard the hoofs and the creaking leather of some riders. A middle-aged couple stopped to ask about his luck while he was pulling off his boots. It was the urbanity of the couple that struck Moses – they looked so terribly out of place. They were both of them heavy and gray-headed – the woman dumpy and the man choleric, short-winded and obese. It had been a warm day but they were dressed correctly in dark riding clothes – bowlers, sticks, tattersalls and so forth. All of this must have been very uncomfortable. 'Well, good luck,' the woman said in the cheerful, cracked voice of middle age, and turned her horse away from the stream. Out of the corner of his eye Moses saw the horse rear but by the time he turned his head so much dust had been raised by the scuffle of hoofs that he didn't see how she fell. He ran up the bank and got the fractious horse by the bridle as her husband began to roar: 'Help, help. She's dead, she's dead, she's been killed.' The horse reared again while Moses' hand was on the bridle. He let go and the hack galloped off. 'I'll go for help, I'll go for help,' the husband roared. 'There's a farm back there.' He cantered off to the north and the dust settled, leaving Moses with what seemed to be a dead stranger.

She was on her knees, face downward in the dirt, the tails of her coat parted over the broad, worn seat of her britches and her boots toed in like a child's, so stripped of her humanity, so defeated – Moses remembered the earnest notes of her voice – in her attempt to enjoy the early summer day, that he felt a flash of repugnance. Then he went to her and more out of consideration for his own feelings than anything else – more out of his desire to return to her the form of a woman than to save her life – he straightened out her legs and she rolled with a thump onto her back. He rolled up his coat and put it under her head. A cut in her forehead, over the eye, was bleeding and Moses got some water and washed the cut, pleased to be occupied. She was breathing, he noticed, but this exhausted his medical knowledge. He knelt beside her wondering in what form and when help would come. He lighted a cigarette and looked at the stranger's face – pasty and round and worn it seemed with such anxieties as cooking, catching trains and buying useful presents at Christmas. It was a face that seemed to state its history plainly – she was one of two sisters, she had no children, she could be inflexible about neatness and she probably collected glass animals or English coffee cups in a small way. Then he heard hoofs and leather and her bereaved husband bore down in a cloud of dust. 'There's nobody at the farm. I've wasted so much time. She ought to be in an oxygen tent. She probably needs a blood transfusion. We've got to get an ambulance.' Then he knelt down beside her and put his head on her breast, crying, 'Oh my darling, my love, my sweet, don't leave me, don't leave me.'

Then Moses ran up the path to his car and, driving it a little way through the woods, he got it onto the loose dirt of the bridle path where the man still knelt by his wife. Then, opening the door, they managed together to lift her into the car. He started back for the road, the wheels of the car spinning in the loose dirt, but he was able to keep it moving and was cheered when they got onto the black-top road. There were choking and grunting sounds of grief from the back seat. 'She's dying, she's dying,' the stranger sobbed. 'If she lives I'll repay you. Money is no consideration. Please hurry.'

'You know you both seem pretty old for horseback riding,' Moses said.

He knew there was a hospital in the next village and he made good time until he got stuck, on the narrow road, behind a slow-moving truck loaded with live chickens. Moses blew his horn but this only made the truck driver more predatory and how could Moses communicate to him that the thread of a woman's life might depend on his consideration? He passed the truck at the crown of a hill but this only excited the driver's malevolence and, roaring downhill, his chicken crates swaying wildly from side to side, he tried, unsuccessfully, to repass Moses. They had come down at last into the leafy streets of the village and the road to the hospital. Many people were walking at the side of the road and then Moses saw signs nailed to the trees advertising a hospital lawn party. They were out of luck. The hospital was surrounded by the booths, lights and music of a country fair.

A policeman stopped them when they tried to approach the hospital and waved them toward a parking lot. 'We want to get to the hospital,' Moses shouted. The policeman leaned toward them. He was deaf. 'We have a woman here who is dying,' the stranger cried loudly. 'This is a matter of life and death.' Moses got past the policeman and through the fair, approaching a brick building, darkened by many shade trees. The place was shaped like a Victorian mansion and may have been one, modified now by fire escapes and a brick smokestack. Moses got out of the car and ran through an emergency entrance into a room that was empty. He went from there into a hall where he met a gray-haired nurse carrying a tray. 'I have an emergency in my car,' he said. There was no kindliness in her face. She gave him that appalling look of bitterness that we exchange when we are too tired, or too exacerbated by our own ill luck, to care whether our neighbors live or die. 'What is the nature of the emergency?' she asked airily. Another nurse appeared. She was no younger but she was not so tired. 'She was thrown by a horse, she's unconscious,' Moses said. 'Horses!' the old nurse exclaimed. 'Dr Howard has just come in,' the second nurse said. 'I'll get him now.'

A few minutes later a doctor came down the hall with a second nurse and they wheeled a table out of the emergency room down a ramp to the car and Moses and the doctor lifted the unconscious woman onto this. They accomplished this in a summer twilight, surrounded by the voices of hawkers and the sounds of music that came from the fair beyond the trees. 'Oh, can't somebody stop this?' the stranger asked, meaning the music. 'I'm Charles Cutter. I'll pay any amount of money. Send them home. Send them home. I'll pay for it. Tell them to stop the music at least. She needs quiet.'

'We couldn't do that,' the doctor said quietly, and with a marked upcountry accent. 'That's how we raise the money to keep the hospital running.' In the hospital they began to cut off the woman's clothes and Moses went into the hallway, followed by her husband. 'You'll stay, you'll stay a little while with me, won't you?' he asked Moses. 'She's all I have and if she dies, if she dies I don't know what I'll do.' Moses said that he would stay and wandered down the ball to an empty waiting room. A large, bronze plaque on the door said that the waiting room was the gift of Sarah P. Watkins and her sons and daughters, but it was difficult to see what the Watkins family had given. There were three pieces of imitation-leather furniture, a table and a collection of old magazines. Moses waited here until Mr Cutter returned. 'She's alive,' he sobbed, 'she's alive. Thank God. Her leg and her arm are broken and she has a concussion. I've called my secretary and asked them to send a specialist on from New York. They don't know whether she'll live or not. They won't know for twenty-four hours. Oh, she's such a lovely person. She's so kind and lovely.'

'Your wife will be all right,' Moses said.

'She isn't my wife,' Mr Cutter sobbed. 'She's so kind and lovely. My wife isn't anything like that. We've had such hard times, both of us. We've never asked for very much. We haven't even been together very much. It couldn't be retribution, could it? It couldn't be retribution. We've never harmed anyone. We've taken these little trips each year. It's the only time we ever have together. It couldn't be retribution.' He dried his tears and cleaned his spectacles and went back down the hall.

A young nurse came to the door, looking out at the carnival and the summer evening, and a doctor joined her.

'B_2 thinks he's dying,' the nurse said. 'He wants a priest.'

'I called Father Bevier,' the doctor said. 'He's out.' He put a hand on the nurse's slender back and let it fall along her buttocks.

'Oh, I could use a little of that,' the nurse said cheerfully.

'So could I,' the doctor said.

He continued to stroke her buttocks and desire seemed to make the nurse plaintive and in a human way much finer and the doctor, who had looked very tired, seemed refreshed. Then, from the dark interior of the place, there was a wordless roar, a spitting grunt, extorted either by extreme physical misery or the collapse of reasonable hope. The doctor and the nurse separated and disappeared in the dark at the end of the hall. The grunt rose to a scream, a shriek, and to escape it Moses walked out of the building and crossed the grass to the edge of the lawn. He was on high land and his view took in the mountains, blackened then by an afterglow – a brilliant yellow that is seen in lower country only on the coldest nights of February.

In the trees on his left the fair or carnival had hit its gentle, countrified stride. An orchestra on a platform was playing 'Smiles' and on the second chorus one of the players put down his instrument and sang a verse through a megaphone. Strings of lights – white and faded reds and yellows – were hung from booth to booth to light, with the faint candle power of these arrangements, the dark of the maples. The noise of voices was not loud and the men talking up hamburgers and fortune's wheel called with no real insistence. He walked over to a booth and bought a paper cup of coffee from a pretty country girl. When she had given him his change she moved the sugar bowl an inch this way and that, looked at the doughnut jar with a deep sigh and pulled at her apron. 'You're a stranger?' she asked. He said that he was. The girl moved down the counter to wait on some other people who were complaining about the chilly mountain dusk.

In the next booth a young man was pitching baseballs at a pyramid of wooden milk bottles. His aim and his speed were superb. He stared at the milk bottles, drawing back a little and narrowing his eyes like a rifleman, and then winged a ball at them with the energy of sheer malevolence. Down they came, again and again, and a small crowd of girls and bucks gathered to watch the performance but when it was ended and the pitcher turned toward them they said so long, so long, Charlie, so long, and drifted away, arm in arm. He seemed to be friendless.

Beyond the baseball pitcher there was a booth selling flowers that had been picked in the village gardens and there were wheels and a bingo game and the wooden stand where the musicians continued without a break their selection of dance music. Moses was surprised to find them so old. The pianist was old, the saxophone player was bent and gray and the drummer must have weighed three hundred pounds, and they seemed attached to their instruments by the rites, conveniences and habits of a long marriage.

When they had finished their last set a man announced some local talent and Moses saw a child, at the edge of the platform, waiting to go on. She seemed to be a child but when the band played her fanfare she lifted up her hands, shuffled into the light and began a laborious tap dance, counting time painfully and throwing out to the audience, now and then, a leering smile. The taps on her silver shoes made a metallic clang and shook the lumber of the platform and she seemed to have left her youth in the shadows. Powdered, rouged, absorbed in the mechanics of her dance and the enjoinder to seem flirtatious, her freshness was gone and all the bitterness and disappointments of a lascivious middle age seemed to sit on her thin shoulders. At the end she bowed to the little applause, smiled her tart smile once more and ran into the shadows where her mother was waiting with a coat to put over her shoulders and a few words of encouragement and when she stepped back into the shadows Moses saw that she was no more than twelve or thirteen.

He threw his paper cup into a can, and finishing his circuit of the carnival saw, walking through the deep grass smell and the summer gloom, a group, a family perhaps, in which there was a woman wearing a yellow skirt. The color of the skirt set up in him a yearning, a pang that put his teeth on edge, and he remembered that he had once loved a girl who had a skirt of the same color although he could not remember her name.

'I want a specialist, a brain specialist,' Moses heard his friend shouting when he returned to the hospital. 'Charter a plane if it's necessary. Money is no consideration. If he wants a consultant, tell him to bring a consultant. Yes. Yes.' He was using a telephone in an office across the hall from the waiting room that had been given by the Watkins family and where it had grown dark without anyone's bothering to turn on a lamp. Only a few lights seemed to burn in the hospital at all. The bereaved and elderly lover sat among covered typewriters and adding machines and when he had finished his conversation he looked up to Moses and either because the light caught his spectacles or because his mood had changed, he seemed very officious. 'I want you to consider yourself on my payroll as of this morning,' he said to Moses. 'If you have other engagements to fulfill you can cancel them, confident that I will more than make this worth your while. The hospital has given me a room for the night and I want you to go back to the inn and get my toilet articles. I've made out a list,' he said, passing such a list to Moses. 'Estimate your mileage and keep track of the time and I will see that you are amply reimbursed.' Then he picked up the telephone and asked for long distance and Moses stepped out into the dark hall.

He had nothing better to do and he was glad to drive back to the inn, not so much from a commendable sense of charity and helpfulness as from his desire to draw into a sensible perspective the events of the last few hours. Back at the inn he gave the manager – like a true Wapshot – the most meager account of what had happened. 'She was in an accident,' he said. He went upstairs to the room that had been occupied by poor Mr Cutter and his paramour. All the things on the list were easy to find – everything but a bottle of rye but after looking in the medicine cabinet and behind the books in the shelves he looked under the bed and found a well-stocked bar. He had a drink of Scotch himself in a toothbrush glass. Back at the hospital Mr Cutter was still on the telephone. He put his hand over the mouthpiece. 'Now you get some sleep, my boy,' he said mingling paternalism with officiousness. 'If you don't have a place, go back to the inn and ask them to give you a room. Report back here at nine o'clock. Remember that money is no consideration. You're on my payroll.' Moses went back to the bridle path to get his fishing tackle, which he found unharmed except for a fall of dew, and spent the night in his rented shack.

CHAPTER 26

The next day at dusk, Mr Cutter's paramour regained consciousness, and in the morning Moses arranged to have his car driven to New York and flew to the city with Mr Cutter and the patient in a chartered ambulance plane. He was not quite sure where he stood on Mr Cutter's payroll, but he had nothing better to do. He went to Coverly's address as soon as he got to New York, not knowing that his brother was on Island 93. Betsey was there and he took her out to dinner. She was not the girl he would have married, but he found her likable enough. A day or so later he had an interview with Mr Cutter and a few days later he was enrolled in the Fiduciary Trust Company Bond School at a better salary than he had received in Washington and with a more brilliant future. The letter Leander wrote to him in Washington lay on the hall floor of his apartment and it went like this:

'Slight mishap to Topaze on 30th. All hands removed with dry feet. Sank in channel and was removed as navigational hazard by Coast Guard on Tues. Beached and patched at Mansion House. She's at your mooring now (Tern's) and has been at same since mishap. Afloat but not seaworthy. Beecher estimates cost of repairs at $400. Till empty here and Honora very unco-operative. Can you help? Please try my son and see what you can do. These are d——d difficult days for your old father.

'Topaze gone, how will I fare? Geezer as old as me begins to cherish his time on this earth but with Topaze gone days pass without purpose, meaning, color, form, appetite, glory, squalor, regret, desire, pleasure or pain. Dusk. Dawn. All the same. Feel hopeful sometimes in early morning but soon discouraged. Sole excitement is to listen to horse races on radio. If I had a stake could quickly recoup price to repair Topaze. Lack even small sum for respectable bet.

'Was generous giver myself. On several occasions gave large sums to needy strangers. One-hundred-dollar bill to cab starter at Parker House. Fifty dollars to old lady selling lavender at Park Street Church. Eighty dollars to stranger in restaurant who claimed son needed operation. Other donations forgotten. Cast bread upon waters, so to speak. No refund as of today. Tasteless to remind you but never spared the horses with family. Extra suit of sail for Tern. Three hundred dollars for dahlia bulbs. English shoes, mushrooms, hothouse posies, boat club dues and groaning board consumed much of windward anchor.

'Try to help old father if within means. If not, feel out acquaintances. There is one easy spender in every group of men. Sometimes gambler. Topaze good investment. Has shown substantial profit for every season, but one. Grand business expected in Nangasakit this year. Good chance of returning loan by August. Regret handkerchief tone of letter. Laugh and the world laughs with you. Weep and you weep alone.'

The mooring that Leander mentioned was a mushroom anchor and chain in the river at the foot of the garden, and the old launch could be seen from there. Mrs Wapshot stared at the *Topaze* one afternoon when she was picking sage. She felt a stirring in her mind and her body that might mean that she was going to have a vision. Now in fact so many of Mrs Wapshot's imaginings had come true that she was entitled to call them visions. Years and years ago, when she was walking by Christ Church, some force of otherness seemed to stop her by the vacant lot that adjoined the church and she had a vision of a parish house – red brick with small-paned casement windows and a neat lawn. She had begun her agitation for a parish house that afternoon and a year and a half later her vision – brick for brick – was a reality. She had dreamed up horse troughs, good works and pleasant journeys to have them materialize oftener than not. Now, coming back from the garden with a bouquet of sage, she looked down the path to the river where the *Topaze* lay at her mooring.

It was a gray afternoon along the coast, but not an unexciting one – there might be a storm, and the prospect seemed to please her, as if she held on her tongue, like a peppercorn, the flavor of the old port and the stormy dusk. The air was salty and she could hear the sea breaking at Travertine. The *Topaze* was dark, of course, dark and she seemed unsalvageable in that light – one of those hulks that we see moored by coal yards in city rivers, kept afloat through some misguided tenderness or hope, wearing sometimes a For Sale sign and sometimes the last habitation of some crazy old hermit whose lair is pasted up with pearly-skinned and spread-legged beauties and whose teeth are pulled. The first thing that crossed her mind when she saw the dark and empty ship was that she would not sail again. She would not cross the bay again. Then Mrs Wapshot had her vision. She saw the ship berthed at the garden wharf, her hull shining with fresh paint and her cabin full of light. She saw, by turning her head, a dozen or more cars parked in the cornfield. She even saw that some of them had out-of-state license plates. She saw a sign nailed to the elm by the path: VISIT THE SS TOPAZE, THE ONLY FLOATING GIFT SHOPPE IN NEW ENGLAND. In her mind she took the path down the garden and crossed the wharf to board the ship. Her cabin was all new paint (the life preservers were gone), and lamps burned on many small tables, illuminating a cargo of ash trays, cigarette lighters, playing-card cases, wire arrangements for holding flowers, vases, embroidery, hand-painted drinking glasses and cigarette boxes that played 'Tales from Vienna Woods' when you opened them. Her vision was in detail and splendidly lighted and warm as well, for she saw a Franklin stove at one end of the cabin with a fire in the grate and the perfume of wood smoke mingled with the

smell of sachets, Japanese linen and here and there the smell
of tallow from a lighted candle. The SS *Topaze,* she thought
again, The Only Floating Gift Shoppe in New England, and
then she let the stormy dusk reclaim the dark ship and went
very happily into the house.

CHAPTER 27

Leander did not understand why Theophilus Gates would not lend him enough money to have the bow of the *Topaze* repaired while he would loan Sarah all the money she wanted to turn the old launch into a floating gift shop. That is what happened. The day after her vision Sarah went to the bank and the day after that the carpenters came and began to repair the wharf. The salesmen began to arrive – three and four a day – and Sarah began to stock the *Topaze,* spending money, as she said herself, like an inebriated sailor. Her happiness or rapture was genuine although it was hard to see why she should find such joy in a gross of china dogs with flowers painted on their backs, their paws shaped in such a way that they could hold cigarettes. There may have been some vengefulness in her enthusiasm – some deep means of expressing her feelings about the independence and the sainthood of her sex. She bad never been so happy. She had signs painted: VISIT THE SS TOPAZE, THE ONLY FLOATING GIFT SHOPPE IN NEW ENGLAND, and posted at all the roads leading into the village. She planned to open the *Topaze* with a gala tea and a sale of Italian pottery. Hundreds of invitations were printed and mailed.

Leander made a nuisance of himself. He broke wind in the parlor and urinated against an apple tree in full view of the boats on the river and the salesmen of Italian pottery. He claimed to be aging swiftly and pointed out how loudly his bones creaked when he stooped to pick a thread off a carpet.

Tears streamed capriciously from his eyes whenever he heard a horse race on the radio. He still shaved and bathed each morning, but he smelled more like Neptune than ever and clumps of hair grew out of his ears and nostrils before he could remember to clip them. His neckties were stained with food and cigarette ash, and yet, when the night winds woke him and he lay in bed and traced their course around the dark compass, he still remembered what it was to feel young and strong. Deluded by this thread of cold air he would rise in his bed thinking passionately of boats, trains and deep-breasted women, or of some image – a wet pavement plastered with yellow elm leaves – that seemed to represent requital and strength. I will climb the mountain, he thought. I will kill the tiger! I will crush the serpent with my heel! But the fresh winds died with the morning dusk. There was a pain in his kidney. He could not get back to sleep and he would limp and cough through another day. His sons did not write him.

On the day before the *Topaze* opened as a gift shop, Leander paid a call on Honora. They sat in her parlor.

'Would you like some whisky?' Honora asked.

'Yes, please,' Leander said.

'There isn't any,' Honora said. 'Have a cookie.'

Leander glanced down at the plate of cookies and saw they were covered with ants. 'I'm afraid ants have gotten into your cookies, Honora,' he said.

'That's ridiculous,' Honora said. 'I know you have ants at the farm, but I've never had ants in this house.' She picked up a cookie and ate it, ants and all.

'Are you going to Sarah's tea?' Leander asked.

'I don't have time to spend in gift shops,' Honora said. 'I'm taking piano lessons.'

'I thought you were taking painting lessons,' Leander said.

'Painting!' Honora said scornfully. 'Why I gave up my painting in the spring. The Hammers were in some financial difficulty so I bought their piano from them and now Mrs Hammer comes and gives me a lesson twice a week. It's very easy.'

'Perhaps it runs in the family,' Leander said. 'Remember Justina?'

'Justina who?' Honora asked.

'Justina Molesworth,' Leander said.

'Why, of course I remember Justina,' Honora said. 'Why shouldn't I?'

'I meant that she played the piano in the five and ten,' Leander said.

'Well, I have no intention of playing the piano in the five and ten,' Honora said. 'Feel that refreshing breeze,' she said.

'Yes,' Leander said. (There was no breeze at all.)

'Sit in the other chair,' she said.

'I'm quite comfortable here, thank you,' Leander said.

'Sit in the other chair,' Honora said. 'I've just had it reupholstered. Although,' she said as Leander obediently changed from one chair to the other, 'you won't be able to see out of the window from there and perhaps you were better off where you were.'

Leander smiled, remembering that to talk with her, even when she was a young woman, had made him feel bludgeoned. He wondered what her reasons were. Lorenzo had written somewhere in his journal that if you met the devil you should cut him in two and go between the pieces. It would describe Honora's manner although he wondered if it wasn't the fear of death that had determined her crabwise progress through life. It could have been that by side-stepping those things that, through their force – love, incontinence and peace of mind – throw into our faces the facts of our mortality she might have uncovered the mystery of a spirited old age.

'Will you do me a favor, Honora?' he asked.

'I won't go to Sarah's tea if that's what you want,' she said. 'I've told you I have a music lesson.'

'It isn't that,' Leander said. 'It's something else. When I die I want Prospero's speech said over my grave.'

'What speech is that?' Honora asked.

'Our revels now are ended,' Leander said, rising from his chair. 'These our actors, as I foretold you, were all spirits and are melted into air, into thin air.' He declaimed, and his declamatory style was modeled partly on the Shakespearians of his youth, partly on the bombast and singsong of prize-ring announcements and partly on the style of the vanished horsecar and trolley-car conductors who had made an incantation of the place names along their routes. His voice soared and he illustrated the poetry with some very literal gestures. '. . . and, like the baseless fabric of this vision, the cloud-capped towers, the gorgeous palaces, the solemn temples, the great globe itself, yea, all which it inherit, shall dissolve, and, like this insubstantial pageant faded, leave not a rack behind.' He dropped his hands. His voice fell. 'We are such stuff as dreams are made on, and our little life is rounded with a sleep.' Then he said good-by and went.

Early the next morning Leander saw that there would be no sanctuary or peace for him in the farm that day. The stir of a large ladies' party – magnified by the sale of Italian pottery – was inescapable. He decided to visit his friend Grimes, who was living in an old people's home in West Chillum. It was a trip he had planned to make for years. He walked into St Botolphs after breakfast and caught the bus to West Chillum there. It was on the other side of Chillum that the bus driver told him they had reached the Twilight Home and Leander got off. The place from the road looked to him like one of the New England academies. There was a granite wall, set with sharp pieces of stone to keep vagrants from resting. The drive was shaded with elms, and the buildings it served were made of red brick along architectural lines that, whatever had been intended when they were built, now seemed very gloomy. Along the driveway Leander saw old men hoeing the gutters. He entered the central building and went to an office, where a woman asked what he wanted.

'I want to see Mr Grimes.'

'Visitors aren't allowed on weekdays,' the woman said.

'I've just come all the way from St Botolphs,' Leander said.

'He's in the north dormitory,' she said. 'Don't tell anyone I said you could go in. Go up those stairs.'

Leander walked down the hall and up some broad wooden stairs. The dormitory was a large room with a double row of iron beds down each side of a center aisle. Old men were lying on fewer than half the beds. Leander recognized his old friend and went over to the bed where he was lying.

'Grimes,' he said.

'Who is it?' The old man opened his eyes.

'Leander. Leander Wapshot.'

'Oh Leander,' Grimes cried and the tears streamed down his cheeks. 'Leander, old sport. You're the first friend to come and see me since Christmas.' He embraced Leander. 'You don't know what it's like for me to see a friendly face. You don't know what it's like.'

'Well, I thought I'd pay you a little call,' Leander said. 'I meant to come a long time ago. Somebody told me you had a pool table out here so I thought I'd come out and play you a little pool.'

'We have a pool table,' Grimes said. 'Come on, come on, I'll show you the pool table.' He seized Leander's arm and led him out of the dormitory. 'We've got all kinds of recreation,' he said excitedly. 'At Christmas they sent us a lot of gramophone records. We have gardens. We get plenty of fresh air and exercise. We work in the gardens. Don't you want to see the gardens?'

'Anything you say, Grimes,' Leander said unwillingly. He did not want to see the gardens or much more of the Twilight Home. If he could sit quietly for an hour somewhere and talk with Grimes he would feel repaid for the trip.

'We grow all our own vegetables,' Grimes said. 'We have fresh vegetables right out of the garden. I'll show you the garden first. Then we'll play a little pool. The pool table isn't in very good shape. I'll show you the gardens. Come on. Come on.'

They left the central buildings by a back door and crossed to the gardens. They looked to Leander like the rigid and depressing produce gardens of a reformatory. 'See,' Grimes said. 'Peas. Carrots. Beets. Spinach. We'll have corn soon. We sell corn. We may grow some of the corn you eat at your table, Leander.' He had led Leander into a field of corn that was just beginning to silk. 'We have to be quiet now,' he said in a whisper. They went through the corn to the edge of the garden and climbed a stone wall marked with a No Trespassing sign and went into some scrub woods. They came in a minute to a clearing where there was a shallow trench dug in the clay.

'See it?' Grimes whispered. 'See it? Not everybody knows about it. That's potter's field. That's where they bury us. These two men got sick last month. Charlie Dobbs and Henry Fosse. They both died one night. I had an idea what they were doing then but I wanted to make sure. I came out here that morning and I hid in the woods. Sure enough, about ten o'clock this fat fellow comes along with a wheelbarrow. He's got Charlie Dobbs and Henry Fosse in it. Stark naked. Dumped on top of one another. Upside down. They didn't like each other, Leander. They never even spoke to one another. But he buried them together. Oh, I couldn't look. I couldn't watch it. I've never felt right after that. If I die in the night they'll dump me naked into a hole side by side with somebody I never knew. Go back and tell them, Leander. Tell them at the newspapers. You were always a good talker. Go back and tell them. . . .'

'Yes, yes,' Leander said. He was backing through the woods, away from the clearing and his hysterical friend. They climbed the stone wall and walked through the corn patch. Grimes gripped Leander's arm. 'Go back and tell them, tell them at the newspapers. Save me, Leander. Save me. . . .'

'Yes, I will, Grimes, yes, I will.'

Side by side the old men returned through the garden and Leander said good-by to Grimes in front of the central building. Then he went down the driveway, obliged to struggle to give the impression that he was not hurried. He was relieved when he got outside the gates. It was a long time before the bus came along and when one did appear he shouted, 'Hello there. Stop stop, stop for me.'

He could not help Grimes; he could not, he realized when the bus approached St Botolphs and he saw a sign, VISIT THE SS TOPAZE, THE ONLY FLOATING GIFT SHOPPE IN NEW ENGLAND, help himself. He hoped that the tea party would be over but when he approached the farm he found many cars parked on the lawn and the sides of the driveway. He swung wide around the house and went in at the back door and up the stairs to his room. It was late then and from his window he could see the *Topaze* – the twinkling of candles – and hear the voices of ladies drinking tea. The sight made him feel that he was being made ridiculous; that a public spectacle was being made of his mistakes and his misfortunes. He remembered his father then with tenderness and fear as if he had dreaded, all along, some end like Aaron's. He guessed the ladies would talk about him and he only had to listen at the window to hear. 'He drove her onto Gull Rock in broad daylight,' Mrs Gates said as she went down the path to the wharf. 'Theophilus thinks he was drunk.'

What a tender thing, then, is a man. How, for all his crotch-hitching and swagger, a whisper can turn his soul into a cinder. The taste of alum in the rind of a grape, the smell of the sea, the heat of the spring sun, berries bitter and sweet, a grain of sand in his teeth – all of that which he meant by life seemed taken away from him. Where were the serene twilights of his old age? He would have liked to pluck out his eyes. Watching the candlelight on his ship – he had brought her home through gales and tempests – he felt ghostly and emasculated. Then he went to his bureau drawer and took from under the dried rose and the wreath of hair his loaded pistol. He went to the window. The fires of the day were burning out like a conflagration in some industrial city and above the barn cupola he saw the evening star, as sweet and round as a human tear. He fired his pistol out of the window and then fell down on the floor.

He had underestimated the noise of teacups and ladies' voices and no one on the *Topaze* heard the shot – only Lulu, who was in the kitchen, getting some hot water. She climbed the back stairs and hurried down the hall to his room and screamed when she opened the door. When he heard her voice Leander got to his knees. 'Oh, Lulu, Lulu, you weren't the one I wanted to hurt. I didn't mean you. I didn't mean to frighten you.'

'Are you all right, Leander? Are you hurt?'

'I'm foolish,' Leander said.

'Oh, poor Leander,' Lulu said, helping him to his feet. 'Poor soul. I told her she shouldn't have done it. I told her in the kitchen many times that it would hurt your feelings, but she wouldn't listen.'

'I only want to be esteemed,' Leander said.

'Poor soul,' Lulu said. 'You poor soul.'

'You won't tell anyone what you saw,' Leander said.

'No.'

'You promise me.'

'I promise.'

'Swear that you won't tell anyone what you saw.'

'I swear.'

'Swear on the Bible. Let me find the Bible. Where's my Bible? Where's my old Bible?' Then he searched the room wildly, lifting up and putting down books and papers and throwing open drawers and looking into book shelves and chests, but he couldn't find the Bible. There was a little American flag stuck into the mirror above his bureau and he took this and held it out to Lulu. 'Swear on the flag, Lulu, swear on the American flag that you won't tell anyone what you saw.'

'I swear.'

'I only want to be esteemed.'

CHAPTER 28

Although the administration of Island 93 was half military and half civilian, the military, having charge of transportation, communication and provisions, often dominated the civilian administrators. So Coverly was called to the military communications office one early evening and handed a copy of a cable that had been sent by Lulu Breckenridge. YOUR FATHER IS DYING. 'Sorry, fellow,' the officer said. 'You can go to communications but I don't think they'll do anything for you. You're signed up for nine months.' Coverly dropped the cable into the wastebasket and walked out of the office.

It was after supper and the latrines were being fired and the smoke rose up through the coconut palms. In another twenty minutes the movies would begin. When Coverly had gone a little way beyond the building he began to cry. He sat down by the road. The light was changing and the light goes quickly in the islands and it was that hour when the primitive domesticity of a colony of men without women begins to assert itself: the washing, letter-writing and the handicrafts with which men preserve some reason and dignity. No one noticed Coverly because there was nothing unusual in a man sitting by the side of the road and no one could see he was crying. He wanted to see Leander and cried to think that all their plans had taken him to the flimflam of a tropical island a little while before the movies began while his father was dying in St Botolphs. He would never see Leander again. Then he decided to try to go home and dried his tears and walked to the transportations office. There was a young officer there who seemed, in spite of Coverly's civilian clothes, disappointed not to have him salute. 'I want some emergency transportation,' Coverly said.

'What's the nature of the emergency?' Coverly noticed that the officer had a tic in his right cheek.

'My father is dying.'

'Have you any proof of this?'

'There's a cable at communications.'

'What do you do?' the officer asked.

'I'm one of the Tapers,' Coverly said.

'Well, you might get excused from work for a week. I'm sure you can't get any emergency transportation. The major's at the club but I know he won't help you. Why don't you go and see the chaplain?'

'I'll go and see the chaplain,' Coverly said.

It was dark then and the movies had begun and all the stars hung in the soft dark. The chapel was about a quarter of a mile from the offices and when he got there he could see a blue gasoline lamp above the door and behind the lamp a large sign that said WELCOME. The building was a considerable tribute to human ingenuity. Bamboo had been lashed into a scaffolding and this was covered with palm matting – all of it holding to the conventional lines of a country church. There was even a steeple made of palm matting and there was an air of conspicuous unpopularity about the place. The doorway was plastered with WELCOME signs and so was the interior and on a table near the door were free stationery, moldy magazines and an invitation for rest, recreation and prayer.

The chaplain, a first lieutenant named Lindstrom, was there, writing a letter. He wore steel – rimmed GI spectacles on a weak and homely face, and he was a man who belonged to the small places of the earth – to little towns with their innocence, their bigotry and their devilish gossip – and he seemed to have brought, intact to the atoll, the smell of drying linen on a March morning and the self-righteous and bitter piety with which he would thank God, at Sunday dinner, for a can of salmon and a bottle of lemonade. He invited Coverly to sit down and offered him some stationery and Coverly said he needed help.

'I don't remember your face,' Lindstrom said, 'so I guess you're not a member of my congregation. I never forget a face. I don't see why the men don't come here and worship. I think I have one of the nicest chapels in the West Pacific and last Sunday I only had five men at the service. I'm trying to see if I can't get one of the photographers to come down from headquarters and take a picture of the place. I think there ought to be a photograph of this chapel in *Life* magazine. I have to share it with Father O'Leary, but he didn't give me much help when there was work involved. He didn't seem to care where his men worshiped. He's over to the officers' mess, playing poker right now. It's none of my business how he spends his time but I don't think a minister of the gospel ought to play cards. I've never held a playing card in my hand. Of course it's none of my business, but I don't approve of the methods he uses to get his congregation together, either. He had twenty-eight men here last Sunday. I counted them. But you know how he did it? There was a whisky ration last Saturday and he went down and pulled the men out of line and made them come to confession. No confession, no whisky. Anybody could fill up a church if they did things like that. I put out the stationery and the magazines and I painted the Welcome signs myself and whenever my wife sends me cookies – my wife bakes oatmeal cookies; she could make a fortune if she wanted to open a bakery – now when my wife sends me cookies I put them in a dish out here but that's as far as I'll go.'

'I want some emergency transportation,' Coverly said. 'I want to go home. My father's dying.'

'Oh, I'm sorry, my boy,' Lindstrom said. 'I'm very sorry. I can't get you emergency transportation. I don't know why they send people to me. I don't know why they do this. You can go and see the major. A man got some emergency transportation last month. At least that's what I heard. You go to the major and I'll pray for you.'

The major was playing poker and drinking whisky at the officers' club and he left the card table gruffly, but he was an amiable or sentimental drinker, and when Coverly said that his father was dying he put an arm around his shoulder, walked him over to the transportation office and got a clerk out of the movies to cut his orders.

He left before dawn in an old DC-4, covered with oil and with a picture of a bathing beauty painted on its fuselage. He slept on the floor. They got to Oahu in the disorder of a hot summer dusk with more lightning playing in the mountains. He left for San Francisco in a transport at eleven the next night. There was a crap game and the uninsulated plane was very cold and Coverly sat in a bucket seat, wrapped in a blanket. The drone of the motors reminded him of the *Topaze* and he fell asleep. When he woke the sky was a rosy color and the flight clerk was passing out oranges and saying that he could smell the land wind. A solid cloud ceiling broke as they neared the coast and they could see the burned summer hills of San Francisco. A few hours after clearing military customs Coverly hitched a ride on a bomber to Washington and went from there to St Botolphs on the train. He took a taxi from the station out to the farm in the middle of the morning and saw, for the first time, the signs on the main road on the elm tree, VISIT THE SS TOPAZE, THE ONLY FLOATING GIFT SHOPPE IN NEW ENGLAND. He got out of the cab and looking around he saw his father, searching for four-leaf clovers in the meadow by the river, and he ran to him, 'Oh, I knew you'd come, Coverly,' Leander called. 'I knew that you or Moses would come,' and he embraced his son and laid his head on his shoulder.

PART
THREE

CHAPTER 29

At the turn of the century there were more castles in the United States than there were in all of Merrie England when Gude King Arthur ruled that land. The search for a wife took Moses to one of the last of these establishments to be maintained – the bulk of them had been turned into museums, bought by religious orders or demolished. This was a place called Clear Haven, the demesne of Justina Wapshot Molesworth Scaddon, an ancient cousin from St Botolphs who had married a five-and-ten-cent-store millionaire. Moses had met her at a cotillion or dance that he had gone to with a classmate from Bond School and through her had met her ward, Melissa. Melissa seemed to Moses, the instant he saw her, to be, by his lights, a most desirable and beautiful woman. He courted her and when they became lovers he asked her to marry him. So far as he knew, this sudden decision had nothing to do with the conditions of Honora's will. Melissa agreed to marry him if he would live at Clear Haven. He had no objections. The place – whatever it was – would shelter them for the summer and he felt sure that he could prevail on her to move into the city in the fall. So one rainy afternoon he took a train to Clear Haven, planning to love Melissa Scaddon and to marry her.

The conservative sumptuary tastes that Moses had formed in St Botolphs had turned out to coincide with the sumptuary tastes of New York banking, and under his dun-colored raincoat Moses wore the odd, drab clothes of that old port. It was nearly dark when he set out, and the journey through the northern slums, and the rainfall catching and returning like a net the smoke and filth of the city, made him somber and restive. The train that he took ran up the banks of the river and, sitting on the land side of the car, he watched a landscape that in the multitude of its anomalies would have prepared him for Clear Haven if he had needed any preparation, for nothing was any more what it had aimed to be or what it would be in the end and the house that had meant to express familial pride was now a funeral parlor, the house that had meant to express worldly pride was a rooming house, Ursuline nuns lived in the castle that was meant to express the pride of avarice, but through this erosion of purpose Moses thought he saw everywhere the impress of human sweetness and ingenuity. The train was a local and the old rolling stock creaked from station to station, although at some distance from the city the stops were infrequent and he saw now and then from the window those huddled families who wait on the platform for a train or a passenger and who are made by the pallid lights, the rain and their attitudes to seem to be drawn together by some sad and urgent business. Only two passengers remained in the car when they reached Clear Haven and he was the only one to leave the train.

The rain was dense then, the night was dark and he went into a waiting room that held his attention for a minute for there was a large photograph on the wall, framed in oak, of his destination. Flags flew from the many towers of Clear Haven, the buttresses were thick with ivy and considering what he went there for it seemed far from ridiculous. Justina seemed to have had a hand in the waiting room for there was a rug on the floor. The matchboard walls were stained the color of mahogany and the pipes that must heat the place in winter rose gracefully, two by two, to disappear like serpents into holes in the ceiling. The benches around the walls were divided at regular intervals with graceful loops of bent wood that would serve the travelers as arm rests and keep the warm

hams of strangers from touching one another. Stepping out of
the waiting room he found a single cab at the curb. 'I'll take
you up to the gates,' the driver said. 'I can't take you up to
the house but I'll leave you at the gates.'

The gates, Moses saw when he got out of the taxi, were
made of iron and were secured with a chain and padlock.
There was a smaller gate on the left and he went in there
and walked through the heavy rain to the lights of what he
guessed was a gatehouse or cottage. A middle-aged man came
to the door – he was eating – and seemed delighted when
Moses gave his name. 'I'ma Giacomo,' he said. 'I'ma Giacomo.
You comea with me.' Moses followed him into an old garage,
rank with the particular damp of cold concrete that goes so
swiftly to the bone. There, in the glare, stood an old Rolls-
Royce with a crescent-windowed tonneau like the privy at
West Farm. Moses got into the front while Giacomo began
to work the fuel pump and it took him some time to get
the car started. 'She'sa nearly dead,' Giacomo said. 'She'sa no
good for night driving. Then they backed like a warship out
into the rain. There were no windshield wipers or Giacomo
did not use them and they traveled without headlights up a
winding drive. Then suddenly Moses saw the lights of Clear
Haven. There seemed to be hundreds of them – they were
so numerous that they lighted the road and lifted his spirits.
Moses thanked Giacomo and carried his suitcase through the
rain to the shelter of a big porch that was carved and ribbed
like the porch of a cathedral. The only bell he saw to ring was
a contraption of wrought-iron leaves and roses, so fanciful and
old that he was afraid it might come down on his head if he
used it, and he pounded on the door with his fist. A maid let
him in and he stepped into a kind of rotunda and at the same
time Melissa appeared in another door. He put down his bag,
let the rain run out of the brim of his hat and gathered his
beloved up in his arms.

His clothes were wet and a little rancid as well. 'I suppose you
could change,' Melissa said, 'but there isn't much time... .' He
recognized in her look of mingled anxiety and pleasure the

suspense of someone who introduces one part of life into another, feeling insecurely that they may clash and involve a choice or a parting. He felt her suspense as she took his arm and led him across a floor where their footsteps rang on the black-and-white marble. It was unlike Moses, but to tell the truth he looked neither to the left where he heard the sounds of a fountain nor to the right where he smelled the sweet earth of a conservatory, feeling, like Cousin Honora, that to pretend to have been born and bred in whatever environment one found oneself was a mark of character.

He was in a sense right in resisting his curiosity, for Clear Haven had been put together for the purpose of impressing strangers. No one had ever counted the rooms – no one, that is, but a vulgar and ambitious cousin who had spent one rainy afternoon this way, feeling that splendor could be conveyed in numbers. She had come up with the sum of ninety-two but no one knew whether or not she had counted the maid's rooms, the bathrooms and the odd, unused rooms, some of them without windows, that had been created by the numerous additions to the place, for the house had grown, reflecting the stubborn and eccentric turns of Justina's mind. When she had bought the great hall from the Villa Peschere in Milan she had cabled the architect, telling him to attach it to the small library. She would not have bought the hall if she had known that she would be offered the drawing room from the Château de la Muette a week later, and she wrote the architect asking him to attach this to the little dining room and advising him that she had bought four marble fountains representing the four seasons. Then the architect wrote saying that the fountains had arrived and that since there was no room for them in the house would she approve his plans for a winter garden to be attached to the hall from Milan? She cabled back her approval and bought that afternoon a small chapel that could be attached to the painted room that Mr Scaddon had given her on her birthday. People often said that she bought more rooms than she knew how to use; but she used them all. She was not one of those collectors who let their prizes rot in warehouses. On the same trip she had picked up a marble floor and some columns in Vincenzo but the most impressive addition to Clear Haven that she was able to find on that or any of her later trips were the stones and timbers of the great Windsor Hall. It was to this expatriated hall now that Melissa took Moses.

Justina sat by the fire, drinking sherry. She was, by Leander's reckoning, about seventy-five then, but her hair and her eyebrows were ink black and her face, framed in spit curls, was heavily rouged. Her eyes were glassy and shrewd. Her hair was raised off her forehead in a high construction, plainly old-fashioned and reminding Moses of the false front on the Cartwright Block in St Botolphs. It was the same period. But she reminded him mostly of what she had been – a foxy old dancing mistress.

She greeted Moses with marked disinterest but this was not surprising in a woman whose distrust of men was even more outspoken than Cousin Honora's. Her dress was rich and simple and her imperious and hoarse voice ranged over a complete octave of requited social ambitions. 'The Count D'Alba, General Burgoyne and Mrs Enderby,' she said, introducing Moses to the others in the room. The count was a tall, dark-skinned man with cavernous and hairy nostrils. The general was an old man in a wheel chair. Mrs Enderby wore a pince-nez, the lozenge-shaped lenses of which hung so limply from the bridge of her nose that they gave her a very dropsical look. Her fingers were stained with ink. Melissa and Moses went to some chairs by the fire but these were so outrageously proportioned that Moses had to boost himself up and found, when he was seated, that his legs did not reach the floor. A maid passed him a glass of sherry and a dish in which there were a few old peanuts. The sherry was not fit to drink and when he tasted it Melissa smiled at him and he remembered her accounts of Justina's parsimony and wished he had brought some whisky in his suitcase. Then a maid stood in a distant doorway and rang some chimes and they went down a hall into a room that was lighted with candles.

The dinner was a cup of soup, a boiled potato, a scrap of fish and some kind of custard, and the conversation, that was meant to move at Justina's dictates, suffered from the fact that she seemed either tired, absent-minded or annoyed by Moses' arrival. When the general spoke to her about the illness of a friend she expressed her fixed idea about the perfidiousness of men. It was her opinion that the husband of her friend was responsible for the illness. Unmarried women – she said – were much healthier than wives. When the meal was finished they returned to the hall. Moses was still hungry and he hoped that there was some breakdown in the kitchen arrangements and that if he did live at Clear Haven he would not be expected to get along on such meager fare. Justina played backgammon with the general and the count sat down at the piano and started a medley of that lachrymose music that is played for cocktails and that is so limpid in its amorousness, so supine and wistful in its statement of passion that it will offend the ears of a man in love. Suddenly all the lights went out.

'The main fuse is gone again,' Justina said, rolling her dice in the firelight.

'Can I fix it?' Moses asked, anxious to make a good impression.

'I don't know,' Justina said. 'There are plenty of fuses.'

Melissa lighted a candle and Moses followed her down a hall. They could hear a babble of voices from the kitchen where the servants were striking matches and looking for candles. She opened a door into a further corridor and started down a steep flight of worn, wooden stairs into a cellar that smelled of earth. They found the fuse box and Moses changed the old fuse for a new one, although he noticed that the wiring was in some cases bare or carelessly patched with friction tape. Melissa blew out her candle and they returned to the hall, where the count had resumed his forlorn music and where the general hitched his wheel chair up to Moses and led him to a glass case near the fireplace where there were some moldy academic robes that the late

Mr Scaddon had worn when he was given an honorary degree from Princeton.

It pleased Moses to think that the palace and the hall stood four square on the five-and-ten-cent stores of his youth with their appetizing and depraved odors. His most vivid memories were of the girls – the girl with acne at the cosmetic counter, the full-busted girl selling hardware, the indolent girl in the candy department, the demure beauty selling oilcloth and the straw-haired town whore on probation among the wind-up toys – and if there was no visible connection between these memories and the hall at Clear Haven the practical connection was inarguable. Moses noticed that when the general spoke of J. P. Scaddon he avoided the phrase 'five-and-ten-cent store' and spoke only of merchandising. 'He was a great merchant,' the general said, 'an exceptional man, a distinguished man – even his enemies would admit that. For the forty years that he was president of the firm his days were scheduled from eight in the morning until sometimes after midnight. When I say that he was distinguished I mean that he was distinguished by his energies, his powers of judgment, his courage and imagination. He possessed all these things to an unusual degree. He was never involved in any shady deals and the merchandising world as we see it today owes something to his imagination, his intelligence and his fine sense of honor. He had, of course, a payroll that employed over a million people. When he opened stores in Venezuela and Belgium and India his intention was not to make himself or his stockholders any richer, but to raise the standard of living generally. . . .'

Moses listened to what the general said but the thought that he would lay Melissa had given to that day such stubborn light and joy that it was an effort to keep his ardor from turning to impatience while he listened to this praise of the late millionaire. She was beautiful and it was that degree of beauty that fills even the grocery boy and the garage mechanic with solemn thoughts. The strong, dark-golden color of her hair, her shoulder bones and gorge and the eyes that appeared black at that distance had over Moses such a power that, as he watched her, desire seemed to darken and gild her figure like the cumulative coats of varnish on an old painting, and he would have been gratified if some slight hurt had befallen her, for that deep sense of involvement we experience when we see a lovely woman – or even a woman with nothing left to her but the loveliness of intent – trip on the iron steps of a train carriage or on a curbing of the street – or when, on a rainy day, we see the paper bag in which she is carrying her groceries home split and rain down around her feet and into the puddles on the sidewalk oranges, bunches of celery, loaves of bread, cold cuts wrapped in cellophane – that deep sense of involvement that can be explained by injury and loss was present with Moses with no explanation. He had half risen from his chair when the old lady snapped:

'Bedtime!'

He had underestimated the power of desire to draw his features and he was caught. From under her dyed eyebrows Justina looked at him hatefully. 'I'm going to ask you to take the general to his room,' she said. 'Your room is just down the hall so there won't be any inconvenience. Melissa's room is on the other side of the house' – she said this triumphantly and made a gesture to emphasize the distance –'and it's not convenient for her to take the general up. . . .'

The stamp of desire on his face had betrayed him once and he did not want to be betrayed by disappointment or anger and he smiled broadly – he positively beamed – but he wondered how, in the labyrinth of rooms, he would ever find his way to her bed. He could not go around knocking on all the doors nor could he open them on screaming maids or the figure of Mrs Enderby taking off her beads. He might stir up a hornet's nest of servants – even the Count D' Alba – and precipitate a scandal that would end with his expulsion from Clear Haven. Melissa was smiling so sweetly that he thought she must have a plan and she kissed him decorously and whispered, 'Over the roof.' Then she spoke for the benefit of the others. 'I'll see you in the morning, Moses. Pleasant dreams.'

He pushed the general's chair into the elevator and pressed the button for the third floor. The elevator rose slowly and the cables gave off a very mournful sound, but filled again with stubborn joy Moses was insensitive to the premonitory power of such lifts and elevators – the elevators in loft buildings, castles, hospitals and warehouses – that, infirm and dolorous to hear, seem to touch on our concepts of damnation. 'Thank you, Mr Wapshot,' the old man said when Moses had wheeled his chair to the door. 'I'll be all right now. We're very glad to have you with us. Melissa has been very unhappy, very unhappy and unsettled. Good night.' Back in his own room Moses shucked his clothes, brushed his teeth and stepped out onto the balcony of his room, where the rain still fell, making in the grass and the leaves a mealy sound. He smiled broadly with a great love of the world and everything in it and then, in his skin, started the climb over the roofs.

This seemed to be the greatest of the improbabilities at Clear Haven but considering what it was that he sought, to be a naked man scrambling over the leads presented nothing that was actually very irregular or perplexing. The rain on his skin and hair felt fresh and soft and the chaos of wet roofs fitted easily into the picture of love; and it was the roofs of Clear Haven, to be seen only by the birds or a stray airplane, where the architect had left bare the complexity of his task – in a sense his defeat – for here all the random majesty of the place appeared spatchcocked, rectified and jumbled; here, hidden in the rain, were the architect's secrets and most of his failures. Peaked roofs, flat roofs, pyramidal roofs, roofs inset with stained-glass skylights and chimneys and bizarre systems of drainage stretched for a quarter of a mile or more, shining here and there in the light from a distant dormer window like the roofs of a city.

As far as he could see in the rainy dark the only way to get to the other side of the house lay past this distant row of dormers and he had started for them when a length of wire, stretched knee-high across a part of the roof, tripped him up. It was an old radio aerial, he guessed charitably, since he was

not hurt, and started off again. A few minutes later he passed
a rain-soaked towel and a bottle of sun-tan lotion and still
further along there was an empty bottle of vermouth, making
the roof seem like a beach on which someone, unknown he
felt sure to Justina, had stretched out his bones in the sun. As
he approached the ledge to the first lighted dormer he saw
straight into a small room, decked with religious pictures,
where an old servant was ironing. The lights in the next
window were pink, and glancing in briefly he was surprised
to see the Count D'Alba standing in front of a full-length
mirror without any clothes on. The next window was Mrs
Enderby's and she sat at a desk, dressed as she had been at
dinner, writing in a book. He had gone out of the range of
her desk light when his right foot, seeking a hold, moved off
into nothing but the rainy dark and only by swinging and
throwing his weight onto the slates did he keep from falling.
What he had missed was an airshaft that cut straight through
the three stories of the hall and that would have been the end
of him. He peered down at this, waiting for the chemistry
of his alarmed body to quiet and listening then to see if Mrs
Enderby or the others had heard the noise he made when he
threw himself down. Everything was quiet and he made the
rest of his climb more slowly, swinging down at last onto the
balcony of Melissa's room where he stood outside her window,
watching her brush her hair. She sat at a table by a mirror and
her nightgown was transparent so that even in the dim light
of the room he could see the fullness of her breasts, parting
a little as she leaned toward the mirror.

'You're drenched, my darling, you're drenched,' she said.
Her look was opaque and wanton; she raised her mouth to
be kissed and he unknotted the ribbons of her gown so that
it fell to her waist and she drew his head down from her lips
to salute her breasts. Then, naked and unshy, she crossed the
floor and went into the bathroom to finish her toilet and
Moses listened to the noises of running water and the sounds
of opening and closing drawers, knowing that it was sensible
for a lover to be able to estimate these particular delays. She

came back, walking he thought in glory and turning out the lights that she passed on her way, and at dawn, stroking her soft buttocks and listening to the singing of the crows, she told him that he would have to go and he climbed in his skin back over the chaos of roofs.

It was daybreak then and Moses, unable to sleep, dressed and went out. Coming down the stairs, he saw in the strong light of morning that everything sumptuous was dirty and worn. The velvet padding on the banister was patched, there were cigar ashes on the stair carpet and the needlepoint bench at the turning was missing a leg. Coming down into the rotunda Moses saw a large gray rat. They exchanged a look and then the rat – too fat or arrogant to run – moved into the library. Crystals were missing from the chandelier, bits of marble from the floor were gone and the hall seemed like an old hotel where expensiveness and elegance had been abandoned by its company to old men, old women and the near poor. The air was stale and the chests that stood at regular intervals along the wall were ringed white from glasses. Most of the chests were missing a claw or a piece of hardware. Continuing along the hall Moses realized that he had never seen so many chests and he wondered what they contained. He wondered if the Scaddons had bought them by mail, ordered them from some dealer or succumbed to a greed for these massive, ornate and, so far as he knew, useless things. He wondered again what they contained but he did not open one and let himself out a glass door onto a broad lawn.

The women that Moses loved seemed to be in the morning sky, gorged with lights, in the river, the mountains and the trees, and with lust in his trousers and peace in his heart he walked happily over the grass. Below the house there was an old-fashioned Roman plunge with a marble curb and water spouting out of lions' mouths and, having nothing better to do, Moses took a swim. A day that had begun brilliantly darkened suddenly and it began to rain, and Moses went back to the house to get some breakfast and talk with Justina.

*

Moses had written to Leander about Justina and Leander had replied without a salutation and with this title: 'The Rise of a Mercenary B—ch.' Under the heading he had written: 'Justina; daughter of Amos and Elizabeth Molesworth. Only child. Father was sporting gent. Good-looker but unable or unwilling to meet domestic obligations. Deserted wife & child. Was never heard from. Elizabeth supported self and daughter as dressmaker. Worked day & night. Ruined eyesight. Mouth always full of pins. Little Justina was changeling from onset or so it appeared to me. Marked taste for queenly things. Scraps of velvet. Peacock feathers, etc. Only childhood game ever indulged in was to play queen in topshelf finery. Out of place in such a town as St Botolphs. Subject to much ridicule. Was taken on as apprentice dancing mistress by Gracie Tolland. Held sway in Eastern Star Hall above drugstore; feed store also. Place smelled of floor oil. Later played piano for movies in old Masonic Temple and J. P. Scaddon five & dime store. Waltz me around again Willie. Piano always badly out of tune.

'J. P. Scaddon then competing with Woolworth and Kresge. Millionaire but not above visiting backwoods stores. Beheld Justina tickling the ivories. Love at first sight! Transported same to New York. Amy Atkinson served as duenna. Later married Justina. Newspaper accounts omitted any mention of St Botolphs, dressmaking mother, dancing mistress. Appeared to have sprung full-grown into high society. Justina well equipped to scrap for social position in New York bear pit. Became benefactress of Dog & Cat Hospital. Often photographed in newspaper, surrounded by grateful bow-wows. Was once asked to contribute small sum of money to local Sailor's Home. Refused. Anxious to keep severance of ties with home-place in good condition. No children. Hobnobbed with dukes and earls. Entertained royalty. Opened big house on Fifth Avenue. Also country place. Clear Haven. All dreams come true.'

Later in the morning Moses found Justina in the winter garden – a kind of dome-shaped greenhouse attached to one of the extremities of the castle. Many of the window lights were broken and Giacomo had repaired these by stuffing bed pillows into the frames. There seemed to have been flower beds around the walls in the past and in the center of the room were a fountain and a pool. When Moses entered the room and asked to speak with her, Justina sat down in an iron chair.

'I want to marry Melissa.'

Justina touched that façade of black hair that was like the Cartwright Block and sighed.

'Then why don't you? Melissa is twenty-eight years old. She can do what she wants.'

'We would like your approval.'

'Melissa has no money and no expectations,' the old woman said. 'She owns nothing of value but her beads. The resale value of pearls is very disappointing and they're almost impossible to insure.'

'That wouldn't matter.'

'You know very little about her.'

'I only know that I want to marry her.'

'I think there are some things about her past that you should know. Her parents were killed when she was seven. Mr Scaddon and I were delighted to adopt her – she has such a sweet nature – but we've had our troubles. She married Ray Badger. You knew that?'

'She told me.'

'He became an alcoholic through no fault, I think, of Melissa's. He had some very base ideas about marriage. I hope you don't entertain any such opinions.'

'I'm not sure what you mean.'

'Mr Scaddon and I slept in separate rooms whenever this was possible. We always slept in separate beds.'

'I see.'

'Even in Italy and France.'

'It will be some time before we can hope to travel,' Moses said, hoping to change the subject.

'I don't think Melissa will ever be able to travel,' Justina said. 'She's not left Clear Haven since her divorce.'

'Melissa's told me this herself.'

'It seemed a confining life for a young woman,' Justina said. 'Last year I bought her a ticket to go around the world. She was agreeable, but when all her luggage had been brought aboard and we were drinking some wine in her cabin she decided that she couldn't go. Her distress was extreme. I brought her back to Clear Haven that afternoon.' She smiled at Moses. 'Her hats went around the world.'

'I see,' Moses said. 'Melissa's told me this and I would like to live here until our marriage.'

'That can be arranged. Is your father still alive?'

'Yes.'

'He must be very old. My memories of St Botolphs are not pleasant. I left there when I was seventeen. When I married Mr Scaddon I must have received a hundred letters from people in the village, asking for financial help. This did nothing to improve my recollections. I did try to be helpful. For several years I took some child – an artist or a pianist – and gave them an education, but none of them worked out.' She unclasped her hands and gestured sadly as if she had dropped the students from a great height. 'I had to let them all go. You lived up the river, didn't you? I remember the house. I suppose you have some heirlooms.'

'Yes.' Moses was unprepared for this and he answered hesitantly.

'Could you give me some idea of what they are?'

'Cradles, highboys, lowboys, things like that. Cut glass.'

'I wouldn't be interested in cut glass,' Justina said. 'However, I've never collected Early American furniture and I've always wanted to. Dishes?'

'My brother Coverly would know more about this than I,' Moses said.

'Ah yes,' Justina said. 'Well, it does not matter to me whether you and Melissa marry. I think Mrs Enderby is in her office now and you can ask her to set a date. She will send out the invitations. And be careful of that loose stone in the floor. You might trip and hurt yourself.' Moses found Mrs Enderby and after he listened to some frowsty memories of her youth on the Riviera she told him that he could be married in three weeks. He looked for Melissa but the maids told him she had not come down and when he started to climb the stairs to her part of the house he heard Justina's voice at his back. 'Come down, Mr Wapshot.'

Melissa didn't come down until lunch and this meal, although it was not filling, was served with two kinds of wine and dragged on until three. After lunch they walked back and forth on the terrace below the towers like two figures on a dinner plate and looking for some privacy in the gardens they ran into Mrs Enderby. At half-past five, when it was time for Moses to go and he took Melissa in his arms, a window in one of the towers flew open and Justina called down, 'Melissa, Melissa, tell Mr Wapshot that if he doesn't hurry he'll miss his train.'

After work on Monday Moses packed his clothing in two suitcases and a paper box, putting in among his shirts a bottle of bourbon, a box of crackers and a three-pound piece of Stilton cheese. Again he was the only passenger to leave the train at Clear Haven but Giacomo was there to meet him with the old Rolls and drive him up the hill. Melissa met him at the door and that evening followed the pattern of his first night there except that the fuses didn't blow. Moses wheeled the general to the elevator at ten and started once more over the roofs, this time on such a clear, starlit night that he could see the airshaft that had nearly killed him. Again in the morning at dawn he climbed back to his own quarters and what could be pleasanter than to see that heavily wooded and hilly countryside at dawn from the high roofs of Clear Haven. He went to the city on the train, returned in the evening to Clear Haven, yawned purposefully during dinner and pushed the old general to the elevator at half-past nine.

CHAPTER 30

While Moses was eating these golden apples, Coverly and Betsey had settled in a rocket-launching station called Remsen Park. Coverly had only spent one day at the farm. Leander had urged him to return to his wife – and had gone to work himself at the table-silver factory a few days later. Coverly had joined Betsey in New York and, after a delay of only a few days, was transferred to this new station. This time they traveled together. Remsen Park was a community of four thousand identical houses, bounded on the west by an old army camp. The place could not be criticized as a town or city. Expedience, convenience and haste had produced it when the rocket program was accelerated; but the houses were dry in the rain and warm in the winter; they had well-equipped kitchens and fireplaces for domestic bliss and the healthy need for national self-preservation could more than excuse the fact that they were all alike. At the heart of the community there was a large shopping center with anything you might want – all of it housed in glass-walled buildings. This was Betsey's joy. She and Coverly rented a house, furnished even to the pictures on the walls, and set up housekeeping with the blue china and the painted chairs that Sarah sent them from St Botolphs.

They had been in Remsen Park for only a little while when Betsey decided that she was pregnant She felt sick in the morning and stayed in bed late. When she got up, Coverly had gone to work. He had left coffee for her in the kitchen and had washed his own dishes. She ate a late breakfast, sitting at the kitchen window so that she could see the houses of Remsen Park stretching away to the horizon like the pattern on a cloth. The woman in the house next door came out to empty her garbage. She was an Italian, the wife of an Italian scientist. Betsey called good morning to her and asked her to come in and have a cup of coffee but the Italian woman only gave her a sullen smile and returned to her own kitchen. Remsen Park was not a very friendly place.

Betsey hoped that she would not be disappointed in her pregnancy. Her mind seemed to strike an attitude of prayer, as involuntary as the impulse with which she swore when she slammed her finger in a window. Dear God, she thought briefly, make me a mother. She wanted children. She wanted five or six. She smiled suddenly, as if her wish had filled the kitchen with the love, disorder and vitality of a family. She was braiding the hair of her daughter, Sandra, a beautiful girl. The other four or five were in the room. They were happy and dirty and one of them, a little boy with Coverly's long neck, was holding in his hands the halves of a broken dish, but Betsey had not scolded him, Betsey had not even frowned when he broke the dish, for the secret of his clear, resilient personality was that his growth had never been impeded by niggardly considerations. Betsy felt that she had a latent talent for raising children. She would put the development of personality above everything. The phantom children that played around her knees had never received from their parents anything but love and trust.

When the housework was done it was time for Betsey to take the iron out and have the cord repaired. She walked out of Circle K and down 325th Street to the shopping center and went into the super market, not because she needed anything but because the atmosphere of the place pleased her. It was vast and brightly lighted and music came down from the high blue walls. She bought a giant jar of peanut butter to the strains of the 'Blue Danube' and then a pecan pie. The cashier seemed to be a pleasant young man. 'I'm a stranger here,' Betsey said. 'We've just moved from New York. My husband's been out in the Pacific. We have one of those houses in Circle K and I just wondered if you could give me some advice. My ironing cord is frayed, it just gave out the day before yesterday when I was doing my husband's shirts, and I just wondered if you happened to know of an electrical-appliance or repair store in the vicinity that might fix it for me so that I could have it tomorrow because tomorrow's the day when I do my big shopping and I thought I could come in here and buy my groceries and then pick up the iron on my way home.'

'Well, there's a store four, no five doors down the street,' the young man said, 'and I guess they can fix it for you. They fixed my radio for me once and they're not highway robbers like some of the people's come in here.' Betsey thanked him kindly and went out into the street and wandered along to the electrical store. 'Good morning,' Betsey said cheerfully, putting her iron on the counter. 'I'm a stranger here and when my ironing cord went yesterday while I was doing my husband's shirts I said to myself that I just didn't know where to take it and have it repaired but this morning I stopped in at the Grand Food Mart and that cashier, the nice one with the pretty, wavy hair and those dark eyes, told me that he recommended your store and so I came right over here. Now what I'd like to do is to come downtown and do my shopping tomorrow afternoon and pick up my iron on my way home because I have to get some shirts ironed for my husband by tomorrow night and I wondered if you could have it ready for me by then. It's a good iron and I gave a lot of money for it in New York where we've been living although my husband was out in the Pacific. My husband's a Taper. Of course I don't understand why the cord on such an expensive iron should wear out in such a short time and I wondered if you could put on an extra-special cord for me because I get a great deal of use out of my iron. I do all my husband's shirts, you know, and he's high up in the Taping Department and has to wear a clean shirt every day and then I do my own personal things as well.' The man promised to give Betsey a durable cord and then she wandered back to Circle K.

But her steps slowed as she approached the house. Her family of phantom children was scattered and she could not call them back again. Her period was only seven days late and her pregnancy might not be a fact. She ate a peanut-butter sandwich and a wedge of pecan pie. She missed New York and thought again that Remsen Park was an unfriendly place. Late in the day the doorbell rang and a vacuum-cleaner salesman stood in the door. 'Well now, come right in,' Betsey said cheerfully. 'You come right in. I don't have a vacuum cleaner now and I don't have the money to buy one at the moment. We only just moved from New York but I'm going to buy one as soon as I have the money and perhaps if you've got some new attachments I might buy one of those because I'm determined to buy a new vacuum cleaner sooner or later and I'll need the attachments anyhow. I'm pregnant now and a young mother can't do all that housework without the proper equipment; all that stooping and bending. Would you like a cup of coffee? I imagine you must get tired and footsore going around with that heavy bag all day long. My husband's in the Taping Department and they work him hard but it's a different kind of tiredness, it's just in the brain, but I know what it is to have tired feet.'

The salesman opened his sample case in the kitchen before he drank his coffee and sold Betsey two attachments and a gallon of floor wax. Then, because he was tired, and this was his last call, he sat down. 'I was living alone in New York all the time my husband was in the Pacific,' Betsey said, 'and we just moved out here and of course I was happy to make the move but I don't find it a very friendly place. I mean I don't think it's friendly like New York. In New York I had lots of friends. Of course I was mistaken, once. I was mistaken in my friends. You know what I mean? There were these people named Hansen who lived right down the hall from me. I thought they were my real friends. I thought at last I'd found some lifelong friends. I used to see them every day and every night and she wouldn't buy a dress without asking me about it and I loaned them money and they were always telling me how much they loved me, but I was deceived. Sad was the day of reckoning!' The light in the kitchen was dim and Betsey's face was drawn with feeling. 'They were hypocrites,' she said. 'They were liars and hypocrites.'

The salesman packed his things and went away. Coverly came home at six. 'Hello, sugar,' he said. 'Why sit in the dark?'

'Well, I think I'm pregnant,' Betsey said. 'I guess I'm pregnant. I'm seven days late and this morning I felt sort of funny, dizzy and sick.' She sat on Coverly's lap and put her head against his. 'I think it's going to be a boy. That's what it feels like to me. Of course there's no point in counting your chickens before your eggs are hatched but if we do have a baby one of the things I want to buy is a nice chair because I'm going to breast feed this baby and I'd like to have a nice chair to sit in when I nurse him.'

'You can buy a chair,' Coverly said.

'Well, I saw a nice chair in the furniture center a couple of days ago,' Betsey said, 'and after supper why don't we walk around the corner and look at it? I haven't been out of the house all day and a little walk would be good for you, wouldn't it? Wouldn't it be good for you to stretch your legs?'

After supper they took their walk. A fresh wind was blowing out of the north – straight from St Botolphs – and it made Betsey feel vigorous and gay. She took Coverly's arm and at the corner, under the fluorescent street lamp, he bent down and gave her a French kiss. Once they got to the shopping center Betsey wasn't able to concentrate on her chair. Every suit, dress, fur coat and piece of furniture in the store windows had to be judged, its price and way of life guessed at and some judgment passed as to whether or not it should enter Betsey's vision of happiness. Yes, she said to a plant stand, yes, yes to a grand piano, no to a breakfront, yes to a dining-room table and six chairs, as thoughtfully as St Peter sifting out the hearts of men. At ten o'clock they walked home. Coverly undressed her tenderly and they took a bath together and went to bed for she was his potchke, his fleutchke, his notchke, his motchke, his everything that the speech of St Botolphs left unexpressed. She was his little, little squirrel.

CHAPTER 31

During the three weeks before their marriage, Moses and Melissa deceived Justina so successfully that it pleased the old lady to watch them say good night to one another at the elevator and she spoke several times at dinner of Melissa's part of the house as that part of the house that Moses had never seen. Moses's training as a mountain climber kept him from tiring in his nightly trip over the roofs but one evening, when they had wine with dinner and he was hurried, he tripped over the wire once more and sprawled, full-length, on the slates, cutting his chest. Then, with his skin smarting, a deep physical chagrin took hold of him and he discovered in himself a keen dislike of Clear Haven and all its antics and a determination to prove that the country of love was not bizarre; and he consoled himself with thinking that in a few days he would be able to put a ring on Melissa's finger and enter her room at the door. She had, for some reason, made him promise not to urge her to leave Clear Haven, but he felt that she would change her mind by autumn.

On the eve of his wedding Moses walked up from the station, carrying a rented cutaway in a suitcase. On the drive he met Giacomo, who was putting light bulbs into the fixtures along the drive. 'She'sa two hundred feefty light bulbs!' Giacomo exclaimed. 'She'sa likea Saint's Day.' It was dusk when the lights gave Clear Haven the cheerful look of a country

fair. When Moses took the general up the old man wanted
to give him a drink and some advice, but he excused himself
and started over the roofs. He was covering the stretch from
the chapel to the clock tower when he heard Justina's voice,
quite close to him. She was at D'Alba's window. 'I can't see
anything, Niki,' she said, 'without my glasses.'

'Shhh,' D'Alba said, 'he'll hear you.'

'I wish I could find my glasses.'

'Shhhh.'

'Oh, I can't believe it, Niki,' Justina said. 'I can't believe that
they'd disappoint me.'

'There he goes, there he goes,' D'Alba said as Moses, who
had been crouching in the dark, made for the shelter of the
clock tower.

'Where?'

'There, there.'

'Get Mrs Enderby,' Justina said. 'Get Mrs Enderby and have
her call Giacomo and tell him to bring his crow gun.'

'You'll kill him, Justina.'

'Any man who does such a thing deserves to be shot.'

What Moses felt while he listened to their talk was extreme
irritation and impatience, for having started on his quest he
did not have the reserve to brook interruptions, or at least
interruptions from Justina and the count. He was safe in the
shelter of the tower and while he stood there he heard Mrs
Enderby and then Giacomo join the others.

'She'sa nobody there,' Giacomo said.

'Well, fire anyway,' Justina said. 'If there's someone there
you'll frighten them. If there isn't you won't do any harm.'

'She'sa no good, Missa Scaddon,' Giacomo said.

'You fire, Giacomo,' Justina said. 'You either fire or hand
me that gun.'

'Wait until I get something to cover my ears,' Mrs Enderby
said. 'Wait until . . .'

Then there was the ear-clapping blast of Giacomo's crow
gun and Moses heard the shot strike on the roof around him
and in the distance the ring of breaking glass.

'Oh why do I feel so sad?' Justina asked plaintively. 'Why do I feel so sad?' D'Alba shut the window and when his lights were turned on and his pink curtains drawn, Moses continued his climb. Melissa ran to him weeping when he swung down onto the balcony of her room. 'Oh my darling, I thought they'd shot you,' she cried. 'Oh my sweetheart, I thought you were dead.'

Coverly could not get away from Remsen Park, but Leander and Sarah came to the wedding. They must have left St Botolphs at dawn. Emmet Cavis drove them in his funeral car. Moses was delighted to see them and proud, for they played out their parts with the wonderful simplicity and grace of country people. As for the invitations to the wedding – Justina had dusted off her old address book, and poor Mrs Enderby, wearing a hat and a scrap of veiling, had addressed the four hundred envelopes and come to the dinner table for a week with ink-stained fingers and an ink-spotted blouse, her eyes red from checking Justina's addresses against a copy of the *Social Register* that could have been printed no later than 1918. Giacomo mailed the cards with his blessing ('She'sa lovely, Missa Scaddon') and the cards were delivered to brownstones in the East Fifties that had been transformed from homesteads into showrooms for Italian neckties, art galleries, antique dealers, walk-up apartments and offices of such organizations as the English-Speaking Union and the Svenskamerikanska Förbundet. Further uptown and further east the invitations were received by the tail-coated doormen of eighteen- and twenty-story apartment buildings where the names of Justina's friends and peers struck a spark in no one's memory. Up Fifth Avenue invitations were delivered to more apartment houses as well as to institutes of costume design, slapdash rooming houses, finishing schools and to the offices of the American Irish Historical Society and the Sino-American Amity, Inc. They were exposed to the sootfall among other uncollected mail (old bills from Tiffany and copies of *The New Yorker*) in houses with boarded-up front doors. They lay on the battered tables of progressive kindergartens where children could be heard laughing and weeping and they fell into the anonymous passageways of houses that, built with an open hand, had been remodeled with a tight one and where people cooked their dinners in the morning room and the library. An invitation was received at the Jewish Museum, at the downtown branch of Columbia University, at the French and the Jugoslavian consulates, at the Soviet Delegation to the United Nations, at several fraternity houses, actors' clubs, bridge clubs, milliners and dressmakers. Further afield invitations were received by the Mother Superiors of the Ursuline Order, the Poor Clares and the Sisters of Mercy. They were received by the overseers of Jesuit schools and retreats, Franciscan Fathers, Cowley Fathers, Paulists and Misericordia Sisters. They were delivered to mansions remodeled into country clubs, boarding schools, retreats for the insane, alcohol cures, health farms, wildlife sanctuaries, wallpaper factories, drafting rooms and places where the aged and the infirm waited sniffily for the angel of death in front of their television sets. When the bells of Saint Michael's rang that afternoon there were no more than twenty-five people in the body of the church and two of these were rooming-house proprietors who had come out of curiosity. When the time came Moses said the words loudly and with a full heart. After the ceremony most of the guests returned to Clear Haven and danced to the music of a phonograph. Sarah and Leander performed a stately waltz and said good-by. The maids filled the old champagne bottles with cheap Sauternes and when the summer dusk had fallen and all the chandeliers were lighted the main fuse blew once more. Giacomo repaired it and Moses went upstairs and entered Melissa's room by the door.

CHAPTER 32

The rocket-launching sites at Remsen Park were fifteen miles
to the south and this presented a morale problem for there
were hundreds or thousands of technicians like Coverly who
knew nothing about the beginnings or the ends of their
works. The administration met this problem by having public
rocket launchings on Saturday afternoons. Transportation was
furnished so that whole families could pack their sandwiches
and beer and sit in bleachers to hear the noise of doom crack
and see a fire that seemed to lick at the vitals of the earth.
These firings were not so different from any other kind of
picnic, although there were no softball games or band concerts;
but there was beer to drink and children strayed and were
lost and the jokes the crowd made while they waited for an
explosion that was calculated to pierce the earth's atmosphere
were very human. Betsey loved all of this, but it hardly
modified her feeling that Remsen Park was unfriendly. Friends
were important to her and she said so. 'I just come from a
small town in Georgia,' she said, 'and it was a very friendly
place and I just believe in stepping up and making friends.
After all, we only pass this way once.' As often as she made
the remark about passage, it had not lost its strength. She was
born; she would die.

Her overtures to Mrs Frascati continued to be met with
sullen smiles and she invited the woman in the next house –
Mrs Galen – in for a cup of coffee, but Mrs Galen had several

college degrees and an air of elegance and privilege that made Betsey uneasy. She felt that she was being scrutinized and scrutinized uncharitably and saw there was no room for friendship here. She was persistent and finally she hit on it. 'I met the liveliest, nicest, friendliest woman today, honey,' she told Coverly when she kissed him at the door. 'Her name's Josephine Tellerman and she lives on M Circle. Her husband's in the drafting room and she says she's lived on nearly every rocket-launching reservation in the United States and she's just full of fun and her husband's nice too and she comes from a nice family and she asked us why didn't we come over some night and have a drink.'

Betsey loved her neighbor. This simple act of friendship brought her all the delights and hazards of love. Coverly knew how dim and senseless Circle K had seemed to her until the moment when she met Josephine Tellerman. Now he was prepared to hear about Mrs Tellerman for weeks and months. He was glad. Betsey and Mrs Tellerman would do their shopping together. Betsey and Mrs Tellerman would be on the telephone every morning. 'My friend Josephine Tellerman tells me that you have some very nice lamb chops,' she would tell them at the butcher. 'My friend Josephine Tellerman recommended you to me,' she would tell them at the laundry. Even the vacuum-cleaner salesman, ringing her doorbell at the end of a hard day, would find her changed. She would be friendly enough, but she would not open the door. 'Oh, hello,' she would say. 'I'd like to talk with you but I'm very sorry I don't have the time this afternoon. I'm expecting a telephone call from my friend Josephine Tellerman.'

The Wapshots went over to the Tellermans' for a drink one night and Coverly found them friendly enough. The Tellermans' house was furnished exactly like the Wapshots', including the Picasso over the mantelpiece. In the living room the women talked about curtains, and Coverly and Max Tellerman talked about cars in the kitchen while Max made the drinks. 'I've been looking at cars,' Max said, 'but I decided I wouldn't buy one this year. I have to cut down. And I don't really need a car. You see I'm sending my kid brother through college. My folks have split up and I feel pretty responsible for this kid. I'm all he's got. I worked my way through college – Jesus, I did everything – and I don't want him to go through that rat race. I want him to take it easy for four years. I want him to have everything he needs. I want him to feel that he's as good as the next fellow for a few years. . . .' They went back into the living room, where the women were still talking about curtains. Max showed Coverly some photographs of his brother and went on talking about him and at half-past ten they said good night and walked home.

Betsey was no gardener but she bought some canvas chairs for the back yard and some wooden lattice to conceal the garbage pail. They could sit there on summer nights. She was pleased with what she had done and one summer night the Tellermans came over to christen – as Betsey said – the back yard with rum. It was a warm night and most of their neighbors were in their yards. Josie and Betsey were talking about bedbugs, cockroaches and mice. Coverly was speaking affectionately of West Farm and the fishing there. He wasn't drinking himself and he disliked the smell of rum that came from the others, who were drinking a lot. 'Drink, drink,' Josie said. 'It's that kind of a night.'

It was that kind of a night. The air was hot and fragrant and from the kitchen, where he mixed the drinks, Coverly looked out of the window into the Frascatis' back yard. There he saw the young Frascati girl in a white bathing suit that accentuated every line of her body but the crease in her buttocks. Her brother was spraying her gently with a garden hose. There was no horseplay, there were no outcries, there was no sound at all while the young man dutifully sprayed his beautiful sister. When Coverly had mixed the drinks he carried them out. Josie had begun to talk about her mother. 'Oh, I wish you people could have met my mother,' she said. 'I wish you kids could have met my mother.' When Betsey asked Coverly to fill the glasses once more he said they were out of rum. 'Run down to the shopping center and get a bottle, honey,' Josie said. 'It's that kind of a night. We only live once.'

'We only pass this way once,' Betsey said.

'I'll get some,' Coverly said.

'Let me, let me,' Max said. 'Betsey and I'll go.' He pulled Betsey out of her chair and they walked together toward the shopping center. Betsey felt wonderful. It's that kind of a night, was all she could think to say, but the fragrant gloom and the crowded houses where the lights were beginning to go out and the noise of sprinklers and the snatches of music all made her feel that the pain of traveling and moving and strangeness and wandering was ended and that it had taught her the value of permanence and friendship and love.

Everything delighted her then – the moon in the sky and the neon lights of the shopping center – and when Max came out of the liquor store she thought what a distinguished, what an athletic and handsome man he was. Walking home he gave Betsey a long, sad look, put his arms around her and kissed her. It was a stolen kiss, Betsey thought, and it was that kind of a night, it was the kind of a night where you could steal a kiss. When they got back to Circle K, Coverly and Josie were in the living room. Josie was still talking about her mother. 'Never an unkind word, never a harsh look,' she was saying. 'She used to be quite a pianist. Oh, there was always a big gang at our house. On Sunday nights we all used to gather around the piano and sing hymns you know and have a wonderful time.' Betsey and Max went to the kitchen to make drinks. 'She was unhappy in her marriage,' Josie was saying. 'He was a real sonofabitch, there's no two ways about it, but she was philosophical, that was the secret of her success; she was philosophical about him and just from hearing her talk you'd think she was the happiest married woman in the world but he was . . .' 'Coverly,' Betsey screamed. 'Coverly, help.'

Coverly ran down the hall. Max was standing by the stove. He had torn Betsey's dress. Coverly swung at him, got him on the side of the jaw and set him down on the floor. Betsey screamed and ran into the living room. Coverly stood over

Max, cracking his knuckles. There were tears in his eyes. 'Hit me again if you want to, kick me if you want to,' Max said. 'I couldn't punch a hole in a paper bag. That was a lousy thing for me to do, you know, but I just can't help myself sometimes and I'm glad it's over and I swear to God I'll never do it again, but Jesus Christ Coverly sometimes I get so lonely I don't know where to turn and if it wasn't for this kid brother of mine that I'm sending through college I think I'd cut my throat, so help me God, I've thought of it often enough. You wouldn't think, just looking at me, that I was suicidal, would you, but so help me God I am an awful lot of the time.

'Josie's all right. She's a darned good sport,' Max said, still speaking from the floor, 'and she'll stay with me through thick and thin and I know that, but she's very insecure, you know, oh she's very insecure and I think it's because she's lived in so many different places. She gets melancholy, you know, and then she takes it out on me. She says I take advantage of her. She says I don't bring in the money for the food. I don't bring in the money for the car. She needs new dresses and she needs new hats and I don't know what she doesn't need new and then she gets real sore and goes off on a buying spree and sometimes it's six months or a year before I can pay the bills. I still owe bills all over the whole United States. Sometimes I don't think I can stand it any more. Sometimes I think I'm just going to pack my bag and take to the road. That's what I think, I think I'm entitled to a little fun, a little happiness, you know, and so I take a pass here and a pass there but I'm sorry about Betsey because you and Betsey have been real good friends to us but sometimes I don't think I can go on unless I have a little fun. I just don't think I have the strength to go on. I just don't think I can stand it any more.'

In the living room Josie had taken Betsey into her arms. 'There, there, honey,' Josie was saying, 'there, there, there. It's all over. Nothing happened. I'll fix your dress. I'll get you a new dress. He just had too much to drink, that's all. He's got the wandering hands. He's got the wandering hands and he just had too much to drink. Those hands of his, he's always putting them someplace where they don't belong. Honey, this isn't the first time. Even when he's asleep those hands of his are feeling around all the time until they get hold of something. Even when he's asleep, honey. There, there, don't you worry about it any more. Think of me, think of what I have to put up with. Thank God you've got a nice, clean husband like Coverly. Think of poor me, think of poor Josie trying to be cheerful all the time and going around picking up after him. Oh, I'm so tired of it. I'm so tired of trying to make his mistakes good. And if we get a couple of dollars ahead he sends it to this kid brother in Cornell. He's in love with this kid brother, he loves him more than he loves me or you or anybody. He spoils him. It makes my blood boil. He's living up there like a regular prince in a dormitory with his own bathroom and fancy clothes while I'm mending and sewing and scrubbing to save the price of a cleaning woman so that he can send this college boy an allowance or a new sports jacket or a tennis racket or something. Last year he was worried because the kid didn't have an extra-special heavy overcoat and I said to him, I said, Max, I said, now look here. You're worrying yourself sick because he doesn't have a winter coat, but what about me? Did it ever occur to you that I didn't have a good winter coat? Did it ever cross your mind that your loving wife is just as entitled to a coat as your kid brother? Did you ever look at it that way? And you know what he said? He said it was cooler up where this college is than it was in Montana where we was living. It didn't make any impression on him at all. Oh, it's terrible to be married to a man who's got something on his mind like that all the time. Sometimes it just makes my blood boil, seeing how he spoils him. But we have to take the lean with the fat, don't we? Into every real friendship a little rain must fall. Let's pretend it was that, honey, shall we, let's pretend it was just a little rain. Let's go and get the men and drink a friendship cup and let bygones be bygones. Let's pretend it was just a little rain.'

In the kitchen they found Max still sitting on the floor and Coverly standing by the sink, cracking his knuckles, but

Betsey went to Coverly and pleaded with him in a whisper to forget it. 'We're all going to be friends again,' Josie said loudly. 'Come on, come on, it's all forgotten. We're all going into the living room and drink a friendship cup and anyone who won't drink out of the friendship cup is a rotten egg.' Max followed her into the living room and Betsey led Coverly behind. Josie filled a large glass with rum and Coke. 'Here's for auld lang syne,' she said. 'Let bygones be bygones. Here's to friendship.' Betsey began to cry and they all drank from the glass. 'Well, I guess we are friends again, aren't we,' Betsey said, 'and I'll tell you, I'll tell you just to prove it, I'll tell you something I had in the back of my mind and that's even more important to me after this. Saturday is my birthday and I want you and Max to come over for dinner and make it a real celebration with champagne and tuxedos – a regular party and I think it's all the more important now that we've had this little trouble.'

'Oh, sweetheart, that's the nicest invitation anyone's ever given me,' Josie said, and she got up and kissed Betsey and then Coverly and linked her arm in Max's. Max held his hand out to Coverly and Betsey kissed Josie again and they said good night – softly, softly for it was late then, it was after two o'clock and theirs were the only lights burning in the circle.

Josie didn't call Betsey in the morning and when Betsey tried to call her friend either the line was busy or no one answered, but Betsey was too absorbed in the preparations for the party to care much. She bought a new dress and some glasses and napkins and on the night before the party she and Coverly ate supper in the kitchen in order to keep the dining space clean. Coverly had to work on Saturday and he didn't get home until after five. Everything was ready for the party. Betsey had not put on her new dress yet and was still wearing her bathrobe with her hair in pins but she was excited and happy and when she kissed Coverly she told him to hurry and take his bath. The table was set with one of the cloths, the old candlesticks and the blue china from West Farm. There were dishes of nuts and other things to eat with cocktails on all the tables. Betsey had laid out Coverly's clothes and he took a shower and was dressing when the telephone rang. 'Yes, dear,' Coverly heard Betsey say. 'Yes, Josie. Oh. Oh, then you mean you can't come. I see. Yes, I see. Well, what about tomorrow night? Why don't we put it off until tomorrow night? I see, oh I see. Well, why don't you come tonight for just a little while? We can bundle Max up in blankets and you could leave right after dinner if you wanted. I see. I see. Yes, I see. Well, good-by. Yes, good-by.'

Betsey was sitting on the sofa when Coverly came back to the living room. Her hands were in her lap, her face was haggard and wet with tears. 'They can't come,' she said. 'Max is sick and has a cold and they can't come.' Then a loud sob broke from her but when Coverly sat down and put an arm around her she resisted him. 'For two days I haven't done anything but work and think about my party,' she cried. 'I haven't done anything else for two days. I wanted to have a party. I just wanted to have a nice little party. That's all I wanted.'

Coverly kept telling her that it didn't matter and gave her a glass of sherry and then she decided to call the Frascatis. 'All I want now is to have a little party,' she said, 'and I have all this food and maybe the Frascatis would like to come. They haven't been very neighborly but maybe that's because they're foreigners. I'm going to ask the Frascatis.'

'Why don't we forget the whole thing?' Coverly said. 'We can eat our supper or take in a movie or something. We can have a good time together.'

'I'm going to ask the Frascatis,' Betsey said, and she went to the telephone. 'This is Betsey Wapshot,' she said cheerfully, 'and I've meant to call you again and again but I've been a bad neighbor, I'm afraid. We've been so busy since we've moved in that I haven't had the time and I'm ashamed of myself for having been such a bad neighbor but I just wondered if you and your husband wouldn't like to come over tonight and have supper with us.'

'Thank you but we already had supper,' Mrs Frascati said. She hung up.

Then Coverly heard Betsey calling the Galens. 'This is Betsey Wapshot,' she said, 'and I'm sorry I haven't called you sooner because I've wanted to know you better but I wondered if you and your husband would like to come over tonight for supper.'

'Oh, I'm terribly sorry,' Mrs Galen said, 'but the Tellermans – I think they're friends of yours – Max Tellerman's young brother has just come home from college and they're bringing him over to see us.'

Betsey hung up. 'Hypocrite,' she sobbed. 'Hypocrite. Oh she'd break her back, wouldn't she to get in good with the Galens and she just wouldn't tell me, her best friend, she just wouldn't have the nerve to tell me the truth.'

'There, there, sugar,' Coverly said. 'It isn't that important. It doesn't matter.'

'It matters to me,' Betsey cried. 'It's a matter of life and death to me, that's what it is. I'm going over there and see, I'm just going over there and see if that Mrs Galen's telling me the truth. I'm just going over there and see if that Max Tellerman's sick in bed or if he isn't. I'm just going over there and see.'

'Don't, Betsey,' Coverly said. 'Don't, honey.'

'I'm just going over there and see, that's what I'm going to do. Oh I've heard enough about this brother of his but when it comes time to introduce him around their old friends aren't good enough. I'm going over and see.' She stood – Coverly tried to stop her, but she went out the door. In her bathrobe and slippers she marched, bellicosely, up the street to the next circle. The Tellermans' windows were lighted, but when she rang the bell no one answered and there was no sound. She went around to the back of the house where the curtains on the picture window hadn't been drawn and looked into their living room. It was empty but there were some cocktail glasses on the table and by the door was a yellow leather suitcase with a Cornell sticker on it. And as she stood there in the dark it seemed that the furies attacked Betsey; that through every incident – every moment of her life – ran the cutting

thread, the wire of loneliness, and that when she thought she
had been happy she had only deceived herself for under all
her happiness lay the pain of loneliness and all her travels and
friends were nothing and everything was nothing.

She walked home and later that night she had a miscarriage.

CHAPTER 33

Betsey was in the hospital for two days and then she came home but she didn't seem to get better. She was unhappy as well as sick and Coverly felt that she was pushing some kind of stone that had nothing to do with their immediate life – or even with her miscarriage – but with some time in her past. He cooked her supper each night when he came home from the laboratory and talked or tried to talk with her. When she had been in bed for two weeks or longer he asked her if he could call the doctor. 'Don't you dare call the doctor,' Betsey said. 'Don't you dare call the doctor. The only reason you want to call the doctor is to have him come and prove that there isn't anything wrong with me. You just want to embarrass me. It's just meanness.' She began to cry but when he sat on the edge of the bed she turned away from him. 'I'll cook the supper,' he said. 'Well, don't cook anything for me,' Betsey said. 'I'm too sick to eat.'

When Coverly stepped into the dark kitchen he could see into the Frascatis' lighted kitchen where Mr Frascati was drinking wine and patting his wife on the rump as she went between the stove and the table. He slapped the Venetian blinds shut and, finding some frozen food, cooked it after his fashion, which was not much. He put Betsey's supper onto a tray and took it into her room. Fretfully she worked herself up to a sitting position in the pillows and let him put the tray on her lap but when he went back into the kitchen she called after him, 'Aren't you going to eat with me? Don't you want to eat with me? Don't you even want to look at me?' He took his plate into the bedroom and ate off the dressing table, telling her the news of the laboratory. The long tape he had been working on would be done in three days. He had a new boss named Pancras. He brought Betsey a dish of ice cream and washed up and walked down to the shopping center to buy her some mystery stories at a drugstore. He slept on the sofa, covered with an overcoat and feeling sad and lewd.

Betsey remained in bed another week and seemed more and more unhappy. 'There's a new doctor at the laboratory, Betsey,' Coverly said one night. 'His name is Blennar. I've seen him in the cafeteria. He's a nice-looking fellow. He's a sort of marriage counselor, and I thought . . .'

'I don't want to hear about him,' Betsey said.

'But I want you to hear about him, Betsey. I want you to talk with Dr Blennar. I think he might help us. We'll go together. Or you could go alone. If you could tell him your troubles . . .'

'Why should I tell him my troubles? I know what my troubles are. I hate this house. I hate this place, this Remsen Park.'

'If you talked with Dr Blennar . . .'

'Is he a psychiatrist?'

'Yes.'

'You want to prove that I'm crazy, don't you?'

'No, Betsey.'

'Psychiatrists are for crazy people. There's nothing wrong with me.' Then she got out of bed and went into the living room. 'Oh, I'm sick of you, sick of your earnest damned ways, sick of the way you stretch your neck and crack your knuckles and sick of your old father with his dirty letters asking is there any news, is there any good news, is there any news. I'm sick of Wapshots and I don't give a damn who knows it.' Then she went into the kitchen and came out with the blue dishes that Sarah had sent them from West Farm and began to break them on the floor. Coverly went out of the living room on

to the back steps but Betsey followed him and broke the rest
of the dishes out there.

On the day after they were married they had gone out
to sea in a steamer of about the same vintage as the *Topaze*
but a good deal bigger. It was a fine day at sea, mild and fair
and with a haze suspended all around them so that, but for
the wake rolled away at their stern, their sense of direction
and their sense of time were obscured. They walked around
the decks, hand in hand, finding in the faces of the other
passengers great kindliness and humor. They went from the
bow down to the shelter of the stern where they could feel the
screw thumping underfoot and where many warm winds from
the galley and the engine room blew around them and they
could see the gulls, hitchhiking their way out to Portugal. They
did not raise the island – it was too hazy – and warped in by
the lonely clangor of sea bells they saw the place – steeples
and cottages and two boys playing catch on a beach – rise up
around them through the mist.

The cottage was far away – a place that belonged to
Leander's time – a huddle of twelve or sixteen cottages, so
awry and weather-faded that they might have seemed thrown
up to accommodate the victims of some disaster had you not
known that they had been built for those people who make a
pilgrimage each summer to the sea. The house they went to was
like West Farm, a human burrow or habitation that had yielded
at every point to the crotchets and meanderings of a growing
family. They put down their bags and undressed for a swim.

It was out of season, early or late, and the inn and the gift
shop were under lock and key and they went down the path,
hand in hand, as bare as the day they were born with no
thought of covering themselves, down the path, dust and in
some place ashes and then fine sand like the finest sugar and
crusty – it would set your teeth on edge – down onto the
coarser sand, wet from the high tide and the sea, ringing then
with the music of slammed doors. There was a rock offshore
and Betsey swam for this, Coverly following her through the

rich, medicinal broths of the North Atlantic. She sat naked on the rock when he approached her, combing her hair with her fingers, and when he climbed up on the rock she dived back into the sea and he followed her to shore.

Then he could have roared with joy, kicked up his heels in a jig and sung a loud tune, but he walked instead along the edge of the sea picking up skimmers and firing them out to beyond the surf where they skittered sometimes and sometimes sank. And then a great sadness of contentment seemed to envelop him – a joy so fine that it gently warmed his skin and bones like the first fires of autumn – and going back to her then, still picking skimmers and firing them, slowly, for there was no rush, and kneeling beside her, he covered her mouth with his and her body with him and then – his body raked and exalted – he seemed to see a searing vision of some golden age that bloomed in his mind until he fell asleep.

The next night when Coverly came home, Betsey had gone. The only message she left him was their canceled savings-account bankbook. He wandered around the house in the dim light. There was nothing here that she had not touched or rearranged, marked with her person and her tastes, and in the dusty light he seemed to feel a premonition of death, he seemed to hear Betsey's voice. He put on a hat and took a walk. But Remsen Park was not much of a place to walk in. Most of its evening sounds were mechanized and the only woods was a little strip on the far side of the army camp and Coverly went there. When he thought of Betsey he thought of her against scenes of travel – trains and platforms and hotels and asking strangers for help with her bags – and he felt great love and pity. What he could not understand was the heaviness of his emotional investment in a situation that no longer existed. Making a circle around the woods and coming back through the army camp and seeing the houses of Remsen Park he felt a great homesickness for St Botolphs – for a place whose streets were as excursive and crooked as the human mind, for water shining through trees, human sounds at evening, even Uncle Peepee pushing through the privet in his bare skin. It was a long walk, it was past midnight when he got back, and he threw himself naked onto their marriage bed that still held the fragrance of her skin and dreamed about West Farm.

Now the world is full of distractions – lovely women, music, French movies, bowling alleys and bars – but Coverly lacked the vitality or the imagination to distract himself. He went to work in the morning. He came home at dark, bringing a frozen dinner which he thawed and ate out of the pot. His reality seemed assailed or contested; his gifts for hopefulness seemed damaged or destroyed. There is a parochialism to some kinds of misery – a geographical remoteness like the life led by a grade-crossing tender – a point where life is lived or endured at the minimum of energy and perception and where most of the world appears to pass swiftly by like passengers on the gorgeous trains of the Santa Fe. Such a life has its compensations – solitaire and star-wishing – but it is a life stripped of friendship, association, love and even the practicable hope of escape. Coverly sank into this emotional hermitage and then there was a letter from Betsey.

'Sweetie,' she wrote, 'I'm on my way back to Bambridge to see Grandma. Don't try to follow me. I'm sorry I took all the money but as soon as I get work I'll pay it all back to you. You can get a divorce and marry somebody else who will have children. I guess I'm just a wanderer and now I'm wandering again.' Coverly went to the telephone and called Bambridge. Her old grandmother answered. 'I want to speak with Betsey,' Coverly shouted. 'I want to speak with Betsey.' 'She ain't here,' the old lady said. 'She don't live here any more. She done married Coverly Wapshot, and went to live with him somewheres else.' 'I'm Coverly Wapshot,' Coverly shouted. 'Well, if you're Coverly Wapshot what you bothering me for?' the old lady asked. 'If you're Coverly Wapshot why don't you speak to Betsey yourself? And when you speak to her you tell her to get down on her knees to say her prayers. You tell her it don't count unless she gets down on her knees.' Then she hung up.

CHAPTER 34

And now we come to the unsavory or homosexual part of our tale and any disinterested reader is encouraged to skip. It came about like this. Coverly's immediate superior was a man named Walcott but in charge of the whole Taping Department was a young man named Pancras. He had a sepulchral voice, beautifully white and even teeth and he drove a European racing car. He never spoke to Coverly beyond a good morning or an encouraging smile when he passed through the long Tapers' room. It may be that we overestimate our powers of concealment and that the brand of loneliness and unrequital is more conspicuous than we know. In any case, Pancras suddenly approached Coverly one evening and offered him a ride home. Coverly would have been grateful for any company, and the low-slung racing car had a considerable effect on his spirits. When they turned off 325th Street onto Circle K, Pancras said he was surprised not to see Coverly's wife on the doorstep. Coverly said she was visiting in Georgia. Then you must come home and have supper with me, Pancras said. He throttled the car, and off they roared.

Pancras' house was, of course, exactly like Coverly's, but it was near the army post and stood on a larger piece of land. It was elegantly furnished and a pleasant change for Coverly from the disorder of his own housekeeping. Pancras made him a drink and began to butter Coverly's parsnips. 'I've wanted to talk with you for a long time,' he said. 'Your work is excellent — brilliant in fact — and I've wanted to say so. We're sending someone to England in a few weeks — I'm going myself. We want to compare our tapings with the English. And we want someone who can get along, of course. We need someone personable, someone with some social experience. There's a good chance that you might make the trip if you're interested.'

These words of esteem made Coverly happy, although Pancras showered on him so many open and lingering glances that he felt uneasy. His friend was not effeminate; far from it. His voice was the deepest bass, his body seemed to be covered with hair and his movements were very athletic, but Coverly somehow had the feeling that if he was touched on the bun he would swoon. He could see that it was ungrateful and dishonest to accept the man's charming house and his hospitality while he entertained suspicions about his private life; and to tell the truth he was thoroughly enjoying himself. Coverly could not contemplate the consummation of any such friendship but he could enjoy the atmosphere of praise and tenderness that Pancras created and in which he seemed to bask. The dinner was the best meal Coverly had eaten in months and after dinner Pancras suggested that they take a walk through the army garrison and into the woods. It was exactly what Coverly would have liked to do and so they walked out in the evening and made a circle through the woods, talking in friendly and serious voices about their work and their pleasure. Then Pancras drove Coverly home.

In the morning, before he had started work, Walcott warned Coverly about Pancras. He was queer. This news excited in Coverly bewilderment, sadness and some stubbornness. He felt as Cousin Honora felt about the cart horse. He did not want to be a cart horse, but he did not want to see them exposed to cruelty. He did not see Pancras for a day or two and then one evening, when he was about to eat his dinner from the pot, the racing car roared into K Circle and Pancras rang the bell. He took Coverly back to his own house for supper and they walked again in the woods. Coverly had never found anyone so interested in his recollections of St Botolphs and he was happy to be able to talk about the past.

After another evening with Pancras it was apparent to Coverly what his friend's intentions were, although he did not know how to behave himself and saw no reason why he should not eat dinner with a homosexual. He claimed to himself to be innocent or naive, but this pretense was the thinnest. The queer never really surprise us. We choose our neckties, comb our hair with water and lace our shoes in order to please the people we desire; and so do they. Coverly had enough experience in friendship to know that the exaggerated attentions he was receiving from Pancras were amorous. He meant to be seductive and when they took their walk after supper he seemed to emanate a stir of erotic busyness or distress. They had come to the last of the houses and had reached the army installation – barracks and a chapel and a walk lined with whitewashed stone and a man sitting on a step hammering out a bracelet from a piece of rocket scrap. It was the emotional no man's land of most army posts – tolerable enough in the push of war, but now more isolated and lonely than ever. They walked through the barracks area into the woods and sat down on some stones.

'We're going to England in ten days,' Pancras said.

'I'll miss you,' Coverly said.

'You're coming,' Pancras said. 'I've arranged the whole thing.'

Coverly turned to his companion and they exchanged a look of such sorrow that he thought he might never recover. It was a look that he had recoiled from here and there – the doctor in Travertine, a bartender in Washington, a priest on a night boat, a clerk in a shop – that exacerbating look of sexual sorrow between men; sorrow and the perverse wish to flee – to piss in the Lowestoft soup tureen, write a vile word on the back of the barn and run away to sea with a dirty, dirty sailor – to flee, not from the laws and customs of the world but from its force and vitality. 'Only ten more days,' his companion sighed, and suddenly Coverly felt a dim rumble

of homosexual lust in his trousers. This lasted for less than a
second. Then the lash of his conscience crashed down with
such force that his scrotum seemed injured, at the prospect
of joining this pale-eyed company, wandering in the dark like
Uncle Peepee Marshmallow. A second later the lash came
down again – this time for having scorned a human condition.
It was Uncle Peepee's destiny to wander through the gardens
and Coverly's vision of the world must be a place where this
forlornness was admitted. Then the lash crashed down once
more, this time at the hands of a lovely woman who scorned
him bitterly for his friend and whose eyes told him that he
was now shut away forever from a delight in girls – those
creatures of morning. He had thought with desire of going
to sea with a pederast and Venus turned her naked back on
him and walked out of his life forever.

It was a withering loss. Their airs and confessions, their
memories and their theories about the atomic bomb, their
secret stores of Kleenex and hand lotion, the warmth of
their breasts, their powers of succumbing and forgiveness, that
sweetness of love that had passed his understanding – was gone.
Venus was his adversary. He had drawn a mustache on her
gentle mouth and she would tell her minions to scorn him.
She might allow him to talk to an old woman now and then,
but that was all.

It was in the summer – the air was full of seed and pollen
– and with that extraordinary magnification of grief – he
might have been looking through a reading glass – Coverly
saw the wealth of berries and seed pods in the ground around
his feet and thought how richly all of nature was created to
inseminate its kind – all but Coverly. He thought of his poor,
kind parents at West Farm, dependent for their happiness, their
security, their food upon a prowess that he didn't have. Then
he thought of Moses and the wish to see his brother was
passionate. 'I can't go to England with you,' he told Pancras.
'I have to go and see my brother.' Pancras was supplicatory
and then downright angry and they came out of the woods
in single file.

In the morning Coverly told Walcott that he didn't want
to go to England with Pancras and Walcott said this was all
right and smiled. Coverly looked back at him grimly. It was
a knowledgeable smile – he would know about Pancras – it
was the smile of a Philistine, a man content to have saved his
own skin; it was the kind of crude smile that held together
and nourished the whole unwholesome world of pretense,
censure and cruelty – and then, looking more closely, he saw
that it was a most friendly and pleasant smile, the smile at the
most of a man who recognizes another man to have known
his own mind. Coverly asked for two days' annual leave to go
and visit Moses.

He left the laboratory at noon, packed a bag and took a
bus to the station. Some women were waiting on the platform
for the train but Coverly averted his eyes from them. It was
not his right to admire them any more. He was unworthy
of their loveliness. Once aboard the train he shut his eyes
against anything in the landscape that might be pleasing, for
a beautiful woman would sicken him with his unworthiness
and a comely man would remind him of the sordidness of the
life he was about to begin. He could have traveled peaceably
then only in some hobgoblin company of warty men and
quarrelsome women – some strange place where the hazards
of grace and beauty were outlawed.

At Brushwick the seat beside him was occupied by a gray-
haired man who carried one of those green serge book bags
that used to be carried in Cambridge. The worn green cloth
reminded Coverly of the New England winter – a simple and
traditional way of life – going back to the farm for Christmas
and the snow-dark as it gathered over the skating pond and
the barking of dogs way off. With the book bag between them,
the stranger and Coverly began to talk. His companion was a
scholar. Japanese literature was his field. He was interested in
the *Samurai Sagas* and showed Coverly a translation of one.
It was about some homosexual samurai and when Coverly
had absorbed this his traveling companion produced some
prints of the samurai in action. Then the valves of Coverly's

heart felt abraded and he seemed to listen at his organs, as
we will at a door, to see if there was any guilty arousal there.
Then, blushing like Honora – coloring like any spinster who
finds the whole sky–high creaking edifice of her chastity
shaken – Coverly grabbed for his suitcase and fled to another
car. Feeling sick, he went to the toilet, where someone had
written on the wall in pencil a homosexual solicitation for
anyone who would stand by the water cooler and whistle
'Yankee Doodle.' How could he refresh his sense of moral
reality; how could he put different words in Pancras' mouth
or pretend that the prints he had been shown were of geisha
crossing a bridge in the snow? He stared out of the window
at the landscape, seeking in it, with all his heart, some shred
of usable and creative truth, but what he looked into were the
dark plains of American sexual experience where the bison
still roam. He wished that instead of going to the MacIlhenney
Institute he had gone to some school of love.

He saw the entrance and the pediment of such a school
and imagined the curriculum. There would have been classes
on the moment of recognition; lectures on the mortal error
of confusing worship with tenderness; there would have been
symposiums on indiscriminate erotic impulses and man's
complex and demoniac nature and there would have been
descriptions of the powers of anxiety to light the world with
morbid and lovely colors. Representations of Venus would
be paraded before them and they would be marked on their
reactions. Those pitiful men who counted upon women to
assure them of their sexual nature would confess to their sins
and miseries, and libertines who had abused women would
also testify. Those nights when he had lain in bed, listening to
trains and rains and feeling under his hip bread crumbs and
the cold stains of love – those nights when his joy overshot his
understanding – would be explained in detail and he would
be taught to put an exact and practical interpretation on the
figure of a lovely woman bringing in her flowers at dusk
before the frost. He would learn to estimate sensibly all such
tender and lovely figures – women sewing, their laps heaped

with blue cloth – women singing in the early dark to their children the ballads of that lost cause, Charles Stuart – women walking out of the sea or sitting on rocks. There would be special courses for Coverly on the matriarchy and its subtle influence – he would have to do make-up work here – courses in the hazards of uxoriousness that, masquerading as love, expressed skepticism and bitterness. There would be scientific lectures on homosexuality and its fluctuating place in society and the truth or the falsity of its relationship to the will to die. That hairline where lovers cease to nourish and begin to devour one another; that fine point where tenderness corrodes self-esteem and the spirit seems to flake like rust would be put under a microscope and magnified until it was as large and recognizable as a steel girder. There would be graphs on love and graphs on melancholy and the black looks that we are entitled to give the hopelessly libidinous would be measured to a millimeter. It would be a hard course for Coverly, he knew, and he would be on probation most of the time, but he would graduate. An upright piano would play 'Pomp and Circumstance' and he would march across a platform and be given a diploma and then he would go down the stairs and under the pediment in full possession of his powers of love and he would regard the earth with candor and with relish, world without end.

But there was no such school, and when he got into New York, late that night, it was raining and the streets around the station seemed to exhale an atmosphere of erotic misdemeanor. He got a hotel room and, looking for the truth, decided that what he was was a homosexual virgin in a cheap hotel. He would never see the resemblance he bore to Cousin Honora, but, as he cracked his knuckles and stretched his neck, his train of thought was like the old lady's. If he was a pederast he would be one openly. He would wear bracelets and pin a rose in his bottonhole. He would be an organizer of pederasts, a spokesman and prophet. He would force society, government and the law to admit their existence. They would have clubs – not hole-in-the-wall meeting places, but straight-forward organizations like the English-Speaking Union. What bothered him most was his inability to discharge his responsibilities to his parents, and he sat down and wrote Leander a letter.

A morning train took Coverly out to Clear Haven and when he saw his brother he thought how solid this friendship was. They embraced – they swatted one another – they got into the old Rolls and in a second Coverly had dropped from the anguish of anxiety to a level of life that seemed healthy and simple and reminded him only of good things. Could it be wrong, he wondered, that he seemed, in spirit, to have returned to his father's house? Could it be wrong that he felt as if he were back at the farm, making some simple journey down to Travertine to race the *Tern?* They passed the gates and went up through the park while Moses explained that he was living at Clear Haven only until autumn; that it had been Melissa's home. Coverly was impressed with the towers and battlements, but not surprised since it was a part of his sense of the world that Moses would always have better luck than he. Melissa was still in bed, but she would be down soon. They would have a picnic at the pool. 'This is the library,' Moses said. 'This is the ballroom, this is the state dining room, this is what they call the rotunda.' Then Melissa came down the stairs.

She took Coverly's breath away; her golden skin and her dark-blond hair. 'It's so nice to meet you,' she said, and while her voice was pleasant enough it could never be compared to the power of her appearance. She seemed a triumphant beauty to Coverly – an army with banners – and he couldn't take his eyes off her until Moses pushed him toward a bathroom where they put on their bathing trunks. 'I think we'd better wear hats,' Melissa said. 'The sun's terribly bright.' Moses opened a coat closet, passed Melissa a hat and, rummaging around for one himself, brought down a green Tyrolean hat with a brush in the band. 'Is this D'Alba's?' he asked. 'Lord, no,' Melissa said. 'Pansies *never* wear hats.' It was all that Coverly needed. He plunged into the coat closet and grabbed the first hat he saw – an old Panama that must have belonged to the late Mr Scaddon. It was much too big for him – it drooped down over his ears – but with at least this one symbol of his male virility intact he walked behind Moses and Melissa down toward the pool.

Melissa didn't swim that day. She sat at the edge of the marble curb, spreading the cloth for lunch and pouring the drinks. There was nothing she did or said that did not charm and delight poor Coverly and incline him to foolishness. He dived. He swam the length of the pool four times. He tried to do a back dive and failed, splashing water all over Melissa. They drank martinis and talked about the farm, and Coverly, who was not used to liquor, got tipsy. Starting to talk about the Fourth of July parade he was sidetracked by a memory of Cousin Adelaide and ended up with describing the rocket launchings on Saturday afternoons. He didn't mention Betsey's departure and when Moses asked for her he spoke as if they were still living happily together. When lunch was finished he swam the length of the pool once more and then lay down in the shade of a boxwood tree and fell asleep.

He was tired and didn't know, for a moment, when he woke where he was, seeing the water gush out of the green lions' heads and the towers and battlements of Clear Haven at the head of the lawn. He splashed some water on his face. The picnic cloth was still spread on the curb. No one had removed the cocktail glasses or the plates and chicken bones. Moses and Melissa were gone and the shadow of a hemlock tree fell across the pool. Then he saw them coming down the garden path from the greenhouse where they had spent some pleasant time and there was such grace and gentleness between them that he thought his heart would break in two; for her beauty could arouse in him only sadness, only feelings of parting and forsakenness, and thinking of Pancras it seemed that Pancras had offered him much more than friendship – that he had offered him the subtle means by which we deface and diminish the loveliness of a woman. Oh, she was lovely, and he had betrayed her! He had sent spies into her kingdom on rainy nights and encouraged the usurper.

'I'm sorry we left you alone, Coverly,' she said, 'but you were sleeping, you were *snoring*. . . .' It was late, it was time for Coverly to dress and catch his train.

Any railroad station on Sunday afternoon seems to lie close to the heart of time. Even in midsummer the shadows seem autumnal and the people who are gathered there – the soldier, the sailor, the old lady with flowers wrapped in a paper – seemed picked so arbitrarily from the community, seem so like those visited by illness or death, that we are reminded of those solemn plays in which it appears, toward the end of the first act, that all the characters are dead. 'Do your soft shoe, Coverly,' Moses asked. 'Do your buck and wing.' 'I'm rusty, brother,' Coverly said. 'I can't do it any more.' 'Oh, try, Coverly,' Moses said. 'Oh, try . . .' Cloppety, cloppety, cloppety went Coverly up and down the platform, ending with a clumsy shuffle-off, a bow and a blush. 'We're a very talented family,' he told Melissa. Then the train came down the track and their feelings, like the scraps of paper on the platform, were thrown up pellmell in a hopeless turbulence. Coverly embraced them both – he seemed to be crying – and boarded the train.

When he got back to the empty house in Remsen Park there was a reply from Leander to the letter he had written his father from New York. 'Cheer up,' Leander wrote. 'Writer not innocent, and never claimed to be so. Played the man to many a schoolboy bride. Woodshed lusts. Rainy Sundays. Theophilus Gates tried to light farts with candle ends. Later President of Pocamasset Bank and Trust Co. Had unfortunate experience in early manhood. Unpleasant to recall. Occurred after disappearance of father. Befriended stranger in gymnasium. Name of Parminter. Appeared to be good companion. Witty. Comely physique. Writer at loneliest time of life. Father gone. Hamlet away. Brought Parminter home for supper on several occasions. Old mother much taken by elegant manners. Fine clothes. I'm glad you have a gentleman for a friend, says she.

Parminter brought her posies. Also sang. Good tenor voice. Gave me a pair of gold cuff links on birthday. Sentimental inscription. Tickled pink. Me.

'Vanity was my undoing. Very vain of my physique. Often admired self in mirror, scantily clad. Posed as dying gladiator. Discobolus. Mercury in flight. Guilty of self-love, perhaps. Retribution might be what followed. Parminter claimed to be spare-time artist. Offered to pay writer hard cash for posing. Seemed like agreeable prospect. Happy at thought of having shapely limbs appreciated. Went on designated night to so-called studio. Climbed narrow staircase to bad-smelling room. Not large. Parminter there with several friends. Was asked to undress. Cheerfully complied. Was much admired. Parminter and friends commenced to undress. Appeared to be pederasts.

'Writer grabbed britches and made escape. Rainy night. Anger. Perturbation. Poor cod appeared to be seat of mixed feelings. Up and down. Felt as if same had been put through clothes wringer. Such feelings gave rise to question: Was writer pederast? Sex problems hard nut to crack in 19th-century gloom. Asked self: Was pederast? In shower after ball games. Swimming in buff with chums at Stone Hills. In locker room asked self: Was pederast?

'Had no wish to see Parminter after exposé. Not so easy to shake. Appeared at home on following evening. Unregenerate. Unashamed. Posies for old mother. Sloe-eyed looks for me. Unable to explain situation. Might as well tell mother moon was made of green cheese. Far from ignorant in regards to such things since St Botolphs produced several such specimens but never seemed to cross mind that gentleman friend belonged in such category. Writer unwilling to meet situation with meanness. Agreed to eat supper with Parminter at Young's Hotel. Hoped to preserve climate of speckless reason. Gentle parting at crossroads. You go that way. I'll go this.

'Parminter in high-low spirits. Eyes like hound dog. Itchy tea-kettle. Drank much whisky. Ate little food. Writer made parting speech. Hoped to continue friendship, etc. Net result was like poking adder with sharp stick. Recriminations.

Threats. Cajolery. Etc. Was asked to return gold cuff links. Accused of flirtatiousness. Also of being well-known pederast. Paid share of check and left dining room. Went to bed. Later heard name being called. Gravel on window. Parminter in back yard calling me. Thought then of slop pail. Sin of pride, perhaps. Hellfire in offing. Everything in due course. Opened door of commode. Removed lid of chamberpot. Ample supply of ammunition. Carried same to window and let figure in yard have both barrels. Finis.

'Man is not simple. Hobgoblin company of love always with us. Those who hang their barebums out of street-front windows. Masturbate in YMCA showers. Knights, poets, wits in this love's flotsam. Drapers. Small tradesmen. Docile. Cleanly. Soft-voiced. Mild of wit. Flavorless. Yearn for the high-school boy who cuts the grass. Die for the embraces of the tree surgeon. Life has worse trouble. Sinking ships. Houses struck by lightning. Death of innocent children. War. Famine. Runaway horses. Cheer up my son. You think you have trouble. Crack your skull before you weep. All in love is not larky and fractious. Remember.'

CHAPTER 35

It would be, Moses thought, a sentimental summer, for they could hear fountains in their room and she made his bed a kind of Venice and who cared about the watery soups and custards that they mostly seemed to get for dinner? Melissa was loving and contented and how could Justina make any of this her province? A few days after the wedding Mrs Enderby called Moses into her office and said that he would be billed three hundred dollars a month for room and board. He apprehended then that loving a woman who could not move from a particular place might create some problems, but this was only an apprehension and he agreed politely to pay the toll. A few nights later he returned from Bond School and found his wife, for the first time since he had known her, in tears. Justina's wedding present had arrived. Giacomo had removed their capacious and lumpy marriage bed and replaced it with twin beds – narrow and hard as slate. Melissa stood at the door to her balcony, weeping over this, and it appeared to Moses then that he might have overlooked the depth of the relationship between his golden-skinned wife and that truculent and well-preserved crone, her guardian. He dried her tears and thanked Justina for the beds at dinner. After dinner he and Giacomo put the twin beds back into the storeroom where they had been and returned the old bed. Watching Melissa undress that night (he could see past her shoulder in the moonlight the lawns and the gardens and the plunge) and resisting the thought that these ramparts were real for her, that she should think that the thorns on the roses that surrounded the walls were piercing, he asked if they could leave before autumn and she reminded him that he had promised not to ask this.

A few mornings later, going to his closet, Moses discovered that all his suits were gone but the soiled seersucker suit he had worn the day before. 'Oh, I know what's happened, darling,' Melissa said. 'Justina's taken your clothes and given them to the church for a rummage sale.' She got out of bed, wearing nothing, and went anxiously to her own closet. 'That's what she's done. She's taken my yellow dress and my gray and my blue. I'll go down to the church and get them back.'

'You mean she's taken my clothes for a rummage sale without asking?'

'Yes, darling. She's never understood that everything in Clear Haven isn't hers.'

'How long has this been going on?'

'For years.'

As it happened Melissa was able to buy their clothes back from the church for a few dollars and with this forgotten he was able to take up his sentimental life. Moses had long since forgotten the dislike of Clear Haven that had formed in his mind when he stumbled on the roof and it began to seem to him an excellent place for the first months of his marriage, for even the benches in the garden were supported by women with enormous marble breasts and in the hall his eye fell repeatedly on naked and comely men and women in the pursuit or the glow of love. They were on the needlepoint chairs, they reached for one another from the tops of the massive andirons, they supported the candles for the dinner table and the bowl of the glass from which Justina drank the water for her pills. He seemed to work even the lilies in the garden into his picture of love and when Melissa picked them and carried them in her arms like lumber, their truly mournful perfume falling this way and that, he kicked up his heels with joy. Night after night they drank some whisky in their room, some sherry in the hall, sat through the wretched dinner and then went together down to the plunge, and they were excusing themselves one evening after dinner when Justina said:

'We're going to play bridge.'

'We're going swimming,' Moses said.

'The pool lights are broken,' Justina said. 'You can't swim in the dark. I'll have Giacomo fix the lights tomorrow. Tonight we'll play bridge.'

They played bridge until after eleven and, in the company of the old general, the count and Mrs Enderby, it was a stifling evening. When Moses and Melissa excused themselves on the next night Justina was ready. 'The pool lights aren't fixed yet,' she said, 'and I feel like some more bridge.' Playing bridge that night and the night after, Moses felt restless, and it appeared to him to be significant that he was the only one who left Clear Haven; that since his wedding he had not seen a strange or a new face in the house and that, so far as he knew, not even Giacomo ever left the grounds. He complained to Melissa and she said that she would ask some people for drinks on Saturday and she asked Justina's permission on the next night at dinner. 'Of course, of course,' Justina said, 'of course you want to have some young people in, but I can't let you entertain guests until I've had the rugs cleaned. I'm having estimates made and they ought to be cleaned in a week or two and you can have your little party.' On Saturday morning Justina announced through Mrs Enderby that she was tired and would spend the week end in her room, and Melissa, encouraged by Moses, telephoned three couples who lived in the neighborhood and asked them for drinks on Sunday. Late Sunday afternoon Moses laid a fire in the hall and brought the bottles out of their hiding place. Melissa made something to eat and they sat on the only comfortable sofa in the room and waited for their guests.

It was a rainy afternoon and the rain played on the complicated roofs of the old monument a pleasant air. Melissa turned on a lamp when she heard a car come up the drive and she went down the hall and through the rotunda. Moses heard her voice in the distance, greeting the Trenholmes, and he gave the fire a poke and stood as a couple, who were made by their youthfulness and their pleasant manners to seem innocuous, came into the room. Melissa passed the crackers and when the Howes and the Van Bibbers joined them the vapid music of their voices mingled pleasantly with the sounds of the rain. Then Moses heard from the doorway the horse, strong notes of Justina's voice.

'What is the meaning of this, Melissa?'

'Oh, Justina,' Melissa said gallantly. 'I think you know all these people.'

'I may know them,' Justina said, 'but what are they doing here?'

'I've asked them for cocktails,' Melissa said.

'Well, that's very inconvenient,' Justina said. 'This day of all days. I told Giacomo he could take up the rugs and clean them.'

'We can go into the winter garden,' Melissa said timidly.

'How many times have I told you, Melissa, that I don't want you to take guests into the winter garden?'

'I'll call Giacomo,' Moses said to Justina. 'Here, let me get you some whisky.'

Moses gave Justina her whisky and she sat on the sofa and regarded the dumb-struck company with a charming smile. 'If you insist on inviting people here, Melissa,' she said, 'I wish you ask my advice. If we're not careful the house will be full of pickpockets and hoboes.' The guests retreated toward the door and Melissa walked them out to the rotunda. When she returned to the hall she sat down in a chair, not beside Moses, but opposite her guardian. Moses had never seen her face so dark.

The rain had let up. Close to the horizon the heavy clouds had split as if they had been lanced and a liquid brilliance gorged through the cut, spread up the lawn and came through the glass doors, lighting the hall and the old woman's face. The hundred windows of the house would glitter for miles.

Ursuline nuns, bird watchers, motorists and fishermen would admire the illusion of a house bathed in flame. Feeling the light on her face and feeling that it became her, Justina smiled her most narcissistic smile – that patrician gaze that made it seem as if all the world were hung with mirrors. 'I only do this because I love you so, Melissa,' she said, and she worked her fingers loaded with diamonds, emeralds and glass in the light that was fading.

Then the stillness of a trout pool seemed to settle over the room. Justina seemed to make a lure of false promises and Melissa to watch her shadow as it fell through the water to the sand, trying to find in her guardian's larcenous words some truth. Justina's face gleamed with rouge and her eyebrows shone with black dye and it seemed to Moses that somewhere in the *maquillage* must be the image of an old woman. Her face would be seamed, her clothes would be black, her voice would be cracked and she would knit blankets and sweaters for her grandchildren, take in her roses before the frost and speak mostly of friends and relations who had departed this life.

'This house is a great burden,' Justina said, 'and I have no one to help me bear it. I would love to give it all to you, Melissa, but I know that if you should predecease Moses he would sell it to the first bidder.'

'I promise not to,' Moses said cheerfully.

'Oh, I wish I could be sure,' she sighed. Then she rose, still beaming, and went to her ward. 'But don't let there be any hard feeling between us, sweet love, even if I have broken up your little party. I warned you about the rugs, but you've never had much sense. I've always been able to wrap you around my fingers.'

'I won't have this, Justina,' Moses said.

'Keep out of this, Moses.'

'Melissa is my wife.'

'You're not her first husband and you won't be her last and she's had a hundred lovers.'

'You're wicked, Justina.'

'I'm wicked, as you say, and I'm rude and I'm boorish and I discovered, after marrying Mr Scaddon, that I could be all these things and worse and that there would still be plenty of people to lick my boots.' Then she turned to him again her best smile and he saw for once how truly powerful this old dancing mistress had been in her heyday and how she was like an old Rhine princess, an exile from the abandoned duchies of upper Fifth Avenue and the dusty kingdoms of Riverside Drive. Then she bent and kissed Melissa and removed herself gracefully from the room.

Melissa's lips were drawn as if to check her tears. Moses went to her eagerly, thinking that he could take her out of the atmosphere of breakage that the old woman had left in the room, but when he put his hands on her shoulders she twisted out of his reach.

'Would you like another drink?'

'Yes.'

He put some whisky and ice in her glass.

'Shall we go up?'

'All right.'

She walked ahead of him; she didn't want him at her side. The encounter had damaged her grace and she sighed as she walked. She held her whisky glass in both hands before her like a grail. She seemed to emanate weariness and pain. It was her charming custom to undress where she could be seen but this evening she went instead to the bathroom and slammed the door. When she returned she was wearing a drab gray dress that Moses had never seen before. It was shapeless and very old; he could tell because there were moth holes in it. A row of steel buttons, pressed to look like ships in full sail, ran from the tight neck to the sagging hem, and the shape of her waist and her breasts was lost in the folds of gray cloth. She sat at the dressing table and removed her earrings, her bracelets and pearls, and began to brush the curl out of her hair.

Now Moses knew that women can take many forms; that it is in their power in the convulsions of love to take the shape of any beast or beauty on land or sea – fire, caves, the sweetness of haying weather – and to let break upon the mind, like light on water, its most brilliant imagery, and it did not dismay him that this gift for metamorphosis could be used to further all kinds of venal and petty schemes for self-aggrandizement. Moses had learned that it was wise to keep in mind the guises most often taken by the women he loved so that when a warmhearted woman appeared suddenly, for some reason of her own, to have become a spinster he would be prepared and in not much danger of losing the hopefulness that sustained his patience, for while women could metamorphose themselves at will he found that they could not sustain these impersonations for long and that if he could endure, patiently, a disguise or distemper or false modesty, it would soon wear thin. Now he watched the changes that had come over his golden-skinned wife, trying to discover what it was that she represented.

She represented chastity – an infelicitous and implacable chastity. She represented an unhappy spinster. She glanced scornfully at where he had let his clothes drop to the floor, averting her eyes at the same time from where he stood in his skin. 'I wish you would learn to pick up your things, Moses,' she said in a singsong voice that he didn't recognize at all. It had in it the forced sweetness of a lonely and a patient woman, forced by a reduction of circumstances to take care of a dirty boy. When she had done what she could to take the softness out of her hair she stood and moved in little steps toward the door.

'I'm going down.'

'If you'll wait a minute, darling.'

'I think if I go *down* now I might be able to help. After all, the poor servants have a great deal to do.' Her smile was pure hypocrisy. She drifted out of the room.

Moses' determination to see through this clumsy disguise put him into a position that verged on foolishness and while he dressed his lined face shone with false cheer. She would have exhausted the part by midnight, he thought, so his yearning would have to wait until then; but there it was, a sense of fullness and strength that seemed to increase in the lamplight. When he went down to the hall he noticed that the bottles he had foolishly left there had been appropriated by Justina and that he would never see them again. He had a glass of bad sherry and a peanut. Melissa was among the lemon trees, twisting off the dead leaves. Even as she did this she seemed to sigh. She was a poor relation now, a shadowy figure, not meant to play a large part in life but philosophically resigned to small things. When she had finished cleaning up the lemon trees she took an ash tray off the table and emptied it – conspicuously – into the fire. When the chimes rang she pushed the general's chair to the door, first tucking the blanket tenderly around his legs, and at the table she picked at her food and talked about the dog-and-cat hospital.

They played bridge until ten, when Melissa yawned daintily and said that she was tired. Moses excused himself and was disheartened to see with what small steps she preceded him down the hall. At the stairs he put his arm around her waist – he had to feel for it in the folds of her drab dress – and kissed her cheek. She did not try to move out of his arm. Up in their room when he closed the door, shutting out the rest of the house, he watched to see what she would do. She went to a chair and picked up a circular sent from a dry-cleaning firm in the village and began to read this. Moses lifted the paper lightly out of her hands and kissed her. 'All *right*,' she said.

He took off his clothes, jubilantly, thinking that in another minute she would be in his arms, but she went instead to her dressing table, tipped many pins out of a small gold box, separated a strand of hair with her fingers, coiled it, laid it flat against her skull and pinned it there. He hoped that she would make only a few curls and he looked at the clock, wondering if it would be ten or fifteen minutes. He liked her hair to be full and he watched with a feeling of foreboding as she took strand after strand, coiled it and laid it flat with a pin against her skull. This did not delay or alter his hopefulness or lessen his need, and trying to distract himself he opened a magazine and looked at some advertisements, but with the kingdom of love so soon to be his the pictures had no meaning. When the hair over her brow was all secured to her skull she started on the sides and he saw that he had a considerable wait ahead of him. He sat up, swung his feet onto the floor and lighted a cigarette. The sense of fullness and strength in his groin was at its apex, and cold baths, long walks in the rain, humorous cartoons and glasses of milk would not help him – she had begun to pin up the hair at the back of her neck – when the feeling of fullness changed subtly to a feeling of anguish that spread from his loins deep into his bowels. He put out his cigarette, drew on some pajama pants and wandered out onto the balcony. He heard her close the bathroom door. Then, with a sigh of real misery, he heard her start to run the water for a bath.

It never took Melissa less than three quarters of an hour to bathe. Moses could often wait cheerfully for her, but his feelings that night were painful. He remained on the balcony, picking out by name the stars that he knew and smoking. When, three quarters of an hour later, he heard her pull the plug in the tub he returned to the room and stretched out, his yearning rising to new summits of purity and happiness, on the bed. From the bathroom he could hear the clink of bottles on glass and the opening and closing of drawers. Then she opened the bathroom door and came out – not naked but dressed in a full, heavy nightgown and busily running a piece of dental floss between her teeth. 'Oh, Melissa,' he said.

'I doubt that you love me,' she said. It was the thin, dispassionate voice of the spinster and it reminded him of thin things: smoke and dust. 'I sometimes think you don't love me at all,' she said, 'and of course you put much too much emphasis on sex, oh much too much. The trouble is that you don't have enough to think about. I mean you're really not interested in business. Most men are intensely interested in their business. J. P. used to be so tired when he came home from work that he could hardly eat his dinner. Most men are too tired to think about love every morning and every afternoon and every night. They're tired and anxious and they lead normal lives. You don't like your job and so you think about sex all the time. I don't suppose it's because you're really depraved. It's just because you're idle.'

He heard the squeaking of chalk. His bower was replaced with the atmosphere of a schoolroom and his roses seemed to wither. In the glass he saw her pretty face – opaque and wanton – formed to express passion and sweetness, and thinking of her capabilities he wondered why she had put them down. That he presented difficulties – the flights and crash landings of a sentimental disposition – that he sometimes broke wind and picked his teeth with a kitchen match, that he was neither brilliant nor beautiful belonged in the picture – but he did not understand. He did not understand, picking back over her words, what right she had to make the love that kept his mind open, and that made even the leaking of a rain gutter seem musical, a creation of pure idleness.

'But I love you,' he said hopefully.

'Some men bring work home from the office,' she said. 'Most men do. Most of the men that I know.' Her voice seemed to dry as he listened to it, to lose its deeper notes as her feelings narrowed. 'And most men in business,' she went on thinly, 'have to do a lot of traveling. They're away from their wives a lot of the time. They have other outlets than sex. Most healthy men do. They play squash.'

'I play squash.'

'You've never played squash since I've known you.'

'I used to play.'

'Of course,' she said, 'if it's absolutely necessary for you to make love to me I'll do it, but I think that you ought to understand that it's not as crucial as you make it.'

'You've talked yourself out of a fuck,' he said bleakly.

'Oh, you're so hateful and egotistical,' she said, swinging her head around. 'Your thinking is so crude and mean. You only want to hurt me.'

'I wanted to love you,' he said. 'The thought of it has made me cheerful all day. When I ask you tenderly you go to your dressing table and stuff your head with pieces of metal. I felt loving,' he said sadly. 'Now I feel angry and violent.'

'And I suppose all your bad feelings are directed towards me?' she asked. 'I've told you before that I can't be all the things you want. I can't be wife, child and mother all at once. It's too much to ask.'

'I don't want you to be my mother and my child,' he said hoarsely. 'I have a mother and I will have children. I won't lack those things. I want you to be my wife and you stuff your head with pins.'

'I thought we had agreed before,' she said, 'that I can't give you everything you want . . .'

'I have no stomach for talk,' he said. He took off his pajamas and dressed and went out. He walked down the driveway and took the back road to the village of Scaddonville. It was four miles and when he got there and found the streets dark he turned back on a lane that went through the woods where the mildness of a summer night seemed at last to replace his vexation. Dogs in distant houses heard his footsteps and went on barking long after he had passed. The trees moved a little in the wind and the stars were so numerous and clear that the arbitrary lines that form the Pleiades and Cassiopeia in her chair seemed nearly visible. There seemed to be some indestructible good health in a dark path on a summer night – it was a place and a season where it was impossible to cherish bad feeling. In the distance he saw the dark towers of Clear Haven and he returned up the driveway and went to bed. Melissa was asleep and she was asleep when he left in the morning.

Melissa was not in their room when he returned in the evening and looking around him hopefully for some change in her mood he saw that their room had been given a thorough cleaning. This in itself might have been a good sign but he saw that she had taken the perfume bottles off her dressing table and thrown out all the flowers. He washed and put on a

soft coat and went down. D'Alba was in the hall, sitting in the
golden throne, reading a Mickey Mouse comic and smoking a
big cigar. His taste in comics was genuine but Moses suspected
that the rest of the picture was a pose – a nod toward J. P.'s
tradition of near-illiterate merchant princes. D'Alba said that
Melissa was in the laundry. This was a surprise. She had never
gone near the laundry since Moses knew her. He went down
that shabby hall that cut away from the rest of the house like
a backstage alley and down the dirty wooden stairs into the
basements. Melissa was in the laundry, stuffing sheets into a
washing machine. Her golden hair was dark with steam. She
didn't reply when Moses spoke to her and when he touched
her she said, 'Leave me alone.'

She said that the bedding in the house had not been washed
for months. The maids kept drawing from the linen closets
and she had found the laundry chute full of sheets. Moses
knew enough not to suggest that she send the sheets to a
laundry. He could sense that cleanliness was not her purpose.
She had successfully discredited her beauty. She must have
found the dress she was wearing in a broom closet and her
golden-skinned arms were red with hot water. Her hair was
stringy and her mouth was set in an expression of extreme
distaste. He loved her passionately and when he saw all of this
his face fell.

Other than the dark brown photograph of her mother,
sitting in a carved chair, holding a dozen roses head down,
he did not know her family. The parents, the aunts, uncles,
brothers and sisters to whom we can sometimes trace a change
of character were unknown to him and if she was overtaken
now by the shadow of some aunt it was an aunt he had never
seen. Watching her stuff sheets into the washing machine he
wished briefly, for once, that her status had not been that of
an orphan. Her energies seemed penitential and he would let
it go at that. He had not fallen in love with her because of her
gift with arithmetic, because of her cleanliness, her reasonable
mind or any other human excellence. It was because he
perceived in her some extraordinary inner comeliness or grace

that satisfied his needs. 'Don't you have anything to do but sit there?' she asked sorely. He said yes, yes, and went up the stairs.

Justina met him in the hall with great cordiality. Her eyes were wide and her voice was an excited whisper when she asked if Melissa was in the laundry. 'Perhaps we should have told you before you married,' she said, 'but you know that Melissa has been very, very –' the word she wanted was too crude and she settled for a modulation – 'she has never been very tractable. Come,' she said to Moses, 'come and have a drink. D'Alba has some whisky, I think. We need something more than sherry tonight.' The picture she evoked was cozy and although Moses felt the naked edge of her mischievousness he had nothing better to do than walk in the garden and stare at the roses. He went down the hall at her side. D'Alba produced a bottle of whisky from underneath the throne and they all had a drink. 'Is she having a breakdown?' D'Alba asked. They were halfway through the soup when Melissa appeared, wearing her broom-closet dress. When she came to the table Moses stood but she did not look in his direction and she did not speak during the meal. After dinner Moses asked if she would like to take a walk but Melissa said that she had to hang out the sheets.

Justina met Moses at the door the next night with a long and an excited face and said that Melissa was ill. 'Indisposed perhaps would be a better word,' she said. She asked Moses to have a drink with her and D'Alba but he said that he would go up and see Melissa. 'She's not in your room,' Justina said. 'She's moved to one of the other bedrooms. I don't know which one. She doesn't want to be disturbed.' Moses looked first into their bedroom to make sure she was not there and then went down the hall, calling her name loudly, but there was no reply. He tried the door of the room next to theirs and looked into a room with a canopied bed but at some time in the past a large piece of the ceiling had fallen and fragments of plaster hung from this cavity. The curtains were drawn and the damps of the room were sepulchral – ghostly he would

have said if he had not had such a great scorn for ghosts. The
next door that he opened led into an unused bathroom – the
tub was filled with newspapers tied into bundles – and the
room was lighted luridly by a stained-glass window, and the
next door that he opened led into a storeroom where brass
bedsteads and rocking chairs, oak mantelpieces and sewing
machines, mahogany chiffoniers with rueful lines and other
pieces of respectable and by-passed furniture were stacked up
to the ceiling, antedating, he guessed, Justina's first glimpse of
Italy. The room smelled of bats. The next door opened into
an attic where there was a water tank as big as the plunge
and there was an aeolian harp attached to the next door
that he opened and asthmatic and airy as the music was it
made his flesh rough when it began to ring as it would have
been roughened by the hissing of an adder. This door led to
the tower stairs and he climbed them up and up to a large
raftered room with lancet windows and no furniture and
over the mantelpiece this motto in gold: LOOK AWAY FROM
THE BODY INTO TRUTH AND LIGHT. He ran down the tower
stairs and had opened the door of a nursery – Melissa's, he
guessed – and another bedroom with a fallen ceiling before
the foolish music of the aeolian harp had died away. Then
with so much stale air in his nose and his lungs he opened
a window and stuck his head out into the summer twilight
where he could hear, way below him, the sounds of dinner.
Then he opened a door into a room that was clean and light
and where Melissa, when she saw him, buried her face in
the pillows and cried when he touched her, 'Leave me alone,
leave me alone.'

Her invalidism, like her chasteness, seemed to be an
imposture, and he reminded himself to be patient, but sitting
at a window, watching the lawns darken, he felt very forlorn
at having a wife who had promised so much and who now
refused to discuss with him the weather, the banking business
or the time of day. He waited there until dark and then went
down the stairs. He had missed his dinner but a light was still
burning in the kitchen, where a plump old Irishwoman, who

was mopping the drainboards, cooked him some supper and set it on a table by the stove. 'I guess you're having trouble with your sweetheart,' she said kindly. 'Well, I was married myself to poor Mr Reilly for fourteen years and there's nothing I don't know about the ups and downs of love. He was a little man, Mr Reilly was,' she said, 'and when we was living out in Toledo everybody used to say he was runty. He never weighed over a hundred and twenty-five pounds and look at me.' She sat down in a chair opposite Moses. 'Of course I wasn't so heavy in those days but towards the end I would have made three of him. He was one of those men who always look like a little boy. I mean the way he carried his head and all. Even now, just looking out of the train window sometimes in a strange city I see one of these little men and it reminds me of Mr Reilly. He was a menopause baby. His mother was past fifty when he was born. Why, after we was married sometimes we'd go into a bar for a beer and the barkeep wouldn't serve him, thinking he was a boy. Of course as he got old his face got lined and towards the end he looked like a dried-up little boy, but he was very loving.

'He never seemed to be able to get enough of it,' she said. 'When I remember him that's the way I remember him — that sad look on his face that meant he was loving. He always wanted his piece and he was lovely — lovely things he'd say to me while he caressed and unbuttoned me. He liked a piece in the morning. Then he'd comb his hair on the left side, button up his britches and go off to a good day's work in the foundry, so cheerful and cocky. In Toledo he was coming home for his dinner in the middle of the day and he liked a piece then and he couldn't go to sleep without his piece. He couldn't sleep. If I woke him up in the middle of the night to tell him I heard burglars downstairs there was no use my talking. The night Mabel Ransome's house burned down and I stayed up watching the fire until two in the morning he never listened to what I said. When thunderstorms woke him at night or the north wind in winter he'd always wake up in a very loving mood.

'But I didn't always feel like loving,' she said sadly. 'Heartburn or gas would get me down and then I had to be very careful with him. I had to choose me words. Once I refused him without thinking. Once when he commenced to gentle me I spoke roughly to him. Forget about it for a little while Charlie, I says. Helen Sturmer tells me her husband don't do it but once a month. Why don't you try to be like him? Well, it was like the end of the world. You should have seed the way his face got dark. It was terrible to behold. The very blood in his veins got dark. I never seed him so crossed in my whole life. Well, he went out of the house then. Come suppertime he isn't home. I went to bed expecting him to come in but when I wakes up the bed is empty. Four nights I wait for him to come home but he don't show up. Finally I put this advertisement in the paper. This was when we was living in Albany. Please come home Charlie. That's all I say. It cost me two-fifty. Well, I put the advertisement in on Friday night and on Saturday morning I hear his key in the lock. Up the stairs he comes all smiles with this big bunch of roses and one idea in his mind. Well it's only ten o'clock in the morning and my housework isn't half done. The breakfast dishes are in the sink and the bed isn't made. It's very hard for a woman to be loving before her work is done but even with the dust all over the tables I knew my lot.

'Sometimes it was a hardship for me,' she said. 'It kept me from ever broadening my mind. There's lots of important things he kept me from seeing, like after the war when the parade went right by our windows with Marshal Foch and all. I looked forward to that parade but I never got to see it. He was on top of me when Lindbergh flewed the Atlantic and when that English king, whatever his name was, put down his crown for love and made a speech about it over the radio I never heard a word of it. But when I remember him now that's the way I remember him – that sad look on his face that meant he was loving. He never seemed to be able to get enough of it and now, God bless the poor man, he's lying in a cold, cold grave.'

It was not until Saturday that Melissa came down, and, asking her to walk with him after dinner, Moses noticed how she hesitated at the door to the terrace as if she apprehended that the summer night might end her imposture. Then she joined him but she kept a meaningful distance between them. He suggested that they go down through the garden, hoping that the smell of roses and the sound of fountains would prevail, but she continued to keep a protective distance between them although when they left the garden she took a path through some pine woods that he had not seen before and that ended in a plot that turned out to be the animal cemetery. Here were a dozen headstones, overgrown with weeds, and Moses followed Melissa, reading the inscriptions:

> Here lie the bones and feathers of an amiable bird,
> A cold December twilight saw his fall.
> His voice, raised in sweet song, was never heard,
> Because the bird was very small.

> Here lie the bones of Sylvia Rabbit.
> She was sat on by Melissa Scaddon on June 17th
> And died of contusions.

> Here lie the bones of Theseus the Whippet.

> Here lie the bones of Prince the Collie,
> He will be missed by One and All.

> Here lie the bones of Hannibal.

> Here lie the bones of Napoleon

> Here lie the bones of Lorna, the kitchen cat.

The lot exhaled the power of a family, Moses thought, and the glee they took in their own nonsense, and looking from the headstones to Melissa's face he saw hopefully that her expression seemed to be softened by the foolish graveyard, but he decided to take his time and followed her out of the lot down a path to the barns and greenhouses when they both stopped to hear the loud, musical singing of some night bird. It sounded in the distance, on the early dark, with the brilliance of a knife, and Melissa was captivated. 'You know J. P. wanted to have nightingales,' she said. 'He imported hundreds and hundreds of nightingales from England. He had a special nightingale keeper and a nightingale house. When we came back from England the first thing we did on the boat after breakfast was to go down into the hold and feed mealy worms to the nightingales. They all died. . . .'

Then looking past her, to the roof of the barn where the night bird seemed to be perched, Moses saw that it was not a bird at all; it was the plaintive song of a rusty ventilator as it turned on the night wind; and feeling that this discovery might change the sentimental mood that the twilight, the graveyard and the song promised he led her hurriedly into the old greenhouse and made a bed of his clothing on the floor. Much later that night, when they had returned to the house, and Moses, his bones feeling light and clean with love, was waiting for sleep he had every reason to wonder if she had not transformed herself into something else.

This suspicion was renewed the next night when he stepped into their room and found her on the bed wearing a single stocking and reading a love story she had borrowed from one of the maids and when he kissed her and joined her where she lay her breath smelled, not unpleasantly, of candy. But on the next night, walking across the lawns from the station, Moses was reminded of those noisome details in her past that Justina liked to dwell on. She was on the terrace with Jacopo, one of the young gardeners. She was cutting Jacopo's hair. Even at a distance the sight made Moses uneasy and sad, for the insatiableness that he adored left the possibilities of inconstancy open and he conceived for Jacopo a hatred that was murderous. Lewd and comely and laughing while she snipped and combed his hair, he seemed to Moses to be one of those figures who stand outside the brightly lighted centers of our consciousness and defeat our love of candor and our confidence in the sweetness of life, but Melissa sent Jacopo away when Moses joined them and displayed her affection for Moses brilliantly in greeting him and he did not worry about the gardener or anything else until, a few nights later, walking down the hall, he heard laughter from their bedroom and found Melissa and a stranger drinking whisky on the balcony. This was Ray Badger.

Now the dubiousness of visiting a former wife did not, Moses supposed, concern him. His rival, if Badger was still a rival, had a hard-finish suit, a cast in one eye and patent-leather hair. He meant to be charming, when Moses joined them, but the memories he shared with Melissa – he had fed the nightingales – were confined to the past at Clear Haven and Moses was kept out of the conversation. Melissa had seldom mentioned Badger and if she had been unhappy with him it did not show that evening. She was delighted with his company and his recollections – delighted and sad, for when he had left them she spoke sentimentally to Moses about her former husband. 'He's just like an eighteen-year-old boy,' she said. 'He's always done what other people wanted him to do and now, at thirty-five, he's just realized that he never expressed himself. I feel so *sorry* for him. . . .' Moses reserved judgment on Badger and found at dinner that Justina was his advocate. She did not speak to her guest and seemed to be in a deeply emotional state. She announced that she was selling all her paintings to the Metropolitan Museum. A curator was coming for lunch the next day to appraise them. 'There is no one I can trust to keep my things together,' she said. 'I can't trust any of you.'

Badger gave Moses a cigar after dinner and they went together out onto the terrace. 'I suppose you wonder why I've come back,' Badger said, 'and I may as well explain myself. I'm in the toy business. I don't know whether you knew that or not, and I've just had an unusually lucky piece of business. I've got the patent on a penny bank – it's a plastic reproduction of an old iron bank – and Woolworth's given me an order for sixty thousand. I have a confirmation for the order in New York. I've invested twenty-five thousand of my own in the thing, but right now I've got a chance to pick up a patent on a toy gun and I'll sell my interest in the bank for fifteen thousand. I was wondering who to sell it to and I thought of you and Melissa – I read about your marriage in the paper – and I thought I'd come out here and give you the first chance. On the Woolworth order alone you'll double your investment and you can count on another sixty thousand from the stationery stores. If you could get over to the Waldorf late tomorrow afternoon for a drink I'll show you the patent and the design and the correspondence from Woolworth.'

'I wouldn't be interested,' Moses said.

'You mean you don't *want* to make any money? Oh, Melissa will be very disappointed.'

'You haven't talked this over with Melissa.'

'Well, not *really,* but I know that she'll be very disappointed.'

'I haven't fifteen thousand dollars,' Moses said.

'You mean to tell me that you don't have fifteen thousand Dollars?'

'That's right,' Moses said.

'Oh,' Badger said. 'What about the general? Do you know if he's worth anything?'

'I don't know,' Moses said. He followed Badger back into the hall and saw him give the old man a cigar and push his wheel chair out onto the terrace. When Moses repeated the conversation to Melissa it did not change her sentimental feelings for Badger. 'Of course he's not in the toy business,' she said. 'He's never really been in any business at all. He just tries to get along and I feel so sorry for him.'

The fact that Justina was parting with her art treasures because she knew no one trustworthy made the next day both elegiac and exciting.

Mr Dewitt, the curator, was due at one and it happened to be Moses who let him into the rotunda. He was a slight man who wore a brown felt hat that was so many sizes too small for him that he looked like Boob McNutt. Moses wondered if he hadn't picked out the wrong hat at a cocktail party. His face was slender and deeply lined – he tipped his head a little as if his baggy eyes were nearsighted – and the length and triangularity of his nose were extraordinary. This thin and angular organ seemed elegant and lewd – a vice, a penance, a gift of the devil's – and reinforced a general impression of elegance and lewdness. He must have been fifty – the bags under his eyes couldn't have been formed in a shorter time – but he carried himself gracefully and spoke with a little impediment as if a hair had gotten onto his tongue. 'Not pork, not pork!' he exclaimed, sniffing the stale air of the rotunda. 'I'm simply pasted together.' When Moses assured him that they would have chicken he put on some horn-rimmed glasses and, looking around the rotunda, noticed the big panel at the left of the stairs. 'What a charming forgery,' he cried. 'Of course I think the Mexicans make the most charming forgeries, but this is delightful. It was made in Zurich. There was a factory there in the early nineteen hundreds that turned them out by the carload. The interesting thing is their lavish use of carmine. None of the originals are nearly as brilliant.' Then some smell in the rotunda turned his mind back to the thought of lunch. 'You're sure it isn't pork?' he asked again. 'My tummy is a wreck.' Moses reassured him and they went down the long hall to where Justina was waiting for them. She was triumphantly gracious and sounded all those rich notes of requited social ambition that made her voice seem to carry up into the hills and down to the shadow of the valleys.

Mr Dewitt clasped his hands when he saw all the pictures in the hall but Moses wondered why his smile should be so fleeting. He carried his cocktail over to the big Titian.

'Astonishing, astonishing, perfectly astonishing,' Mr Dewitt said.

'We found that Titian in a ruined palace in Venice,' Justina said. 'A gentleman at the hotel – an Englishman, I recall – knew about it and showed us the way. It was like a detective story. The painting belonged to a very old countess and had been in her family for generations. I don't clearly recall what we paid her but if you will get the catalogue, Niki?'

D'Alba got the catalogue and leafed through it. 'Sixty-five thousand,' he said.

'We found the Gozzoli in another hovel. It was Mr Scaddon's favorite painting. We found it through the assistance of another stranger. I believe we met him on a train. The painting was so dirty and so covered with cobwebs when we first saw it and hung in such a dark room that Mr Scaddon decided against it but we later realized that we could not be too particular and in the morning we changed our minds.'

The curator sat down and let D'Alba fill his glass and when he turned to Justina she was reminiscing about the dirty palace where she had found the Sano di Pietro.

'These are all copies and forgeries, Mrs Scaddon.'

'That's impossible.'

'They're copies and forgeries.'

'The only reason you're saying this is because you want me to give my pictures to your museum,' Justina said. 'That's it, isn't it? You want to have my pictures for nothing.'

'They're worthless.'

'We met a curator at the Baroness Grachi's,' Justina said. 'He saw our paintings in Naples where they were being crated for the steamer. He offered to vouch for their authenticity.'

'They're worthless.'

A maid came to the door and rang the chimes for lunch, and Justina stood, her self-possession suddenly refreshed. 'We will be five for lunch, Lena,' she told the maid. 'Mr Dewitt won't be staying. And will you telephone the garage and tell Giacomo that Mr Dewitt will walk to the train?' She took D'Alba's arm and went down the hall.

'Mrs Scaddon,' the curator called after her, 'Mrs Scaddon.'

'There isn't much you can do,' Moses said.

''How far is it to the station?'

'A little over a mile.'

'You don't have a car?'

'No.'

'And there aren't any taxis?'

'Not on Sunday.'

The curator looked out the window at the rain. 'Oh this is outrageous, this is the most outrageous thing I've ever experienced. I only came as a favor. I have an ulcer and I have to eat regularly and it will be four o'clock before I get back into the city. You couldn't get me a glass of milk?'

'I'm afraid not,' Moses said.

'What a mess, what a mess, and how in heaven's name could she have supposed that those paintings were authentic? How could she have fooled herself?' He gave up with a gesture and started down the hall to the rotunda, where he put on the little hat that made him look like Boob McNutt. 'This may kill me,' he said. 'I'm supposed to eat regularly and avoid excitement and physical exertion. . . .' Off he went in the rain.

When Moses joined the others at lunch there was no talk at all and the silence was so oppressive that his hearty appetite showed some signs of flagging. Suddenly D'Alba dropped his spoon and said tearfully, 'My lady, oh my lady!'

'Document,' Justina snapped. Then she swung her head around to Badger and said fiercely, 'Please try and eat with your mouth shut!'

'I'm sorry, Justina,' Badger said. Maids cleared off the soup plates and brought in some chicken but at the sight of the dish Justina waved it away. 'I can't eat a thing,' she said. 'Take the food back to the kitchen and put it into the icebox.' Everyone bowed his head, sorry for Justina and bereft of a meal, for on Sunday afternoons the iceboxes were padlocked. She put her hands on the edge of the table, glaring heavily at Badger, and rose. 'I suppose you want to get into town, Badger, and tell everyone about this.'

'No. Justina.'

'If I hear a word out of you about this, Badger,' she said, 'I'll tell everyone I know that you've been in *prison*.'

'Justina.'

She started for the door, not bent but straighter than ever, with D'Alba in tow, and when she reached the door she threw out her arms and cried, 'My pictures, my pictures, my lovely, lovely pictures.' Then D'Alba could be heard opening and closing the elevator doors and there was the mournful singing of the cables in the shaft as she went up.

It was a gloomy afternoon and Moses spent it studying syndicalism in the little library. When it began to get dark he shut his books and wandered through the house. The kitchen was empty and clean but the iceboxes were still padlocked. He heard music from the hall and thought that D'Alba must be playing, for it was cocktail music; the languid music of specious sorrow and mock yearning, of barroom twilights and unfresh peanuts; of heartburn and gastritis and those paper napkins that cling like wet leaves to the foot of your cocktail glass – but when he stepped into the room he saw that it was Badger. Melissa sat beside him on the piano bench and Badger was singing dolefully:

I've got those guest-room blues,
I'm feeling blue all the time,
I've got those guest-room blues,
Surrounded by things that aren't mine.
The bed is lumpy and has sprained my back,
And I hear the choo-choo whistling that will take me back,
I've got those guest-room blues . . .

When Moses approached the piano they both looked up. Melissa sighed deeply and Moses felt as if he had violated the atmosphere of a tryst. Badger gave Moses a jaded look and closed the piano. He seemed to be in an emotional turbulence that Moses was at some pains not to misunderstand. He got up from the piano bench and walked out onto the terrace, a figure of grief and unease, and Melissa turned her head and followed him with her eyes and all her attention.

Now Moses knew that if we grant men vestigial sexual rites – that if the ease of his stance when a hockey stick was first put into his hands, if the pleasure he took in the athletic equipment in the closet at West Farm or the sense, during a football scrimmage on a rainy day, of looking, during the last minutes of light and play, deep into the past of his kind, had any validity – there must be duplicate rites and ceremonies for the opposite sex. By this Moses did not mean the ability to metamorphose swiftly, but something else, linked perhaps to the power beautiful women have of evoking landscapes – a sense of rueful distance – as if their eyes had come to rest on a horizon that had never been seen by any man. There was some physical evidence for this – their voices softened and the pupils of their eyes dilated, and they seemed to be recollecting some distaff voyage over distaff waters to a walled island where they were committed by the nature of their minds and their organs to some secret rites that would refresh their charming and creative stores of sadness. Moses did not expect ever to know what was going on in Melissa's mind but as he saw her pupils dilate now and a deeply thoughtful cast fall over her beautiful face he knew that it would be hopeless to inquire. She was recalling the voyage or she had seen the horizon and the effect of this was to stir up in her vague and stormy longings, but that Badger seemed to fit somehow into her memories of the voyage was what made him anxious.

'Melissa?'

'Justina is so mean to him,' Melissa said, 'and she has no right to be. And you don't like him.'

'I don't like him,' Moses said, 'that's true.'

'Oh, I feel so sorry for him.' She got up from the bench and started for the terrace after Badger. 'Melissa,' Moses said, but she was gone in the dark.

It was about ten o'clock when Moses went upstairs. The door to their room was locked. He called his wife's name and she didn't reply and then he was enraged. Then some part of him that was as unsusceptible to compromise as his sexual pride was inflamed and this rage seemed to settle in his gut like stone. He pounded on the door and tried to break the lock with his shoulders and was resting from these exertions when the cold air, coming through the space between the door and the sill, reminded him that Badger was sleeping in the room where he had slept when he first made his trip over the roofs.

He ran down the back stairs and across the rotunda and took the old elevator to the bedrooms on the other side of the house. Badger's door was shut but when he knocked no one answered. When he opened the door and stepped in the first thing he heard was the loud noise of rain from the balcony. There was no sign of Badger in the room. Moses went out onto the balcony and swung up onto the roof and sure enough, about a hundred yards away from him and moving very cautiously, bent at the waist and sweeping the air around his feet with his hands like a swimmer (he must have been tripped up by the old radio wire), was Badger. Moses called his name. Badger began to run.

He seemed to know the way; he steered clear of the airshaft anyhow. He ran toward the pyramidal roof that the chapel made and then turned right and ran along the pitched slate roof of the hall. Moses came around the other side but Badger retreated and got back onto the straightaway and began running toward D'Alba's lighted dormer. Halfway across the flat roof Moses outstripped him and clapped a hand on his shoulder.

'It isn't what you think,' Badger said. Then Moses hit him and down Badger went on his bum and he must have sat on a nail because he let out such a hoarse, loud roar of pain that the count stuck his head out of a window.

'Who's there, who's there?'

'It's Badger and me,' Moses said.

'If Justina hears about this she'll be wild,' the count said. 'She doesn't like people to walk on the roofs. It makes leaks. And what in the world are you doing?'

'I'm on my way to bed,' Moses said.

'Oh, I wish you'd give a civil answer to a sensible question once in a while,' the count said. 'I'm terribly, terribly tired of your sense of humor and so is Justina. It's a terrible comedown for her to have people like you in the house after having spent her life in the highest society including royalty, and she told me herself . . .' The voice got fainter as Moses continued along the ledge to above Melissa's balcony, his feelings blasted with anger. Then he sat on the roof with his feet in the rain gutter for half an hour, composing an obscene indictment of her intractableness and seeming to release this into the night until the stony rage in his gut diminished. Then, realizing that if he was to find any usable truth in the situation, he would have to find it in himself, he swung down onto the balcony, undressed and got into bed where Melissa was asleep.

But Moses had wronged Badger. There had not been a lecherous thought in his head when he started over the roofs. He had been very drunk. But there was some magnanimity in the man – a trace of the raw material of human excellence – or at least enough scope in his emotions to set the scene for a conflict, and when he woke early the next morning he reproached himself for his drunkenness and his crazy schemes. He could see the world out of his window then all blue and gold and round as a bull's eye but all the sapphire-colored lights in heaven merely chilled Badger's spirit and excited in him a desire to retire into some dark, badly ventilated place. The world, in the partial lights of early morning, appeared to him as hypocritical and offensive as the smile of a door-to-door salesman. Nothing was true, thought Badger; nothing was what it appeared to be, and the enormity of this deception – the subtlety with which the color of the sky deepened as he dressed – angered him. He got down through the rotunda without meeting anyone – not even a rat – and telephoned Giacomo, although it was not six o'clock, and Giacomo drove him to the station.

The early train was a local and all the passengers were night-shift workmen, returning home. Looking into their tired and dirty faces Badger felt a longing for what he thought to be their humble ways. If he had been brought up simply his life would have had more meaning and value, the better parts of his disposition would have been given a chance to develop and he would not have wasted his gifts. Shaken with drink and self-reproach, he felt it was plain that morning that he had wasted them beyond any chance of their renewal, and images of his earlier life – a high-spirited and handsome boy, bringing in the terrace furniture before a thunderstorm – rose up to reinforce his self-condemnation. Then at the nadir of his depression light seemed to strike into Badger's mind, for it was the force of his imagination rebelling against utter despair, to raise white things in his head – cities or archways at least of marble – signs of prosperity, triumph and splendor.

Then whole palladia seemed to mushroom beneath Badger's patent-leather hair, the cities and villas of a younger world, and he made the trip into the city in a hopeful mood. But sitting over his first cup of coffee in the hole-in-the-wall where he lived Badger saw that his marble white civilizations were helpless before invaders. These snowy, high-arched constructions of principle, morality and faith – these palaces and memorials – were overrun with hordes of war-whooping, half-naked men, dressed in the stinking skins of beasts. In they rode at the north gate and as Badger sat huddled over his cup, he saw one by one his temples and palaces go. Out the south gate rode the barbarians, leaving poor Badger without even the consolation of a ruin; leaving him with a nothingness and with his essence, which was never much better than the perfume of a wood violet gone.

'Mamma e Papa Confettiere arrivan' domani sera,' Giacomo said. He was screwing light bulbs once more into the long string of fixtures that were hung in the trees of the driveway. Melissa met Moses sweetly at the door as she had done on his first night there and told him that some old friends of Justina's were arriving on the next night. Mrs Enderby was in the office, telephoning invitations, and D'Alba was running around the hall in an apron, giving orders to a dozen maids that Moses had never seen before. The place was upside down. Doors were thrown open onto bat-smelling parlors and Giacomo took the bed pillows out of the broken windows in the winter garden where palm trees and rose bushes were being unloaded from trucks. There was no place to sit down and they had sandwiches and drinks in the hall where the Scaddonville Symphony Orchestra (eight ladies) undressed the harp of its cracked mackintosh and tuned their instruments. Then the glee of the old upside-down palace on the eve of a party reminded Moses of West Farm, as if this house, like the other, lay deep in their consciousness – even in the dreams of the fly-by-night maids, who exhumed and burnished the old rooms as if they were improving their wisdom. Bats were found in the big basement kitchens and two of the maids came screaming up the stairs with dish towels over their heads but this small incident discouraged no one and only seemed to heighten the antic atmosphere, for who, these days, was rich enough to have bats in their kitchen? The big chests in the cellar were filled with beef and wine and flowers and all the fountains played in the gardens and water poured out of the green-mouthed lions in the plunge and a thousand lights or more burned in the house and the driveway was beaded with lights like a country fair and lights burned here and there in the garden, forlorn and unshaded like the lights in rooming-house hallways and with all the doors and windows open at ten or eleven and the night air suddenly cold and a thin moon in the sky over the broadest lawns Moses was reminded of some wartime place, some poignance of furlough and leave-takings, headlines and good-by dances in beery ports like Norfolk and San Francisco where the dark ships waited in the roads for the lovers in their beds and none of it might ever happen again.

And who were Mamma and Papa Confettiere? They were the Belamontes, Luigi and Paula, the last of the *haut monde* of the *prezzo unico botteghe*. She was the daughter of a Calabrian farmer and Luigi was spawned in the back of a Roman barbershop that smelled of violets and old hair, but at the age of eighteen he had saved enough money to stock a *prezzo unico* store. He was the Woolworth, he was the Kress, he was the J. P. Scaddon of Italy and had made himself into a millionaire with villas in the south and castles in the north by the time that he was thirty. He had retired in his fifties and for the last twenty years had motored around Italy with his wife in a Daimler, throwing hard candies out of the windows of their car to the children in the street.

They left Rome after Easter (the date was announced in the newspapers and the radio) so that a crowd would have gathered outside the gates of their house for the first free candy of the season. They drove north toward Civitavecchia, scattering candy to the left and the right – a hundred pounds here, three hundred pounds there – circumventing Civitavecchia and all the larger cities on their route for they had once nearly been torn limb from limb by a crowd of twenty thousand children in Milan and had also caused serious riots in Turin and Leghorn. Piedmont and Lombardy saw them and southward they traveled through Portomaggiore, Lugo, Imola, Cervia, Cesena, Rimini and Pesaro, tossing out handfuls of lemon drops, peppermints, licorice sticks, anise and horehound drops, sugar plums and cherry suckers along streets that, as they climbed Monte Sant' Angelo and came down into Manfredonia, had begun to be covered with fallen leaves. Ostia was shut when they passed there and shut were the hotels of Lido di Roma, where they scattered the last of their store to the children of fishermen and caretakers, turning northward and home again under the fine skies of a Roman winter.

Moses took a suitcase to work in the morning and rented a suit of tails at lunch. He walked up from the station to the hall in a late summer dusk when the air already smelled of autumn. Then he could see Clear Haven in the early dark with every one of its windows lighted for Mamma and Papa

Confettiere. It was a cheerful sight and, letting himself in at the terrace doors, he was cheered to see how the place bad been restored, how shining and quiet it was. A maid who came down the hall with some silver on a tray walked stealthily and, other than the sound of the fountain in the winter garden and the hum of water rising in some pipes within the walls, the house was still.

Melissa had dressed and they drank a glass of wine. Moses was standing in the shower when all the lights went out. Then every voice in what had been a hushed place was raised in alarm and dismay and someone who was stuck in the old elevator cage began to pound on the walls. Melissa brought a lighted candle into the bathroom and Moses was pulling on some trousers when the lights went on again. Giacomo was around. They drank another glass of wine on the balcony, watching the cars arrive. Jacopo was directing them to park on the lawns. God knows where Mrs Enderby had found the guests, but she had found enough for once and the noise of talk, even from the third floor, sounded like the October sea at Travertine.

There must have been a hundred people in the hall when Moses and Melissa went down. D'Alba was at one end and Mrs Enderby at the other, steering servants toward people with empty glasses, and Justina stood by the fireplace beside an elderly Italian couple, swarthy, egg-shaped, merry and knowing, Moses discovered when he shook hands with them, not a word of English. The dinner was splendid, with three wines and cigars and brandy on the terrace afterward, and then the Scaddonville Symphony Orchestra began to play 'A Kiss in the Dark,' and they all went in to dance.

Badger was there, although he had not been invited. He walked up from the station after dinner and hung around the edges of the dance floor, a little drunk. He could not have said why he had come. Then Justina saw him and the corrosive glance she gave him and the fact that she was not wearing any jewelry reminded Badger of his purpose. That evening

had for him the savor of a man who finds his destiny and
adores it. This was his finest hour. He went upstairs and started
once more over those roofs (he could hear the music in the
distance) that he had crossed often enough for love himself,
but that he crossed now with a much deeper sense of purpose.
He headed for Justina's balcony at the north end of the house
and entered that big chamber with its vaulted ceiling and
massive bed. (Justina never slept in this; she slept on a little
cot behind a screen.) The decision against her jewelry must
have been made suddenly for it was all heaped on the cracked
and peeling surface of her dressing table. He found a paper
bag in her closet – she collected paper and string – and filled
this with her valuables. Then, trusting in Divine Providence,
he left boldly by the door, went down the stairs, crossed the
lawns with the music growing fainter and fainter and caught
the 11:17 into the city.

When Badger boarded the train he had no idea of how he
would dispose of the jewelry. He may have thought of prying
some of the stones out of their settings and selling them. The
train was a local – the last – taking back to the city people
who had been visiting friends and relations. They all seemed
tired; some of them were drunk; and, sweating and sleeping
fitfully in the overheated coach, they seemed, to Badger, to
share a great commonality of intimacy and weariness. Most
of the men had taken off their hats but their hair was matted
with the pressure of hat brims. The women wore their finery
but they wore it awry and their curls had begun to come
undone. Many of them slept with their heads on the shoulders
of their men, and the smells – and the looseness of most of
the faces he saw – made Badger feel as if the coach was some
enormous bed or cradle in which they all lay together in a
state of unusual innocence. They shared the discomforts of the
coach, they shared a destination and for all their shabbiness
and fatigue they seemed to Badger to share some beauty of
mind and purpose, and looking at the dyed red head of the
woman in front of him he attributed to her the ability to
find, a shade below the level of consciousness, an imagery of

beauty and grandeur like those great, ruined palladia that rose
in Badger's head.

He loved them all – Badger loved them all – and what
he had done he had done for them, for they failed only in
their inability to help one another and by stealing Justina's
jewelry he had done something to diminish this failure. The
red-headed woman in the seat in front moved him with love,
with amorousness and with pity, and she touched her curls so
often and with such simple vanity that he guessed her hair had
just been dyed and this in turn touched him as Badger would
have been touched to see a sweet child picking the petals off
a daisy. Suddenly the red-headed woman straightened up and
asked in a thick voice, 'Wassa time, wassa time?' The people in
front of her to whom the question was addressed did not stir
and Badger leaned forward and said that it was a little before
midnight. 'Thank you, thank you,' she said with great warmth.
'You're a genemun after my own heart.' She gestured toward
the others. 'Won't even tell me what time is because they
think I'm drunk. Had a liddle accident.' She pointed to some
broken glass and a puddle on the floor where she seemed to
have dropped a pint bottle. 'Jess because I had a liddle accident
and spilled my good whisky none of these sonofbitches will
tell me time. You're a genemun, you're a genemun and if I
didn't have a little accident and spill my whisky give you a
drink.' Then the motion of Badger's cradle overtook her and
she fell asleep.

Mrs Enderby had given the alarm twenty minutes after
the theft and two plain-clothes men and an agent from the
insurance company were waiting for Badger when he got
off the train in Grand Central. Wearing tails, and carrying
a paper bag that seemed to be full of hardware, he was not
hard to spot. They followed him, thinking that he might lead
them to a ring. He walked jubilantly up Park Avenue to Saint
Bartholomew's and tried the doors, which were locked. Then
he crossed Park Avenue, crossed Madison and walked up Fifth
to Saint Patrick's, where the doors were still open and where
many charwomen were mopping the floors. He went way

forward to the central altar, knelt and said his Lamb of God. Then – the rail was down and he was too enthralled to think of being conspicuous – he walked across the deep chancel and emptied his paper bag on the altar. The plain-clothes men picked him up as he left the cathedral.

*

It was not one o'clock when the police department called Clear Haven to tell Justina that they had her jewelry. She checked the police list against a typewritten list that had been pasted to the top of her jewel box. 'One diamond bracelet, two diamond and onyx bracelets, one diamond and emerald bracelet,' etc. She tried the policeman's patience when she asked him to count the pearls in her necklace, but he did. Then Papa Confettiere called for music and wine. 'Dancinga, singinga,' he shouted, and gave the ladies' orchestra a hundred-dollar bill. They struck up a waltz and then the fuses blew for the second time that night.

Moses knew that Giacomo was around – he had seen him in the halls – but he went to the cellar door anyhow. A peculiar smell surrounded him but he didn't reflect on it and he didn't notice the fact that as he went down the back hallway sweat began to pour off his body. He opened the cellar door onto a pit of fire and a blast of hot air that burned all the hair off his face and nearly overcame him. Then he staggered down the hall to the kitchens where the maids were cleaning up the last of the dishes and asked the major-domo if anyone was upstairs. He counted off the help and said that no one was and then Moses told them to get out; that the house was on fire. (How Mrs Wapshot would have been disappointed with this direct statement of fact; how cleverly she would have led the guests and servants out onto the lawn to see the new moon.)

Then Moses called the fire department from the kitchen telephone, noticing, as he picked up the receiver, that much flesh had been burned off his right hand by the cellar doorknob. His lips were swollen with adrenaline and he felt peculiarly at ease. Then he ran down to the hall where the guests were still waltzing and told Justina that her house was burning. She was perfectly composed and when Moses stopped the music she asked the guests to go out on the lawn. They could hear the bull horn in the village beginning to sound. There were many doors onto the terrace and as the guests crowded out of the hall, away from the lights of the party, they stepped into the pink glow of fire, for the flames had blown straight up the clock tower and while there were still no signs of fire in the hall the tower was blazing like a torch. Then the fire trucks could be heard coming down the road toward the drive and Justina started down the hall to great them at her front door as she had greeted J. C. Penney, Herbert Hoover and the Prince of Wales, but as she started down the hall a rafter somewhere in the tower burned loose from its shorings, crashed through the ceiling of the rotunda and then all the lights in the house flickered and went out.

Melissa called to her guardian in the dark and the old woman joined them – now she seemed bent – and walked between them out to the terrace where D'Alba and Mrs Enderby took her arms. Then Moses ran around to the front of the house to move the cars of the guests. They seemed to be all that was worth saving. 'For the last six nights I been trying to discharge my conjugal responsibilities,' one of the firemen said, 'and every time I get started that damned bull horn . . .' Moses bumped a dozen cars down over the grass to safety and then went through the crowd, looking for his wife. She was in the garden with most of the other guests and he sat beside her at the pool and put his burned hand into the water. The fire must have been visible for miles then, for crowds of men, women and children were climbing over the garden walls and pouring in at all the gates. Then the Venetian room took fire and, saturated with the salts of the Adriatic, it bloomed like paper, and the iron works of the old clock, bells and gears had begun to crash down through the remains of the tower. A brisk wind carried the flames deep into the northwest and then slowly the garden and the whole valley began to fill up with a bitter smoke. The place burned until dawn and looked, in the morning light with only its chimneys standing, like the hull of some riverboat.

Later the next afternoon Justina, Mrs Enderby and the count flew to Athens and Moses and Melissa went happily into New York.

*

But Betsey returned, long before this. Coming home one night Coverly found his house lighted and shining and his Venus with a ribbon in her hair. (She had been staying with a girl friend in Atlanta and had been disappointed.) Much later that night, lying in bed, they heard the sounds of rain and then Coverly put on some underpants and went out the back door and walked through the Frascatis' yard and the Galens' to the Harrows', where Mr Harrow had planted some rose bushes in a little crescent-shaped plot. It was late and all the houses were dark. In the Harrows' garden Coverly picked a rose and then walked back through the Galens' and the Frascatis' to his own house and laid the rose between Betsey's legs – where she was forked – for she was his potchke once more, his fleutchke, his notchke, his little, little squirrel.

PART
FOUR

CHAPTER 36

In the early summer both Betsey and Melissa had sons and
Honora was as good as or better than her word. A trust
officer from the Appleton Bank brought the good news to
Coverly and Moses and they agreed to continue Honora's
contributions to the Sailor's Home and the Institute for the
Blind. The old lady wanted nothing more to do with the
money. Coverly came on from Remsen Park to New York
and planned with Moses to visit St Botolphs for a week end.
The first thing they would do with Honora's money was to
buy Leander a boat and Coverly wrote his father that they
were coming.

Leander gave up his job at the table-silver company with the
announcement that he was going back to sea. He woke early
on Saturday morning and decided to go fishing. Struggling,
before dawn, to get into his rubber boots reminded him of
how rickety his limbs – or what he called his furniture – had
gotten. He twisted a knee and the pain shot and multiplied
and traversed his whole frame. He got the trout rod, crossed
the fields and started fishing in the pool where Moses had
seen Rosalie. He was absorbed in his own dexterity and in
the proposition of trying to deceive a fish with a bird's feather
and a bit of hair. The foliage was dense and pungent and in
the oaks were whole carping parliaments of crows. Many of
the big trees in the woods had fallen or been cut during his
lifetime but nothing had changed the loveliness of the water.

Standing in a deep pool, the sun falling through the trees to
light the stones on the bottom, it seemed to Leander like
an Avernus, divided by the thinnest film of light from that
creation where the sun warmed his hands, where the crows
carped and argued about taxes and where the wind could be
heard; and when he saw a trout it seemed like a shade – a
spirit of the dead – and he thought of all his dead fishing
companions whom he seemed cheerfully to commemorate
by wading this stream. Casting, gathering in his line, snagging
flies and talking to himself, he was busy and happy and he
thought about his sons; about how they had gone out in the
world and proved themselves and found wives and would now
be rich and modest and concerned with the welfare of the
blind and retired seamen and would have many sons to carry
on their name.

That night Leander dreamed that he was in strange country.
He saw no fire and smelled no brimstone but he thought that
he was walking alone through hell. The landscape was like the
piles of broken and eroded stone near the sea but in all the
miles he walked he saw no trace of water. The wind was dry
and warm and the sky lacked that brilliance that you see above
water, even at a great distance. He never heard the noise of
surf or saw a lighthouse although the coasts of that country
might not have been lighted. The thousands or millions of
people that he passed were, with the exception of an old man
who wore some shoes, barefoot and naked. Flint cut their feet
and made them bleed. The wind and the rain and the cold
and all the other torments they had been exposed to had not
lessened the susceptibility of their flesh. They were either
ashamed or lewd. Along the path he saw a young woman but
when he smiled at her she covered herself with her hands, her
face dark with misery. At the next turn in the path he saw
an old woman stretched out on the shale. Her hair was dyed
and her body was obese and a man as old as she was sucking
her breasts. He saw people astride one another in full view of
the world but the young, in their beauty and virility, seemed
more continent than their elders and he saw the young, in

many places, gently side by side as if carnality was, in this strange country, a passion of old age. At another turn in the path a man as old as Leander, in the extremities of eroticism, approached him, his body covered with brindle hair. 'This is the beginning of all wisdom,' he said to Leander, exposing his inflamed parts. 'This is the beginning of everything.' He disappeared along the shale path with the index finger up his bum and Leander woke to the sweet sounds of a southerly wind and a gentle summer morning. Separated from his dream, he was sickened at its ugliness and grateful for the lights and sounds of day.

Sarah said that morning that she was too tired to go to church. Leander surprised everyone by preparing to go himself. It was a sight, he said, that would make the angels up in heaven start flapping their wings. He went to early communion, happily, not convinced of the worth of his prayers, but pleased with the fact that on his knees in Christ Church he was, more than in any other place in the world, face to face with the bare facts of his humanity. 'We praise thee, we bless thee, we worship thee, we glorify thee,' he said loudly, wondering all the time who was that baritone across the aisle and who was that pretty woman on his right who smelled of apple blossoms. His bowels stirred and his cod itched and when the door at his back creaked open he wondered who was coming in late. Theophilus Gates? Perley Sturgis? Even as the service rose to the climax of bread and wine he noticed that the acolytes' plush cushion was nailed to the floor of the channel and that the altar cloth was embroidered with tulips but he also noticed, kneeling at the rail, that on the ecclesiastical and malodorous carpet were a few pine or fir needles that must have lain there all the months since Advent, and these cheered him as if this handful of sere needles had been shaken from the Tree of Life and reminded him of its fragrance and vitality.

On Monday morning at about eleven the wind came out of the east and Leander hurriedly got together his binoculars and bathing trunks and made himself a sandwich and took the Travertine bus to the beach. He undressed behind a dune and

was disappointed to find Mrs Sturgis and Mrs Gates preparing
to have a picnic on the stretch of beach where he wanted to
swim and sun himself. He was also disappointed that he should
have such black looks for the old ladies who were discussing
canned goods and the ingratitude of daughters-in-law while
the surf spoke in loud voices of wrecks and voyages and the
likeness of things; for the dead fish was striped like a cat and
the sky was striped like the fish and the conch was whorled
like an ear and the beach was ribbed like a dog's mouth and
the movables in the surf splintered and crashed like the walls
of Jericho. He waded out to his knees and wetted his wrists
and forehead to prepare his circulation for the shock of cold
water and thus avoid a heart attack. At a distance he seemed
to be crossing himself. Then he began to swim – a sidestroke
with his face half in the water, throwing his right arm up like
the spar of a windmill – and he was never seen again.

CHAPTER 37

So, coming back to give him a boat, his sons heard the words said for those who are drowned at sea. Moses and Coverly drove down from New York without their wives and arrived in the village late on the day of the service. Sarah did not cry until she saw her sons, and held out her arms to be kissed, but the manners and the language of the village helped to sustain her. 'It was a very long association,' she said. They sat in the parlor and drank some whisky where Honora joined them, kissed the boys and had a drink herself. 'I think you make a great mistake to have the service at the church,' she told Sarah. 'All his friends are dead. There will be no one there but us. It would be better to have it here. And another thing. He wanted Prospero's speech said over his grave. I think you boys had getter go to the church and speak with the rector. Ask him if we can't have the service in the little chapel and tell him about the speech.'

The boys drove over to Christ Church and were let into an office where the rector was trying to work an adding machine. He seemed impatient at the little help Divine Providence gave him in practical matters. He refused Honora's requests gently and firmly. The chapel was being painted and could not be used and he could not approve introducing Shakespeare into a holy service. Honora was disappointed to hear about the chapel. This anxiety about the empty church was the form her grief seemed to take.

She looked old and bewildered that day, her face haggard and leonine. She got some shears and went into the fields to cut flowers for Leander — loosestrife, cornflowers, buttercups and daises. She worried about the empty church all through lunch. Going up the church steps she took Coverly's arm — she clutched it as if she was tired or frail — and when the doors were opened and she saw a crowd she stopped short on the threshold and asked in a loud voice, 'What are all these people doing here? Who are all these people?'

They were the butcher, the baker, the boy who sold him newspapers and the driver of the Travertine bus. Bentley and Spinet were there, the librarian, the fire chief, the fish warden, the waitress from Grimes' bakery, the ticket seller from the movie theater in Travertine, the man who ran the merry-go-round in Nangasakit, the postmaster, the milkman, the stationmaster and the old man who filed saws and the one who repaired clocks. All the pews were taken and people were standing at the back. Christ Church had not seen such a crowd since Easter.

Honora raised her voice once during the service when the rector began to read from St John. 'Oh no,' she said loudly. 'We've always had Corinthians.' The rector changed his place and there seemed to be no discourtesy in this interruption for it was her way and in a sense the way of the family and this was the funeral of a Wapshot. The cemetery adjoined Christ Church and they walked behind Leander, two by two, up the hill to the family lot in that stupefaction of grief with which we follow our dead to their graves. When the prayers were finished and the rector had shut his book Honora gave Coverly a push. 'Say the words, Coverly. Say what he wanted.' Then Coverly went to the edge of his father's grave and although he was crying he spoke clearly. 'Our revels now are ended,' he said. 'These our actors, as I foretold you, were all spirits and are melted into air, into thin air. We are such stuff as dreams are made on, and our little life is rounded with a sleep.'

*

After the service the boys kissed their mother good-by and promised to return soon. It would be the first trip they made and Coverly did return, on the Fourth of July, with Betsey and his son, William, to see the parade. Sarah closed her floating gift shop long enough to appear on the Woman's Club float once more. Her hair was white and only two of the founding members remained, but her gestures, the sadness of her smile and the air of finding that the glass of water on her lectern tasted of rue were all the same. Many people would remember the Independence Day when some hoodlum had set off a firecracker under Mr Pincher's mare.

Honora was not there and after the parade when Coverly telephoned to see if he could bring Betsey and the baby to Boat Street Honora put him off. He was disappointed, but he was not surprised. 'Some other time, Coverly dear,' she said. 'I'm late now.' A novice at observing her might have guessed that she was late for her piano lessons but as soon as she had mastered 'The Jolly Miller' she had shut the lid on her piano and become a baseball fan. What she was late for was the starting pitch at Fenway Park. She had arranged with a cab driver in the village to drive her to and from the games once or twice a week when the Red Sox were in Boston.

She wears her three-cornered hat and her black clothes to the game and climbs up the ramp to her seat in the balcony with the ardor of a pilgrim. The climb is long and she stops at a turn to catch her breath. She clasps one hand, her fingers outspread, to her breast, where the noise of respiration is harsh. 'Can I help you?' a stranger asks, thinking that she is sick. 'Can I help you, lady?' but this gallant and absurd old woman does not seem to hear him. She takes her seat, arranges her program and her score card and taps a Catholic priest who is sitting near her on the shoulder with her stick. 'Forgive me, Father,' she says, 'if I seem remiss in my use of language, but I do get carried away. . . .' She sits in the clear light of harmlessness and as the game proceeds she cups her hands to her mouth and shouts, 'Sacrifice, you booby, *sacrifice!*' She is the image of an old pilgrim walking by her lights all over the world as she was meant to do and who sees in her mind a noble and puissant nation, rising like a strong man after sleep.

Betsey loved the floating gift shop and spent most of the afternoon there with Sarah, admiring the fish-net floats, mounted to hold ivy, the hand-painted flatirons and coal scuttles, the luncheon sets from the Philippines and the salt and pepper shakers shaped like dogs and cats. Coverly walked alone through the empty rooms of the farm. There would be a thunderstorm. The light was getting dim and the telephone in the hall had begun to ring erratically, sensitive to every random charge of electricity. He saw the threadbare rugs, the bricks, neatly encased in scraps of carpeting, that would keep the doors from slamming now that the wind had begun to rise, and on a corner table an old pewter pitcher, filled with bayberry and bittersweet, all covered with dust. In the storm light the fine, square rooms stood for a way of life that seemed to be unusually desirable, although it could have been the expectancy of the storm that accounted for the intensity of Coverly's feeling. Memories of his childhood could be involved and he could remember those thunderstorms – Lulu and the dog hidden in the coat closet – that plunged the sky, the valley and the rooms of the house into darkness and how tenderly they felt for one another, carrying buckets and pitchers and lighted candles from room to room. Outside he could hear the tossing noise of the trees, and the teakwood table in the hall – that famous barometer – made a creaking sound. Then, before the rain began, the old place appeared to be, not a lost way of life or one to be imitated, but a vision of life as hearty and fleeting as laughter and something like the terms by which he lived.

But Leander got the last word. Opening Aaron's copy of Shakespeare, after it had begun to rain, Coverly found the place marked with a note in his father's hand. 'Advice to my sons,' it read. 'Never put whisky into hot water bottle crossing borders of dry states or countries. Rubber will spoil taste.

Never make love with pants on. Beer on whisky, very risky. Whisky on beer, never fear. Never eat apples, peaches, pears, etc. while drinking whisky except long French-style dinners, terminating with fruit. Other viands have mollifying effect. Never sleep in moonlight. Known by scientists to induce madness. Should bed stand beside window on clear night draw shades before retiring. Never hold cigar at right-angles to fingers. Hayseed. Hold cigar at diagonal. Remove band or not as you prefer. Never wear red necktie. Provide light snorts for ladies if entertaining. Effects of harder stuff on frail sex sometimes disastrous. Bathe in cold water every morning. Painful but exhilarating. Also reduces horniness. Have haircut once a week. Wear dark clothes after 6 P.M. Eat fresh fish for breakfast when available. Avoid kneeling in unheated stone churches. Ecclesiastical dampness causes prematurely gray hair. Fear tastes like a rusty knife and do not let her into your house. Courage tastes of blood. Stand up straight. Admire the world. Relish the love of a gentle woman. Trust in the Lord.

penguin.co.uk/vintage